NEVERLAND'S DARLINGS
BOOK ONE

Shadow
A DARK PETER PAN RETELLING

EMBERLY JADE

Contents

Dedication		VII
Author's Note		IX
Content Warnings		XI
Prologue		3
1.	Chapter One	11
2.	Chapter Two	17
3.	Chapter Three	25
4.	Chapter Four	35
5.	Chapter Five	43
6.	Chapter Six	49
7.	Chapter Seven	63
8.	Chapter Eight	69
9.	Chapter Nine	77
10.	Chapter Ten	85

11.	Chapter Eleven	91
12.	Chapter Twelve	103
13.	Chapter Thirteen	111
14.	Chapter Fourteen	123
15.	Chapter Fifteen	131
16.	Chapter Sixteen	141
17.	Chapter Seventeen	151
18.	Chapter Eighteen	159
19.	Chapter Nineteen	169
20.	Chapter Twenty	179
21.	Chapter Twenty-One	187
22.	Chapter Twenty-Two	195
23.	Chapter Twenty-Three	205
24.	Chapter Twenty-Four	215
25.	Chapter Twenty-Five	223
26.	Chapter Twenty-Six	231
27.	Chapter Twenty-Seven	241
28.	Chapter Twenty-Eight	251
29.	Chapter Twenty-Nine	259
30.	Chapter Thirty	267
31.	Chapter Thirty-One	279
32.	Chapter Thirty-Two	289
33.	Chapter Thirty-Three	297

34. Chapter Thirty-Four   305

35. Chapter Thirty-Five   315

36. Chapter Thirty-Six   325

37. Chapter Thirty-Seven   331

38. Chapter Thirty-Eight   341

39. Chapter Thirty-Nine   351

40. Chapter Forty   359

41. Chapter Forty-One   369

42. Chapter Forty-Two   377

43. Chapter Forty-Three   387

44. Chapter Forty-Four   397

45. Chapter Forty-Five   407

46. Chapter Forty-Six   413

47. Chapter Forty-Seven   421

48. Chapter Forty-Eight   429

Epilogue   433

Acknowledgements   435

About the author   437

For those of us who crushed on Jeremy Sumpter as Peter Pan when we were young,
only to fall in love with Killian Jones from Once Upon a Time when we grew up.
Then found dark romance and realized you like them even darker.
I see you... Neverland awaits your arrival.

Author's Note

This story is a work of fiction loosely based on the tale we all know and love as Peter Pan. I have twisted this tale into something almost unrecognizable and dark. My Neverland is full of Fae and monsters from your nightmares.

The little faeries you grew to love are now dark and nefarious beings willing to eat you here, literally and figuratively.

This story is set in modern times. The Darling children, having been raised in the 80s and 90s, are now full-grown adults who live in the real world, but played in Neverland with Peter while growing up.

This series follows four couples. Three are MF pairings and one is MM.

Please read the Trigger Warning page and do not take it lightly.

If you are still on board with me...

Welcome to Neverland

Content Warnings

This story is not a normal retelling of Peter Pan. This goes deep into Fae lore and my own wicked imagination.
Please consider your own mental health and well-being before going forth into Neverland.

In this trilogy, there are scenes of:

Kidnapping
Stalking
Murder/Sacrifices
Mentions of Suicide
Torture
Human/Sex Trafficking(Child and Adult— the child sex trafficking is talked about, grooming is on page)
Child Slaves/Abuse
Rape (on and off page)
Drugs/Alcohol (Manufacturing, Trafficking, and the use of, both forced and not)

Exhibitionism/Voyeurism

Masturbation

Anal Play

Blood Play

Consensual Non-Consent

Dubious Consent

Somnophilia

Cannibalism

If you have made it this far and still want to visit the nefarious Fae of
Neverland,
Captain James awaits your arrival on the ship...

Tick... Tock...

Tick... Tock...

Ooooh, Little Shadow...

Tick... Tock...

Come home...

Tick...

Come home, Little Shadow...

Tock...

Prologue

Jane

One Year Ago

The ice in my glass was melting and the drink I had just downed wasn't making me forget my horrible week.

"Come on, Jane. You know you want to try it. It's just a little blow to let the steam off from the hell at the hospital this past week. You don't even work for the next few days!" Juliette yelled in my ear over the music vibrating around us.

Staring at the line of Dust on the table before us, I pondered how much trouble I would get into if I was caught. Dust was a new drug on the scene, and as far as I knew, nothing bad had come of anyone who had tried it.

The two men across from us had their legs spread and arms laid across the back of the black, leather couch they were sitting on. They looked nice enough, but the fact that they had the drugs told me it was a facade and they were probably more dangerous than they looked.

Glancing over to Jules, she just shrugged her shoulders as she finished the last bit of vodka cranberry in her glass and leaned down, inhaling the substance.

"It isn't that bad, babes. You really should try it," she said as she sat back against the sofa.

Guilt gnawed at my gut, knowing my career would be on the line if I was caught. I always put my career and my patients before my own needs, but Jules was right. It had been hell this week. I had lost two of my patients to the diseases that ravaged their poor little bodies and there was nothing I could do about it. They had been fighting for a long time. Trying to console their parents was hard to do when your own heart was breaking.

Staring at the line of sparkling white on the table before me, I was at war with myself. The alcohol in my system was telling me it was just a line, it wasn't going to do much, maybe get my mind off my horrendous week and my aching heart for the kids I couldn't save. Even if it was nothing but a temporary fix, my still half-sober mind was screaming at me to skip it.

"Jane? Are you okay? You don't have to do it, but it'll probably help." I heard Jules' slurred voice through my muddled thoughts. Fuck it. Leaning down, I picked up the used straw and inhaled. The burn in my sinuses was foreign, but not too untowardly. Sitting back, I looked up at the men we were seated with. A look of satisfaction crossed their faces as if we had just done exactly what they wanted us to do. Regret sat heavy in my gut at my decision to partake in the drug.

Juliette was already laid back across the leather couch, a dazed look on her face, the drug hitting her system fast. Shit, how strong was this stuff? Grabbing her hand, I shook her until she looked at me. "How are you feeling?"

"Light as a feather. Do you see the little faeries flying around?" she asked, her hand dancing in the air, following a path I didn't understand. Searching the area where she was pointing, I saw nothing but dust motes flickering the different colors of the strobe lights hitting them.

"No, I don't," I answered, fear flitting through me. If she was seeing things, what was going to happen to me?

Jules stayed glued to the spot she was in, barely moving. Once in a while, a smile would creep on her face as she stared at the same spot she had pointed out earlier.

Tick... Tock...

What the fuck was that? The ticking of a clock came unbidden and loud as hell. Where the fuck was a clock that big in this place?

"Did you all hear that?" I asked, frantically searching for something I knew wasn't there.

"Probably just the Dust..." the blonde man answered, leaning on his knees as he sat forward.

Taking in Jules, she was half passed out next to me, totally relaxed and enjoying whatever high she was on. Apparently, we were having two different experiences.

Tick... Tock...

The ticking was loud, echoing through my head.

My mind was whirling with thoughts and questions, but my body was slow to respond to anything. I was sluggish. It was as if trying to move my hand was the same as lifting a fifty-pound weight. It hurt.

"What are the side effects of it?" I slurred, trying to get the question out of my mouth.

The men grinned, their incisors pointed into fangs, as they moved closer to us. "Hallucinations for the most part," the dark-haired one answered, running his hand through his hair, pointed ears peeking through the curls.

The blonde's gaze bore into mine. His eyes glowed a deep blue as he stood up, terror seizing my insides. "Maybe we should go outside and get some air." His hair reflected the blue and pink lights, giving him a more ethereal look. Like he didn't belong here.

TICK... Tock...

Shaking my head, I turned my attention back to Jules. The drugs must be affecting me, that's all. Like Jules over here, thinking she's seeing faeries. The idea of going outside was a good idea, but my gut clenched at the idea of the two guys going with us. The look the two guys were giving had fear sinking into my bones. My hands shook as I leaned over to get Jules' attention.

"Hey, Jules, want to go outside? Think you can make it to the front?"

"No need, we can go to the roof," Blondie interjected. "It's much quieter up there, and we'll be alone for you two to work through your haze."

A cold shiver ran down my spine, settling in my lower back at the thought of going to the roof. Something wasn't right, but I was too far into my haze to figure out what.

TICK... Tock...

A grimace crossed my face at the unbidden ticking resounding through my head. What the fuck is that? It must be the drugs. It had to be.

Both men were standing over us as fear drove through my middle. The effort to move my body was too much. It felt like I was weighed down with sandbags and being pulled in the wrong direction.

Their glowing eyes widened as they flashed their fangs in malevolent smiles. The danger emanating from them had my mind screaming to move, but my body wasn't listening. These men were not what they seemed to be. No. They looked to be something straight from my nightmares, and there was no way in fucking hell I wanted to go with them anywhere.

TICK... TOCK...

Once again, the incessant ticking grew louder, making me grimace. The pain of the shouting clock echoed through my head, fighting with the bass of the club that shook my body.

A hand came around my upper arm and lifted me to my feet. "Come on, we'll take you two to get some fresh air and work this little bit of Dust out of your systems," the dark-haired man said as Blondie lifted Jules into his arms.

TICK! TOCK!

No. No!

There was no way we were going with them. I feebly tried to pull on my arm, but the man's grip was like steel, hard and bruising. "Let me go! I don't want to go up there!" I slurred loudly as panic started to set in, hoping to garner any attention from anyone to help. Pulling back on his grip, I planted my feet, but the man was just too strong and my body too weak to fight. He dragged me to the door to our right with almost no effort on his part.

"Don't fight me," the man growled out between his clenched teeth. "We don't need you making a scene."

But that's exactly what I wanted. Opening my mouth to scream, I was suddenly silenced as the man picked me up and threw me over his shoulder like I weighed nothing. Trying to fight the drug in my system to lift my hands to fight him, I couldn't move. The harder I tried, the heavier I felt.

TICK! TOCK! TICK! TOCK!

Sweat dripped down the side of my fevered cheek as ice-cold terror slid through my body like knives, wracking another shiver from me. I could only imagine what the two men would do to us when they got us alone. My mind raced at the thought of dying at the hands of the two men who had us in their grasps. Having no way to fight them brought a fresh bout of panic flooding through me, settling low in my stomach and making me nauseous.

Hopelessness and terror had sunk into my bones as I heard a door open. Butterflies of dread beat against my sternum, urging me to do something. Anything.

My heart plummeted to my feet as another man came up behind the man carrying me, his features blurred in the dark.

Tick... Tock...

"Is there someplace you two are taking these ladies?" The man's voice almost floated through the space, with a sharp edge of menace in his tone.

The man tensed underneath me as he turned to face the newcomer. "Just to the roof to get some air, is all," the blond man stated, clearly not affected by the man's tone.

"It doesn't look to me as if they really want to. And the girl you are holding is straight passed out. So, let's try that again." This time, his voice promised violence as tension rose in the space around us, thickening into a battle of wills.

Blondie looked between the dark-haired man and the newcomer. Growling to himself, the man handed Juliette over to him and stalked off back into the club. My muscles tensed as I waited to be put back down. Surely, this man wasn't going to take me when the other man gave up.

Tick...

Pain shot through my body as I landed in a heap on the ground at the man's feet. Something wet dripped down my face as I lay on the floor, riding out the pain, trying to make sense of what had just happened.

Jules was suddenly at my side, groaning in pain as the sound of fists hitting flesh and scuffling echoed around us.

"Touch them again and you both die," the newcomer stated as I heard the groans of a pained man.

"Whatever, Barrington. It's Drake you'll need to deal with, not us. We were just doing as we were told," the man that had dropped me spat.

"Hey, Cap, what's the hol—What the fresh fuck is this?" A new voice joined the mix, my head spinning with the commotion going on around me.

"Nothing. Madok here was just leaving," the one called Cap said.

I heard shuffling as I felt a pair of arms lift me into their hold.

"Come on, we'll let them sleep this off in my room. I'll tell Drake what happened and we'll return to the ship."

Ship? I must seriously be hearing things... What ship?

The man smelled of tobacco and the sea. It was an interesting combination because we were so far from any tropical place. Inhaling his scent, I curled into the man's chest, totally at ease with him.

The last thing I thought before sleep took over my exhausted body, was the ticking had finally stopped.

Chapter One

Jon

Present Day

Going into the morgue at night was unnerving.

There's a reason I hated being around dead bodies. Seeing enough growing up, one would think it would give you a nonchalant stance on it. It does not.

It's one thing to defend yourself from cannibals trying to make you their next meal and quite another to see a dead body lying on a steel table, being readied to be cut open and examined, that it made shivers coast down my spine.

Maybe it was because I was running from that exact fate as a child that made me hate the job of a coroner. But the fact that I was interested in the brain and had no problem with it must say something about my character. I went into the study of neurology because of the man-eaters and the things I had experienced as a child.

Did I imagine the things I had experienced as a kid? Sadly, no.

Did I decide to work on the actual brain instead of going into psychiatry because of what I have seen? Yes.

Did I want to avoid getting into my head and discovering things I never wanted to know about myself? Also, yes.

Will I tell people of my adventures as if they are faerytales so I do not get thrown into the asylum? Let's just say I have found that some things are better left as fables than to be told as truth.

Taking a breath and steadying my nerves, I opened the door to the morgue and scanned the area. Letting out the breath that I was holding in fear of seeing an opened-up corpse, I made my way over to the sink on the far side of the room and scrubbed my hands and arms as if prepping for surgery. Which, I guess I was, in a sense.

All gloved up, I walked over to the refrigerator in my surgical suit, where I had been told the brains were in. I let my eyes wander around the room, settling on the row of horizontal freezers that I knew held the bodies of the people's brains I was about to examine. It was a bit nerve-racking to think that these people had been brought down to just bits and pieces to be examined and weren't actual beings anymore—just flesh and bone, frozen in time.

This was the first time I was ever asked by the police to examine the dead, as if they didn't trust what our coroner said about them. As if one were to assume that this wasn't the first body found in this manner and they were grasping at straws to bring in a brain expert to do the autopsy. I am not one to make assumptions, but it is the one thing that makes the most sense to me.

After opening the jar and setting the gray matter on the cold, metal table, I grabbed my instruments and was about to start slicing vertically when the door hissed open, sending a jolt of fear through my body and making me jump.

A laugh rang through the room as I looked up and saw the coroner herself walk in, sending butterflies skittering through my chest. Isabella was a beautiful woman, short and curvy. Her dark hair ran down her back, complementing her olive skin tone. I'd be lying if I said I wasn't attracted to her—far from it. She was just my type, but the fact that she liked to play with dead bodies made me fear her just a little bit. "You should warn a person before just walking into a room that holds nothing but dead people," I said, getting my breathing back to a normal rhythm. Whether it was from the jump scare or the fact that this gorgeous creature had walked in was to be determined.

"Maybe you shouldn't be so worried about zombies." She chuckled. "Dead people aren't the ones to fear, my dear doctor. It's the live ones that will kill you."

She wasn't wrong. But good Gods, having someone walk in while you thought you were alone, slicing into a brain while surrounded by freezers of corpses, was distressing in the least.

"I have seen weirder things than zombies, so it isn't in the realm of impossibilities."

"What do you mean? Zombies are impossible, my dear doctor. We should all agree that once someone is dead, they're dead."

"And some things that should be impossible and improbable have been known to happen. I would like to believe there is still a little magic left in the world. Whether or not that makes me slightly insane, I guess that's my problem."

Isabella looked at me with questions in her eyes and a slight smile on her lips. Her cheeks were slightly flushed as she gazed at me. A picture of her bent over as I fucked her tight cunt flashed through my mind. It wouldn't be the first time I had done something like that in the hospital, but the fact that this was a morgue and I was wrist-deep in a brain had me hesitating.

No. I wasn't going to ruin this investigation for her by fucking her on one of the exam tables. Clearing my throat of the sudden desire clogging it, I changed the subject. "I thought I was going to be doing this myself." I didn't want to delve deeper into what could very well become a good conversation and then drinks and some great sex. I needed to stay on task, but her big, dark eyes looking at me across the room distracted the hell out of me.

"I need to be here and record everything you are doing and what you find, which I doubt is anything new to me. You won't find anything abnormal," she stated matter-of-factly, as if our odd conversation hadn't happened. Probably for the best, seeing how this was a police investigation and the talk of magic made me look less like an expert in my field and more like a lunatic needing therapy.

"Why do you say that?" I asked, watching her get scrubbed up and grabbing the camera off her desk.

"Because all of them are the same. It's just that they are normal, healthy, seemingly happy people who all decided they would jump off a roof on a random Tuesday. I'm not saying they all happened simultaneously, but you get what I mean. There's no rhyme or reason as to why they would do it."

"Has anyone looked into their medical histories and seen any discrepancies or patterns between them?" I asked, my curiosity piqued as I made the first slice into the now-warming brain on the table. But if it is as she says it is, then there is no reason for me to be doing this other than for the police to get an outside source and a second opinion from an expert.

"We have. There's nothing suggesting anything of the sort. It's all a really odd case that the police want to be handled as soon as possible, but I can't find a medical reason for any of it."

"No drugs or alcohol?"

"No drugs. Some have alcohol and some don't. There wasn't enough in their systems to suggest they would commit suicide. But probably had a good time on the town before coming home and falling off the roof."

What she was saying made no sense. There had to be an explanation somewhere. After examining the first brain, I found nothing abnormal, as she had expected. The next two were just the same.

"The only way I would be able to tell if there was something neurologically wrong would be if I had a victim still alive that I would be able to do a scan on," I said to her as she recorded everything. If she was giving this to the police, it's pretty much going to tell them to find a person before they jump so I can get them into an EEG or MRI as soon as they bring them in. Which was going to be impossible, but one could hope.

Putting all the instruments away, I cleaned up the area as Isabella plugged the recording into the computer and started uploading it straight away. The woman was like a machine. Everything was carefully done, in its place, and done as fast as possible. Another reason we wouldn't get along. Outside of the hospital, I was looking for adventure and the next adrenaline high I could find. A problem, probably, stemming from my fucked-up childhood.

Why I was looking for reasons not to ask this woman out was beyond me. Yes, she was gorgeous and probably a great lay, but I was an emotionally unavailable wreck who hadn't let a woman past my bed in the past twenty-some years. Only one would do it, and she decided that I wasn't enough for her.

Being reminded of that, I cleared my throat and decided to take a shot. It wasn't like the ghost of my past was doing me any favors in the present. "Would you like to go out for drinks? I have a spot and would love some company. We could discuss this," I said, pointing around the room, "more in-depth. See if there is anything you're missing."

Isabella looked up at me, her honey eyes calling to me as desire swirled around my middle, lashing to get out. A small smile curled her lips as mischief filled her gaze. "Sure, let me finish this report and go home and change out of these bloody clothes. Eight, okay?"

Triumph filled my being. Blood rushed straight south at the thought that I might get lucky tonight and bring this little, tempting creature to my bed. "Eight is perfect." A smirk crossed my lips as mirth filled my eyes. This was going to be a great night. A great night, indeed.

Chapter Two

JANE

"Jane! Hurry up! The cab will be here any minute!"

Jolting, I smeared the eyeliner across my face as Jules' screamed down the hall.

"Fuck!" I don't have time for this. Quickly blotting the offending line off my face, I leaned toward the mirror again, focusing on making a straight cat eye as the sound of heels clicking against the hardwood floors became louder.

"What is taking you so long? You're usually the first one ready," Jules said, her hands on her ear as she placed a dangled earring. Her dark hair was curled over her shoulders. She was wearing a black halter dress with sequins galore and strappy, red heels.

"I don't know. Just nervous, I guess." Truthfully, I didn't know what it was. My skin was clammy and I felt slightly fevered. Nerves were the closest thing I could put the butterflies of dread in my stomach to.

"About what? Getting your weekly fuck in the back of a club by a fine-ass man? I'm confused."

Throwing down the eyeliner, I looked myself over in the mirror, my gut twisting and butterflies running rampant. I know it wasn't about James. He and I had been going steady the past year since the incident, but something wasn't right and my intuition told me something was up. I just couldn't place what.

Shaking myself from my musings, I turned around to check my back. My emerald green dress fell to mid-thigh, the back open with gold chains laying against my tanned skin, my blonde curls falling in a waterfall against it all. Turning back around, I grabbed the glitter spray and let it rip. The more glitter, the better, I always say.

Jules giggled from the doorway and a smile crept on my face. "You definitely make sure every woman there knows he's taken when he leaves that place. The amount you use every week, I don't know how the man doesn't shit glitter."

The laugh rolled through my belly at the visual that came unbidden of James, the big, overly buff man shitting glitter for days. Gods, to see him that way would make my year.

Alas, we don't see each other outside of the club except at the hospital when he visits his niece. Those visits have become fewer and far between in the last few months, and they didn't sit right with me. I would say something, but being the girl's nurse and his lover put me in a hard spot of overstepping patient boundaries and into a more caregiver role than I think he wants me to be in.

Pushing Jules out of the way, I made my way back down the hall to my room to grab my heels as the honk of a car horn sounded from outside.

"I'll be outside. Hurry up!" Jules rushed down the stairwell, grabbing her clutch as she ran out the door to catch the cab.

Groaning to myself, I strapped the black heels on as I took one last look in the mirror hanging on my door. I looked hot. But the feeling that something was amiss had bile settling in the bottom of my throat, the acrid taste burning the back of my tongue.

Maybe we shouldn't go.

This is the same feeling I had last year before Jules and I got into trouble at the club. Nothing has happened since then. Even Arron and Madok have kept their distance since that night. Never coming close or their gaze lingering too long. Whatever James said to them kept them at bay and I was thankful for it. Again, I shook myself to try and rid my body of the feeling of doom.

"Mom! We're leaving! We'll be back in a little bit!" I yelled through the house as I came down the stairs.

"You two be careful!" I heard as I closed the door behind me, turning the key in the lock as I left. It was the one rule my mother had that we always abided by growing up. All the windows and doors stay locked, especially at night. Mom had this weird superstition about faeries coming and stealing people away to this place called Neverland. It was one of her quirks, but it made for great stories and didn't hurt anything. It was all poppycock, but I still did as she wished. I haven't been stolen by a faery yet, so she must be right on some level, right?

A roll of thunder clapped from overhead as the cab driver honked at me to hurry up, only adding to my trepidation.

Jules was on her phone as I got in the back of the car. Running my fingers through my hair, I got comfortable for the twenty-minute ride it should take to get to Magique.

"So, do you think you're going to meet anyone tonight? Or are you just hanging around until my rendezvous with James is done?" I laughed.

"I have a few guys already waiting for us at the bar. They'll have our drinks ready for us when we get there," she stated absently as she kept texting.

"And you trust them?"

Jules scoffed, "Yes. They won't do anything to our drinks. I've hung out with them before. They are all pretty chill. You'll like them. Maybe one of them will catch your eye and you can forget about James."

My heart sank. "Why would I do that?"

"He's a walking red flag. He only sees you on Fridays and rarely comes to see his niece at the hospital anymore. The man probably has a wife and kids somewhere, and you're his booty call."

I felt like I had been slapped in the face, the sting of hurt piercing through me. I had never thought about James like that, and now that it was out in the open, I couldn't *not* see it. My heart sank straight to my feet as my excitement about seeing James dimmed and anger surged through my veins. "You don't mean that," I spat.

"I do. I know you're in love with the man, but you two aren't going anywhere from where I am standing. You've been doing this for over a year and it hasn't changed. You really should look into other men to date. Hell, James hasn't taken you on a real date. Ever," she answered, her eyes on me as I took in what she was saying.

The truth of her words spun around me as I sank back into the leather seat, wishing it would swallow me whole. How long had she been thinking about this? Why did she bring it up now?

"We should discuss this when we get home. I just want to have fun," I said quietly, my heart in my throat as tears threatened to choke me. I would not cry over this. I would not let this revelation ruin my night.

"I am just saying the guys that we're meeting up with are hot, so keep your options open. If anything, make the man jealous," she prodded as she sank back into her seat. I turned to stare out at the passing streetlights.

She wasn't wrong.

And I think that's what stung the most.

Tick... Tock...

The cab slowed as we got closer to the bar. The line outside was already around the block with people dying to get in. The thing about this club was you needed a membership or reservations to get in. We just happened to be the lucky few who got free memberships when the place first opened and have maintained our status to keep it. James may have had something to do with it, as well, but I wasn't going to ponder that right now.

Paying the fare, we got out of the cab, glancing down the block at all the gorgeous people waiting to get in. That was another thing about this place. It had a strict dress code. Cocktail dresses and heels for the women. Ties and slacks for the men. It made the place stand out and made everyone feel like they could be somebody if they caught the right person's attention.

Arms locked together, Jules and I strode up to the door. The bouncer with a clipboard and headset nodded our way as we walked past. The sounds of whispers, groans, and complaints that we skipped the line were something I had gotten used to and now ignored.

A huge man came barreling out the door as I went to grab the handle, nearly knocking Jules and me off our feet. My heart raced in my chest at the adrenaline. His hair was dark brown, almost auburn, with eyes the color of ice. A huge scar ran down the left side of his face, which should have marred his features, but instead made him more handsome and just this side of menacing.

"I'm sorry, ladies. Here you go. I hope you two have a lovely night," he said, holding the door open. A smile plastered on his face, mirth playing in his eyes, had us both stopped, our jaws agape.

"Thank you!" Jules answered as she grabbed my arm, pulling me into the dark entryway as a dark chuckle followed us. "Oh, my Gods! Did you see that man?!"

"Yes, Jules, I saw him." I laughed as we waited in line to pass through the second door.

"That man could bend me in half and eat me anytime." She fanned her face, her dark hair bouncing about her shoulders. Shaking my head, I laughed at her panting after a man that we would probably never see again.

The bass hit me as we walked through the door, thrumming through my body and vibrating the floors. The club was already packed as we made our way through the throng of hot, sweaty bodies to the bar.

Tick... Tock...

Stupid ticking. Always when I entered this place. I would almost put it down to PTSD, but my gut twisted at the thought. Whatever.

"Julie!" I heard over the music.

"Nate!" Jules let go of my arm, rushing toward a group of four guys standing at the bar, leaving me to fend for myself.

Rolling my eyes, I pressed forward, slowly making my way in her direction in no real hurry to meet these guys. Our earlier conversation still echoed in my head and I was ill-inclined to meet whoever these guys were to appease her thoughts on my relationship. As true as they were, I didn't like the idea of meeting men to keep my options open. It felt too much like cheating. And that was not something I would ever do.

Sighing to myself, I ignored the twisting sensation in my gut as I caught up to the group. Jules was standing in between the four guys as if she belonged, two drinks in her hands. Handing one off to me, I quirked an eyebrow at her, questioning whether it was safe to drink or not.

Jules rolled her eyes in time with her hips as she swayed to the music. "It's safe. I watched the bartender make it, just for you."

Mouthing *thank you*, I took a huge gulp, the sweetness of the rum and coke coating my tongue. The muscles in my shoulders and neck relaxed slightly as I took in the men surrounding me.

Two were blonde and clean-cut, totally not Jules' type nor mine. They were too pretty and gave off jock from high school who didn't know what to do with the rest of their lives. Maybe they did and I was just being a judgmental asshole. Most likely.

The guy standing between the two blondes had a shock of blue hair, an eyebrow piercing, and tattoos everywhere. This guy screamed mentally unstable, but seeing as he was hanging with the boys from next door, I had to wonder if he was nuts or if they were.

Mentally slapping myself, I turned to the last guy, the one Jules was hanging on, and I understood why she wasn't letting him go. Towering over the rest of the guys, he had broad shoulders and dark hair with a five o'clock shadow. The name Nate didn't fit him. He seemed more like Dante or something you'd read in mafia romance, but I guess you can't really choose your name, can you?

Slurping down the rest of my drink, I slammed it down against the bar. If I was going to have to play Jules' game of entertaining one of these men, I would need more booze. And confidence. Because I was quite sure a man upstairs was going to be pissed when he saw what I was doing tonight.

Hell, maybe Jules was right and I could turn it into something that worked *for* me. A little bit of jealousy never hurt anybody, right? And maybe it'll make James want to do something about our non-relationship relationship.

Signaling the bartender for another, I waited impatiently while Jules introduced me to the guys. Blonde number one was Tony and blonde number two was Brad. Fitting, I thought to myself, mentally rolling my eyes. Brandon was the tattooed one.

My mood was going down the toilet fast and I needed another drink if I was going to try and make James jealous of one of these guys. My best luck would be with Nate, but seeing as Jules had laid claims, I looked over the other guys. One of the blondes would do.

"On B's tab?" the bartender yelled across the bar at me.

Shaking my head, I picked up my drink. "Just mine. The rest of the guys are on their own."

"Oh, I wouldn't dare. Good luck with this." The bartender's finger was pointing at the gang surrounding me. "B's going to be pissed when he catches sight of it."

I sure hoped so.

Chapter Three

WENDY

The storm was raging outside the nursery window, lightning striking in the distance and the distant roll of thunder jolted me out of my thoughts. It had been twenty-four years to the day that Peter disappeared from our lives. I was sitting here, reminiscing as I do every year, in the same spot he had always appeared since we were little.

The ice in my drink had melted, and the sweat on the glass had made my hands wet and clammy. Staring down into the watered-down whiskey, I sighed, lifted the glass to my lips, and shot the shit down. Waste not, want not, isn't that what they say?

Staring back out the window, I watched the rivulets of rain run down the stained glass, letting my memories take hold once more.

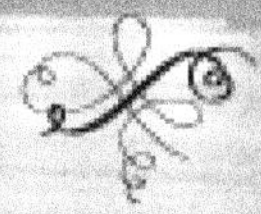

"I can't stay... Tink says Neverland is changing without me there..."

The words I knew that would come out of Peter's mouth at some point sank into me, chipping at the armor I had vaulted around my heart. There was no keeping Peter Pan. He was as free-spirited as the rest of the Fae in Neverland. But my damned heart didn't get the message and fell for the boy anyway.

Keeping the tears at bay, I gazed up at the boy-turned-man. I don't know when it happened, but he had grown up just as he always said he wouldn't. And I couldn't say whether he regretted it or not.

"Go..." I say, choking on the tears that threatened to spill. "Neverland needs you. I knew I could never keep you."

Peter gripped the bottom of my chin lightly, forcing me to look into his eyes. "I don't know if I will ever be able to return. Tinkerbelle says the island is in bad shape. But if you should ever need me, wish upon the second star. Neverland will hear your wish."

If my heart could sink any further than it already had, it would be in hell. Or was I already there? Was this hell? To have the man you loved most tell you that he can't come back? That you were going to be alone from now on?

Peter pulled me to him, wrapping his arms tightly around me as tears fell from my eyes. His head was resting upon mine as I listened to his heartbeat, wishing this moment would never end.

I didn't want him to leave.

I didn't want this to ever end.

Whatever was happening in Neverland, I should be a part of, too.

Leaning down, he kissed me, his tongue brushing against mine, and I lost it. I returned his kiss with as much passion and love as I could. I would force all that I felt into that kiss so he would always remember me.

Remember us.

Feeling Peter's arms loosen from around me, I knew our time was done. Both of us were left panting and wanting more. To finish what we started.

But Neverland calls.

Pulling away from me, he stood on the ledge of the window, keeping eye contact with me. My heart dropped as he stepped off the ledge, as it did every time he did it. Even knowing he would fly back up to hover right outside the sill for a few more seconds, blowing a kiss through the window, before he took off to that star in the sky.

"Neverland will always hear my wish."

No. No, it didn't. I had been wishing upon that star for as long as I could remember now to let Peter come home, and still, he never came. It was nothing but a fucking lie to placate a broken heart.

The doorbell ringing shook me from the darkness of my thoughts. Who the hell would be ringing my door this late at night?

Making my way down to the flat's entryway, my thoughts flew in a million different directions. Jane and Julie were out and had a key, so I knew it wasn't them. Jon was at the hospital. Not that he would have needed to be here this late. He had his own flat. So, who the hell?

Peering through the peephole, my heart rattled in my chest as I stared at a man I had never seen before.

Opening the door just a crack, I peeked at the man standing on the front stoop. His hair was wet from the rain, and it was cut long on top and short on the sides. His ice-blue eyes peered at me through the crack, a long scar marring his otherwise handsome face.

"Wendy?" his voice was deep and ragged. Trepidation slid down my spine at my name. Who the hell?

"Yes... Who are you?" The man's clothes told me he wasn't from these parts. It was a stormy autumn night. He should at least be wearing a coat.

The man took a deep breath as if bracing himself for what was about to leave his lips. "It's your brother."

Opening the door, I took in the man in front of me. His shoulders were wide and muscled, very much like Jon's. His hair was the same color as mine, even wet. Gazing into his eyes, though, the look of a lost boy trying to find his way home struck me.

"Michael!!" I threw myself into his unsuspecting arms, barely catching me.

"Wendy." He laughed into my shoulder. His body had become hardened from the years that he lived in Neverland. "Gods, I've missed you guys," he said as his arms fell and I ushered him in the door.

"Let me grab some towels and get you dried. I have some of Jon's clothes here if you'd like to change..." I said as I showed him the living area and quickly went up the stairs.

"It's fine. I don't have a lot of time." He sat on the hearth of my fireplace, careful not to get the furniture wet. A habit we all had from childhood after playing in the mud and rain.

Michael. He's alive after all these years. And grown up. How? When did he come back? Where is Peter?

The questions swirled through my mind faster than I could try to comprehend them. The only thing taking hold was the fact that my brother was still alive after all these years of being stuck in Neverland. And he was home.

Coming back into the living area with the towels, Michael observed the pictures of Jane and Julie that I had hung on the walls. From their first dances to their graduations and everything in between, I loved those two girls with all my heart.

Julie became Jane's best friend when they were quite small, and the two have been inseparable ever since. Nothing could tear them apart. When her parents left her when she was a teen, I took her in, no questions asked. I never had a problem with her. She kept her grades up and stayed out of trouble for the most part. I never asked her why her parents left her. It was a burden that she faced herself and one I hoped I helped her with.

Michael was staring at the one photo of all three of us at the Eiffel Tower, his fingers twitching as he stared at the photograph. We went to Paris as a graduation hurrah. It was one of the best times we ever had together.

"These girls... are they yours?" he asked, his voice ragged, his eyes shifting to mine. His shoulders were tensed as he made eye contact.

"Yes. They are mine." My heart beat in my chest, pounding against my ribcage. Something was wrong. The way he was staring at the pictures set off alarm bells in my head.

"I have nieces?" he sounded befuddled and heartbroken. Sorrow crossed his features, but was just as quickly gone, masked back into one of indifference, as he turned to me.

"Yes." My already-aching heart was slowly shattering into tiny shards. He had no idea of the lives we had created for ourselves here, while we just assumed he was having the time of his life in Neverland. The scars on his face and his behavior told another story.

"Do they know about me?" he asked, needing to know that he hadn't been forgotten, clearly written in his features. The Lost Boy that returned home shone through for a moment in time.

"Yes. They know we had a brother and that he went missing when we were kids."

Nodding, he turned back to the pictures, his demeanor back to that of almost stone. "Do they know about Neverland?"

"I think I need a drink. Would you like one?" I asked, changing the subject instead. I wasn't ready for this discussion. This deep dive into my world when he was being so guarded, himself.

Michael searched my face as if I was going to answer all the questions he was asking of me. Finally, he nodded and I left the room to grab a much-needed glass of whiskey.

This is not what I thought would happen if I had ever met up with Michael again. Explaining my life and my daughters' lives to a man who had been dead for the past twenty-some years.

Running my shaking hands through my hair, I took in a deep breath, trying to calm myself. It's just my brother.

But you haven't seen him in over twenty years and you have no idea his true intentions here, I thought to myself, pouring myself a shot into a glass and shooting it.

"Taking shots without me, huh?"

Spinning around, my heart beat wildly in my chest. "Jesus! You scared the living piss out of me!"

Chuckling, he strode into the room, making himself a glass and shooting it back. "I know I am the last person on Earth you ever thought you would ever see again." He smirked, his eyes twinkling in the dim light being cast from over the stove. "But I didn't come here to pry into your life. We need to talk about Neverland."

Nodding, I turned and went back to the living area and sat on the couch. "Before you come in here, can you grab my drink? Actually... Bring the whole bottle. We are going to sit and talk."

Michael grumbled to himself as he made his way into the living area and handed me my glass. I peered over the rim as I took a sip, letting the burn of the alcohol sit on my tongue and seep into my taste buds. Closing my eyes, I savored the smoky flavor before swallowing. Feeling a bit of the tension leave my shoulders, I opened my eyes to see my brother staring at me intently. Studying me. Wariness settled at the nape of my neck, the hairs on end as we stared at each other.

"How have you been, Wendy? Like really been?" he asked, concern lacing his voice as he broke the silence.

"Tired," I said with a sigh. "I wish I could escape this dull life and return to Neverland."

"No. That's out of the question." He shook his head violently, putting the glass down with enough force to slosh some of his drink onto the coffee table, fear settling itself into my gut. "It's become too dangerous for you. If I could stay here, I would," he said, dismayed.

"Then why don't you? Just don't go back," I say, both genuinely curious and frightened by what his answer could be.

"Because if I try, Barrington will come looking for me and the first place he will turn to for information will be Tink herself. If she were to find out I was living there this whole time, I wouldn't just be dragged back to be killed, but she would take her time with it. Hell, she'd probably bring me back to life, repeatedly, for the fun of it because she is that psychotic."

"Tink? Where the hell is Peter?" I asked, frightened about this revelation.

"Wendy," he said tentatively, as if he might break me with what he was about to say, "he's been missing for as long as I have been there. I have only returned because I found a way to do so. Peter is gone, probably dead, at this point. And I don't think I have much time left, either," Michael said in a breathy rush.

"What does Tinkerbelle have to do with all of this?" I ask, my voice hushed.

"The Fae have taken over the island, Wendy. Since Pan died, they have had free reign of Neverland, making it a place that nightmares are made of."

My heart sank with every word Michael said. No. Peter couldn't be dead. Neverland would die as well. That's what he had always told me. That he and the island were one. If one dies, the other goes as well. He had to be alive. Searching my feelings, I wanted so badly to believe that he was still alive, but the fact of the matter was, he hadn't been back. He left. And the last time he left, he had said goodbye.

"I want to go. I want to go find him," I stated, damn everything else. Peter needed me.

"No, Wendy. I have friends who have been looking for him all over the island. He is nowhere. There is nowhere we haven't looked. I would rather know you are here, safe with your daughters, than know that you are there, somewhere, looking for a dead man."

Shaking, I got to my feet. Anger, fear, and concern warred within me, battling to be the main component of what I should be. "You should go." I shakily sighed. I just wanted to be alone. I needed to work through all this information and decide for myself what to do next. Which was probably nothing, seeing how I had no way to get to Neverland.

Michael got up from his seat and made his way over. He went to wrap his arms around me in a hug, but I flinched. Hurt crossed his face, but understanding followed quickly behind as he nodded. He knew he had not only hurt me, but barred me from even coming to help.

Hearing the door close behind him, I hurled the glass in my hand at the wall, the glass shattering to mirror the pieces of my heart. I thought I had sewn myself back together and that nothing would be able to tear me apart again.

I was wrong. With just a few words, Michael had ripped my insides out and tore them to shreds. Hot tears streamed down my face as the grief I wouldn't allow myself to feel all those years ago came rolling in.

Grabbing the bottle of whiskey, I sank against the couch and let my emotions roll through me, taking sips of the liquor, letting it add to the burn that I was already feeling.

After sitting there for Gods knew how long, a knock came to me in my self-deprecating stupor. The fact that I hadn't locked the door after Michael left had me moving towards the door, the bottle of whiskey still in my hand.

Stumbling down to the entryway, I passed a mirror and was half tempted not to open the door. My eyes were puffy and red, mascara was running down my cheeks in streaks, and my nose was bright and sore. Setting the bottle down on the table under the mirror, I quickly wiped what I could from my face. I turned toward the door and the knocking that was still coming from the other side. I blew out a shaky breath and opened it.

Blinking, I took in the man that stood on my front stoop.

The man on my step was not from here, not that I could tell, and fear made me take a step back, even in my drunken state. His clothes told me more than anything. His pants were a light linen and were ripped in spots. His shirt was also made of a fine quality of linen, but again, it was torn and, I hoped, wasn't splattered in blood. His hair would probably be a dirty blonde if it was washed, but the smell. The smell of horrible

BO and old blood permeated the air around me, swallowing my senses and forcing a gag from my throat.

"Wendy Darling?" the man rasped out, like his voice box didn't work right. The scar along his neck explained why it didn't.

Backing up another step, my hand on the knob about to close the door, I went to say no, but something stopped me. What would be the chances that the way I needed to get to Neverland would land on my doorstep looking for me? Slim to none.

Still not answering the man's question, because the answer could mean my life or death, I just stared at him. Slightly in awe and slightly in disgust. The man didn't seem to be bothered by my perusal of him and went to grab a pouch on his hip.

"Where did you get that?" I asked. The pouch looked oddly familiar. One that Toodles used to hold his marbles and would never let anyone touch. To see this man with it gave me pause. Something wasn't right, but I had had too much to drink and couldn't quite piece together what I was missing.

The man ignored me and emptied what looked like pixie dust into his hand. Oh, my Gods, I thought. He was going to fly me to Neverland. Instead, he blew the dust into my face, forcing me to cough at the burn of the foreign substance as I inhaled. Then, all went black.

Chapter Four

LILY

The bar was empty for a Friday night. I would have been worried about being caught, but seeing as I have watched him for years and he has yet to spot me, I wasn't concerned.

A few men were at the pool tables in front of the door, having a good time, semi-blocking my view. But their distraction was just enough that, walking in, you wouldn't notice a single woman in the back.

Sitting in the back corner booth, the shadows from the poorly lit lamps kept me hidden. The water in front of me was half empty, and I was beginning to wonder if he was going to show up. It would be out of his routine not to show, but he works in a hospital, so he could have had something come up.

Grumbling to myself, I realized that I was wasting my time. I glanced at the clock sitting above the bar, which I learned a long time ago was set ten minutes ahead to get drunks out of the bar before closing time. I had twenty minutes before I made my way to the real reason I was in London.

Watching a couple pay their tab, their hands intertwined and desire painted on their faces, my mind wandered to what it would be like to have that—to have someone just for myself, to love and desire me for me and not what I can give them.

You did have that, I berated myself. *You just gave it up without a fight.*

Sighing, I brought the water to my lips and let the coolness run down my throat, quenching the fire of regret inside me. I needed a drink, but the stuff here isn't the same as Neverland. I would rather have my full wits about me while in London than not. Especially if I had to deal with *him* at some point.

My right leg started bouncing under the table as impatience got the best of me. Fuck this. He wasn't showing, and the longer I put off seeing Drake, the worse it was going to be for me, especially if he found out why I kept him waiting.

But I needed to see him. I needed to see his face, to see that he was still alive.

Standing, I grabbed my leather jacket off the hook at the end of the booth and threw it over my shoulders, covering all the swirls of ink that covered my body. He wasn't going to show and I needed to get going. I threw a couple of bills on the table for the trouble of taking up space. I went to make my way to the door, until the bells went off and I was staring at the man I had been waiting for.

There was a woman on his arm and a smile painted on his face. Jealousy wound through my middle at the thought that the mystery woman had his attention and I could do nothing about it. Backing up, I sat back down in my booth and pressed myself against the shadows, trying to blend in as much as possible.

From afar, Jon's hair looked black, but up close, you realize it was just this shade of brown. It reminded me of dark chocolate, soft as silk from what I remembered. He had grown up from when we were children. His gangly limbs as a teenage boy turned into a tall man of lean muscle with a straight, white smile that oozed charm and sex appeal. His jaw was sharp, covered in a five o'clock shadow, and his nose was still slightly crooked from when it broke when we were playing in Skull Rock, which only added to his charm.

His hand was brushing against the woman's back, bringing her to the bar to grab a drink. I needed to leave before he spotted me, but watching him be happy tore me apart and set a boiling rage through my veins.

That should be me. I should be the one on his arm. I should be the one smiling and drinking with him. I should be the one with his arms wrapped around me.

The thoughts swirled through my mind, growing my agitation about the situation like an itch under my skin. The need to claw it out and run from the sight in front of me made the water in my stomach turn.

Logically, I couldn't be mad at him for wanting female company, but how I felt about it made it much worse. I never stopped loving him, but circumstances changed and I had to do what was best for the both of us. Whether he knew it or not, I saved him.

Grumbling to myself, I crawled out of the booth when his back was turned towards me and was focused on the mystery woman. Ire slipped through me again, heating my veins with jealousy once more. Gritting my teeth, I walked slowly toward the door, slipping behind the men playing pool to conceal myself.

That was a mistake.

"Hey, hey, pretty lady. Was watching you over there, watching us play. You wanna go at it?" The man in front of me tried handing me one of the pool cues. His foul-smelling breath fanned my face, making me choke back a cough. I didn't have time for this.

"No, thank you. I need to get going." Going for a polite dismissal, I didn't want to bring more attention to myself. It was already quiet in here. Just one wrong move would alert Jon to my presence and I was trying to avoid that at all costs.

"Oh, come on, baby girl, we all were watching you. We know you want to play." The innuendo wasn't lost on me and bile rose in my throat at the thought that they wanted to fuck me.

I was tall for a woman, but my athletic build tends to make me look like an easy prize, especially if you don't consider all the weapons I always carried on myself. Looking around at the other men standing around the table, I took into account that almost all of them were around six feet tall and close to two hundred pounds. I could take one or two of them, but all five of them at once wasn't going to be a feat I was going to be able to master on my own.

Letting out a breath, I tried to make my way past the man, but he blocked my path once more. Apparently, ignoring the man wasn't going to help me, either.

The man grabbed my upper arm, squeezing just enough to make me wince. "Come on, one game won't kill you," he growled as he turned me towards the table. A couple of other bar patrons were starting to notice the commotion and fear slid along my spine that I might get caught. No, I was going to be caught anyway I looked at it.

Rolling my eyes to the ceiling, I moved closer to the table, keeping my eyes on the other men surrounding me. This is not how my night was supposed to go.

Wrestling my arm free of the man's grip, I tried to turn around but found I was pinned against the table as the man ground his hard cock against my ass. Clenching my teeth as I gripped the edge of the pool table, I slammed my head backward into the man's nose, the pain ricocheting through my skull. His screams of pain brought a slight smile to my face as he backed away. Quickly, I grabbed the knife that I had sheathed to my thigh and brought it up between his thighs.

"Now... since you decided to ruin my night, here's a piece of advice," I whispered in his ear, thrusting the knife up just enough for him to stand higher on his toes. "Don't touch women just because you want to. You never know which one is crazy enough to cut your balls off."

The other men had backed off while the man in front of me was now a whimpering mess. Fucking pussy.

Stepping back, I turned to leave when *his* voice rang out, making my body tense immediately. Fuck all.

Ignoring my name being called, I made my way to the door and flung it open, stepping out into the cool air and feeling the crispness against my heated skin. Turning quickly, I made my way to the alley that was two blocks up. My heels rang out against the sidewalk, alerting anyone nearby about where I was, but nothing was to be done about it.

The bang of the bar door slamming open behind me made my shoulders tense. Fucking hell. I wasn't going to chance turning around and see who it was that had followed me. It could be one of the men who was looking for vengeance for their friend, or worse, it could be Jon.

Dipping into the well of magic inside me, I let it flow through my veins. I tried not to use my magic in London. It was too easy to get caught, but desperation filled me with the need to move fast.

The alley was just ahead, sweat beaded my brow as I felt my magic reach out to my fingertips, sparks spewed off in intervals as I neared my destination.

"Hey. HEY!" a man's voice called out behind me, making me quicken my steps into a near jog. I knew that voice. Had heard it so many times in my dreams. I longed to hear my name from his lips again, but that was not to be.

My heart quickened as my breath started to come out in pants. I needed to get out of here. Needed to escape from him.

My magic buzzed under my skin, itching to be let free. My fingertips were nearly numb, waiting for the perfect spot to open the portal. Finally, the alley came up and I turned, thrusting my hand in front of me. I let the magic flow and created an opening between time and space.

"LILY, STOP!" Jon's voice rang out.

As I stepped through the opening, tears sprung into my eyes. Turning to close it, to bring my magic back into my being, I saw Jon staring at me, his eyes full of wonder and hurt.

Shaking my head, I closed my palm into a fist and the portal closed with a snap. The last thing I heard was his voice ring out once more.

"LILY!"

I could feel the bass through the roof of the old building vibrating my ass. Considering how the club was set up, it made sense to have it here instead of in the middle of town, where most other bars and clubs were closer to the colleges. When one deals in the laundering of money, drugs, and sex, it would make sense to have a spot right on the Thames.

One, it was beautiful. Sitting on the roof, the feel of the night air up here had a freshness in the air you couldn't find anywhere else in this Godsforsaken city. Two, easy distribution center. Quick in and out of the basement, everything was set. No one sees anything. Three, the building itself is old, like centuries old, and is on an old leyline. It comes quite handy when you use magic to transport goods.

Gazing up at the star in the sky I called home, I sighed. Coming here always made me more grateful for where I live. Less people, less noise. The politics were probably just as high, but the simplicity of living was easier as long as you obeyed the Fae.

The creaking of the roof door came from behind me, the line of light making my shadow shoot out over the roof. Getting to my feet, I turned to see the man I had been waiting for.

Drake was impeccable, as always. Not one hair was out of place, not one wrinkle on his suit. I would say he never did anything to break the image he put out to the world, but then again, I knew what he was capable of and wasn't going to cross that line again. He could make you hurt without lifting a finger.

Nodding my head, I let him approach me. He may know he holds all the power here, but he also gives me a little sense of dignity in this situation.

Turning back to look at the skyline, I waited until he was in my peripheral before speaking. "So, I have another shipment I need to pick up, I am assuming."

He nods his ascent. "Yes. But it will still take me a few days to get it together. There's been a hiccup I wasn't expecting. But the payment will be ready in two days." His hand grazed my arm, raising goosebumps along my body, a shiver coasting down my spine. "You know, I miss you, my sweets. Maybe you could stay the next couple of nights and take the shipment when it's ready. It would give us plenty of time to get reacquainted."

I suppressed the shudder that wound through me at the thought of what he wanted. "I need to get back to the island. My magic is waning and I can't stay very long." The excuse was flimsy, but I wasn't lying. Fae could always smell lies, so I had to be careful of how I spoke to him. Over the years, I have become quite proficient at it.

A sigh came from his lips. "You know, as my wife, I should be able to fuck you whenever I want," he growled out next to me. "But here we are, distant strangers, both pawns to someone who we both despise. If we spent time together, we'd be able to get out of this predicament."

A sigh rang through me this time. "No. Nothing would change. The fact that I hate you should be enough for you to get the hint. You have plenty of pussy within those walls to keep you satisfied." I dipped back into the well of magic within, pulling on the string to create a portal home.

"They aren't you. I just want my wife."

I turned to look him in the eye. "That sounds like a you problem. I'll be back in two days to pick up the payment."

I opened the portal behind me and stepped inside. Still holding eye contact with my estranged husband, I closed the hole in front of him.

Chapter Five

JAMES

The club was crowded, as would be expected for a Friday night. The bass thumping from the speakers pounded through my body as I went to the offices upstairs. Seeing the office door closed, I turned to the balcony overlooking the crowd of glittering faces. Neon bounced off of the crystals on the writhing, dancing bodies below, creating a sea of want and lust in the air that was hard to ignore.

My eyes kept searching the sea of bodies until I pinpointed the blonde head I was looking for. My cock twitched at the sight of Jane in her little, emerald green dress that hugged her body to perfection and left nothing to the imagination. Her eyes were closed as her hips swayed to the music, her arms in the air. The bouncing light of the strobes glinting off the glitter she had on her body made her look more like the Fae at home than anything human.

I leaned against the railing, watching her enjoy herself. She was a bright star in my world of darkness. When I found her in the club a year ago, I never would have thought that the little sprite would be such a firecracker when under pressure. Finding her and her friend in the arms of Arron and Madok stoked a fury in me that I still cannot explain.

She was mine, and no one was to touch what was mine. She may not know it, but she was my little obsession. After that night, I wanted to know as much about her as possible, only to find out there was little to know. She grew up with a single mom and now lives with her uncle. Her other uncle was determined legally dead as he had been missing for over twenty years, and she worked hard to get where she was. I was surprised when I found out she was one of the nurses on my niece's floor in the hospital she was in. I was even more surprised when my niece told me that Jane was her favorite. Paying off the heads to make sure she was her main nurse was of little consequence.

She came to the club to let off steam from her work week, which worked out in my favor. I could always keep an eye on her. The only problem I had ever seen happen to her was that one night. I don't know what exactly happened, but Drake and I came to an understanding about it. And now, she wouldn't ever have a problem coming here again.

Watching her writhe and dance to the rhythm on the dance floor was enough to make my cock stand at attention. Knowing what she felt and sounded like writhing beneath me wasn't helping the situation. I was so busy keeping my eyes on her that I didn't notice the man come up behind her until he was wrapped around her and keeping time to her rhythm.

Blind rage heated my veins as my vision darkened, my hands clenched into fists as I gnashed my teeth together. Everything in my being told me to go down there and lay claim to what was mine, but the one in control, the side that never lets the rage out of its cage, knows better than to do so. Not only would Drake beat the ever-loving fuck out of me, but I would run the risk of scaring off Jane. Not that a little scare wouldn't do her some good, but I prefer to punish her indiscretions differently. A way that is beneficial for both of us. The thoughts of what I was going to do to her made my already hard cock strain against my jeans.

Taking a deep, steadying breath, I opened my eyes and found she was staring straight at me. She had a small smirk on her lips as her tongue darted out to wet them. She raised her arms and put them around the man. She knew what she was doing. She was daring me to do something about it and my control was already on a tight leash. Fucking tease.

I watched as the man's hands moved down her body, grabbing her hips and pulling her against him. Maybe taking both of his hands as a reminder not to touch what wasn't his wasn't such a bad idea. The thought brought a dark smile to my face.

"Cap? Drake is ready for you," a female said from behind me, pulling me from my thoughts of breaking every bone in the man's hands.

Grinding my teeth, I turned and strode into the Fae's office.

Drake's office was like walking back into the jungles of Neverland. The walls were lined with plants of all shapes and sizes. Heat lamps and humidifiers were placed to keep the environment perfect for them to flourish in a place they were never meant to be.

There was a desk sitting directly opposite the door when you walked in made of dark mangroves, which completed the jungle theme. Behind the desk was Drake, impeccably dressed in a freshly pressed, black-on-black suit, not a wrinkle in sight. The dark-skinned Fae was hard to see in the dimly lit room. The only thing giving him away was his glowing, gold eyes. No matter how hard he tried to glamor himself, those always remained. His power was almost too much to be completely hidden away, even here in London.

Motioning to the leather chairs sitting in front of his desk, his low voice carried across the room. "I am assuming everything went smoothly."

Settling into the chair, I let the coolness of the leather sink into my skin, a slight reprieve from the heat and humidity of the room. "You would assume correctly. The men are moving everything as we speak and we should be ready to depart in a few hours."

"Good. I need you to report back to Tink that her product is failing. We need stronger doses if she wants her payments. She will get the one owed to her, but the Dust isn't strong enough for the humans. They have become resistant to it."

Nodding my ascent, I noted to send Smee on that little errand. I hated the palace and Tink would take the news better from him than me. Always had.

Drake started shuffling some papers around his desk as if there was anything on there that would pertain to me. "I do have something to discuss with you that would pertain to a certain little nurse of yours."

My hackles rose at the mention of Jane. If the man even thought about doing anything to her, Fae or not, he was going to be seriously hurt. "What about her?" I asked, surprising myself at how even-keeled I sounded, which warred with the straight-up hostility I felt towards the man right now.

"I have police reports here that show you have been leaving men carved up outside my club. Now, you know I can't have that."

"They shouldn't be touching what isn't theirs to touch." Nonchalance rolled off my tongue. "The men were lucky that they were left alive. I might have to rectify that if it's a problem."

Drake's power rolled into me like a freight train, pressing me into the chair. The sudden loss of breath had my heart racing and fear settling into my bones. "Yes, well, you either need to keep your hands to yourself and stop scaring off my patrons or you will have to talk to Tink about it, because it is starting to cause a slight problem with getting product out. And we both know she isn't as merciful as I am. This is your only warning." The threat of violence as his power kept rolling into me made my teeth clench. "Are we at an understanding?"

His power had me struggling to breathe, as if he had a hand clenched around my throat, squeezing the life out of me. Barely able to move, I slowly nodded my head in ascent and the squeezing ceased immediately.

"Good." Drake flicked his wrist and the door opened behind me. My cue to leave. "Any more trouble and it won't be you getting the brunt end of it."

The threat of Drake even thinking about laying a hand on Jane had boiling rage flowing through me. "Don't even think about touching her," I growled out. "Anything happens to her, and there is nothing that will stop me from raising hell on this plane or the other."

"Who said anything about her? Don't you have a sick niece?" The Fae had a sick and twisted smile plastered on his face, and my stomach dropped as I felt all the blood rush out of mine. "Yes. I know of her. So, now that you know the gravity of the situation, I would suggest you be on your best behavior and leave my patrons alone."

I grabbed the door handle and slammed the door closed as I left the Fae's office, not giving a rat's ass if the door closed behind me or not. The urge to punch something had been growing since I first saw the unknown man touching my woman, and now the looming threat that both of my girls were in danger because of my actions in protecting them made everything in the club seem hazy. All I could think about was finding someone to take my anger out on.

The metal stairs shook as I made my way down them. A drink was in order if I wanted to see this night through with little violence. In the corner, where the bar met the wall, stood Jane, a drink in hand. It looked like a second drink sat next to her as if she knew I was on my way.

Coming up behind her, I studied the way her hips moved to the rhythm of the music almost subconsciously. Her right leg had a tattoo of a crocodile that wound up and around and ended with its head on her ribcage. The emerald green dress she was wearing was backless and ended right above her ass. Her blonde curls looked slightly frizzed from the humidity in the club, and probably from fuck nuts dancing behind her, but they still looked soft enough to entice me to wrap my hands around them and pull her head back, exposing her neck to me. Mmmm... there's an idea. Coming up, I ran my hand along her spine and leaned into her ear. "Hello, love."

Chapter Six

JANE

Purposely teasing James earlier was probably a bad idea, but at the time, I didn't care. He never comes down to dance with me, always up on that balcony watching. Sometimes a little push was needed to get you what you wanted.

He had been coming here every weekend since that night over a year ago and our relationship bloomed into what it is now, but I still couldn't tell you exactly what that was. Friends with benefits? I couldn't say we were dating as we didn't do anything outside the club. Even when he visits the hospital to see Alis, which is few and far between anymore, he keeps it very professional. It was so impersonal that one wouldn't even guess that we had a sexual relationship outside of the hospital.

Jules was right. The whole thing was a red flag.

Glancing down at the rum and Coke in my hand, I asked for a second drink, a whiskey on the rocks for James, whenever he got down here. Glancing up at the clock by the doors, I saw it was a little after midnight. I was leaving if he wasn't down here in the next fifteen minutes. I had a shift tomorrow and didn't want to be here until sunrise.

The sensation that someone was behind me made me tense up. A hand started to caress my back, putting my body on alert until the sound of his voice in my ear immediately had me relaxing into his touch.

"Hello, love," he practically purred, making my insides clench at the thought of what else he could do with his tongue. I was putty in his hands, and he knew it.

"James..." I sighed, my breath hitching as he traced his fingers up and down my spine, making a shiver coast through my body at his touch.

"I see you like to defy me and let others touch what is mine." He continued his pattern on my back, stopping right above where my dress covered my ass. His teasing touch was slowly creating an inferno of desire that I knew, at some point tonight, he would deliver on. The only question was when.

"James, it was just a dance." I tried turning into him, but he pressed himself into me, his chest into my back. He pushed me into the bar, his hands on either side of me, barring me from escaping him.

"And his hands were in places that only mine should touch, were they not?" Anger tinged his voice as he growled into my ear. It shouldn't turn me on, his possessiveness of me, but my damned body didn't get that message as desire pooled between my thighs. His hard cock was pressed against my ass and I pushed myself back against him, playing with fire. His answering groan in my ear had me glancing over my shoulder, his lips close enough to capture with my own. Licking my lips, his eyes darted to watch my tongue, darkening when he backed up suddenly.

Pulling me by the waist, he sat down on the empty stool next to us, planting me between his thighs. Still standing, I felt his left hand making its way under my dress. "Did you want him to touch you here?" he asked as he lightly moved his finger over my pussy, making my thighs clench.

I could feel a blush rising to my cheeks as I thought about what he was asking. A challenge. Did I want that man to touch me? No. Did James know this? Yes. But what answer was going to get me fucked the way I had been craving all week?

"What if I did?" I asked, defiance flashing through me. If you're going to play the tease, you should see it all the way through, right?

A chuckle sounded from behind me as I felt him leave a kiss on the middle of my back and his fingers pinched hard against my clit. A gasp left my throat as he stood up and pressed himself back against me. "You're playing with fire, darling. I have half a mind to fuck you in front of everyone here so they all know who you belong to, but I think you would enjoy that too much." Moving the piece of lace out of the way, he circled my clit lightly, my thighs clenching around his hand and an answering wetness coated his fingers. "Oh... my naughty little croc. Were you getting turned on by having me watch you?" he asked as he pushed a long finger inside me.

A moan left my lips at the sudden intrusion, a blush creeping up my neck. Fear that we would get caught wound through my middle as James curled his finger and pressed against that spot he knew would bring me to my knees, making me forget where we were. My hands clenched around the glass of rum in my hand. I felt his cock twitch against my ass and my pussy clenched around his finger. It was good that he was behind me or I would have collapsed immediately.

"Hey, baby, you ready for the next dance?" Tony came up and asked, completely oblivious to what was happening. His eyes were glazed over and red. Whether it was just from alcohol or the other drugs that ran through this place, I wouldn't know.

"Yeah, *baby*, are you ready?" James whispered in my ear, but his eyes were focused on the man beside us. If looks could kill, Tony would have been dead on the spot. James removed his finger, giving me a sense of reprieve to handle the situation. Until he grabbed my hip hard and plunged a second one inside me, sending a shock to my system. A gasp left my lips as I felt myself clench hard around him.

My breath was shaky, and all I could think of was how James was making me feel. I never, in my twenty-three years, had been so turned on in my life by a man standing there trying to have a conversation with me as I was getting finger fucked by a god. I gripped my glass tighter and said as evenly as I could manage, "No. I am going to enjoy my drink and catch up with my friend here."

A low grunt sounded from behind me as he pulled his fingers from inside me and slapped my pussy, making me gasp again. Guess he didn't like being called a friend.

"Are you okay?" Tony asked. Concern crossed his face as if he was just figuring out what was happening before him. I prayed he didn't. "If you need help, you can tell me."

He was a bold motherfucker. I had to give him that.

"She's fine. Now leave us," James snapped at him, his fingers going back to slowly circle my clit, wetness seeping down my thighs.

"I am fine," I choked out, taking a sip of my rum and Coke. "Just haven't seen each other in a long time and would like to be left alone to catch up. Thank you, though," I said, trying to diffuse the situation. I knew James was protective of me, but sometimes he could take it too far. I would prefer he turn his attention back to me than the imbecile who wouldn't take a hint.

Tony eyed the both of us, worry marring his features as he contemplated his next move.

"You got your answer. Leave us be." James practically growled at the man.

The man just nodded and backed away, glaring at him the whole time. If he knew what was best for him, he would leave us alone for the rest of the night.

James groaned as he pushed his fingers back inside me. My moans were drowned out by the bass thumping loudly, vibrating our bodies. "Good girl," he whispered in my ear, sending a shiver down my spine. Another answering wetness coated his hand, his cock hardening even more so against my ass.

Thrusting his fingers in and out of me, he pulled me back, flush up against him, back to chest, giving him more room to play. Bending my neck back against his shoulder, he looked into my lust-filled gaze and lowered his lips to mine, giving my lips a light brush. "That was a fabulous performance, darling. I believe that deserves a reward." He smiled as he kept up the rhythm and kissed me like he was a drowning man and I was his air. My thighs started quivering as he kept on thrusting in and out of me. Using his thumb, he brushed over my clit, once... twice... He swallowed my groans of pleasure as he let me ride out my orgasm, holding me up against the bar.

Pulling his finger out of me, he finally turned me around to be able to gaze at him straight on. His eyes were dark with desire as he raised his hand, which was sticky with my cum, and put his fingers in his drink, stirring the ice around, taking a long swallow while keeping his eyes on mine.

My eyes widened at what I was watching him do. My brain finally caught up to me and my body flushed at the realization of what we had just done. I can't believe I let him fuck me at the bar. I let him finger fuck me while a man was talking to me. I could feel the heat in my cheeks burning as embarrassment filled my being.

What if we were caught?

No, we were, but the man was too belligerent to know what was going on.

This isn't what I wanted. I needed to talk to him. To know where we stood. To know I wasn't just a fuck. To know that I meant something to him.

Pulling his face down to mine, I licked a small drip of his whiskey off his bottom lip, sucking until he moaned into me. Pleasure raced through me that I could make this man as needy as he does me.

"I want to talk to you." I leaned into his ear, hopeful he could hear me over the noise.

Watching concern cross his face, he nodded. "Let's go to the back." James grabbed my hand and pulled me in the direction of the private rooms. This was where we always went. The thoughts of what he might have had planned for me had my pussy throbbing again and my mind going blank.

Tick...

The security guard glanced at us as we approached the red door leading to the private rooms and nodded, letting us through.

The hallway was dark and empty, the light of a camera winking at the other end. Smiling to himself, James pulled me flush up against him, pressing me against the wall with my hands pinned above my head.

"They can see us," I protested as he pressed against me, my eye catching the camera.

"That's the point, love." He put his thigh between my legs, settling right into the spot that had my eyes rolling into the back of my head, and I forgot about the camera. My breasts were pressed up against his chest, my eyes hooded as desire and lust rushed through me. My tongue slipped out to wet my suddenly dry lips, and his mouth crashed into mine in a clash of teeth and tongue.

He tasted of whiskey and my own sweetness. His tongue slid against mine in a fight for dominance, one that I gave in to freely.

A moan escaped me as he slowly moved a hand up my side, lightly cupping my breast in his hand, molding it to his pleasure. He pinched my nipple, rolling it between his fingers, shooting pleasure straight to my core.

Bringing his hands down to cup my ass, he lifted me in the air and I instinctively wrapped my legs around his waist, my hands diving into his hair. My dress rode up to my hips as I ground down against his bulge. "What was it you wanted to ask me?" He ground against me, my mind going blank as he hit just the right spot. A moan poured out of me as he pulled back, his lust-filled gaze boring into mine. "We aren't going any further until you talk," he murmured as his hand slowly grasped my throat, my pulse fluttering beneath his fingertips.

Reality came tumbling down as I realized what we were doing. That he was so easily able to distract me from my main focus. He was fire, enticing and dangerous, and I was a moth tempted to be burned by his desires. We were dancing a fine line between lust and more, but I couldn't do this anymore. I couldn't stand by and be his plaything. Jules was right. I deserved better.

Taking a breath, I lowered my shaking legs to stand. I wasn't going to have this talk wrapped around him, grinding against his cock. I needed to stand up for myself, which meant standing on two legs. I wasn't going to go into that room if all he wants is his weekly fuck. Plenty of girls here would gladly take him up on his offer. So why me?

His eyes widened at my sudden change of demeanor. Letting go of me, he took a step back himself. "What's wrong?" Concern filled his voice as his forehead creased in worry, creating a deep line between his brows.

My heart pounded against my ribcage, fighting to get free, as my palms started to sweat. I could do this. I needed to do this. "What are we doing? What are we?" I asked, my heart in my throat, afraid that all of this was for naught.

Surprise lifted his eyebrows and was just as quickly replaced with anger, his features darkening into a low fury. "What brought this about?" he asked, his voice lower than normal, raking a shiver down my spine.

He went to move toward me and I jumped. His eyes lowered into slits, pissed that I had flinched at his approach. Slowly, he moved one hand to the door, opening it and ushering me inside to slam it shut behind us.

I knew the room's layout by heart. There was a couch straight to the left of the door, a coffee table in front of it, and a mini bar to the right. Off in the far-right corner was a bathroom and in the center of the room was a massive bed with black, linen sheets.

Grabbing me, he pressed me against the wall, his hands on either side of my head. He bracketed me in, sending a shot of fear through me. Had I angered him that much that he would hurt me? No. He would never do that. Would he? I had never seen him angry, and the look of malevolence in his eyes had me cowering.

Should I have not asked? No. It needed to be addressed.

The tension in the room rose as he glowered down at me. Straightening myself to my full height, I pushed my fear and doubts aside. I refused to be cowed by him. I deserved to know.

Leaning down, his breath fanned my face as his lips barely grazed mine. "You are mine, Jane. I have no intention of ever letting you go. So get any of those stupid little ideas out of your head," he whispered against my lips, sending a shiver of desire through me. "I don't know where you got the idea that you were anything else, but you better lose it," he ground out.

He thought he owned me? What the hell kind of horse shit was that? "I am not some whore to be owned," I snapped, glaring back at him.

"Ohhh, love." He grasped my throat, a light touch, slightly pressing down on me as my pulse fluttered back to life beneath his palm. "You are *my* whore. And I don't share what's mine."

Shaking my head, I fought the urge to bend to his will. "No. If that's all I am to you, then we are done. I deserve better than that," I said flatly, pushing all of my emotion out of my voice. My heart was slowly cracking into pieces. Tiny shards that were being held together by thin threads, but I wasn't going to be his toy.

A flush crept up James' neck, his features slowly mottling into a rage, sending another shot of fear through me. Fuck. Letting go of my throat, he scooped low, grabbing my legs and throwing me over his shoulder as if I were weightless.

"What the hell!" I slapped his lower back as he strode across the room. "James!" *Slap.* "Put." *Slap.* "Me." *Slap.* "Dow—" I screeched as I bounced onto the bed. I flailed to get my hair out of my face, trying to place where the hell he was. I felt a hand grab my ankle, pulling me forward until I was sitting at the edge of the bed.

Pinching my chin between his fingers, he leaned down into my face. "We are going to get one thing straight here, Jane. You don't have a choice." Removing his fingers from my chin, he slowly traced the hollow of my throat as tears formed in my eyes. He was fucking insane.

"I refuse to be just a weekly fuck, James. I am done being your toy..." I said quietly, praying my low tone would keep the beast burning in his eyes at bay.

Picking me up, he sat himself down, pulling me into his lap as my legs wrapped back around him. I didn't want to have this conversation like this. It was too close, my body still singing from earlier. Resting my hands against his chest, he gripped my hips harshly. Slowly moving my body against his creating a slow burn that could easily catch into a fiery storm if we weren't careful.

"Look at me, love." Bringing my gaze to meet his, my breath caught in his stare. "You are not a toy. But you are mine." Moving his hand around, it found its way to my soaked panties, toying with my clit beneath the fabric. A low moan rolled from my chest as he kept playing with me. "This beautiful body? Mine." *Flick.* "Your pussy? Mine." *Flick.* "Your heart? Mine," he growled as he captured my lips between his, forcing my mouth open to his onslaught of desire, anger, and, beneath it all, desperation.

Throwing my head back, I ground myself against him, craving the friction he had been stoking in me. I needed something to bring some sort of relief. Pulling back from him, I gazed into the blue storms that were his eyes. "James... I need to know. Is there anyone else?" I pressed my lips to his neck, feathering kisses toward his ear. My breath caught in my chest, my heart pounding, waiting for his answer.

"No... Only you." Running his hands up my back, he slid the straps of my dress off my shoulders as he kissed and licked his way down my throat and collarbone. Pushing the dress down over my breasts to pool at my waist, his mouth went straight to one nipple as he kneaded and massaged the other, sending waves of pleasure through me. Arching my back to give him more access, I pull on his hair, my only grip on reality. A groan escaped him as he laved my breasts with attention, vibrating the already hardened peak. His eyes gazed up at mine, blown wide with angry desire. "Anything else, baby girl?" He nipped at the underside of my breast, sending chills through me.

"James... please..." I moaned his name, grinding harder onto his jeans, my pussy weeping for relief. I couldn't think anymore. He made it clear that I wasn't going anywhere and neither was he.

Chuckling, he moved his hand back between my thighs. "What is it you want, Jane? Use your words." His lips brushed against mine lightly, just a tease, building an inferno that needed to be satisfied by any means necessary at this point.

"I need you..." I gasped as he pinched my clit. Gods, this man would be the death of me. Who cared if he was a walking red flag? The way he made me feel was beyond this world.

"You need what?" He nipped my bottom lip. He could keep this up all night, he'd done it before. Watching me get the point of just a needy thing, just for him, begging him for any type of relief.

"I need you... please... please..." I whispered, moving my hands down from his chest to his jeans, trying to unsnap them, but he wouldn't let me move to get to him.

Flipping us, he pulled my dress off as he kissed his way down my neck and between my breasts, fondling them as he made his way to my navel. "Anything for my girl..." He pulled on my piercing quickly before nipping his way down my hip to my core. Peering up at me, he slid a finger through my folds as I bucked into his hand, silently pleading for more. Grinning, he lowered his head and traced his tongue up and down my slit, taking his sweet time tasting me before sucking my clit into his hot mouth.

Hot pleasure raced down my spine and straight to my core as he sucked, licked, and nipped at me, bringing me close to the brink of release before he moved his mouth south, a cry of displeasure escaping me as I felt a smile form on his face.

"Impatient little thing tonight, aren't you?" he asked against my thigh as he kissed the sensitive skin there, his five o'clock shadow rubbing against it.

Squirming beneath him, I ignored his question and pushed his head back against my weeping cunt, needing his mouth on me. Moaning at my response, he delved his tongue deep into me, thrusting in and out, pinning my hips down and pressing on my lower stomach.

My breath hitched and came in pants, wetness coating his tongue. Pushing a finger inside and curling up, I clenched down around him and my legs started quivering again.

"You gonna come again for me, love?" he rasped.

Grabbing his head again, I pushed him back to where I needed him. "Don't stop..." I gasped out.

Giving me one long lick from bottom to top, he chuckled against my skin. "You don't tell me what to do." He moved up my body, purposely denying my release.

"That's not fair," I growled out my frustration as I moved my hand down my body and quickly circled my clit. I almost purred at the satisfaction that brought me. Just a couple more flicks and I'll—

James moved quickly, grabbing my hands and, once again, pinned them above my head. "Did I say you could touch yourself?" he growled in my ear as a shiver of anticipation ran down my spine.

I knew there was frustration written on my face. There was no hiding it. My body was aching and he was playing with me like I was his favorite toy. "No," was all I said, knowing if I said more, I'd be punished.

"Then don't." He got up and slid his pants down, his long, hard length popping free of its restraint.

Lying back down on top of me, he slid his tip up and down my slit, coating himself in my slick. I arched into him, my breasts high, almost as an offering. He lowered his head and took one of my nipples into his mouth, biting softly as he notched himself at my center.

My eyes rolled back as I mewled from the pleasure of finally feeling him against me. Slowly, he pressed inside me, my walls clenching around him tightly, and he threw his head back. "Fuck, woman, you will be the death of me one day," he ground out. He slowly pulled back and thrust deeply inside me, filling me fully.

"James, please... I'm almost there." My legs wrapped around his hips as I pulled him deeper and my arms wound around him. scratching long lines down his back that were surely going to be there long after we were done.

Grunting his approval, he moved faster. My hardened peaks rubbed against his lightly haired chest, our gazes locked. He lowered his mouth to mine, sweeping his tongue across my bottom lip. "Now, darling, you may touch yourself. I want to watch as you make yourself come all over my cock."

Doing as he asked, I quickly flicked my clit, once... twice... the third time sent me soaring. My screams of relief echoed around us as James kept up a punishing pace until he found his release, finishing inside me.

Slowly coming down from my high, James had laid his head on my chest, listening to my heartbeat come back to normal levels. "It's been a long time. Gods, I've missed you," he whispered.

"It's only been a week." I laughed, my hands making small, gentle circles up and down his back, completely sated and content.

"You have no idea how long a week can be," he answered, his arms tightening around me as I fell asleep in his arms.

Chapter Seven

Jon

Lily was here. My heart still raced at the thought that she was right there. Was it a coincidence? It was obvious she was trying not to be seen, but the men hassling her made her out. Lucky for me, or I never would have known.

My thoughts were still wandering when Isabella and I stopped in front of her door. "Are you okay?" she asked quietly.

I should be asking her that. I hadn't said much since I got back to the bar. The shock of seeing Lily, the portal, and the bar fight put a real damper on the evening. What was I supposed to tell her? *Oh, sorry, that was just my ex? And I ran after her?* What a great date this turned out to be.

"Oh, yes. I'm just disappointed that our time together ended early. I am sorry about that, by the way. I have never seen that happen there in the whole time I have been drinking at that bar," I rambled, praying that she didn't bring up Lily.

"Oh, that wasn't my first time witnessing a bar fight. The first time the lady won, maybe." My heart clenched at the mention of Lily in a fight. Isabella smiled softly up at me before continuing. "Did you know her?"

There it was.

My sharp intake of breath no doubt clued her in that was the wrong question to ask, but she just stared, waiting patiently for me to think of my reply. I don't know if I am grateful for that or not. It would have been almost easier if she had just taken the hint to let it lie, but Isabella was not anything but thorough.

"Yes. She was a childhood friend," was the only thing I could think of to say. I didn't want to ruin this night with her any more than it already was. It wasn't a lie. We were friends—until we became more, and then nothing.

She just nodded and turned towards the door, her key in hand. I could tell she wanted more of an explanation than that, but there was nothing more to tell. I couldn't talk about my childhood, especially where Lily was concerned. It was not only complicated, but half of it sounded delusional. There was no way to explain it without sounding insane.

As she stepped inside the flat, Isabella sighed. She turned and looked back at me, running her fingers through her hair. Hair that I wanted to feel a few hours ago myself and now thought it was not just a bad idea, but the idea turned me off altogether. She wasn't Lily. "Don't forget to get those reports to me as soon as you can. The police are going to want to know your findings." Disappointment showed through her voice at the way the whole night ended. It was probably for the best we kept ourselves professional.

I nodded my agreeance on the matter, as if what she stated was, in fact, what I was thinking. "Yes, I will. Again, I am so sorry about what happened tonight." Shoving my hands in my pockets, I shrugged my shoulders. There wasn't much else to say.

"Yes. Well, good night, doctor," she said quietly as she closed the door, the lock latching felt like a blow.

Grimacing to myself, I turned to go back to my car. The storms must have finally made their way to this part of town as the rain drizzled down to add to my despair. The warmth of the interior did little to rid the chill from my bones.

Why was Lily here? How long has she been coming to London? Hell, how long had she been sitting in that bar? There was no way it was a coincidence. I didn't believe in them. Everything happened for a reason and she had one. But how am I to find out what it was? She literally ran from me.

Taking the turn for my drive, I pressed the button for the garage and pulled in without much thought. My house was on the larger side, as I have found to like space. Whenever we returned from Neverland, the smallness of our flat felt like it was pressing in on me. I much preferred the openness of my space now. The ability to breathe without feeling like someone else would bump into you was welcoming.

As I stepped into the foyer, the clambering of claws against the wood floors as Dixie, my Doberman puppy, came barreling through the house. She was as clumsy as could be, but she was one of the things I loved coming home to most. She was always here waiting impatiently for treats and pets. She reminded me of our dog, Nana, when we were young. Having passed away years ago, I finally decided to get a dog of my own. If not just for companionship, but to be alert of intruders when Jane was here, not that she was great at it. If someone threw her a chicken nugget, they'd be her new best friend.

I ruffled her behind the ears, her soft fur tickling my fingers. Going into the kitchen, I grabbed a rawhide for her and filled her water dish, hoping to keep her occupied for the night. She sat, impatiently waiting for me to hand her the treat, her tail wagging furiously beneath her. I let her grab it from me and she bounded back through the house to Gods knew where to settle in, giving me a chance to go upstairs and get cleaned up.

Hell, I wanted to wash away the night. To forget it even happened.

Striding into the master, I headed straight to the bath, shedding my clothes along the way. They were suffocating in a way that made my skin itch and my lungs burn. Only a reminder of what the night had brought me. Memories, questions, and disappointment.

The temperature of the water was scalding as I stepped underneath its spray, letting it burn away the long-buried memories that kept coming forth in my mind.

Seeing Lily, Gods, it had been so long. A grown woman now, full of curves and bite, came to the fore. She wasn't a woman to be trifled with, that was for sure. Heat slid through my body, settling low, my cock thickening at the thought of her.

Fuck.

Grabbing the base of my staff, I slowly pumped myself up and down, the memory of her ass swaying as she walked away from me bright in my mind's eye. Imagining that I had caught up to her and could feel her full, plump lips beneath mine, tangling my tongue with hers, had a groan rumble through my chest. I pumped myself faster as I thought of her silky hair running through my fingers as I slid myself inside her tight cunt. Heat built up in my lower back as I felt myself ready to come. The thought of her coming around my cock, spasming and screaming my name, had me calling out hers in the shower as I came harder than I had in a long time.

Shuddering under the now-cooling water, I cleaned myself up and shook myself from my thoughts. I hadn't done that in a long time, especially to her. There was no doubt in my mind that I would see her again. And when I did, I wasn't letting her go.

Stepping out of the shower, I let the water drip from my body as I looked at myself in the mirror. What the fuck was wrong with me? Pining after a woman who chose another man over me?

I heard Dixie barking from downstairs, knocking me out of my reverie. Odd. Who the hell would be at my house this late at night? Throwing on a black tee and some jeans, I padded down to the front foyer to find her growling at the door.

"Good girl." I patted her head as I opened the door. A man I hadn't ever seen before stood before me. His hair was disheveled, sopping wet from the storm. A long scar slashed through his face, but his eyes. I would never forget my brother's eyes. "Michael?"

"Jon," he answered, his voice gruff.

Pulling my brother in for a hug, I gripped him as memories of Neverland took hold. He was alive. Laughing, we stepped back, taking each other in. He was as tall as I was and just as built. Mine from the gym and rock climbing on the weekends. Him, survival of the fittest.

Stepping into the house, Michael peered around, looking for what, I was not quite sure.

"We thought you were dead," I stated. My heart was pounding wildly, but felt ten times bigger than it had a few moments ago.

"I had almost died so many times I lost count. But here I am, still kicking ass," he answered as he followed me to the kitchen.

"Did Pan finally bring you back?" I grabbed two glasses from the cabinet and a bottle of scotch. This was worth celebrating.

"Pan's dead."

I stilled, the blood rushing through my ears the only thing I could hear. "What do you mean, Pan's dead? How are you here if he isn't?"

"The ship. I joined up with Barrington and was able to get off here for a few hours. I just wanted to let you and Wendy know. Neverland is dying. I—I'm probably not coming back. I just wanted to see you guys one last time."

"Then stay! Why do you have to go back?!" Confusion warred inside of me as grief for my friend descended into my chest.

"It's a long story. But Barrington will look for me if I don't return soon." Michael gripped me and held on for a long moment. "Gods, I missed you two."

"Don't go back. We can figure this out." Pulling back, Michael stood tall in front of me, no longer the boy I remembered, but a pirate.

"I can't, but tell my nieces that I love them. Wendy is in bad shape. You might want to check on her. She didn't take the news of Pan very well."

Gripping the sides of the counter, I counted to ten. He visited Wendy. Fuck.

I nod. "I'll check on her in the morning. Give her time to process."

"Thank you."

And just like that, my brother was gone as quickly as he had come.

Chapter Eight

JANE

The ride home from the club was quiet. My ears were still slightly ringing, but my body ached in the most delicious of ways. Jules was slumped over and half-passed out in the seat beside me, the passing streetlights casting shadows over her still form.

My time together with James had been getting more and more intense as time wore on, and I am not quite sure how I felt about it. The man had me in a chokehold. Whenever he was around, my body instantly reacted to his, like electricity through my veins at his touch, and I melded to his whims in his hands. He was danger, wrapped in lust and sin.

The taxi had stopped in front of the house, bringing me out of my deep thoughts. After paying the driver, I shook Jules awake and stepped out onto the sidewalk. The cool autumn night was damp from the recent rain with a bite to the air from the breeze coasting off the street.

Goosebumps coasted down my arms as the car pulled away from the curb, and we stumbled our way up to the front steps. Our aching feet sloshed through the small, cold puddles to get there, adding to their pain.

Jules sat on the front stoop, waiting for me to get the key out, her dress slightly askew and her legs spread, like she gave no fucks about who saw what. Good thing it was late and we were the only ones out on the street. As I went to pass her to unlock the door, I felt her cold fingers grasp my ankle, halting me. "What is that?" Jules slurred as she picked up a small bag that I had almost stepped on. Hell, I would have tripped on it in my bumbling state.

Bending at the knee, I stooped down to get a better look at what it was, my brain sloshing at the movement, and noticed it was a small marble bag. What the hell was it doing here? The design on it was something I had never seen before. Swirls of leaves, vines, and flowers in white across the dark blue, almost black, silk fabric caught the light as I took it from Jules to get a better view. As I did, a sprinkling of sparkling, white powder fell out of the bag. Fear clutched at my heart as I recognized it for what it was.

Dust.

Fuck, fuck, fuck, fuck, fuck...

I dropped the fabric immediately, rubbing my hands down my dress, my ass hitting the concrete hard as I tried to get the vile drug off of me. Flashbacks of that night came to mind as my breath caught in my throat.

No, no, no. I didn't ingest it. I didn't breathe it in. I am fine.

I am fine.

My thoughts spun as I stood up to go inside, turned towards the door, and found it slightly ajar.

Mom.

The fear that had been choking me earlier was now full-blown terror, my heart racing as drops of rain from the roof dripped onto my face. "Julie, stay here. I'm going to find Mom."

Pushing the door open slowly, my heart in my throat as I found the sprinkling of Dust all over the walls and floor of the entryway. Pressing the door all the way open, I saw the table was askew from where it normally sits and Mom's favorite whiskey was toppled over, dripping all over the floor.

She must have been having a bad night if she had been drinking that much. Worry wormed through me at that thought. What had set her off to be drinking straight out of the bottle? She was depressed earlier, but not that bad.

"Mom?" I called out, the quiet hush of the house my only answer.

"Where's Mom?" I heard Jules from the front.

"Just stay there, Julie!"

Jules came staggering in behind me, a gasp leaving her lips as she took in the scene I was staring at. "We need to find Mom," she slurred, reiterating what I was already trying to do.

Shaking my head, I picked my way across the carpet, trying to avoid getting either the drug or the whiskey on me. I made my way to the living area, where the desk was pulled apart and the glass flower vase shattered on the floor with water and flowers strewn across the room.

Pulling my phone out, I dialed the only person I could think of to help. The ringing stopped as a deep, sleep-ridden voice answered.

"Uncle Jon? Uncle Jon?!" I called out, panic ringing through my voice.

"Jane? What's wrong?" I could hear him shuffling around, probably trying to find his glasses.

"Someone was here... the house—" I started, panic filling me that the person might still be here. "Mom... she's gone..." I trailed off as I slowly made my way to the staircase. If the intruder was still here, they would have heard me by now. But seeing as Mom was missing, they were probably gone as well.

"Don't move. Don't go anywhere, Jane. Go outside and wait for me there." I heard my uncle distantly as I peeked up the stairs, clothes scattered everywhere.

"I'm going upstairs. I need to see—"

"JANE! GO OUTSIDE!" I heard him yell into the phone, panic and fear evident in his voice, matching mine.

Ending the call, I grabbed the banister with shaking hands. I could do this. I could do hard things.

"Should we be going up there?" I jumped as terror skidded down my spine. I had forgotten Jules had followed me into the house.

Placing a hand on my now racing heart, I glanced behind me to see Jules waiting on my decision. Peering back up to the top of the stairs, my knees started shaking and sweat lined my brow. "We need to check and make sure she's not up there. She could be hurt," I stated, more for my own sake than hers.

Step by step, I passed pictures of the three of us at plays, recitals, and graduations. Some of the pictures were of Jules and me playing or at parties. It was like walking through a tunnel of memories, which may indeed be just that—memories.

I don't know what I am going to find at the top, but worry and dread slid through my veins, making it hard to breathe. There wasn't much up here but clothes that looked to have been dragged out of the rooms. It was the rooms I was more concerned with. You can't hide in a hallway, but you can in a bedroom.

Stopping outside the first room on the right, Mom's room, I peered inside. "Mom?"

"Sshhh! You don't wanna call out her name?!" Jules frantically tried shushing me. "What if the perp is still here?"

"I am more concerned about my mother than some piece of shit that broke into my house. I'll deal with whatever may pop out. Besides, it's two against one. Odds are in our favor," I whispered back, trying to keep Jules under control. Her drunk ass needed to be outside, but again, drunk.

Turning on the light, Mom's room was torn apart. Everything was off the bed and her clothes were thrown everywhere, from the dresser to the closet. Even her jewelry was scattered along the floor.

Pulling myself out of the carnage, I forced Julie to move on to the next room. Her room.

"Oh, that son of a bitch!" she screeched as she took in the destruction that had been wrought in her space. "Imma kill him! Where is the fucker? He's gonna die..." Jules stomped around the room, searching high and low, stumbling and falling as she took in all her belongings.

"Is anything missing?" I asked, trying to keep her occupied.

"I don't know!" she cried as she sat in a cluster of dresses on the floor. Truthfully, I wouldn't know if most of this destruction was from her before we left or the intruder. She was a tornado in human form most days, reminding me that maybe it wasn't all that bad.

Sighing, I took a step back as I moved down to my room. My room used to be what Mom called the nursery, and it was in worse shape than the two rooms before. My dresser and bed were in pieces. My pillows were torn apart, the fluff in places I never thought it could land. My clothes were strewn all over, a few of them slashed through and cut to pieces.

Too much. It was too much.

Bile clawed up my throat as I flew down the hall to the bath, throwing up everything that I had.

I don't know what I had done, nor why my room was the main source of their violence. But it was quite apparent that I was the main target and Mom was just collateral.

I didn't know how much time had passed. The cool tile against my cheek let me know I was still at home, but I was too exhausted to be bothered to move. Where to anyway? Everything was torn apart. What could they have been looking for?

"Jane? Julie?" I heard my uncle from a distance, but couldn't muster the energy to call out.

"Jane?!" I heard again. Blinking to try and bring myself back to the present, I forced my arms under my body and grunted as I pressed my body into a sitting position. "Jane! Oh, my Gods, are you alright?" Uncle Jon rushed into the bathroom as I rested myself against the wall, the room spinning. Nothing like throwing up all the alcohol you drank on a surge of adrenaline to get you semi-sober.

"She's gone. The house—" I cried into his shoulder as he picked me up. "We aren't going to worry about it right now. We are getting you two home and then we'll talk," he stated as he jostled me into his arms and made our way down the stairs, glass crunching under his shoes as he headed to the door.

Outside, it had started raining again. The drops that pelted against my feverish skin felt like little knives trying to pierce their way into my soul and cleanse it of this night.

"I found it! He didn't take it!" Jules yelled from inside the house.

"Found what?" Uncle Jon asked me, perplexed, as he turned around so we could see what she was screaming about. My uncle's face flushed ten shades of purple as he caught sight of what Jules' most prized possession was.

A pink and purple dildo, the length of her forearm, was proudly thrusted in the air as she twirled in drunken happiness. "Mr. C. Duction!"

Embarrassment flooded through me at the sight of my best friend on the stoop of our house, waving around this enormous dick.

"Oh fuck, sorry, Uncle Jon!" Jules ran back into the house, her face red as a tomato, as if she had just realized who was there.

Giggles came unbidden as my uncle settled me into the passenger seat. "There are some things I don't need to know about you two. And that was one of them." He shook his head as if trying to shake the image that was probably burned into his brain. I know it was mine. But Gods, it was funny.

Jules came back outside, quiet and still red-faced. "I am so sorry," she apologized as she passed Uncle Jon, climbing into the back of the car.

"It's alright. We all make mistakes," he grumbled as he made his way back up to the door to lock it.

Watching out the window, my vision blurred from exhaustion as I saw him bend down and pick up the bag I had left on the front step. The need to tell him to be careful burned within me, but the night's events had caught up to me and I felt myself slowly slipping into unconsciousness.

Chapter Nine

MICHAEL

The ship was sitting in the river by the club, swaying gently in waves. Being from Neverland, the Crimson Krok was cast in faery dust, making it invisible to the human eye except for those who knew how to look for it.

The crew was all accounted for and we were all waiting for our most illustrious leader. Knowing him, he was probably balls deep in some random pussy I didn't want to know about. But being late was starting to become a habit of his and was going to lead to trouble if he didn't stop worrying about getting his dick wet while here.

I understood his reasoning behind not fucking any of the women in Pirate's Cove, but it was irritating waiting on him to finish his business while we were all watching the time tick by and the stars slowly fade from view. If we waited much longer, we'd be stuck here until tomorrow night, and *that* was not something we could do.

I climbed the rigging, making myself comfortable on the yardarm, right below the crow's nest, giving me a good viewpoint of the crew below and of anyone coming up to the ship. Pulling my dagger from its sheath, I ran the sharpening stone along its blade. It was already plenty sharp, but the action was more calming for my nerves than the actual necessity of it.

Seeing Wendy and Jon for the first time since I left made me realize that a lot has changed since I lived here. I missed them horribly, but since I went missing all those years ago, I couldn't just show back up and act as if nothing happened. It was easier this way.

I had to tell them about Neverland. I don't know what possessed me to do so, but my gut twisted at the thought that they would come searching for me one day and find nothing there. The island of dreams was gone. Telling them that Pan was dead was the hardest thing I have had to do in a long time. His death still haunted me. But if I knew Wendy, she deserved to know the man she was in love with died. I had been searching the island high and low for the man. The man who once hung dreams for all of us to live upon died with all our hopes and wishes with him.

Spotting a hulking figure walk out of the back door to the club, I shook myself from my musings and stopped sharpening my blade. Barrington was a formidable fellow and had had his fair share of run-ins with the Fae on the island, leaving him with a slight limp on his left leg. That was how I recognized him.

The Fae had become insidious creatures that liked to cause harm to anything they could. Running out of beings to torture on Neverland, they weaponized pixie dust and turned it into a type of drug for humans to consume. What they get out of it, I had no idea. I know that Barrington was brought to Neverland to ferry the Dust back and forth, but other than that, I tried to stay out of the politics of the island. The less you knew, or the less you talked about knowing, the better for your health.

The way Barrington was walking though, I knew something was amiss. Or he'd struck out and didn't get what he was looking for. That thought brought a smirk to my lips. The poor man couldn't get laid.

I shook my head and kept watch as he lumbered his way across the gangplank, the crew at the ready to lift it and make way. Dawn was drawing close and our time here was getting short. The longer it took for us to leave port, the more likely we would be stuck here. The faery dust keeping us invisible would only last for so long.

"Smee!" Cap yelled out, impatience clear in his tone. Rolling my eyes, I got to my feet and grabbed the nearest rope, sticking my dagger between my teeth and waited until he was just under me. As he strode past the main mast, I quietly slid down the rope, landing silently behind him.

Should I do this? Probably not. He could easily kill me or try to anyways, but it was my favorite pastime to irritate the living fuck out of the man. "Yes, Cap'n?" I leaned against the mast, picking dirt out from under my nails with my knife.

The man stiffened and let out an aggravated breath that I had snuck up on him. Again. "Do you always need to do that?" he grated between his teeth before turning around to face me.

Lifting a shoulder, I looked him up and down. He looked like he got what he came for. His hair was unusually mussed, his swagger was a bit looser, and the glitter falling off his clothes was a for sure tell. A smirk crawled across my face. He must have gotten laid by the looks of it, which meant there was something else afoot, and it probably didn't bode well for us. "I get great satisfaction out of it, though you really shouldn't let someone sneak up on you. Bad form, you know?" I teased, trying to lighten his mood.

"Good thing I trust you with my life then, huh?" Hands on his hips, he looked around. "Everything ready to go?"

I nodded. "We're just waiting on you, Cap. Dawn is almost here. We need to move. Fast," I said, making a dig at him that he was late, again.

He just nodded and made his way up to the helm, completely ignoring my statement. Gritting my teeth, I followed him to await his cue. Barking out orders, the crew got ready to drop the sails. The timing needed to be perfect to make sure we made our way into the sky and not into the bridges that crossed the river.

The ship lurched away from the docks, cutting through the water with ease. Setting the course, Barrington let go of the helm and started yelling to the crew to get ready. I headed down to the deck, keeping watch on the riggings to make sure everything would unravel easily. That was my duty, besides keeping everyone in line. I had a natural affinity for ropes and knots, so it made sense to make me responsible for them.

"NOW!" he shouted, and all at once, the crew flew into a flurry of motion and the riggings let go seamlessly. I grabbed hold of one of the ropes flying past and flew into the air, being caressed by the cool night air. It was the closest thing to flying that I get to feel anymore.

Landing on the top beam, I balanced myself, slowly making my way to the crow's nest and made myself at home. The ship had lifted into the air and was flying toward the Tower of London before we banked hard to the right, heading straight to the second star.

Settling in and leaning against the top of the main mast, the cool air rushing past us flowed over me, leaving goosebumps in its wake. On our way back to the island, the sea of stars was always something to admire. The swirls of purple, blue, and green clouds of gases parted as if we were sailing through the seas.

Closing my eyes, I went back to the conversation I had with Wendy. She had kids. Two daughters. I had nieces. I was flabbergasted that she had moved on from Pan and had a family. I never saw pictures of a man, though. Which was peculiar, but from what I could gather, men weren't all they were cracked up to be anymore.

The distant sounds of shouting coming from below brought me out of my reverie. What the hell? Usually, we all took naps, or played dice or cards on our way back, as it was quiet, smooth sailing until we reached Pirate's Cove.

Peering over the side, I watched as a man was brought forth from below deck. Furrowing my brow, I leaned further over the edge to hear what was going on. The wind hurtling past made everything from below muffled, irritating the fuck out of my nerves and making me itch.

Carefully studying the scene, I caught sight of two men bringing up a woman from below. Her head was hanging low. She didn't look conscious, or even lucid, about what was going on around her.

Shock flared through me when recognition hit me. I grabbed one of the riggings and slid down to the deck, burning my hands along the way. Too fast, but necessary. I can put ointment on them later, but getting to Wendy was more important.

Barrington approached the man, a dagger hung loosely from his fingertips. "Tsk, tsk. One would think after playing with the Fae for so long, you would know better than to bait me. Now," he put his knife under the man's chin, blood trailing from the bite of it, "you are going to the brig for stowing away on my ship and for kidnapping. I am quite sure the Fae will be quite happy to know that I have found the man they are looking for."

I don't know what I missed and didn't quite care. The man could die for bringing Wendy here for all I cared. My eyes stayed on the men holding my sister, their grips not gentle and most likely going to leave bruises. My lips curled at the thought.

Looking closely at her, I noticed her skin was unusually pale and her light freckles stuck out like sore spots. There was sweat lining her brow and her breathing was shallow. Anger that the mystery man had done something to her had me clenching my teeth.

"How 'bout the woman? What shall we do with her?" one of the men asked, running his dirty fingers through her auburn curls, his nose buried in her neck as he slowly raised his head and dragged his tongue up her cheek.

Disgust rolled through me as rage boiled through my veins. A growl escaped my throat as I unsheathed my dagger, stepping toward the man, not allowing him a chance to recant his statement. Sliding my blade across his throat, blood spewed like a fountain, covering both me and Wendy in its wake. The man's eyes were wide with shock as he choked and coughed on his own blood. Heaving him back, I let him fall overboard into the gaseous clouds that flowed past, leaving him to die in the void of space.

No one touched a woman like that on this ship. They had plenty of pussy back in the harbor. This just spoke out to this man's character and I wasn't having it. Even worse, she was my own flesh and blood, and that just would not do. I protected my own.

"I think you all got the message. Touch her and die." Cap's eyebrow was cocked at me, but said nothing further. "Bring her to my quarters. We'll let her rest up there."

Stepping up to the man holding Wendy's prone body, I lifted her into my arms and strode towards the captain's room.

Blood from the crewman slid down my chest and pooled into her blouse, more than what was already soaked into it. Grimacing at my lack of tact, I realized I was going to have to bathe her at some point, and that was just not something I wanted to do. I would have to find one of the women on board to do the task.

Barrington was on the far end of his room, watching me intently as I laid her down on his bed. Grimacing again, I turned towards the man who held a question on his face, but was keeping silent.

I moved to his side, grabbed one of his glass tumblers, and poured myself two fingers of his whiskey, shooting it down and letting it burn away at the adrenaline still roiling through me.

"Who is she?" he asked quietly.

I sighed, knowing this was going to bring hell to us all. I stared out the back windows, watching the clouds and stars pass us by, wondering if, by some miracle, I could get her back to London before the island felt her presence.

No. We were in for our biggest adventure yet.

"My sister," was all I could muster to say before I turned and walked out of his room.

Chapter Ten

WENDY

The sway of the bed I was on made my stomach turn and my head pound. This has got to be the worst hangover I have ever had. I don't even remember drinking that much.

My eyes were glued shut, with what felt like sandpaper, and my tongue was stuck to the roof of my mouth. My arms felt like lead held them down and my body ached all over. What happened?

Groaning, I thought back to what I did remember.

Jane and Julie leaving for the night.

A man on my doorstep.

No. Michael.

Michael was alive.

Peter was dead.

Neverland was dying.

Then, all went blank.

Dread slid through me. Something wasn't right, but I couldn't quite place what it was. What the fuck? How am I missing part of my night?

Breathing deep, I caught the scent of the ocean and the sound of gulls hit my ears. Fear snaked its way through my brain. I pried my eyes open, groaning as I forced my arms to my face to rub the tired away and see where I could be. I knew I wasn't home. I lived nowhere near the ocean, and the continued sway told me I wasn't in my bed.

The sun filtered in through a nearby window, blinding me. My hand flew over my face to block it out, leaving me to see spots behind my eyelids as pain flared through my head. "Shit…" I mumbled under my breath, my throat feeling hoarse, as I tried to regain my vision and waited for the pain to subside.

Slowly, this time, I opened my eyes and peered through my fingers, giving myself time to adjust to the brightness outside. Carefully, I crawled my way across the bed closer to the window, taking in where I could possibly be.

The cove was full of life, with people hustling between the wood and metal buildings. The town sat in front of a copse of tropical trees. Laughter filled the air, mingling with the sounds of ocean waves and the sea birds overhead. Looking down, it now made sense why I felt a sway. I was on water, so I must be on a ship of sorts. But how?

Turning my body back around felt like torture. All my muscles were tight and straining against the movement. All I could think of was a long soak in a hot tub, a full body massage, and some Tylenol. But from the looks of where I was, that wasn't going to happen. Sitting up, the room spun, forcing me to close my eyes once more to fight the nausea that came with it. Fuck me.

Slowly, my eyes opened and I took in the room I had slept in. It was all wood. Floors, walls, ceiling. There was what looked to be a sitting area in the middle of the room. To my left was another bank of windows with a huge desk in front of it. To the right of the desk was a collection of bottles, alcohol of sorts, I assumed. To the right of me was a door. Was it locked, though?

Setting my feet on the wood floor, I almost expected it to be unfinished, like I should be watching for splinters. Instead, my toes were met with cool, smooth boards. Why would I think they wouldn't be finished? Everything else seemed nice.

A memory was tickling the back of my mind, but I couldn't concentrate on it to bring it forth. Sighing to myself, I shook my head at the thought. No use giving myself a headache over something I couldn't remember anyway.

A commotion outside the door caught my ear. A man barking orders that I couldn't make out before I heard keys jingle in the lock. So, I was locked in, a captive. Fear gripped my body and I couldn't move. Frozen in place, I watched as the door opened slowly, not a creak to be heard from the hinges.

The man silhouetted in the door frame was big. His shoulders were broad with his waist tapering in slightly. His legs were thick as well, as if he could crush boulders with them. Stepping into the cabin, he closed the door behind him, leaving me alone with this behemoth of a man.

Another wave of dizziness hit me and I couldn't stop myself from swaying forward. I heard the man rush towards me, catching me before I hit the floor.

"Better be careful. Coming down off Dust will make you sicker than a dog." The man's deep voice vibrated through my skull, making me wince.

"Who are you? Where am I?" I croaked, the feeling of knives raking my throat. I needed water. And what the hell was Dust?

"That is an interesting question with an equally compelling answer," the mystery man answered, being quite vague and irritating.

"Can't you answer anything directly?" This infuriating man was eating up my little bit of patience, and the fact that he was still holding me upright wasn't helping.

A dark chuckle was my only answer.

"What so fucking funny?" I sniped as I pushed away from the behemoth. I raised my hand to run it through my hair, getting stuck in the tangles. I was still dizzy, but I wasn't going to let this man help me any more than necessary.

"You remind me of a friend of mine. She doesn't cut corners either and has the mouth of a sailor. Quite fitting, if you ask me," he stated as he turned away from me and headed toward what looked to be the bar in the corner. The clank of the glass hitting the counter and the smell of the whiskey he was pouring made my stomach turn.

No more drinking for me.

Sitting back on the edge of the bed, I studied the man who was my captor. Because what else could he be? His raven hair was long, with waves hanging down to his shoulders. Strays hung over his clear blue eyes that studied me like a specimen he didn't know what to do with. His lips were full, with a five o'clock shadow that traced his sharp jaw. There was an earring in his left ear and a gold chain hanging around his neck. His black shirt looked made of light linen, unbuttoned halfway down his chest, showing off a light dusting of chest hair. The shirt was tucked into a pair of form-fitting pants that looked to be made to move swiftly in, not like jeans. His waist was thick, but most likely, it was all muscle from working on the ship. He was a good-looking guy. Not my type, but still handsome.

His demeanor screamed menacing, but I couldn't bring myself to be afraid. He had just saved me from falling face-first onto the floor and, from all accounts, hadn't harmed me.

"What is Dust?" I asked, breaking the silent stare down. My throat still felt like it was on fire, but I wasn't going to ask for a drink from the bar.

"A drug," was all he said.

"A what? I don't do drugs. I may drink, but no—" I shook my head as confusion barreled through me, causing another wave of nausea to pass. "I wouldn't do it."

"Well, you did. I don't know what else to tell you." He dared to chuckle under his breath.

The thought of raking my nails down this man's face ran through my mind as I got my bearings.

The man turned around, poured something into a different glass, and came toward me. If I could have backed up further, I would have, but I was already against the bed, and lying down in front of this man just wasn't something I was willing to do. Handing me the glass, I gazed into it and saw nothing but what appeared to be water.

"Drink. It's just water."

I took a small sip of the cool, refreshing liquid. The taste brought me back to Neverland. The water was always so crisp and clean. My eyes widened as I asked again, "Who are you? Where am I?"

A dark grin came over the man's face as fear spiked through me. "I am Captain Barrington, dear girl. Welcome to Neverland."

Chapter Eleven

WENDY

Shock radiated through me at the man's statement.

"No," was all I could say, shaking my head in denial. I couldn't fly anymore and Peter never came for me. Gods knew that Michael would never bring me here willingly. He stated that before he left. "I shouldn't be here."

The captain just cocked an eyebrow at me, almost like he found my displeasure amusing. "Shouldn't, and are, are two different things, and one is the truth."

"Or they are both the truth and we are all fucked," I spat at the man as I stumbled across the room and sank into the soft, red cushions of the sofa. The room still spun slightly, but not nearly as bad as before I drank the water.

The captain tilted his head at me as if I had somehow confused him. "Care to explain that statement?" he asked, his eyes narrowed and his jaw clenched.

"I am not talking anymore until I see my brother." I wasn't going to divulge any information to this man. I have no reason to trust him. My brother might, and I will let him decide how much to tell him, but I don't know this man and I refuse to blatantly trust anyone on this island. Not anymore.

"And you assume I know who this supposed brother is?" he asked me, the corner of his lip quirking up into a sly smile.

Oh, he knew. He was just being a dick. Two could play that game.

Silence fell between us, taut and thick, as I refused to say more. The tension grew as we stared at each other, neither of us wanting to break the quiet of the cabin. I brought the glass of water to my lips, taking a sip, not letting go of his gaze until he broke. Barrington blew a breath out of his nose and rolled his eyes before he strode out of the room, slamming the door. A smirk pulled at my lips as he left.

Not knowing if he was going in search of Michael, I laughed under my breath as I got up to lie back down. My head was still pounding, but the room had stopped spinning, for which I was grateful. I don't know what was in the water, but it felt like a miracle drug.

As I climbed back into the bed, I glanced down at myself and, for the first time since waking, realized I wasn't wearing my own clothes. Last night, I wore a light blue long-sleeved shirt and black leggings to relax and be comfortable. Right now, I was wearing a man's long black shirt and pants that weren't mine. What the fuck?

Embarrassment flooded me that Barrington may have changed me, but that begs the question, why? Sighing to myself, I threw the thought out of my head. I wasn't going to think about it. I had enough to deal with and clothes just weren't at the top of my list.

Snuggling beneath the blankets, I let the warmth seep into my body, my eyes growing heavy. I needed sleep to fight off whatever was still in my system. Fuck it, I needed the rest if I was going to find a way home.

Home. Jane. Peter.

Peter.

I could look for Peter.

Michael was going to hate me for this, but the opportunity is right here. I am here, in Neverland. It was the one place I never should have returned to, but maybe fate had a different course for me than everyone else had planned.

With my mind made up, I let my memories of the island take me to sleep as I dreamed of happier times and the man I wasn't giving up on.

Moaning, I turned to the sensation of someone touching me, caressing my breasts. It had been so long since I had last been touched. My nipples hardened as they plucked them into buds. Peter?

No. He was dead.

"That's it, baby girl, you know you want more," a gruff voice said above me.

My eyes popped open in shock as terror seized me.

The man towered over me. His grey eyes were almost white. His bald head was tattooed, the ink moving down his body, not a piece of skin left unmarked. He was huge. Muscles bulged everywhere. His shirt barely fit and his trousers needed mending, not that this man would care. He had a sword on his hip and a gleam of evil in his eyes like he would have no problem taking me out and having his way if he wanted.

Licking his lips, he looked over me appraisingly, making me shudder. "You are a pretty thing. No wonder Cap has kept you locked up. I would, too," the man sneered, once more leering at me, molding my breast to his hand.

Shaking myself of my horror, I scurried to the edge of the bed, out of the man's grasp. "Who are you? What are you doing in here?" I asked, not letting this man see my fear.

Fake bravado was better than none, especially here. I may not have been here since I was a child, but I would assume the same rules apply.

"Cap wants you on deck. I came to wake you." He stepped back nonchalantly. As if what he did would have zero consequences.

"You did more than wake me," I accused, anger running through me, disgust hard on its heels.

He shrugged. "You woke up, didn't you?"

How dare he?!

Scooting to the edge of the bed, I ignored the man as I went past to get to the door. I was going to have a word with "Captain" Barrington about this. This was fucking insane.

Do it. Always do it. Do it enthusiastically, or do it scared. But never show anyone here your fear. The island will feed off it.

"Where are you going, pretty girl?"

"I am going to find the man that is in charge since that is why you assaulted me, right?" Opening the door, I was struck by the transformation of what I assumed used to be Cannibal's Cove.

Forgetting about the menace of a man behind me, I slowly stepped out of the room onto the top deck. My gaze traversed over the ship as awe took over my body. My gaze took to the sky. The sails on the ship were rolled up, letting the stars twinkle and moonlight light up the decks.

My eyes landed on the crow's nest. Closing my eyes, I could almost hear Peter crowing and flying down from the top as I fell through the boards of the nest, nearly hitting the deck. Memories flitted through my mind as I looked around. All of us playing on the beach, outrunning the man-eaters of the island. We never could figure out where they came from, but the beach was their favorite hunting spot. It's probably because all of us played there so often.

"The look on your face tells more than anything you could ever say."

I turned to the voice behind me, my eyes capturing Captain Barrington's. "What do you mean?"

"The look of awe. Like you can't believe you're here. You're lost in your thoughts. The tears in your eyes tell me that they were probably memories."

"They were," I said quietly. Melancholy quickly replaced the anger I had felt just moments before. "I can't believe that I'm back here."

"I can't believe you grew up here," he answered.

Irritation coursed through my veins like an itch I couldn't scratch. "Why would I lie about something as stupid as that? That just makes one ignorant. If I lie, it's to protect myself or someone I love. This place has taken so much from me that there isn't much more it could take."

Barrington's face was still hidden by the hair hanging across his face. He purposely hid his face from me, which made the itch worse, my ire rising. "Neverland couldn't have taken that much from you. You are still breathing. Most don't leave alive. So, I am curious how you escaped mostly unscathed."

"The only thing it hasn't taken is my life. I know that at the end of this, it will have that, too," I say quietly. It was as if saying it out loud would bring Krok's wrath upon me.

Glancing back at the captain, I caught the look of surprise across his face before his mask fell once again. I turned back to stare at what used to be an empty beach. Now, it was a small shantytown full of people. Where did they all come from?

I'll have to ask Michael when I see him. Worry, once again, wormed its way through my middle. Michael hadn't shown his face once since I had been here. Was he okay? Did the captain do something with him?

No. That's doubtful. According to Michael, he relied on him too much. So, where the hell could he be? Did something happen back in London? Fear iced my veins. If so, he was in much more trouble there than here.

"What are you thinking, pretty girl?" the man from earlier sauntered over. Chills swept down my body as he approached.

Not even acknowledging him, I turned back to the captain. "So. Why did I need to be up and out here? This man," I pointed my thumb behind me, "woke me very rudely."

"Ah, yes. Well, Grim isn't very subtle and has apparently taken a liking to you." He snickered.

"Yeah, well, he can get over it. I'm taken."

The pirate named Grim came up behind me. "That's in London. Here... you're free game," he whispered into my ear as a shudder coasted down my spine.

"And that's where you are wrong. Touch me and I'll kill you."

"You can try. It might turn me on, though, *darling*," he said loud enough for everyone to hear, my gut tightening at the use of my surname.

Barrington's face hardened. The thoughts behind his eyes moved fast and I almost couldn't tell what he was thinking. "I don't believe you ever told me your name."

The sudden change in topic spun my thoughts in a different direction. I was going to have to fantasize about Grim's demise later.

Names are powerful things in Neverland. The more the Fae know about you, the more power they have. The warning still warmed through me. *Trust no one.*

"Moira," I said. It wasn't a lie. It was the name I used when I was a child here, my alter ego.

As I said the name aloud, the wind off the sea picked up, blowing my hair across my face and whipping the water into massive waves. The waves crashed into the ship's side, rocking it back and forth, tossing it around the cove and knocking the dock into the sea.

My feet moved to brace against the onslaught of water that had washed up on the deck. The wind started howling through the cove, whipping around me as another wave crashed over the starboard side, knocking my feet out from under me. My head slammed onto the deck, stars filling my vision.

"Fucking hell! Storm incoming!" Barrington shouted.

Blood ran down my face, covering my fingers as I cradled my head. I scrabbled up, grabbed the rail before me, and glanced at the sky. It was still clear, the stars still winking in the dark.

No. The island wanted me to admit who I was. It wanted to hear my name.

"Wendy... My name is Wendy!" I yelled into the wind, praying it was enough to appease the island.

The waves seized immediately and the wind died down to a light breeze. You could almost hear the island sigh. Like a breath on the wind letting itself settle. Neverland was welcoming me home. It was a peculiar feeling and one I wasn't quite sure I wanted.

Wendy...

A breeze flew by me, my name on its breath. Dread filled me with what that could mean for my future.

Grim came up behind me, his sword out and now resting against my throat. "What was that?"

"Yes... curious minds want to know. What was that, *Wendy*?" Barrington questioned, enunciating my name, making me cringe.

"Neverland."

"That's not an answer." Grim's sword pressed closer, now slicing into my skin.

"It is. The fact that you know nothing is not my fault nor my problem," I answered with fake bravado once more, making me more confident than I should be. Fake it until you make it, isn't that what they say?

"Hmm." The captain looked on, apparently not concerned with the fact that his crew was threatening to kill me for no other reason than the island scared him. Fucking pussy.

I just kept my eyes on his, refusing to be the first to break. *"Always keep eye contact. That way, you can anticipate the opponent's next move."* Peter's voice once more came through. This would be hell trying to keep up a facade when your memories wouldn't stay lying down. "I am going to assume you all have heard of me, then. Seeing how your man is more than threatened now that he knows my name."

"I am not scared of you, wretch," he breathed into my ear, pressing the sword's blade tighter against my throat. The sting of it cutting into my skin made a hiss escape my lips.

"Could have fooled me," I gritted out between clenched teeth.

Barrington's eyes darkened as my blood slowly trickled down the blade. "Let her go. I told you no harm comes to my captive." His eyes flicked to the man behind me, rage filling his gaze. "And you are harming her. Don't give me a reason to kill you."

The man slowly released me from his grasp and I took a big inhale of breath, not moving from my spot. That would imply I was afraid, and as much as I was worried the man would kill me if he had the chance, I wasn't going to let him know it.

"You could say you're more of a faerytale here," he said, bringing us back to the original topic of my name. "Come, let's get you off this ship."

"A faerytale in a faerytale. Great."

I glanced back to see Grim was now striding to the crew that was lowering a dinghy to be able to row to shore. I didn't feel all that comfortable with him coming with us, but I guess I didn't have an opinion on the matter. Barrington apparently trusted him.

Nodding, the captain led the way toward the town, leaving me to catch up. I stayed a few feet behind him, taking in the atmosphere. My brain was still trying to catch onto the point that the island had changed so much in the time I had been gone. "Where are we going?" I asked, genuinely curious about the town he was taking me through.

"Somewhere safe," he said, leaving me to stew in my thoughts.

The town looked like it had been built out of the trees they had cut down, but also, pieces looked newer, like there were pieces bought from a lumberyard. I would have to guess that the ship was made of the island to be able to travel back and forth, but it was also used to transfer goods from there to here to make this place habitable.

Most of the walkways were boards covering the sand. It was probably to make it easier to transport goods and not struggle to get through the sand. The sand here was thick and would suck you in if you stood in one spot too long. It was one of the reasons we played here. You couldn't stay still or risk dying, and at the time, we all thought we were invincible, so we loved to play Peter's games, not thinking about the consequences. Should I ask how Barrington had learned about the sand?

The people here mainly were dressed as one would in London. Only a few had garments that stood out as pirates. Everyone was wearing jeans or dark linen capris with t-shirts or blouses. All had boots, though, and all had swords or knives attached to their bodies.

The list of questions in my head overflowed and would fly out of my mouth if I didn't stop wondering about the place. Why did I care about how he got here and why he was here? How did he create this town?

I should have asked him where Michael was, but what if Michael didn't say anything to be able to keep his identity a secret from the Fae? We weren't supposed to be here at all. None of us Darlings were. That was the deal with Tinkerbelle. If we all stayed away from Peter Pan and Neverland, we got to keep our lives. She didn't know Michael was already here and there was no way to contact him.

Barrington suddenly turned further into the island, stopping at a random house. It looked better than the rest in this small town. It had a sturdy foundation with sun-bleached driftwood as the siding. Tall plants lined the front, covering the window-shaped holes, making it look cozy.

Knocking on the door, in what I could only call a code, the door swung open as he ushered me inside, telling Grim to stand outside as a watch. More and more questions came to mind, but I kept quiet.

The smell of freshly made bread and soup wafted through the interior and my stomach grumbled. It reminded me that I hadn't eaten since I left London. I couldn't tell you how long I had been out.

"You can stay here. Your brother should be home shortly and there's food in the kitchen. Also," the captain said before turning toward the door, "don't bother trying to leave. Grim will be waiting right outside the door and we both know he would love the opportunity to get his hands on you."

My stomach sank into my feet at the thought that Grim would be watching over me. A shudder ran through me as Barrington laughed, closing the door behind him.

Chapter Twelve

JAMES

I ground my teeth as irritation wove its way under my skin, like an infection that needed to be purged. I needed a drink to drown out the voice telling me to kill something.

The woman, Wendy, was a fucking faerytale brought to life. Just my fucking luck. She was more of a danger to us than to herself. I should have just let Grim have his way with her when I had the chance, but I didn't want to deal with the wrath of Smee.

When he returned from the palace, that man had a lot of explaining to do. I may be in charge of running Pirate's Cove, but Smee was here way before I was and knew things about the island that made me cringe. I still question how he was still sane when he found me to this day.

The tavern was on a little side street between the ship and the crew's houses, making it a good point for relaxation and fun for any of us. And that is exactly what I needed after the night I'd had.

The sound of a flute dying somewhere seized my ears, the bar going quiet as I walked in. I shook my head as I stalked across the floor to the barmaid, Talia, and she handed me my usual whiskey. Nodding my thanks, I went to sit in my seat in the back corner, voices and music playing once more.

Thinking back to London immediately brought Jane into my thoughts. I couldn't begin to wonder what had gotten into her head that she felt she could walk out on me. The mere thought sent me spiraling into madness and fury.

Smirking, I wondered how she would explain all the marks left on her body when she had to go to work. Just the thought of my mark on her had blood rushing to my cock. I made sure when she left, there was no doubt in anyone's mind that she was spoken for. If I couldn't beat the living shit out of the men who dared touch her, then I'll make sure they know she isn't up for grabs in the first place.

Pulling the ring off my finger, I twisted it in the light. The gold band glinted in the dim light, the emeralds embedded in it reflecting green, reminding me of the girl's eyes. I wish I knew where she was right now, just to watch her try and get that enchanted collar off. Without this ring, she was shit out of luck.

She was mine, even if she didn't want to admit it yet.

The clambering of boots making their way to my table had me putting the ring back on my finger. No way in hell was I letting it off my body.

"Cap, the stowaway is awake and I have the boat readied for you," the man we called Ghost stated. The man had a piercing in his eyebrow and the opposite side of his lip. He had a tattoo of a rose on his neck that was half-hidden by his long, dark hair. His black linen shirt was open halfway down his chest, showing off the scars he had gotten from the island and his life before. He was one of my most trusted men and one of the more ruthless ones.

Nodding, I downed the rest of my drink, following him out of the bar—best to get this interview done. I was half-tempted to have Smee there, but I had a feeling his emotions would get the better of him and he'd end up killing the man. My heart raced at the thought of getting some answers from the man who dared to infiltrate my compound. Irritation flitted under my skin again, stoking the anger I had kept at bay for most of the night. Questions were stirring in the back of my mind that I had been ignoring, but needed to address, churning that anger into a red-hot inferno by the time we got to the dinghy at the mouth of Crocodile Creek.

Steering the small rowboat into the river, we set a course upstream, making a slow but steady headway, which wasn't helping my thoughts. Who was this man? How did he know Wendy even existed? Can I even trust the men in my crew if he wasn't found before we left for London?

Thoughts turned through my head, creating an itch under my skin that only one thing would appease: the man's blood. Chaos. Thinking of everything in store for my prisoner, had an evil grin forming on my face.

The ride up the river was smooth. The trees lining the banks were growing overhead to the point where the moonlight almost couldn't shine through. Vines were hanging low and the sounds of nature were prominent. It would have been a nearly tranquil ride if my thoughts weren't so ominous. Smiling, I almost laughed to myself. When weren't my thoughts of the sinister side? That's the only way I knew to survive.

Arriving at the dock set up on the river's edge, I looked up at the white sheetrock on the side of the riverbank. It was carved into the shape of a skull, but covered in moss and algae from the river. The eyes were bottomless holes glaring at passersby, leaving one with the feeling of being watched. It was perfect to keep unwanted persons away.

Tying the small boat off next to the one sitting in the water, I jumped onto the dock, twinging the nerve in my bad knee, sending a shock of lightning through my leg. A hiss escaped my lips as I limped towards the worn path, trying to ignore the pain radiating through me.

Ferns and vines brushed along my body as the sound of scuttling animals scurrying out of the way hit my ears. It was probably a good thing, too. I wasn't in the mood to deal with whatever decided to hop onto my leg today.

The tunnels were lit by lanterns when used, and today, it was no different. Checking out the first lamp and ensuring there was enough oil, I carefully made my way down the slick rock. As much as I tried to dry the rock, it was always wet. The moss was now worn away after having been trodden on so many times over the years. The walls were dry in spots, but others were covered in slime that I never wanted to touch again. In the moonlight, it would glow, but it wasn't enough to give off light to see, just enough that you knew it was there.

Poisonous. A shiver ran through me at the memory of Smee finding me half-dead from touching the stuff in my first explorations of the island. I owed the man my life, and in return, I got a friend and confidant. But finding out the man had more secrets than he had ever told had me rethinking our friendship. I rubbed my chest at the thought that he didn't tell me that much. Curious at the feeling, I quickly threw it out of my mind. I'm not dwelling on Smee's secrets. He had never betrayed me, but I wouldn't continue it if he didn't trust me explicitly.

The slow trek through the tunnels ended and I felt relief that I would finally be able to get some answers and get out of my head for a while.

The room was square with shelves built into the walls to hold all my tools. The chair was carved out of the rock in the middle of the room and iron shackles were attached to the arms and legs. Iron, in case I ever needed to use it against the Fae, so they wouldn't be able to fight it. The trick was getting them into it.

Two men stood next to the door, Striker and Savage. Both were taller than me and a lot burlier. Striker, on the right, was balding and had tattoos down his body. I don't think there was a spot left on the man that wasn't touched by ink or metal. The man had a thing for pain and reveled in both giving and receiving it. It is something to be greatly admired, but it made me wonder if that's what Striker got off on. What happened to the women he bedded? Not my circus, not my monkeys. As far as I knew, no women have come up missing in Pirate's Cove. In London? Well, that was their problem.

Savage had graying hair that was cut short and missing an eye along his temples. A Fae he had once crossed took it out in a duel, but it wasn't enough to kill the man. Said Fae was no longer among the living. One of the reasons he was one of my most trusted people. If he could take on a Fae and kill him, one wouldn't want him on your bad side.

The prisoner in question was already in the chair, his face swollen and bloodied. One wouldn't recognize him from the man who was aboard my ship a few nights ago. My men were under strict instruction to just hurt him. I wanted to take my time with him and I couldn't if he was dead. The man appeared unconscious. His head lolled forward as if he was asleep.

Walking over to the rat, I grabbed the man's bloodied blonde hair and pulled his head up. The man's eyes opened slightly, but he was unconscious. Damn it.

"I thought you said he was awake?" I gritted between my teeth, irritated that the men had knocked him back out, knowing I was on my way.

"He's asleep. We haven't touched him since we sent Ghost off." The deep timbre of Savage's voice echoed around us, bouncing off the rock walls.

"Hmm..." Glancing over the wall of tools, I grabbed a pair of pliers and a hammer. Grabbing a bucket off the floor, I handed it to Striker. "Water. He's not going to sleep this whole time. That will take the fun out of it." The man just nodded and left the room. "Ghost, I will need you to take care and listen to everything that pours out of this man's mouth. Since Smee is gone, you will be his fill-in."

"Sure thing, Cap." The man's voice was gravelly. Then again, he rarely talked. He was more of a man of action.

Nodding my ascent, I turned back to the prisoner. "Has he said anything in the past few days?"

"No. He says he's going to die anyway. Won't tell us a damned thing," Savage stated, rolling his eyes. I can feel his exasperation about the situation. The man wouldn't have to die. Hell, we wouldn't need to do this at all if he would talk. But that would take my fun away.

Nodding once more, the door to the room creaked open and Striker strode through, the water slightly sloshing over the edges. Motioning toward the man, the bald man flung the water onto the stowaway. Gasping for breath, his eyes widened in fear when he saw who was before him.

The thought that I created terror in him made me very happy.

Good. He should be afraid.

"So, you haven't wanted to talk to my men here about what you were thinking using my ship to kidnap a woman and bring her back here... So here I am, wasting my time to ensure you answer the questions." It's not a lie, but he doesn't need to know that.

The man's eyes widened as he saw the pliers and the hammer held loosely in my grip. Coming behind the chair, I fisted a handful of the man's hair and pulled his head back, exposing his neck. "Now, we are going to start simply with your name because I would like to call you something besides a traitorous rat," I said coolly, grazing the pliers down the man's face.

The man stiffened, but kept his mouth closed.

"Ah. We have decided to be difficult. That's fine. This just means I get to have fun." Opening the pliers, I grabbed hold of the man's ear, pulling just enough to bring immense pain, but not enough yet to begin tearing as his screams filled the room. "As I said, I just want your name."

"Chip! They called me Chip. I don't have a last name."

"And where did you come from, *Chip*?" I took my time enunciating every syllable, pulling a little more on his ear.

"AAAAAH! The castle!" His screams quieted as I released his ear, his breathing coming out in shallow pants as he tried to catch his breath.

I had expected as much, but that doesn't explain a damned thing. "So, Chip from the castle, how did you escape that prison?"

Chip's breathing was fast and his eyes were white with fear. He was going to pass out quickly if I didn't move fast and I had barely gotten started.

"Chiiipp..." I sing-songed. "How did you escape that hellscape?"

"I killed my guardian and found some tunnels that led out to Mermaid Lagoon."

"You didn't get snatched up by those hungry sirens? Impressive."

Taking a deep breath, Chip looked up at the ceiling. "Why don't you just kill me? Get it over with."

"Ah, but see, that's what you don't seem to understand. I need to know what the fuck you were thinking, stowing away on my ship, kidnapping a woman, and bringing her back here."

"It doesn't matter now. I am going to die and she, well, if she makes it back to London, she'll go about her merry life."

I was getting impatient, tapping my thigh with the hammer. I lifted the hammer into the air, bringing it down fast and slamming it down on the man's hand, his screams bringing music to my ears. "Now, Chip. That's not what I asked."

Chip's legs started bouncing, tears and snot streaming down his face, but he remained quiet. What the hell did the Fae do to this man to make him so resilient against torture? I almost gave the man props for lasting so long if it wasn't grating against my nerves that he was fighting me so hard. It has been days since the man had been fed, being beaten in the meantime, and he's still fighting against me.

Raising the hammer again, I hit the same hand again, officially incapacitating it as Chip yelled out, "Her name is Wendy!! She is the one the queen says has Neverland's Shadow! If I bring the Wendy girl to her, I hope she grants me the chance to live and not die with the rest of the Lost Boys."

Surprise at that revelation had me stopping myself mid-swing. Neverland had a shadow? Who were the Lost Boys? More questions to be answered, but not by this man. Not at the moment, anyway.

Moving the hammer claw up under the man's chin, I tipped his head back to look him in the eye. "See now, was that so hard?"

Chapter Thirteen

MICHAEL

Walking into the Fae Castle was always nerve-wracking. Not only was I afraid that they would figure out who I really was, but the magic here was off. It wasn't like the light magic of the island from when I was a child that filled these walls. It was heavy and wrong. It wasn't like coming home, where the atmosphere was welcoming and warm. This was like walking into someone else's house, uninvited and unwanted.

The palace always had a cold air to it. It is not something you'd physically feel, but more of the atmosphere. I would have to knock it to the fact that the walls were made of quartz and the only light filtered down through the skylights.

Right now, it was dim, only moonlight and torches lighting the way, and it was eerie as hell. I hated it. It's why I preferred coming during the day, not that I got to be that lucky today—that and the fact that no one was about. The Fae tend to be nocturnal creatures, which usually made my life a lot easier, but today, the empty halls set my teeth on edge. Where was everyone?

The halls to the palace were long and narrow, and the sound of my boots hitting the black tiled floor echoed all around. Tink was most likely in the throne room, acting as if her reign was the best thing that had ever happened to Neverland. It wasn't and was slowly killing the only place we had to call home. But there was no telling her that. You'd just end up in Mermaid Lagoon as fish bait.

Walking toward the throne room I had assumed *Her Majesty* to be in, my mind wandered back to Wendy. I still needed to talk with her, but every time I looked at her, rage filled me that she was here in the first place. I know it wasn't her fault, but Godsdammit, it was going to be a pain in the ass trying to get her home without Tink finding out she was here. But I have a feeling that our talk was going to just lead to her badgering me into staying to find Peter, and that was a fool's errand. He was gone. Dead. A waste of time that would only lead to us getting into more trouble than we already were with her being here.

Coming to the door that the throne was behind, the laughter of the woman most people on the island feared came through. Well, at least she's in a good mood. Grimacing to myself, I opened the door and let myself in.

The smell of smoky herbs, sweat, and sex filled the air. Automatically, I pulled a handkerchief out of my pocket and wrapped it around my face. I wasn't taking any chances of whatever it was they had burning, getting into my senses. I prefer my head to be straight on my shoulders, not in the clouds. I did Dust once... Never again. You would have to strap me down to a table and force-feed me the shit before I did it voluntarily.

Low moans filled the air around me and I could only guess that I had walked into one of Her Majesty's orgies, which sent a shiver of disgust through my body. I hated walking into these. I was always at war with myself afterward. My body was strung tight, and watching and hearing others getting off as I stood outside was torturous.

Steeling my nerves, I slowly stalked up to the glass throne Tinkerbelle was perched upon. Her strawberry blonde hair was piled on top of her head, the freckles spattered her nose and cheeks flushed with pleasure. Her blue eyes were closed and her head was thrown back against the back of her throne. Her wings were spread wide, but slightly drooped as if she was too into the man in between her thighs to care that they were lying on the floor. The dress she was wearing was a light grey gossamer gown that hid nothing but gave easy access to the pleasures that she was wont to have.

The man that was kneeling between her legs was eating her pussy like his life depended on it. And it probably did. He must have been doing a great job, as she didn't even realize I was standing before her, waiting for her to finish. Her hands were fisted in the man's hair, and moans of pleasure that left her lips sent blood rushing to my cock at the erotic display.

Sighing to myself under my breath, I glanced around at the others tangled in each other's limbs.

They were everywhere. The floor was covered in plush cushions with men and women grinding and moaning their pleasure into the air, making my raging cock harder than it already was. I wasn't quite sure if I was one to enjoy watching, but there was little to do about it. It had been a long time since I had last gotten laid myself. The thought that I could easily join one of the groups crossed my mind, but I refused to lower myself to that.

There was a throuple over by the window. A woman was on her knees before a man, his cock shoved down her throat, as another man was fucking the woman from behind. There was a couple in the air, a man tied up in intricate knots, knots I knew personally, as I enjoyed them myself, as I watched another man hovering behind him, his giant wings keeping him afloat, grabbing the man's cock, whispering in his ear, and fucking his ass.

But looking beyond all that, in the corners of the room, quiet as mice, were teenagers. Kids I had never seen before. Surprise and disgust flitted through me. Children weren't easy to find on the island, and the fact that there were teens here watching this display made bile crawl up my throat, killing any type of mood I was in for a good fuck. They shouldn't be here and shouldn't be watching this.

Turning on my heel to go to one of the nearest kids near me, I was stopped by the sound of Tinkerbelle's voice ringing out. "What are you doing here, Smee? I don't believe I called for you..."

This Tinkerbelle didn't intimidate me nearly as much as when she had her full regalia on and her full power turned out. This Tink made me think of a whore who needed to get her fix. This Tink is just as dangerous. She's only a little more relaxed in this environment. She never got too buzzed that she couldn't still take your life from you with a flick of the wrist.

"Drake sent me."

"And what could possibly be so important that you had to interrupt my party?" she asked, never once lifting her gaze off the man in front of her, her legs still open as he slowly licked her slick.

Clearing my throat, I just went for it. It was going to come down on my head anyway, so I might as well get it over with. "He said to tell you that the Dust isn't strong enough. That the humans are becoming resistant to it and you won't be getting your payment if the humans aren't buying." I had no idea what the payment that Drake had referred to was, and I would prefer to keep it that way, but the darkening of Tink's gaze told me it wasn't good.

A scream rang out from the front of the room and it was silenced just as quickly. The man's head that was between her thighs had been ripped from his body and was now hanging from Tinkerbelle's hand, blood spewing everywhere. The man's body fell backward, blood splattered all over my face and body. The warm fluid was not foreign, but almost comforting. The people that were right in front of the throne were not stopped from their fucking in the least. If anything, the one man licked the blood off the other's face and rubbed it down their bodies, using it as a lubricant. Disgust rolled through my gut. I didn't mind a little blood mixed in my sex, but that was too much.

Almost at once, Tinkerbelle's features morphed into one of rage, her blonde hair turning red, and the room started to shake. Small pieces of the rafters fell to the ground, coating those around us. The faery in front of me was seething, her breath coming in pants. Her hands were shaking in rage as blood and gore slipped down her body. The need to flee coursed through me, but running from her would only heighten her fury, so I stayed still, standing in the carnage she had wrought.

"Is there anything else I can help you with, Smee? " Her voice was even, but the underlying rage had made it deeper than the high-pitched tinkling it usually was.

The thought of letting her know that we had a stowaway on board flitted through my mind, but the thought that she would want to know the whole story had brought me pause. If she had found out Wendy was here, she would have sent for and killed her, no doubt about it.

"No. That was the message."

"Then leave. I will deal with Drake myself."

The jungle was always fucking hot. I don't know if I had gotten to the point of resenting it or if I was just tired of living this life. The way Neverland was now, was not something I would have ever imagined it to become. With Peter, there was always this sense of fun and belonging. Now, it was like walking on eggshells through the forest, praying that the Fae were too engrossed in their deviances to notice you.

Brushing the tree leaves aside as I made my way through the clogged paths of the Never Woods, my mind wandered to what needed to get done. Wendy needed to be taken home. That was a must. Gods know what Tink would do to her if she got her hands on her.

Tinkerbelle always had a sore spot for Wendy. Truthfully, I think the faery was in love with Pan and he didn't return the favor. She hated my sister for the attention that Peter gave her. Jealousy was a cunning bitch that would create the biggest feuds over nothing.

Shaking my head, I continued to make my way to The Sanctuary. James had asked me to set up a meeting between him and Asher, but didn't give me any more information, which would make my life difficult. Asher would want to know details before he went into the meeting, but I didn't have them, which would mean he would make my time here harder. As if being around the Fae wasn't hard enough, the man loved tormenting me, both in and out of bed.

Gritting my teeth, I pressed forward as the end of the woods cleared and what used to be Pixie Hollow came into view.

The sun gleamed off the tiny, abandoned, rotting houses, shining a bright light onto the situation that was now Neverland. I don't know where the new pixies are born anymore. This was where we would be able to watch the pixies frolic and play, especially under the full moons. Now, the silence that echoed in The Hollow was a reminder of better days past.

Glancing up at the main tree in The Hollow, my gaze wandered upward, taking in the new tree house. The tree was huge, nearly as big around as it was tall, and the leaves were different colors of green and gold. Asher had built into it years ago when he defected from Tink. Not that she knows this. She thinks he dislikes the palace life and lives here to keep in the ways of old, which he does. But he also tries to get as many orphaned Fae children out of that environment as he can and keep them here, safe from the morbid toxicity of the castle. The tree house was built into the trunk, around, and up the branches. Some windows peeked out through the leaves and the trunk to let light into the house. It was still early in the morning, so the kids were most likely still sleeping, giving me a little time to find Asher before his hands were full.

Anticipation sang through my veins, blood rushing straight to my thickening cock at the thought of a little alone time with the man, a low groan escaping my lips as I adjusted myself.

Breaking through the last bit of brush, I entered the clearing, making my way over to the door that was carved into the base of the tree. Twisting the wooden door handle, I silently pressed my way into the small entryway and quietly closed the door behind me before heading toward the stairs that would take me up to the main living space of The Sanctuary.

The sounds of tinkling bells came from a nearby alcove and I blew a sigh out of my nose. "Hi, Meera," I murmured, rounding to where she sat on one of the sills. She was one of the last Pixies I knew of. A tiny little sprite with red hair and pink wings, always wearing red flower petals. She looked like a tiny devil from hell, but was the kindest soul ever. "I am guessing that since you are here, Ash knows I'm coming up?"

She nodded her head as she started talking. The only thing reaching my ears were her voice's high-pitched bells. Only other Fae could understand the pixies and it was a pain in the ass most times.

Shaking my head in defeat, I continued climbing the stairs and came face to face with a half-naked Fae man in the middle of the room. My stomach did a flip and my heart pounded harder in my chest. No matter how many times I see this man, I'll always get butterflies.

His bulky but muscular frame, covered in marred tattoos and scars, was facing away from me. His dark, wavy hair fell about his shoulders, arms clasped behind his back with his head bowed. Asher and I were the same height if you didn't count the horns curling out of his head. Those added another six inches, but were great to hold onto when the man was on his knees, taking my cock in his mouth. The image had my already rock-hard staff twitching against my jeans, making me even more uncomfortable, with the perfect solution standing in front of me. Admiring the way his body was at peace, with no tension in his normally solid form, had my mouth watering for a taste.

"I can smell your arousal from here. If you keep staring at my ass, I might have to do something about it." Asher's gruff voice carried across the room. The threat in his words had my anticipation for this visit growing.

"Maybe that's why I am here."

The Fae turned toward me and I was stricken by how magnificent he looked in the morning sun streaming through the windows. Watching the man looking me up and down with appraisal, lust clear in his hooded gaze, I stood my ground as he prowled forward until we were chest to chest. My heart beat against my ribcage as my cock continued to throb in need. Asher slowly lifted his hand, grazing my side and settling on my throat as he squeezed slightly, sending another bolt of need through me as he leaned into my ear. "You forget that I smell your lies as strong as I can your lust. It isn't very becoming on you, Darling," he growled as he pulled back, his gaze landing on my lips before staring into my soul. "Now, why are you here?"

My thoughts raced at the many things I could do and say to get him to move his hand lower to relieve the ache in my loins, but the look in his eyes told me now wasn't the time. "Barrington needs to set up a meeting with you." I let out breathlessly as he tightened his grip on my neck, my pulse fluttering as he moved his other hand slowly to pull my hips toward his, plastering me to him.

"And what exactly would he need from me?" His lips were just a breath away from mine. One small twitch and our mouths would be fused. If there was one thing I needed right now, it was him.

"He didn't say. Just that it was urgent," I whispered, as if talking too loudly would make the man's lips disappear from mine. But I knew this game: if I played his good boy and didn't move until he was ready, I'd be rewarded for my struggles.

"Hmm," Asher hummed as he moved his hand from my hip to the front of my body, playing with the edge of my jeans. Flicking the button it made my cock pulse with need and a moan escaped my lips. "So needy," he said in a whisper as he squeezed my throat at the same time, sealing his mouth over mine. His desire melded with mine in a clash of tongues and teeth and need.

My hands made their way into his hair, locking him to me as our tongues fought for dominance. His grip moved to the short hair at the back of my head, keeping me in place as he bent my neck back, tracing his lips down the hollow of my throat, a low groan rumbling from his chest.

I kept one hand embedded in his hair as I moved the other down his body across the planes of his chest, tracing the scars that I knew by heart. Slowly making my way down his abs to his shorts, I shoved my hand in the waistband and gripped his hard staff in my hand. Another groan rumbled from his chest as I moved my grip up, thumbing the tip, smearing the precum across my fingers as I stroked him once more.

His lips came back up to mine, his tongue tracing my bottom lip before snatching it between his teeth. A moan fell from my lips as he unbuttoned my pants, shoving his hand down to fist my aching cock.

Relief flooded me at the friction until the tinkling of bells entered the room and my stomach plummeted. Our time was up. A flurry of pixie dust surrounded us as Meera pulled on Asher, separating us, annoyance and lust clear on our faces.

The sound of children rushing down the stairs from the floor above shook us both from the need pulsing between us. I shoved my throbbing member back into the confines of my jeans and he threw a shirt on over his massive frame.

We should never have let it get this far with the kids just waking up and my need to get back to the Cove, but damn, I needed him.

Looking down, I saw that my hand was still slick with his precum. Eyeing him from across the room, I sucked my finger into my mouth, relishing the taste that was all Asher.

His gaze heated at the action and his fists were clenched in need. "Tell the captain to meet me at Skull Rock in two days. We can discuss what we need to there," Asher ground out between clenched teeth as he left the room, brushing by me.

Grabbing his arm on his way out, I stopped him. "Soon," was all I said, meeting his gaze. My meaning was clear to him as his shoulders sagged in a little bit of relief.

Soon, I would come here of my own accord and have some much-needed alone time. I knew he needed me as much as I did him, but right now, I needed to get back and deal with Wendy.

Chapter Fourteen

JANE

The pounding in my head was nothing compared to the ache of my body, inside and out. This must be what getting hit by a train felt like.

Groaning, I rolled over and grabbed my phone off the nightstand, seeing a glass of water and two little white pills. I braced my arms beneath me, shaking with the effort. I scooped them up and downed the water, dying of thirst. Which, with my dry cotton mouth, I probably was at this point.

Slowly, my brain fog lifted as memories of last night came pouring into my mind. James fingering me on the dance floor in front of everyone, to our half-assed conversation that didn't get me many answers, then to the mind-blowing sex afterward. The cab ride home and finding a bag of Dust on the doorstep, to finding the house ransacked and Mom missing. My mind flashed to Uncle Jon finding me on the bathroom floor to seeing Jules' dildo.

Giggling at the image that would forever be imprinted in my head, the sudden movement had bile burning my throat as I quickly made my way out of bed to the adjoined bath. The room spun out of control as I barely made it to the toilet and threw up the water I had just inhaled. Shivers racked my body as I tried catching my breath against the rim, my body cradling the bowl as the feeling of hopelessness enveloped me like a hug.

What fucking good am I? My mother was missing, my house was ransacked, and I was so hungover that I couldn't even leave the bathroom. Gods, when did my life become such a mess?

The door to my room creaked open like a hot knife slicing through my eardrums as my uncle appeared in the doorway.

"I see you're awake. Alive might be another story, though." He chuckled as he grabbed a cloth, wetting it before handing it to me. "I already called the hospital and told them you'd be out for the next few days."

Fuck. I totally forgot about work. Guilt wormed its way through my gut that I was letting the kids and my coworkers down. I really needed to get my life in order.

"What did you tell them? That I'm a drunk fuck up?" I asked, berating myself.

"No. I told them the truth. That you had a home invasion last night, you're dealing with the aftermath, and I am staying here to help you. I will need to go in at some point, though. I have some paperwork I need to file before the day's out," he stated matter-of-factly as if a break-in was normal. "Also, it will give you time to heal that collar of hickeys around your neck. I tried to get your necklace off, but I don't know where the key is," he added nonchalantly.

Embarrassment flooded my being, heat rushing into my cheeks, burning me from the inside. Wait... What necklace?

Scrambling to my feet, I stood over the wash basin as Uncle Jon leaned against the doorway, studying me, concern written on his face.

My reflection was a mess. Makeup had run down my face and my curly hair was a rat's nest that would take me forever to untangle. But what sent disbelief and another flood of embarrassment and guilt through my veins was the necklace surrounded by hickeys encompassing my throat.

The necklace itself was beautiful. The thin, black, leather strap was soft and had what looked to be a butterfly pendant hanging at the hollow of my throat. The pair of wings looked like a clear crystal with an emerald body that matched the color of my eyes, holding the wings together. But what was most disconcerting was the locking mechanism at the back of my neck. I didn't have a key to take it off.

Fucking James. Anger boiled in my gut at the thought that he dared to place this on me without asking me, branding me as his property. Fuck him. The hickeys would heal, but this collar, I was going to kill him. Slowly.

"I am guessing you know who gave you the necklace," Jon said softly, his voice soothing the rage sizzling under my skin.

"Yes. And he's going to get an ass-kicking the next time I see him."

"Good," was all he said as he made his way out toward the hall. "I have some food for you and Jules downstairs. I would suggest taking a hot shower and then we can all talk over breakfast."

Nodding my ascent, I grabbed some clothes as he closed the door behind him and made my way to the shower to scrub the life out of my skin and wash the horrible night away.

The smell of hashbrowns, bacon, and eggs filled the air as I descended the stairs, churning my sour stomach into knots. Gods, I was never drinking again.

Stepping into the kitchen, I found my way to the coffee pot, brewing the nectar of the Gods. I took a sip, wincing at the pain that flared in my stomach as the acidic brew hit, but the taste was glorious and I wasn't going to complain.

Turning toward the island, Dixie lay on the floor next to Julie, who looked worse off than me. Her head lay on the counter as if it was the only thing keeping her head on. Uncle Jon placed two plates down and turned to make his own before taking a seat at the end. Trudging my way to the open seat between the two, I sat down and grimaced at both the ache in my body and the smell of the food. I knew it would taste delicious, but my stomach was not up for it.

I started playing with the hashbrowns on my plate, deciding whether I wanted to try eating yet, when my uncle cleared his throat and sent a pointed look in my direction. Sighing, I lifted the fork full of hashbrowns and eggs to my mouth, praying that I wouldn't regret this later.

"So, we need to talk." Uncle Jon's voice broke the silence.

I didn't want to have this conversation with this raging headache, but there was no going around it. "Yeah, we do. Did you ever call the cops about the break-in?" I asked, hoping to steer the conversation from the necklace he kept eyeing.

A sigh fell from his lips as his eyes rolled to the ceiling. Trepidation sank into me. He didn't want to talk about this either. "No, I haven't. There's no need to because I know where your mother is," he stated softly, as if he knew how I would react. "She's in Neverland."

My hand stopped halfway to my mouth, the food on the fork falling off onto the plate as surprise flickered through me, quickly followed by anger. "Neverland isn't real. It's just a faerytale that you guys told us as kids to get us to sleep."

"Wait, what?" Jules raised her head, confusion in her tone.

My uncle's jaw clenched in irritation. "We told you tales from our childhood and what we experienced. None of it was false. It all happened." He pulled out the bag with Dust in it last night, making my body jerk violently as I scrambled out of my chair to get as far from the bag as possible. "That was dramatic," he stated flatly.

"That bag is dangerous. It has Dust in it," I stuttered, unable to believe he was handling it without a care.

"There is nothing in this bag." He turned it upside down and shook it. A squelch squeaked out past my lips as I waited for the horrid drug to sprinkle all over the counter and food.

Except nothing fell out.

Uncle Jon's left eyebrow cocked up and a questioning look crossed his face. "So, do you want to explain to me this irrational fear of this bag or the 'dust' that's in it?"

I could feel my eyes bugging out of my head as I looked at Jules. We hadn't told anyone what happened that night, and Jules remembers almost none of it. I really shouldn't have reacted the way I did, but now that I was here, I didn't have a choice. It was either tell him what I did or tell him what I did. There was no going around it.

"Promise not to freak out?" I sat back down, moving my plate away from me. I wasn't going to chance that even a speck was still in that bag that we couldn't see.

He took a deep breath to steady his nerves. I know I wasn't the easiest kid to handle growing up, and he and my mom did their best to keep both Jules and me on the straight and narrow, but they knew we were always getting into trouble, somehow. It followed us like a plague.

"It was over a year ago now. We only did it once. Do you remember the week that I lost several patients in a row?"

He nodded. "Yeah, that was a rough week for all of us at the hospital. One wasn't just your patient, but mine as well."

"Yeah," I said softly as memories of that week bombarded me. The feelings of hopelessness and being a complete failure for those families came crashing into me once more. Quickly, I blinked away the tears stringing my eyes and pushed my emotions back into the box I kept them in. "Well, Jules and I went out that weekend with a couple of guys we knew from previous times we had been to the club. After hearing about our week, they offered us a line, you know, to take the edge off and let us loosen up and enjoy our time out."

Taking a sip of my now cold coffee, I watched my uncle's face darken, his features construing into one of deep concern. "Did they do anything to you?"

I shook my head. "No, they didn't get a chance to. James found us and helped us out." I wasn't going to tell him the things we saw while we were high or what the men were trying to do when James found us. Uncle Jon was already on edge and it was a time I would much rather forget. Jules was lucky she didn't remember.

"So that was when you met the man who gave you that necklace?" he asked, his gaze hardening on the collar.

"Yeah, where did that come from?" Jules asked from her perch, listening in to the conversation.

My hand flew up and traced the crystal. Knowing James gave it to me calmed me, knowing I had a piece of him wherever I went. However, the fact that I was stuck with it still perturbed me. Ignoring Julie, I answered my uncle, "Yes."

Nodding, he picked up our plates and put them in the sink. "Well, that bag that you are so afraid of is empty. There's nothing in it."

"There was last night. I remember seeing the stuff all over the front entry," I stated snidely. I didn't care what he had to say. I know what I saw.

"It must have been washed away in the rain, then," he said as he shook his head. "That bag is from Neverland. It belonged to an old friend of ours. One of the Lost Boys. Do you remember them?"

Nodding slowly, I thought back to my childhood when he and Mom told us tales of Neverland and the Lost Boys. The boys that never grew up. If I remember correctly, there were six of them.

"Tootles never went anywhere without his marbles. So, the fact that the bag is here, sans the marbles, tells me that something is wrong. Your mom's house being ransacked says that whoever from Neverland came here was looking for something. I am assuming they couldn't find it, so they took your mom instead."

Shaking my head in disbelief at everything Uncle Jon told me, I stood. Worry already gnawed at me, but the blatant lies coming out of my uncle's mouth set me aflame with rage.

"We need to call the cops. There were drugs involved and a kidnapping, and you are telling me it was people from a faerytale?! FAERIES DON'T EXIST!" I screamed across the kitchen at him, letting loose all the anger and frustration I was feeling at the man who helped raise me.

"DON'T SAY THAT! NEVER SAY THAT!" he screamed right back, his face turning red with anger.

Dixie jumped to her feet, putting herself in between me and him, a low growl emanating from her chest. Jules was on her feet, her hand on my arm, bracing for a fight. She didn't grow up in the best of households and wouldn't take abuse of any kind toward her or her loved ones, even if it was someone else she loved.

Uncle Jon threw his hands in the air as fear laced through me, my eyes widening at the fact he was screaming at me. Uncle Jon has never raised his voice to me. Even when I was a trouble-making child, he was always calm. To see him losing his shit over faeries had me second-guessing myself and the claims he was making.

Grabbing the bag from the counter, he stormed out of the kitchen and down the hall. Good riddance.

My heart still raced in my chest as I walked around the kitchen counter, grabbed my still half-full plate out of the sink, and set it on the floor for Dixie. She deserved a treat after what Jon had just done.

"What was he talking about, Jane?" Jules asked, her face white with fear.

"Faerytales."

Shaking my head, I made my way to the coffee pot. My hands, still slightly shaking with the adrenaline rush, had coffee sloshing over the sides of the mug.

Faeries. We were arguing over fucking faeries.

Removing my phone from my back pocket, I went to file a police report. It was better than believing in their tall tales.

"What are you doing?" Jules asked, moving back to the island to sit down.

"Calling the cops. We can't just ignore that Mom is missing and our house was broken into. I don't know what has gotten into Uncle Jon, but he isn't thinking straight," I stated as I sat down next to her.

"Before we do that, can we go over there so I can put away Mr. C.?"

Chapter Fifteen

JON

She didn't understand. She never would. Until she had been there, she would always believe that Neverland was a faerytale. I could tell her until I was blue and she would still not believe it. All would be fine as long as she doesn't say that one phrase out loud.

I didn't want to tell Jane that my supposed-to-be-dead brother and my ex also visited last night. Neverland was here, in London. There was no doubt about it. It finally caught up to us and I didn't know how to explain it to the girls without sounding insane.

Guilt pressed in on me as I sat behind my desk, turning on the computer to warm it up. I can't believe that Jane never told me about what happened last year. I knew she went into a downward spiral after that week, but I didn't realize she went so deep as to try drugs to get her mind off it. Those two girls always had trouble following them.

Dust. What the hell kind of concoction was the world thinking up now?

Browsing the internet, I wasn't coming up with much. How to get rid of dust mites? What is dust made of? There was nothing on a drug that I could find. Maybe she remembered the name wrong?

I grabbed my keys and went to the garage, passing Dixie curled up on the sofa—lazy dog. I did have to give her credit for protecting Jane, though, even if it was against myself.

Gritting my teeth at my lack of composure caused another flare-up of guilt. I have never yelled at the girls in all my years, but something snapped and I couldn't stop myself. Jane was infuriating at times, but today, she knew what buttons to push and pushed them all at once.

Yanking the car door open, I made myself comfortable behind the wheel and pulled out of the drive to make my way to the hospital. My gut was turning with butterflies of dread, the burn of acid crawling up my throat. I wasn't ready to face Isabella after what happened the last night, but I needed to drop off this paperwork to her.

Shame filled my body, heat flushing my cheeks as the burn of guilt flayed me raw at what I had done. How does one explain running into an ex that shouldn't exist in this realm? That I left her at the bar with those men searching for said ex? I had left her at risk of the other men there, and I had no reasonable explanation for it other than pure instinct to chase down Lily.

Still, the pull to find the woman who has haunted my dreams since I came home was as strong as ever. Like a cord that tethers us together, she pulls away and I have this stupid need to follow. It has always been like that. Like two cosmic energies that collided at birth and then separated, we are bound to each other in our separate realms.

I had been to Neverland many times before I met her. I was fifteen when we first met. Even now, it amazes me how I had never met her in the years I had been going back and forth from there.

"Come on, Jon, you're falling behind!! Don't let the man-eaters get you!" I heard Pan's voice up ahead, encouraging us on. The kid was flying and didn't care if any of us got eaten. It was all a game to him. He didn't go home with unexplainable broken bones and scars.

Adding a push into my step, the burn in my lungs made it harder to breathe. The pounding footsteps in the mud behind me sent a rush of adrenaline through my system, spurring me on. Sweat beaded in my hair, and the slap of the leaves from the wet jungle trees wasn't helping, but slowing me down.

The sounds of the Lost Boys up ahead told me I was getting closer to Dead Man's Tree, but the monster behind me was catching up fast.

Rushing past the trees, I garnered a glance back and terror seized my body as the massive being was almost upon me. His eyes were red and his skin a pale gray color, as if lifeless, and his teeth were all jagged points ready to tear into its next meal. Me.

A scream tried crawling its way out of my throat, but I was frozen as the man swiped at me with his claws. At the same time, a hand grabbed my arm and pulled me aside into the forest, away from the trail.

A roar of frustration rang through the jungle air as the girl pulled me along and the trampling through the brush was hushed behind us the further the two of us went.

The girl's hand was in mine, with our fingers intertwined as she pulled me further through the Never Wood. My heart was now racing in my chest for a totally different reason. Not that I hadn't held a girl's hand before, but this was different and I didn't know why. Coming up to a tree, she stopped us and finally turned around for me to see who my savior was.

Her big, dark eyes, outlined by long lashes, were the first thing to catch my attention. Her dark hair was pulled back from her face in a braid, frizzing from the humidity and our hurried running through the woods. Her cheeks were flushed and she was breathing as hard as I was. She was the most beautiful girl I had ever seen.

"Thank you," I panted between breaths, pushing my glasses back up my nose to get a better look at her.

She just shrugged her shoulders as if it was nothing.

"My name is Jon. What's yours?" I asked because I was curious. My need to know who the beautiful creature was before me burned fiercely.

"Tiger Lily."

A horn blasted from behind me shook me out of my reverie and I pulled forward into the hospital lot.

The memory came out of nowhere. I hadn't thought about the first time Lily and I had met in a long time. Hell, there's been a lot of that going around lately. Her coming here has triggered a lot of memories that I wanted to keep buried, but here we were.

The brain is a marvelous thing. It can make you believe in anything, even create memories that never happened. But it also has the power to bury things so deep that you forget about them until something triggers your memory to crack. The fragments of time slip forward and your happy world comes crashing down around you, leaving you scrambling to pick up the pieces of your shattered reality.

I couldn't let my past ruin my future. Hell, even the present. I needed to get my head on straight and bury Lily once and for all. It was a mere coincidence that she was here the night Wendy disappeared. Wasn't it? No. There was no such thing as coincidence, especially regarding Neverland. Everything happens for a reason. I just needed to figure out what.

Shaking my head to rid it of the unbidden memories, I grabbed the file I needed and entered the hospital. The smell of antiseptic and illness filled my senses, welcoming me home. This is where I found peace after all those years in Neverland, taking care of the sick and healing those who could be saved.

Isabella was on the bottom level of the hospital. My heart beat against my ribcage and trepidation filled my being once more. As I approached the elevators to take me down, sweat beaded across my brow and an anxious chill ran down my spine, settling at the base and creating an ache I wanted gone.

It's just a quick trip down. There are no threats down there besides a pissed-off coroner. Nothing to be afraid of.

There's nothing to be afraid of.

I repeated the mantra the whole trip down, and as the elevator doors slid open, I almost believed myself.

The smell of bleach permeated the air, not entirely covering up the smell of death, that told me I was now in no man's land—the morgue. A chill ran down my spine, and I wasn't sure if it was from the cold air being blown into the hall or my fear getting the better of me.

There's nothing to be afraid of.

The ding of the elevator door closing roused me from my ruminations. I slammed a hand onto the door and pressed it open to step off before letting my mind and anxiety take over.

I took a deep breath and forced my feet toward the door at the end of the hall. The sooner I got this done, the sooner I could leave. Isabella wasn't going to kill me. We were colleagues. So why are the butterflies in my stomach saying otherwise?

The door to the morgue itself had a film over it to prevent passersby from seeing the gruesome scenes that may be going on behind the glass. It was also my enemy at the moment because I had no idea what Isabella might be doing behind the window, which left my brain spinning in the many directions I didn't want it to go.

Breathing in through my nose and out my mouth, I enacted the breathing exercises that generally tell my patients to ease their anxiety. Sometimes, I give good advice. I let out my breath and some of the tension in my shoulders as I grabbed the handle and pushed the door open. My mind went blank at the scene before me and flashes of memories took over.

"JON!" Wendy whispered into my ear. "We need to go before the man-eater gets us, too." She pulled on my arm, but I was frozen in fear and curiosity, taking in the scene before us.

The woman was bloody, her hands in the stomach cavity of the Fae that was in front of her. Her chewing was loud enough to be heard across the small field, blood and pieces of flesh falling from her mouth back onto the corpse.

Cold sweat trickled down my face and body as I watched the scene, creating a chill that wracked my gangly frame. My glasses slid down my nose.

Wendy was still pulling on my arm, but I could no longer hear what she was saying. I knew I needed to move, but the ability had left me.

The realization hit me like a freight train. This was real. They really would eat us if given the chance. Neverland wasn't all fun and games. It wasn't a game that Pan had us playing. It was survival of the fittest and our lives were the prize.

"Dr. Darling? Are you alright?" Isabella's voice floated through my consciousness, mixing with the memory of Wendy calling for me to move.

My sight was zeroed in on the stomach in the woman's bloody hands. The sounds of Isabella emptying the stomach into a bowl made my own stomach turn and my insides turned to ice. I screwed my jaw shut as a scream tried to erupt from within. But I held myself silent, letting it ring freely in my mind, my fist tightening on the folder in my hands to keep from running from the scene.

"Dr. Darling?" Again, my name echoed around the room, but the only thing I could see were the flashes of Neverland bouncing through my head like a kaleidoscope of nightmares and memories that wouldn't go away.

"JON!" The loud echo of my name rang through my eardrums, clearing my mind and bringing my attention back to the present situation. My hands loosened from the folder, which was now a twisted mess. I realized I would have to get her new paperwork now that these were almost unusable anymore.

Gritting my teeth, I unclenched my jaw slowly and found her desk on the other side of the body. Nothing could go right today.

Clearing my suddenly parched throat, I made my way into the room and let the door close behind me, sealing me in with the opened-up corpse. Looking at its gray pallor sent more flashes of the man-eaters in Neverland to the front of my mind.

"Jon, are you alright? You're looking pale—ghost white, actually," her assistant, Darren, asked. I had seen the kid around the hospital. He was doing well and was now on his stint in the morgue.

"Never better," I choked out, the lie evident in the air between us. "I just needed to drop off this paperwork, but I might have to reprint it." Disappointment filled me at the thought that I would have to do this again.

All because I couldn't handle dead bodies.

"It should be fine. Just set it on my desk, doctor. I'll look it over later and get a hold of you with any questions I may have," Isabella stated curtly, her tone harsh as she placed the stomach onto a metal pan.

I nodded, took a deep breath, and quickly strode across the room, skirting by the body before laying the crumpled folder on her overly organized desk, looking out of place. Guilt riddled me that I couldn't handle seeing a cadaver. I really should get help for my PTSD, except then I would have to answer questions that would land me in a psych ward, and well, I was avoiding that.

Turning back, I quickly made my way toward the door. The need to leave the enclosed space had become an irritant under my skin. The compulsion to scratch it out festered in my mind like an infection in an open wound. A speck of glitter on the floor caught my eye as I wrapped my hand around the handle. Looking around, I couldn't see anymore with my naked eye, but the speckle brought back up the "Dust" Jane had mentioned earlier. It looked like pixie dust.

I shook my head. Maybe...

I quickly glanced back at the coroner and her assistant, both arms deep in the body. Flashes of the man-eaters flickered through my thoughts. Nope. He's dead. They aren't eating him.

They are not eating him.

Breathing in the stagnant air, the smell of the body wafted through my sinuses, the urge to gag was at the back of my throat. I swallowed down my reflexes to run and walked up to the body, ignoring the fear that gripped my insides, telling me to turn around. As I tamped down my urge to run away, I stopped a few steps from the table, not wanting to contaminate their findings, but I needed to look at the body.

There wasn't much to see. The insides were like any other human, except they were all laid flat on separate surfaces to be put back inside a bag and put back into the body at some point. What I was looking for was the speckle of pixie dust. Seeing how they had already thoroughly washed the body, it was doubtful, but something told me to keep looking.

"Is there something you're looking for, doctor?" Isabella asked, her voice muffled behind the mask.

"Was there any glittery-type substance on her when she came in?" My voice carried evenly, surprising even myself.

"Not that we have note of. Is there something you know that we should be looking for?" she asked, almost accusingly, as if I was holding back information.

"No. My nieces brought to my attention that there's a new drug out called Dust. She said it was shimmery and created hallucinations."

"Sounds like your nieces might have a problem if they know that," she huffed, glaring at me like I was lower than the gum on her shoe, which was granted. "Besides the fact that I have never heard of it and it is nowhere in the databases, they must be mistaken."

"No. I know what they're talking about," Darren interrupted, almost shyly. "It's really hard to come by. The owners of the local clubs only let certain people partake in the party drug, but as far as I know, nothing has come of it. Why did they bring it up?"

"Oh, they were just telling me about their experience at the bar and what they saw. I was curious about what it could be and if there were any known cases with it," I answered, skirting around Jane taking the drug. Not that they would be able to do anything about it now. It had happened over a year ago and couldn't be proven.

Concern furrowed Isabella's eyes as she looked up at me. "I'll look into it. But I don't know what good it'll do."

Nodding my head sharply, I regressed to the door once more and let out a heavy breath. I had done what I came to do. I was still alive and Jane wasn't crazy. There was a drug out there, one that we had no idea what it could do. And Jane and Julie were the only ones able to get their hands on it.

Chapter Sixteen

LILY

Opening the portals had become increasingly difficult. The strain on my mental capacity had been giving me headaches, not to mention the fact that my magic drains so fast it's almost impossible to reopen the portals to return home. I didn't know why it was happening, but I didn't want to bring it to anyone's attention because that meant weakness, and weakness would get you killed.

Focusing again, I pulled forth from the well of magic within my center, letting it fill my being, and focused on where I wanted to end up—the club.

Did I want to go back there? No.

Would I rather stay away from the bastard of a husband of mine? Yes.

Did I have a choice? No.

Drake knew who I was when I was little and spent a lot of time around the tribe, teaching me to trust him and that everything he said was pure gold. It turned out he could spin shit into gold strings of lies that wound into beautiful webs of deceit to get anything he wanted. By the time I was old enough to figure it out, I was already in a marriage with him and my true love had left me.

Focusing back on the magic trying to break free, I let the sparks at my fingertips fly, creating a hole that ripped between the realms. It was just big enough for me to walk through. Barely.

I took and stepped through the rip as apprehension slivered through my being. I hated being here. It was not London exactly, not that I enjoyed it here, but the club itself was eerie when it was closed, making for a long trip.

"You're late."

Gritting my teeth, I turned to the man behind my nightmares. "Well, I figured you could use the extra time to get the rest of your affairs in order. As you said the last time I was here, you needed time to fix a problem. What's just a few extra hours for you, anyway? Don't you live forever? Or was that also bullshit you fed to me as a kid, too?"

Drake's eyes bored into mine, anger simmering just beneath the surface of his cool exterior. "Time is as precious to me as it is to everyone. Why do you feel the need to waste mine? I'll have no idea."

"I'm pretty sure you do. You just don't want to admit fault in your undoing." I walked over to the bar and poured myself two fingers of the rum in the well. It was cheap and probably wouldn't do jack shit to calm my nerves, but it gave me something to do with my hands besides itching to hit him in the face.

He shook his head as he followed me to the bar, stopping so close I could feel the heat of his body against mine. Taking the bottle from my hand, he purposely brushed his fingers against mine, letting them linger longer than was necessary. "Maybe I thought *my wife* would think of other ways to waste my time than to sit in Neverland, pondering when she should interrupt my night."

Letting the shudder blatantly run down my spine, I pulled away from the Fae and rounded back to the front of the bar to put space between us. I hated that he thought he could have me whenever he pleased, which is one of the main reasons I waited until the last minute to pick up the payment. The less time to be here to do the illicit things he would love to do to me. One of these nights, I was going to end up in his bed just to get him to shut the fuck up for a while, but tonight was not that night. I had bigger fish to fry.

"How about we get on with our night? You give me the kids, I'll whisk them away to Neverland, and we can go our separate ways, as always. Makes much more sense to me than you pining away for something you lost long ago."

"I didn't lose anything." He came right up close, his hand closing around my throat. If it weren't him, I'd almost be turned on. Almost. Breath play was one of my kinks, but this man killed anything I may have felt towards him a long time ago and, in doing so, any desire to be with him. "I could easily just take what I want." He tightened his hold. "But I know how much you like control and I am not in the mood to be dominated."

"Poor choice on your part. You probably need it. Remember that you aren't as high and mighty as you think you are," I spit out. Would I do it? Eh... the threat was there, but I would have to be desperate for a release to come to him for it. And as he said, he could take what he wanted. He had before. Some things just can't be fought and his magic overpowers mine every time.

"Careful, pet. I might take it anyway and let you deal with the consequences." He tightened his hold once more, his thumb caressing the side of my throat, feeling my pulse flutter beneath his hand. Gods, I hated him.

"Then I'll just let Tink know that your baser needs precede her and you can deal with her wrath. The evidence would be laid there for her to see. I may have little repercussions over it, as it is my fault for ignoring you. But her needs come first. She will still side with me," I spit out once again.

Drake sneered at me, his head coming down to my neck, smelling my hair and rubbing his nose along the column of my throat. Once, this was nice. Once, this was something I craved. Now? He could get fucked.

Letting go of me, I stumbled backward, dropping my glass and taking in a deep, needed breath. Looking up at the man, all he did was smile. Bastard.

"The children are in the basement. We already sent one ahead. She probably isn't going to last long without her medications, so we just sent her straight to the castle."

How? He can't just create portals. That was my magic. No one else could do it.

He continued, reading my mind. "Don't forget, my darling wife, when we wed, I was bonded to your soul. I can use any magic that you have. Have you been feeling weaker lately?" My eyes shot to where he was standing, an empty spot now as if he had vanished.

That motherfucker. If he wasn't already on my shit list, he was there now.

The basement was cold. There was no dampness in the air, just cool. Why Drake kept the kids freezing was beyond me. I quickly moved down the hall and entered the third door on the right, the door creaking as I opened it. I should tell him to oil those, but the fucker has already pissed me off. He can deal with his rusty hinges.

The kids were all asleep on cots that lined the walls. This time around, the batch looked bigger. Counting the bundles, there were around twenty kids, not including the one he had already sent ahead.

Heat seared through my chest at the reminder. That bastard has been draining me himself and thinks I should sleep with his ass... No, thanks. I am already exhausted, having to replenish my magic more often than necessary because he's been using it without my knowledge. There had to be a way to stop him from doing it or to at least know when he was doing it. I would have to talk to my father about that, but I really didn't want to seek him out.

I walked down the aisle between the bunks and took a quick peek at the kids. Most of them were about the age of six or seven. Lost Boys and Girls. Lost Boys, for short, because the Fae couldn't be bothered. I stopped at a particular bed. The girl's red curls and freckled face had caught my eye. Her breathing was slightly different than the others, more erratic. Touching her hair, I smoothed it down. My touch seemed to calm her down and her breathing slowed back to normal. She must have been having a bad dream. When she woke, it was going to be worse. So much worse.

I don't know precisely what the Fae did with all these kids, but I could harbor a good guess, which made my stomach turn. The Fae were vile creatures who let their tastes run rampant by need and not moral sense. They didn't care. A body was a body until it wasn't of use anymore.

Shaking my head, I brought myself back to the present. There was no sense in saving them. I had tried that once and paid dearly. I have learned many lessons over the years, none of them lightly, and all at a cost.

I brought the wall around my heart back in place and went to open the portal I was going to need. Usually, I had Drake wake the children for me to make this easier, but seeing how he decided to disappear and not want to help me tonight, probably because I refused him, I would have to ask the men on the other side to move them.

As I dipped back into my being, I slowly started pulling on the magic and let it sing through me. The magic flowed out to my fingertips to create the hole in the fabric of space and time. Magic was tricky if you didn't know what you were doing with it. I had been playing with mine for so long that I didn't need to concentrate too hard, but one little mistake and we were all goners.

Once opened, my men were patiently waiting by the old Deadman's Tree. The tree used to be Pan's hideout with the original Lost Boys and the Darling children. One day, the tree was set ablaze, all the Lost Boys dying, and Pan had never been seen or heard from again. No one knew what happened that night and we would probably never get answers. Pan's absence in Neverland has been felt since and we all became a shell of what we once were. It was ironic that the Fae chose this place as the drop-off point for the children, seeing how many deaths surrounded this area.

The area around the tree gave off bad vibrations as if the island itself hated the hole that was left there. I would almost say the area was cursed. You could practically feel the ghosts of the dead Lost Boys chilling the air.

The man closest to me, Wolf, a fitting name as that was his other form, turned and investigated the room. His long, dark hair fell forward, covering his tattooed face. "Where's the Fae?" he asked, his voice reverberating through the room. The portal distorted voices, but his was always more profound and menacing through the rip than most people's.

"Couldn't be bothered today, apparently," I answered, flipping my hair behind my shoulder. I wasn't going into detail about Drake's disappearance. It was my problem, not theirs, and I didn't want anyone worrying about me more than necessary. "I need help. I don't think they'll wake anytime soon without him letting them up, so I need you guys to cross over and carry them, one or two at a time, into the tree. I'll keep the portal open." I needed them to hurry, but I wasn't going to tell them that the bastard of a husband drained me.

All the men nodded and came forward. None of us wanted to do this, but it was this or die. And dying in Neverland was never really dying. You just become a shadow that can't do much. You can't be seen or heard, but you can still feel pain. It was pure hell, from what legends say, and none of us were too keen to find out if those were true or not.

The five of them moved quickly, taking two trips each. After the last of the children were gone, I took one more look to double-check, as I have made that mistake before, leaving a child behind, and that was the last time I did that. Sweat was spotting in my hairline and the portal was starting to waver, the edges sputtering. I needed to hurry. I couldn't hold it open much longer. Double-checking all the kids were in Neverland, I turned back to the portal, my magic officially failing as I stepped through, and it snapped closed behind me.

The children were all in the bunks we had set up underneath the tree. Tears emerged, memories assaulting me as I walked through the old tree house. The corner where we all would have food fights, more often than not. The hammock in the middle of the room where we would take turns swinging on. The room down the hall where Jon and I had snuck our first kiss.

Gods, I hated this place. The Fae had turned a place of memories and fun into a burned-out prison.

All the guys had already left, their jobs done for the night. The Fae would be here in about an hour or two to pick the kids up, I assume, to take them to the castle for whatever whims they may have of them.

I glanced around the room and all the kids were lying on their beds. The one girl still caught my eye. There was something about her, I don't know what, but I knew if I stayed any longer and let my emotions get into it, it wasn't going to help either of us. If I could, I wouldn't do this at all. These children deserved better than to be brought to an island of nightmares.

After I left the cursed tree, I slowly made my way back to the camp. The men had changed into their other forms, primarily wolves, their howls filling the night air. Our tribe was blessed with magic long ago when Neverland was created. The women held the magic that kept the tribe running smoothly, and the men were shapeshifters to protect us. If my magic weren't being sucked away from me by a leech, I would just be able to portal myself home, but this gave me time to think.

The trails I knew by heart were overgrown, and the day's heat had waned into something almost bearable. But the humidity still stuck to the leaves of the trees and ferns, soaking my skin and hair in its dampness, mirroring the well of betrayal I felt.

Drake knew about the bond that gave him access to my magic and had been using it for his own agenda. Now, I wanted to know how long he had been using me for his own gain and if anything we ever had was real in the first place. At one point in time, I did care about the man, but with this revelation, he made sure I would never trust him again.

I shook myself from my dark thoughts and recalled when Jon had almost caught me the other day. It was clear that he had moved on from me. The memory of the woman he was with, touching him, had a spike of jealousy run through my veins, creating an inferno of rage inside.

He was mine.

I didn't care that I had to leave him. It wasn't like I wanted to. I had no choice. It was marry Drake, or they killed Jon. Either way, whether Jon was dead or alive, I was still to be married to the damned Fae.

Agitation burned along my skin with the fact that Jon was over there with someone that wasn't me, while I was stuck with a piece of shit husband who treated me as property more than anything. It had me seeing red.

Stomping through the brush, I finally made my way back home. Ignoring everyone, I went straight to my tent and tore my clothes from my body. Soaked with sweat, I lay on my bed and tried to quiet my mind. Listening to the howls of my people lulled me to sleep.

Rest. I needed rest. Then, I would go back and visit Jon.

Chapter Seventeen

WENDY

"Peter! Come down here! I can't fly like you!"

"Oh, but Wendy-Bird, you can! You just have to remember."

"I haven't flown since the last time you brought me here, remember? I need pixie dust and Tinkerbelle has refused to give me any since we were here last," I stated matter-of-factly.

Tinkerbelle has been quite distant since the last time I was here. I don't remember doing anything to her to make her hate me, but the disgust on her face anytime I'm around is more than enough for me to know I pissed her off somehow.

Shaking my head, I looked up to Peter floating above me, his legs crossed and his chin resting on his fist as if in thought. Trying to figure out how he thought it was a dangerous thing. His train of thought was backward and didn't make sense to me. But he grew up with faeries, and their sense of morality was just as eschewed. I knew he was trying to figure out how to make me fly again, but without the pixie dust, it was impossible.

"I'll go see Tink and ask her why she won't let you use her pixie dust."

"None of the other Lost Boys fly. Why are you adamant that I fly?" I didn't want him to get into it with Tinkerbelle. She was one to hold onto a grudge, whether I knew what that grudge was about or not. Fae were finicky creatures, and I didn't want to start a war with them. Better to leave sleeping dogs lie, as they say.

"Because I want you to go places that only I know, and you have to fly to get there."

"Why don't you just carry me like you did to bring me here?"

"Because it is easier for both of us to fly."

He really wasn't going to let this go. "Well, if you are dead set on this, then go ask her. But I don't think it's a good idea." I cross my arms over my small breasts.

It's been four years since I started visiting Neverland, and each time I come back, I'm just a little bit more grown-up. And each time, I've noticed that the Fae hate me more and more. I don't know if it is because I am growing up, or because Peter spends a lot of time with me when I am here.

"Don't do that." Peter's voice was suddenly different. Deeper.

Looking up to where he was still floating, I saw what he was staring at: my chest. Quirking an eyebrow, I asked, "Stop doing what?"

He came down, landing in front of me. He was taller than I remember and his body was fuller, like other boys my age at home. Taking my arms, he unfolded them in front of me and said, "That. Don't do that."

"Why? I do it all the time."

"You didn't have these before," he said as he cupped my breasts in his rough hands. A shot of arousal flew through me straight to my privates, something I had never felt before. He started to massage them, my nipples hardening into peaks. He moved to play with them, and I let out a small moan. It felt good, and I wanted more...

No. This was wrong.

Putting my hands over his, I removed them from my chest and looked up at him, my eyes wide at the physical contact and what I was feeling. I had never felt anything like that before, and looking down, I saw that Peter was just as aroused as I was at that little bit of contact.

"You shouldn't touch me there. It isn't appropriate." My voice had softened, almost a whisper between us.

"But your reaction says otherwise. It sounded like you liked it. I liked it, too." His voice was husky, filled with lust.

Shaking my head, I tried to clear it of the thoughts of Peter touching me more because Gods did I want him to. "No. It isn't right, Peter. Maybe you're right. You should ask Tink for some dust so I can fly by myself." The fewer chances we have of touching each other, the better.

Nodding, Peter flew off and I was left standing in the middle of his room in the tree house, pondering what the hell just happened. What would have happened if I let him continue touching me.

The pillow under my face was warm and wet. As I swiped the hair out of my eyes, I found it soaked with sweat with my hair tangled, my fingers getting caught in the knots. My body was feverish, but probably more so from the memory than the heat of the day. The room was still slightly cool and felt marvelous against my skin.

Opening my crusted eyes, I looked around the room I was in. The bed was placed on the left side of door, a nightstand on either side of the bed. The bed itself was huge. More than enough room for three people to sprawl upon. What does Michael need such a huge bed for? You know what—I don't want to know. Curtailing my thoughts from that direction, a huge, picturesque window was on the far side of the room, to the right of the door. In front of the window was a desk with a chair behind it. What does he use the desk for?

The stark realization that he had an entire life here that I didn't know about, that I didn't know my brother at all, made my head hurt as a shot of pain went through my heart, cracking it.

My muscles ached from not moving for so long as I crawled to the edge of the monstrous bed. I had been sleeping extremely soundly for being in a place that wanted me dead. I would be more worried about it if I weren't sure the men guarding the door wouldn't let anything through. The men rotated shifts and Grim hadn't been back since his first stint. Thank the Gods.

My feet touched the fur rug that was on the side of the bed, tickling my toes. Rolling my neck, I made myself stand up, the room swaying slightly as blood rushed to my head, but I was still upright. Yay me. Sometimes it was the little things in life.

The smell of food cooking filtered into the room, my stomach grumbling at the delicious scent. I let my nose lead me and followed the smell down the stairs, stopping at the base in a small living area. A couch and rocking chair were placed in the middle with a fireplace on the wall in front of me. A small hallway to the left of the stairs I was still standing on led to the kitchen. My stomach told me to keep following the smell of food, but my brain was telling me no one should be there.

"Michael?" I called out.

"Who's Michael?" a woman's voice rang back.

My heart jumped into my throat. Was I even in my brother's house? Who was in the kitchen?

Slowly making my way down the hall, trepidation filled my being as I walked into the small, but quaint kitchen. Standing at the stove was a beautiful, dark-skinned woman, braids falling from her head down to her butt with beads at the ends and a bandanna across the top of her head. She was tall and thin, but more athletically inclined, as you could see the toned muscle of her arms as she stirred whatever was in the pot. As she turned toward me, I was startled by her bright, blue eyes and a nose ring glinting off the light that filtered in through the windows.

My stomach decided that was the moment it was going to announce that it was still dying of starvation, and we both broke out in laughter.

"It sounds like you're hungry," her soft, southern accent filled the air. She scooped some of what looked to be soup into a bowl and put it on the small island in the middle of the kitchen. "Here, eat this. I made you some chicken soup. Fresh rolls are coming out of the oven in a minute."

Watching the woman move around the kitchen, I realized she knew where everything was. Almost as if she lived here as well. The thought that I was invading her space sent a wave of shame through me. Turning back toward me with a bowl of her own, her black braids swirl about her lithe body as she took a seat.

Flabbergasted, I sat on one of the stools and picked up the spoon that was awaiting me. "I'm Wendy, by the way. The captain didn't tell me anyone else lived here, I am sorry for invading your space." Embarrassment flitted through me, but then I knew it wasn't my fault I didn't know shit about fuck here anymore.

The woman's smile was bright as she went to grab the yeasty rolls out of the oven, the smell of the freshly baked bread making my stomach grumble more than it already was. "Talia," she said by way of introduction, "and I don't live here, not really. I just stay here with Smee sometimes. My place is up the beach a way away. He asked me to come watch over you while he dealt with Neverland business."

The name Smee popped up again. The name niggled at something in my subconscious, but nothing stirred enough to know what. Does Michael not use his real name here? Or are they two separate people and everyone is confused?

Shaking my head, I bent down over the bowl in front of me, the soup piping hot tasted like heaven. I haven't had a soup like this since my mother was alive to make it for us when we got sick. Maybe it was just because someone besides me had made it that made it taste that much better. Or it could be the fact that I was so hungry it didn't matter what was put in front of me. I was going to devour it. The rolls that Talia brought out of the oven sent a wave of heat in my direction that didn't help my still fevered skin, but the smell more than made up for it. My mouth watered at the prospect of fresh rolls to dip into the broth.

"Thank you for the soup. I have no idea how anything works here anymore and was afraid of setting his kitchen on fire when I saw it was a wood stove."

"Oh, it's no problem. It's not very often that I get to cook for someone besides myself and have someone appreciate it."

We ate in silence, enjoying the meal she had made. I took the last of the roll I had, running it over the bottom of the bowl to soak up the last of the broth before popping it in my mouth and savoring the last bite. "Mmmm. That was delicious, Talia." I placed my hand over her dark one and squeezed it. "You are more than welcome to spoil me with your cooking anytime. If I knew I could have been eating food like this the whole time I've been here, I would have come to you sooner." I laughed.

"I don't tell anyone because then they'll put me in the kitchens and I would prefer to bartend. One, coin is better. Two, I would rather keep my hobby a hobby and not my life's work, unlike my sister, who wants to share her cooking with the world. I don't want to do it to the point that I don't enjoy it anymore."

"That makes sense. I wouldn't want to do that, either." I nodded my head in agreeance. "So, I have a lot of questions, but first, I want to shower. I know 'Smee' has to have something around here." I raised my fingers to air quotes because I was still quite confused about who this 'Smee' character was.

"Why did you do that? Do you not know who Smee is?" Talia waved her finger at me, bangles jingling on her wrist.

"No, I don't. The only person I know here, besides you, is my brother and his name isn't Smee."

Her brow furrowed as she contemplated what I was saying. "Smee told me before he left that you were important to him and to watch over you. Are you sure we aren't talking about the same person?"

Confusion must have been clear on my face as I considered what she was saying. Smee... A tingling of memory trying to push itself forward was just out of my reach, creating a headache between my temples. I know I have heard that name before, but for the life of me, I can't remember where or why. Michael must be masquerading under an alias to keep prying ears from knowing his true identity. It was the only explanation and a smart one. I couldn't think of any reason someone would claim me, the island pariah, as important to them if they wanted to live.

Still, I couldn't be too careful about who knew what around here, and even though my instincts were telling me Talia was safe, I couldn't let go of the feeling that I was dancing a charade on thin ice and about to fall through.

Shrugging my shoulders, I looked at the woman who stared at me with a questioning gaze. "Guess we will be finding out who's who around here at some point. I am getting a headache thinking about it and really want a shower. That's all."

The beads on her braids knocked lightly together as she nodded her head and stood up, grabbing our bowls. "What's here is cold water that will freeze your tits off. Even with it being so hot here, I won't even use their shady plumbing. I prefer to use the hot springs."

A memory flashed through my mind at the mention of the hot springs. Peter and I, lying naked on the rocks, our toes in the water. Him gazing down at me, touching me...

I shook my head violently at the flash and my cheeks instantly flushed at the memory. It was the last time I was here and one of my favorite memories to get off to.

"Are you okay? Your cheeks are red."

"Oh, yeah. I just totally forgot about them. I'm embarrassed that I forgot about half of what was on this island," I lied.

A smirk crossed her lips. "Riiight." She didn't say she knew I was lying, which I was thankful for. I didn't want to explain that I had lost my virginity at the springs.

"Let's get going and not waste any more time here. We have a hot spring to dip ourselves into." Talia smiled, her bright white teeth clashing against her dark skin. I swear, they could use her as a night spy.

"Yes, let's. I am feeling like a soaked sponge and probably smell just as bad."

"I am not commenting on that statement." She snickered.

I cringe. "That's just confirming my worst thoughts." I sighed to myself as we made our way to the springs.

Chapter Eighteen

JAMES

Of course, Asher would take his sweet time wanting to meet with me. Being the only Fae on the island I trust, was starting to get to the man's head. Some things must be done more swiftly than at the big-headed man's leisurely pace.

Smee arrived at the ship, saying the Fae would meet with me here today. It gave me little time to prepare, but all I have been doing is thinking. And thinking is dangerous. The only thing on my mind since leaving London has been one thing.

The safety of my girls.

Hopefully, the bull-headed man could help. I am more concerned about Alis' treatment than anything. Hot rage coursed through me at the thought. If Drake even thinks about laying a hand on her, there would be hell to pay. Nothing on this island would stop me from taking the man's head. I dared him to try—one less headache to deal with.

Sitting on the edge of the dock, the water from Crocodile Creek slowly flowed out to the Cove. It was soothing, but it flared my temper at the reminder that everything happens at its own pace, no matter my impatience for things to move faster.

"You know that glaring at the water isn't helping you." A deep voice came from behind and I fought the urge to draw my weapon. He never was one to announce his presence like a normal person. Then again, the Fae weren't normal. Quite the opposite. Stupid is what they were.

"You know, sneaking up on people is bad for your health," I responded, my voice steady, even as my nerves shot through me. The damned Fae and their games.

The man came to sit beside me, my ire rising at his close proximity, but to move meant showing weakness. And I wasn't showing him anything. My jaw clenched as I let out a breath to steady myself, counting down from ten. Not that it would work, anyway. It never did.

"Are we just going to sit here and stare at the fish all day, or are you going to tell me what was so important to drag me away from The Sanctuary?" Asher grumbled. He wasn't as keen on being here as I was. We didn't meet for a good reason. If we were to be caught, it would look like we were conspiring against *Her Majesty*. As true as that might be, we weren't ready to take any action against the damned woman.

"Yes, well, we have a problem." My left knee throbbed as I lurched to my feet, the achiness a reminder I bore that not everyone you trust is your friend, including family.

Especially family.

I turned my back to the man, showing the little bit of trust I had in him, and strode toward the entrance of Skull Rock, letting him play catch up.

The sound of Asher's clothes brushing against the leaves of the path was intentional. He didn't have to make the noise. He was born in the forest and could move through it without a sound. He could blend in with the scenery so well that you wouldn't know he was there unless you knew what to look for, and I still had a hard time finding him most days.

The sound of the creek rushing through the bottom of the cavern echoed around us and drowned out all the noise, creating a perfect hunting spot for predators like myself. The thought that an even bigger predator walked behind me sent a shiver down my spine as I continued down the path. I hated it.

There were only a few more paces before we reached our destination. A small alcove that I had carved out for meetings such as this. Quiet, with enough surrounding noise our conversations couldn't be overheard unless you were in our immediate vicinity. In that manner, you'd probably be dead. Dead men can't tell tall tales or something like that, isn't that what the pirate saying was? A small smirk tilted my lips into a small grin, a quiet chuckle escaping my throat. Sometimes, I amused myself.

"Something funny you want to share with the rest of us?" Asher asked, curiosity dripping from his voice.

"Just my own twisted humor. Nothing that concerns you."

"Just my luck. A pirate captain who listens to voices in his head. What has this island come to?" I could hear the smile in the Fae's voice. At least he was in good spirits. By the end of this meeting, his good humor was most likely to be turned sour.

"Could be worse. I could be insane."

"That is still to be determined."

He wasn't wrong. Psychotic, maybe, but not insane. Not yet, anyway.

The side of the walkway opened on the right to the alcove I was looking for. Slipping inside, I lit the sconces on the wall with my lighter, moving further into the room to the far wall, wet with the glowing moss, being careful not to touch it.

Turning back to Asher, the man filled the space, his horns almost grazing the ceiling. I didn't build the place in mind with a huge Fae coming to visit me, but here we were.

The waves of power coming off the man pressed against my body, making it hard to breathe. Locking my knees, I practiced my breathing to keep myself stable while I waited for him to bring his power back into himself.

Slowly, the room was less stifling as Asher pulled the rest of his powers back to himself, the fire in the sconces flickering as if the air in the room was being depleted as well. It might have been, for all I knew. The Fae's powers here all differed. I gave up a long time ago on trying to learn all the different species and their nuances. If I stayed out of their way, they stayed out of mine.

"Now, what's going on that this couldn't wait? I had to pull some strings to be able to get here." Asher's voice filled the alcove, reverberating along the walls.

"I have a favor to ask."

"Favors with the Fae come with a price. Are you sure you want to pay it?"

My stomach sank to my feet as sweat beaded along my hairline. "What is the price?"

"That depends on the favor. I cannot guarantee the price to be paid. Neverland has its way of working itself out."

I knew that the Fae had prices to pay for their magic, but the fact that Asher didn't set the price had my heart sinking. What if it isn't something I didn't want to pay? What happens to Alis if I don't?

I shook my head, clearing it of all my thoughts. Only Alis and Jane mattered. And if only Alis was here and Jane was not, then Neverland couldn't harm Jane, but Drake could. Especially if he found out I took his bargaining chip, he would turn to the one that was left. Jane. And that just wasn't acceptable. I would rather put my odds against the magic of Neverland than deal with him.

"I need my niece brought here to The Sanctuary. The only problem is she is sick."

"Why? Why does she need to be here? Neverland isn't a place for children and it has never been. But Pan didn't care and brought them here to play anyway," the man scoffed.

Dread crept into my being. Who the hell is Pan?

"Drake has threatened her well-being, and I would rather the man not get his slimy fingers on her." He had his fingers in more pots than he could handle, and he was just adding to the load by threatening mine.

Asher nodded his head. "How sick is she?"

"She has cancer. She is laid up in a hospital and cannot fight someone like him."

"Is she dying? Are you asking me to save her life?"

"She isn't dying. Not yet. She is taking the treatments, but they make her very weak and she sleeps a lot."

"But if I bring her here, she won't have access to that. You would be better off having the island heal her and knowing that she is safe and healthy."

"But what is the price for that?"

Asher shrugged, his body tense. "As I said, Neverland will balance it out in its own way. I can assure you that it will be something you won't like. What are you willing to pay?" His eyes flashed with mischief and malevolence.

There was something the man wasn't telling me. I don't know if he would tell me or spin me more riddles. But I would risk anything to keep my girls safe. And if Alis was healed of her disease in the process, then I was more than willing to pay whatever price the island wanted.

"Can you do it?" I asked, no longer wanting to entertain the man, but we had one more thing to discuss and this was taking too long.

Asher nodded. "As you wish. I will pick her up in the next few days. I need to make some preparations for her to arrive here first."

Nodding my ascent, I pressed forward and motioned for the behemoth of a man to move away from the door. "I appreciate it. But I have something else I would like to show you."

The Fae cocked his head, his horns scraping the ceiling and sending rock down on his head. I barked out a laugh and shook my head as I waited for the man to move through the doorway.

"I hope you know that you will owe me a favor in return," Asher growled out, apparently not happy that I laughed at him. I would care more if he didn't look so ridiculous.

Following him out the door, I started the stroll toward the cell that held Chip. "I had assumed this wouldn't be a one-way street, but it doesn't seem fair that I am paying twice for the same favor. I think after you see what else I have in store for you, you will change your mind."

Asher grunted, slowly making his way behind me. His opinion of me isn't very high, but I wasn't my father, which I have repeatedly proved to him. Asher still doesn't think I bring much value to our tenuous relationship.

After taking a few turns, I slowed my stride, my steps turning sticky as we made our way to the cell door. A coppery tang filled the air that shouldn't have been there. Apprehension and dread had my stomach sinking to my feet. Something was wrong.

"I didn't think you would bring me a sacrifice for this favor." Asher chuckled as we continued forth. "The effort is worth noting, but not necessary."

His nonchalance at this grated on my nerves, like nails scraping down a chalkboard. "No. Something is wrong," I stated as I pulled out my revolver. As much as I loved my sword, this was not the place to use it.

"What do you mean?" Concern laced his words. Sometimes, the man cared.

Ignoring him, I crept along the walkway. My jaw clenched so hard that I gritted my teeth. I tried to keep myself as quiet as possible, which, with sticky shoes, was nearly impossible. Anyone could hear us coming. But if the blood was that tacky, whoever died did a while ago. Trepidation ran down my spine as my shoulders tensed with nerves. My men were under orders to keep the captive alive and they had yet to fail me. The sense of foreboding filled the tunnel with an unease that was palpable.

I halted outside the door, knocking in the pattern to alert my men I was outside. Silence answered my call. My heart crawled into my throat and my nerves were frayed to the bit. I had no patience left. Raising my hand to knock once more, Asher grabbed my forearm from behind.

His finger was to his lip, silencing my retort to him touching me. Following his finger, he pointed to the ground, whereupon a hand lay outside the door—one adorned with gold jewelry that I would recognize anywhere.

Striker.

Pulling back, my fingers gripped the slick doorknob, ignoring the fact that it was covered in blood. Blood of one of my men, no doubt. Fury furrowed red hot through my veins at the audacity and the loss.

The smell of blood and rotted flesh filled the air, forcing me to step back as I nearly gagged from the stench. The fires in the sconces were almost out, the oil having been lit for too long without being refilled. How long ago did this massacre happen?

Blind rage filled my vision as everything turned a hazy red. My breath became erratic as I tried to process what I was seeing. Striker's hands were cut off at the wrists. No. Sawed-off. The flesh around his forearms was uneven and choppy, as if the person doing it didn't know what they were doing. His throat was slit so deep his head was nearly off his shoulders. The spray covered the room in his blood and his eyes were glazed and staring at the ceiling, the look of shock forever etched onto his face.

Savage wasn't in any better shape. His hands were still intact, but the eye he had was gone. His lips were blue, and the rope around his neck was embedded so deep his skin was flayed around it.

In the center of the room, where my captive should have been, was an empty chair, the iron shackles pried apart by the wrench that was lying on the floor nearby.

The acrid taste of bitterness coated my tongue. My face flushed as my hands clenched into fists. The need to throw something, anything, clawed desperately at my limbs and my heart raced out of my chest.

Asher cautiously stepped into the room, his eyes scanning the carnage that was wrought against my men. "Humans didn't do this. It was made to look that way, but the amount of strength it would take to do this..." He shook his head, as if unable to believe what is front of him. "Who was being held captive here?" His eyes landed on the bloodied, empty chair.

"The man's name was Chip. I was going to give him to you in good faith. He said escaped Tink's castle of horrors. Apparently, someone else found him first." I spat at the ground, letting it mix with my men's blood.

Something flashed through Asher's eyes. It was gone so fast I would have thought I had imagined it if I hadn't been around the man enough to know he was pissed.

"I didn't think anyone knew about this system of caverns you had laid out in here?" he asked quietly, fury low in his voice.

"Only the few people I trust."

Asher nodded as if thinking the same thing I was.

Someone was a rat.

Chapter Nineteen

WENDY

The water was hot—so hot that you could see the steam rising from within the woods. The moisture stagnant in the air made it hard to breathe.

The water was the color of turquoise, the deeper parts of the spring turning a purple hue, the bubbles breaking the surface twinkling like diamonds under the steam. I knew it would be clear as glass when I dipped into the water and the warmth would instantly soothe my aching muscles. I could almost hear the water calling my name. Then again, it could be the long-lost memory of mermaids calling me to the depths of Mermaid Lagoon. The white sand along the spring was soft and the long grass surrounding the area swayed lightly in the breeze. A light song played among the reeds, the tune almost too light to hear.

Talia had moved to the water's edge and started stripping out of her clothes. No embarrassment. No shame. No care in the world. Just stripped right down and got in. But, then again, if I had her body, I wouldn't be ashamed to show it off, either. Talia's body was made of sinew muscle with the perfect amount of curve.

Stepping through the reeds, I stripped down to my bra and panties and dipped my paint-chipped toes into the warm water, the heat inviting me deeper. My body wasn't muscled like it used to be from running the island. It was now soft with curves and cellulite, scars from childhood, and stretch marks that come with age and childbearing. I am not ashamed of my body. It has brought me this far in life, but I still was slightly envious of the woman in front of me.

I took a deep breath, dipped under the water to douse my head, and scrubbed the sweat out of my hair. The water was comforting and felt like a hug from the island itself, wrapping me in its embrace and welcoming me home. The warmth seeped into my skin and deep into my bones. The aching muscles relaxed the longer I stayed beneath the water.

Too soon, I was reminded that I was still human and needed to breathe. The burn for air razed my lungs like wildfire. Swimming upwards, I broke the surface, gasping while I moved the hair out of my face. I slipped on the slick rocks beneath my toes as I tried to gain my footing and fell back into the water. A squelch left my lips before I slipped beneath the steam again. The sounds of laughter rang in my ears as I got my bearings, reminding me of the girls.

Thinking about them had worry worming itself back through my thoughts. What if whoever came after me came for them? No. They came searching for me. No one here knew of Jane. And even less of Julie. We took precautions to ensure the girls were hidden from the Fae that might come looking for a reason to hurt me.

I let out a breath and turned to Talia as she swam over to my spot in the spring. This was where Peter and I loved to swim and lie on the rocks, letting the dual suns dry us as we touched and played with each other until our bodies were deliciously sore.

"One would think you had never swum before with your floundering over here." Talia giggled, apparently only seeing my fall into the water and not my graceful swimming techniques.

"I have plenty of experience swimming in this pool." I splashed at her. "I just lost my footing on the rocks."

"Whatever you say. Looked like a fish out of water to me." She splashed back at me. Her laughter rang through the clearing, making my lips quirk up in a smile.

"Maybe that was my plan the whole time. Get everyone to underestimate me, make myself look weak and dumb." I laughed. The idea wasn't a total waste. It would help me, but Tinkerbelle already knew what I was capable of and wouldn't fall for it. Neither would my brother.

Talia chuckled. "We all know better than to underestimate anything here on the island. Especially newcomers."

"Well, I should be one of the people whom you trust. I've been here before and know the layout of Neverland better than anyone else." Except maybe my brother, but that's questionable as well. "But I guess that's up to you to decide. I am not here to prove anything to anyone. I just want to figure out where the hell Peter is."

"Who's Peter?" Talia's face screwed into confusion, her mouth pursed and her nose wrinkled.

"Peter Pan? The boy who grew up here? The man that Neverland is attached to? This isn't the Neverland it was when I was a child. Peter, missing from the island, has created this hellscape and needs to be found to return the island to the way it was." The hair on the nape of my neck rose as a rustling in the trees caught my ear.

We weren't alone. But I didn't know if Talia knew that.

She shrugged her shoulders. "I have no idea what you are talking about. You and Smee probably have a better idea than the rest of us. We were all recruited to help Cap with the ship."

"What is 'Smee's' job around here, anyway?" I asked, curiosity getting the better of me. Any little bit of information I could get on my brother would help me understand what he had gone through since we last saw each other over twenty years ago.

"Smee is Captain Barrington's first mate. His right-hand man, as you will. And that is all I am telling you about it. If he wants you to know, he will tell you." She turned and started swimming back to the shore. Apparently, our time here was done.

A wave of dread wove through me as I watched Talia climb from the water. More rustling came from the tree line and I was now more than ever ready to leave the spring. Someone was watching us, and that didn't bode well.

I needed a weapon.

I groaned as I dipped my head under the water again and returned to the edge. My body felt much better after that long soak. I felt more nimble and less achy. The tension in my shoulders probably wasn't going away anytime soon—too much stress and fearmongering.

Reaching down to the clean clothes we had brought, Talia walked over, already dressed. "We should get going back. Lord knows that if Smee or Cap come back and you aren't at the house, Smee will have both of our heads." She laughed under her breath as if something was funny.

It wasn't.

Just as I pulled on my boots, a shiver slid down my spine as if I was being watched again. The need to have a knife in my hand was almost too much to bear. "Talia? Does anyone else know about this spot?"

"Probably a couple of the men and the Fae. But the men don't come out here very often, as they all bathe in the Cove. The Fae rarely come out of their castle to bother us."

"Castle? Since when was there a castle?"

"What do you mean?"

"When I was a kid, the Fae lived in the trees and the woods. There was no castle," I spat out, flabbergasted at the thought that they had the audacity to build one for themselves.

"Well, there is now."

Logging that information away for me to ponder later, I shook my head, searching the woods for any sign that someone was there. The Fae were tricksters, and if any of them got wind of the fact that I was here, I would be in trouble. And they were excellent at hiding in nature. They were born and thrived there.

Staring into the forest, recollections of pixies playing in my hair as I ran through the trails with Peter and the boys in tow came forth. Pixies. They were small enough to hide and could report whatever they found to Tink. Sweat beaded on my brow at the thought. It was a bad idea to come here. I had no weapons, and my only sort of defense was a woman who said she would protect me. I'm asking for a sword and a gun when I talk to Michael.

I wasn't going without a weapon back into the woods. I trusted Talia, but one woman against however many enemies wasn't the best odds, especially when they wanted something.

Standing up, I looked Talia over, counting the three daggers on her person that I could see, but that didn't include what I couldn't see. She could spare one. "Do you mind lending me a knife?"

Talia's eyebrows rose as if asking such a question was blasphemous. "No. I don't trust you."

"Well, there's something in the woods and I would much rather not be defenseless. I figure one dagger isn't going to hurt you, seeing how many you have on your person. I just need one. I'll give it back before we get to the town."

"Do you plan on stabbing me in the back with it?" she practically snarled. Her change in demeanor had alarm bells ringing loudly in my head, but I'd rather deal with her than be unarmed against whatever was watching us.

"Oh my Gods, why the fuck would I do that?! Fine! I'll just trust you to protect me. But don't be whining when something comes out of the woods and you regret not letting me have something to defend myself." I stomped off into Cannibal Forest, purposely going toward the area the rustling came from. The sense of being watched grew stronger the more I moved into the forest, but, at the moment, I didn't give a damn.

"Wait!!" I heard Talia come from behind. "Goddammit! Wait a minute, Wendy."

I twirled on her. "No. You all want to treat me like I'm the problem around here when the real problem is watching us." I looked down at her dagger as if in a peace offering. Without looking, I grabbed it from her hand and threw it at the tree on my right, never breaking eye contact.

"Fuck," a low groan permeated the woods.

Talia's eyes widened into saucers as she realized I was right. "What... How... How did you..." she stammered.

"I may have been gone for twenty-four years, but some things stay ingrained in you. Like knowing when to throw a knife at a threat and where that threat may be." I sighed. "Peter taught me many things about this island, except when we were kids, we fought off man-eaters, not the Fae. They were our friends at one point." I turned toward the man who was leaning against the tree still, blood pouring out of his chest. "Was there obsidian in your dagger?"

"Yes, it is the one thing Cap demands we have in all our weapons."

"Smart man. I'll have to commend him when we get back." I walked over to the Fae in question and looked up at him. He was quite tall, with horns that sprouted from his forehead and dark eyes that were both in pain and awe.

"Wendy-Bird. It has been a long time," he gritted out between clenched teeth.

"Asher. Why are you here?"

"I could ask you the same question. You have been absent from Neverland for so long we had begun to think you had forgotten about us."

I cocked my head. That wasn't the answer I was expecting. "What do you mean? I was banished. And Peter has not been back to see me. I don't know what you are talking about." I leaned towards him, grabbed hold of the hilt, and pulled. Blood spurting out onto me, coating me in a warmth that I forgot about but welcomed. I would need to contemplate that thought later, alongside another bath. Damn it. I couldn't afford to let my old demons out to play. Not yet, anyway.

"You have no idea. Has Michael not done his job keeping you informed of the goings-on here?" he asked, perplexed.

"Michael," I sneered, "had never come to see me. You act as if I should know things I do not. You are also forgetting I was banished from ever stepping foot back here. So why would I care?"

"You no longer care for Pan?" Asher rubbed his chest where the dagger was a few moments ago, the hole healing slowly, his hand coming away dripping in blood.

"I never said that."

"So, you don't care about Neverland?"

"I said I didn't care about the politics happening here. Neverland will always have a spot in my heart, but why stress about it when you can't do anything about it?" I stated.

A branch snapped behind me, and I remembered Talia was watching and listening to everything. "What do you mean Michael was supposed to keep her apprised of everything happening here? Who the hell is Michael?" she asked.

Glancing over my shoulder as if he was seeing her for the first time, Asher looked her up and down. "Michael is one of your men and abides by his own rules. Even Barrington knows better than to judge his decisions."

"But that means that Cap has no control over him and has free reign to do as he pleases."

Asher nodded, not adding anything else. I filed that information away for later when Michael and I were alone.

"What were you doing out here anyway, Asher?" I asked. "Besides playing peeping tom?"

"He was meeting me." Michael stepped out of the brush and came to stand beside me. "What are you two doing out here? I was worried sick that something happened to you."

"Oh, don't worry about the Wendy-Bird. She still has the knack for throwing daggers and asking questions later, as you so happened upon."

Michael looked over to Asher with all the blood upon his person. His eyes widened quickly in horror before he replaced the surprise with indifference. "Yeah, I forgot that she can be a badass when she wants to be." He smirked. "You must have snuck up on her and she decided to not chance being caught, I take it?" He chuckled, looking up to meet Asher's eyes. The tension was palpable, but I couldn't tell what it was from. The two looking at each other or the fact that Asher had been stabbed.

"I didn't think she would be able to sense me after all these years being gone. I was wrong." He again rubbed his chest. That obsidian must have done a number on him. I would have felt bad if he hadn't snuck up on us in the first place.

"He's lucky I recognized him. I would have shown Talia here how to finish him off if he wasn't someone I knew." I crossed my arms.

"As if I would have let you get that far."

I glared at the man. "Don't tempt me," I spat.

Talia approached me from behind, putting her hand on my shoulder. "Maybe we should go. You're going to need more clothes and another freshening up. And I am quite sure Asher would like to be on his merry way."

"Ah, yes. Take leave, dear Wendy-Bird. But next time we talk, I will ensure you are thoroughly informed of the news in Neverland. Seeing as your brother has kept you in the dark." He glanced over to Michael as his eyes hardened and his jaw clenched.

Michael had been keeping several secrets and it was time for them to be spilled.

Whether he wanted them to or not.

Chapter Twenty

JANE

The cab pulled into the hospital and I took a deep breath, paying the fare to the driver. Pasting on a smile I didn't feel and knew didn't reach my eyes, I passed the security guards and went straight to my floor.

I loved working here. The cancer unit was one of the most challenging places to work in the children's hospital, but it was always awe-inspiring to see the children, who had every right to be miserable, in high spirits. Hope and love were always at their fingertips, even as you watched the diseases they had ravage their tiny bodies.

Tick... Tock...

Gods, that blasted noise in my head. I rarely heard it outside the club, even less in the hospital. The fact that it was becoming a more frequent ring in my head concerned me. It was close to driving me insane.

Gretchen, this unit's head nurse, stood by the main desk. I gritted my teeth and ignored the ticking as I quietly walked past the rooms, which mostly had sleeping children.

Working the night shift was easy. The kids would sleep and occasionally one would call to get a drink or help to the bathroom. For the most part, one got to take in the quiet atmosphere and push away the knowledge that some of these kids may not make it through the next month, week, or day.

Parents were allowed here if we knew their times were drawing close, but for the most part, the parents left when visiting hours were done. To be given that much trust over your child gave me a sense of pride. Given the circumstances, I would do anything to keep my patients safe and as healthy as possible. Most of the parents knew I would call them personally and give them updates throughout the night if they wanted it.

"How is everyone tonight? Seems quiet," I whispered, reaching the desk.

The older lady scowled at her computer. "They're sleeping. Of course, they're quiet," she griped. "For now, anyways. Alis has had a terrible day. We found out her mother died last night, suicide. We aren't telling her that, though, just that it was a bad accident. We had to give her a sedative to make her sleep."

My head snapped up at the mention of Alis. The news of her mother had my stomach sinking to my feet. There was no way that woman took her own life. She lived and breathed for her daughter.

I took a deep breath to calm my slowly fraying nerves. It didn't make sense. "Do we know anything else about her death? I'm assuming the police informed Alis' uncle." My breath caught and butterflies erupted in my stomach at the thought that I would see the man who had turned my world upside down and inside out before the week was up. I wouldn't have to wait until Friday to see him again.

Gods, I was starting to sound like an addict in need of her next fix.

"No. It's confidential because there is a police investigation going on around her death, but it seems fishy to me. I stated as much to the investigator who came up here. As for the uncle, no one has heard from him," Gretchen answered.

My eyebrows rose as surprise hit me, quieting the flutters within. Usually, James was on top of everything for Alis. But then again, he traveled a lot and may not have been told yet or was on his way back.

Tick... Tock...

Ignoring the ticking, I asked, "Okay, how is Alis right now? Has anyone checked on her recently?"

"Her vitals here show she's sleeping, but if it will make you feel better, you can sit with her for a little bit. I'll page you if you're needed."

Nodding, I turned to make my way down to Alis' suite. It was like the woman knew I would need to check on her. Alis and I had a special bond—we always had. From the first time she was brought up here for her first chemo session to now that she is here full-time, we have gotten a lot closer.

I opened the door to her room as quietly as possible, peeking inside to see if she was truly asleep. She was good at remaining still as a statue to keep her vitals down. Her antics had scared me a few times before.

As I came in, the monitors' sounds were normal. I checked all her equipment and made sure she was comfortable. I stooped down to grab her favorite stuffed animal from the floor and placed it beside her as I sat down in the chair her mother usually took.

Tick... Tock...

Her icy touch stunned me as I picked up her hand. Then my brain caught up and I wrapped my warm hands around hers to keep them warm. Chemo will do that to you. Your body will be perpetually freezing all the time.

As I gazed at the little girl, memories flitted through my mind from when I first met her a little over a year ago. Her long, blonde hair and big, blue eyes lined with long lashes would make anyone jealous. I thought she was a little beauty. Now, her hair was all gone. No lashes or eyebrows, either. Her once olive skin was now pale and her body gaunt. Cancer really sucked dick, and the fact that she had to deal with it on top of her mother's death made tears well in my eyes.

Squeezing her hand, I laid a kiss on top. We shouldn't get attached to our patients. It crossed many moral codes, but this girl had my heart from the very beginning and she knew it. As I sat there, watching her sleep, I let my mind wander over the menagerie of events that had happened over the past few days.

Tick... Tock...

I have been told stories about Neverland ever since I was born. Of an island planted in the stars that had mermaids, faeries, natives, and man-eaters. You couldn't grow old on the island and were told of all the adventures you could do. As I grew older, the stories made little sense and I knew they were made up to keep a little girl occupied.

So, my mother being in Neverland was a far stretch. I didn't believe in the faerytales that my mother and uncle had woven for me as a child anymore.

But Mom missing had me worried. She wasn't one to just take off suddenly. She has always been as steady as a rock. I tried to file a missing person's report, but the police wouldn't even come to the house and see the disaster that was left behind. They didn't care.

"We'll make the report, but she's probably off on a bender. That happens more often than you think, miss. If she's gone for more than a week, come back. Then we can talk more."

Anger skirted through me as I recalled the policemen brushing off my complaint. Is this seriously what our world has come to?

Tick... Tock...

What if something actually happened to her? Like what happened to Alis' mom? Because I know for a fact that woman did not commit suicide. That woman would have given her life to save her daughter and my mother was the same.

Worry wormed through me once more. Not that it had ever really left, but seeing as I was concentrating on it, it came back with a vengeance. The need to find her clawed at my insides, demanding I take action when none could be taken.

Even if Mom was in Neverland, there was no way for me to get there. Hell. I wouldn't even know *how* to get there.

Pinpricks shot through my ass, numb from sitting and pondering my life. I stared at a child who was in no shape to help me in any situation, but her presence was a soothing balm that I needed. Checking her vitals once more, I left the room, quietly shutting the door behind me. She didn't need to be around me when I was too caught up in my own life and drama, and I didn't want her to feel the chaos of my mind, even if she was asleep.

As I made my way back to the nurses' station, the hair on the back of my neck stood up on end and goosebumps pricked my skin. The sensation of being watched had me scanning the empty hall behind me. There were cameras everywhere, and Gretchen would have said something about a late-night visitor if there had been one, but the feeling left me unsettled.

I shook off the feeling and leaned over the desk, picking up the pile of cases we had. I knew most of these by heart, but to make sure nothing changed in the past few days was still crucial to my job. Studying one of the other children's files, a clatter came from down the hall.

TICK! Tock...

My ears perked and my gaze shot toward the noise. There was nothing to be seen. Shaking off my uneasiness once more, I went back to studying the file. *There's nothing there, just things settling on the poles and shelves*, I told myself, even as a sliver of fear slid down my spine.

My concentration was shot as I kept one eye on the hall. Something was amiss. The ticking in my head was getting louder and harder to ignore.

As I carefully observed the hall where the noise came from, the soft tinkling of bells came to my ears. Tilting my head, I questioned if the sound was really there. A light sprang from the bookshelf across from Alis' room, quickly pushing the door open and closing it tight.

WHAT THE FUCK WAS THAT?! Did I really just see that?

The computer on the desk started ringing off alarms for Alis almost immediately.

TICK! TOCK!

I sprang to my feet and dashed down the hall, slamming into her door. The hospital doors don't lock, but this wasn't budging. No!!

TICK!! TOCK!!

Moving to the opposite wall, I gave myself a running start and shoved as hard as I could, smashing through the door. The scene before me was almost unreal.

Alis was floating... no, that's not right. Her blankets were cradled around her and she was being lifted in the air by a small light, a tinkling of bells coming from the small thing. There was no way it could hold her.

TICK!! TOCK!! TICK!! TOCK!!

The ticking in my head was banging like a gong now. Cradling my head in my hands, I closed my eyes to the scene before me and slid down the wall. This wasn't happening. That wasn't a faery. It couldn't be.

The scent of the ocean wafted towards me and the feel of a light breeze on my skin made me open my eyes. There, in the middle of the hospital room, was a hole, sparks flying out from the outside rim of it. In the center was what looked to be a beach, complete with palm trees.

Little Shadow...

The name whispered through my mind, paralyzing me. I hadn't heard that nickname since I was a child.

Come home...

A soft moan broke me from my trance. Alis was waking up.

I scrambled up the wall, tearing my gaze away from the hole and toward the little girl. The little light was struggling to fly with her in tow. No! There was no way I was letting her go through that. She would die and I wasn't going to let that happen.

Getting my feet beneath me, I tried to take a step toward the bundle that was James' niece. My feet suddenly felt like they were being held down by bricks. I couldn't seem to get them to move. Looking back to the hole in the room, a man stood there now, if that's what you would call him.

He had long, dark, tangled hair. Cheekbones were sharp enough to cut glass, tattoos and leaves covering most of his body, and horns curving out of his head. Fucking HORNS!

But the look of amusement in the man's eyes shot fear straight through me. Like he *knew* there was nothing I could do to stop him. Reaching through the hole, he grabbed the blanket from the little ball of light.

"NO!! She's sick, you can't take her!" I yelled across the room as if that would stop him.

Holding the girl in his arms, he glanced back up at me, smirking, then looked me up and down like he appreciated what he saw. The man's eyes were dark green, the color of moss in the forest, covered in dark lashes, and full of mirth. He winked before he turned away from me.

The tiny, little light tinkled like bells once more and flew right into the opening after the thing that was there, and the hole was gone with a snap that echoed throughout the room and made my ears ring.

Tick... Tock...

Chapter Twenty-One

TINKERBELLE

The throne was carved out of glass. The back was tall with holes on either side between the arms and back to slide my wings into when I had them on display. The arms and legs were carved into claws that looked like a crocodile's, a token to the beast that once roamed the island, keeping us Fae in check that no longer existed thanks to yours truly. The seat and back had a deep purple, velvet cushion that was comfortable for the most part, but after a while, it still got stiff and the need to move was insistent.

Irritated, I continued listening to the incessant complaint of the Water Fae in front of me about the need for more Lost Boys. I knew the Lost Boys were dying faster than usual, but it wasn't my fault the Fae were getting too violent with their desires and killing their toys.

As I leaned back against the blown glass, I closed my eyes. Rage slowly built inside me, creating a low-burning inferno.

I was tired.

I was tired of listening to the same thing every damned day from everyone. I could only get so many children at a time. You can't just kill people like you used to. There were too many questions and too many ways to get caught.

The puny man's nasal whine grated on my last nerve like nails on a chalkboard, and slowly, my vision turned red. "Enough!!" I yelled at the man, fear crossing his face. His eyes widened as he shut up immediately.

Good Gods, when did we Fae become so weak? To be needy creatures that were happy only when their basest desires were satisfied. We never used to need sex. Hell, we didn't even know what it was until *she* came about.

I shook my head, not wanting to think of the woman who ruined everything and brought myself back to the present situation. "I have heard you. You will get another child when I get one, but you will be put on the wait list with the rest of the people waiting on new toys."

Nodding, the man bowed. "Thank you, Your Highness. " His voice shook and that slight nasal whine still made me cringe.

With a wave of my hand, I dismissed the man and stood from my throne, a cue to my guard that I was done seeing complaints for the time being. Reaching my arms overhead, I felt the stretch move down my body as I crossed behind my chair to the window overlooking the grounds.

The gardens were starting to wither, the leaves dreary and needing something. It couldn't be water or sun. There was plenty of it here. It was magic. Neverland ran on magic and it had been slowly running out since that Wendy girl took Pan from us. Everything changed when that insipid girl arrived.

Flying through London was one of Peter's pastimes. Why? I would never know. Maybe it was because of the air, or the buildings and scenery.

Once in a great while, Peter would find a lost child and bring them back to Neverland with us. They would become one of the Lost Boys until they grew up and had to be brought back. What happened to the children after that? I didn't know and didn't care. They were too old to be in Neverland, so there was no place for them there. As long as Peter stayed with me, that was all that mattered.

As I flew through the air, the wind fluttering against my wings. It didn't smell as fresh as it used to when we first came here. Watching the city change and flourish in ways I wasn't happy with was dismaying. The smog was almost chokingly thick, but alas, I tried my damnedest to keep up with the child flying freely ahead of me.

I spied an open window as I was searching for a place to rest for a minute. When I landed on the sill, the voices of children rang out into the stale air.

"ARRR—Take that, you vermin!"

"I will get you, you pillaged rat!"

I peered into the room and saw two boys with play swords bouncing from bed to bed, sounding like they were playing pirates. As I watched the two play out their game, I knew of the fun the two could have in Neverland with Peter. He could always use some new Lost Boys.

Having caught my breath, I flew off the sill to catch up with Peter. Pulling on his clothes with all my might, I finally grabbed his attention and brought him round to the sill I had found.

Now, there was a girl in the room and the boys were sitting on the bed as she told a story. Listening closely, the girl told stories of Neverland.

Looking at Peter, he was as enraptured by the story as the two boys in the room, leaving me filled with happiness that I had found them. However, there was a small twinge of trepidation inside that I couldn't quite place.

I should have listened to it.

I never should have pointed out the Darling household to Pan. That was the beginning of the end of Neverland as I looked back on it. The Wendy girl cast a spell on him. That's the only explanation.

Magic.

A growl erupted from my chest as guilt and regret filled my being. Before everything started falling apart, I was happy. Before the Darlings, we were whole.

At first, we Fae had no idea what the feeling inside was. It was visceral, carnal, and insistent. The more we ignored the feeling, the worse it became. The need to touch something, someone, anything became an itch none of us could ignore. An emptiness that had roared to life and refused to be filled.

In the beginning, we were able to suppress the fire inside by touching ourselves and each other, bringing each other pleasure that we had never known existed before. But after a few years, we realized it wasn't enough. We needed *more*. I don't even remember how we figured out that human flesh was the best way to quench our desires.

The door to the throne room banged open as if whoever dared to enter had no qualms about my wrath. Only one man would do so. Grifford.

The half-Fae man was useful in accomplishing my dirty deeds. He loved violence beyond measure and, for some odd reason, never feared me. It was both refreshing and annoying.

Turning away from the window and the reminder that Neverland was dying, I returned to my throne, both annoyed that he decided to interrupt my depressing solitude and curious about what made him barge in here like he owned the place.

"Your Majesty, we found him."

My eyebrow cocked as ire ricocheted around my middle. There were quite a few things I was searching for, so what he said didn't clarify anything, but raised my annoyance levels a couple of points.

"The escaped lost boy. We found him." Grifford clarified as two more guards brought in a very broken man. Blood dripped, no—smeared across the floor from where they dragged him. He wasn't going to be of much use to us in the condition he was in. Even if I healed him, there was still the matter of him killing his owner.

Balmont was a great friend and I missed him very much. That and his cock was a wonderful thing to behold. Grief struck through my heart at the reminder that he was no longer with us and bitter anger quickly took its place.

"What would I want to do with the brat that wasn't grateful for what he had? I should have him put down like the mutt he is. He wasn't wanted in London, and he grew up not to be wanted here. Trash. That's what he is. Should have left him to rot and let the island take care of him," I spat. "Because what I am going to do now, is so much worse." A smile crept over my face as I thought of all the fun things I could do to prolong his torment. So he felt everything I did over losing one of my best friends.

"You don't want to know where we found him?" Grifford's voice rang of disappointment. "No, but since you seem to think I need to know, please tell."

"Skull Rock. Captain Barrington had him. The boy mumbled something about shadows and Darlings before passing out."

Red-hot rage boiled in my center at what the man was implicating. "Take him to the dungeons." With a wave of my hand, I dismissed the guardsmen and slowly exited the throne room. The need to be left alone was the only thing on my mind. I didn't want to think, but that was all I left to do anymore.

As I strode through the halls, some of the light that filtered through the glass windows dimmed. Almost as if the island knew what happened in these rooms and halls. It shed less light on the dark parts of the palace, shadowing it and not wanting to spread its light on the darker areas that have become a part of Neverland.

Neverland used to be so bright, happy, and carefree. Now, the island's shadows have come out to play with a chokehold on its inhabitants and they have no plan of letting them go.

I never thought I would be the supreme ruler over Neverland. That was Pan's job, but he had failed us and led us all here. I had to do something before all of Neverland fell into complete ruins and I don't regret any of it. Except maybe not getting my chance to kill the Wendy girl.

Hot and heavy, his betrayal sank into my heart from the memory of him choosing those brats over his home. He was never supposed to grow up and never supposed to know "love." He will never know of all the sacrifices I made to ensure Neverland's survival. He was as good as dead at this point.

Making a sharp turn, I made my way onto the stone steps that led down into the center of the mountain, away from the castle. Few Fae came here anymore after Pan left them. They didn't want to believe in anything anymore, more concerned with their more earthly, carnal desires than what we were created for.

I haven't lost my sense of faith. Not quite yet. Neverland is still alive, barely surviving, but breathing. She just needs her Shadow, her other half. And it is now my mission to find the fucking thing Pan lost.

Irritation flitted through me at the thought. Fucking Pan. How do you lose your fucking Shadow?

Pain radiated through my jaw. I was clenching my teeth so hard, waking me from my stupor. Loosening my fists and taking a calming breath, I filled my being with a little bit of peace that I truly hadn't felt in what felt like eons. What I would give to feel peace again.

Entering the middle of the mountain felt like coming home. The air was cool and damp from the huge ball of floating water in the middle of the room. The magical currents in the room were soft but strong, keeping the water in place. The magic here was so pure you could taste it, like a shower of fresh rain pressing against your senses.

Slowly, I glided across the uneven grounds to the ball of water and power and pushed my hand into it. Searching for what? I wasn't sure. Once, this held all the light and magic needed for Neverland to survive. Now, it was more of a ball of energy with no real purpose.

Sighing, I brought my hand back, not wet as one would expect, and sat on the stone slab directly below it in my favorite meditation pose. After spending so many years here learning how to listen to the island and what it needed, my meditation immediately came to me.

I had connected with Neverland at its source so long ago that I could now use its magic and bring myself power. It was now like second nature to me to just plug myself in and be one with the island. To feel what it feels and see what it sees. To hear what it hea—

Wendy...

The voice of the island, long forgotten to me, shook me to my core. Even worse was that it was saying that bitch of a woman's name.

Instant rage filled my veins and flowed through my being, my magic warring within, creating an inferno of red-hot anger and disgust. And underneath it all, betrayal. Someone had brought her here.

The earlier conversation with my guards about the whereabouts of my missing Lost Boy swirled viciously through my head.

Barrington. That bastard.

My thoughts kept spiraling, moving too fast for me to slow them down. A tornado of everything around me falling into an abyss of nothing brought tears to my eyes.

The reminder that everything was so close to falling apart. From the Fae here not keeping their children alive to the Dust in London—it was all crumbling. Everything I had worked so hard to build was deteriorating at a faster pace than I could ever imagine.

No. I wouldn't let that happen.

Opening my mouth for a breath, a scream escaped my being into the void, unleashing all my pent-up rage into the room to mix and intertwine with the magic of Neverland itself.

Watching the two magics slowly combine, a plan took root. A barely there seed, but just enough life to give me hope.

Getting to my feet, I adjusted my dress and put it back into position. I needed to get to London and start making preparations.

War was coming.

Chapter Twenty-Two

MICHAEL

My living area was reminiscent of the tree house we played in as kids. Dead Man's Tree. I tried to copy the same furniture and the fur rug from memory, so it wasn't exact, but it was close enough. The wood floors were light in color, which contrasted with the dark walls. The fireplace on the far side had wood stacked, ready to burn at any time, but it was more for decoration than actual use. The island was always hot and the coolness of the night was a welcoming reprieve. It was cozy and felt like home.

Wendy was banging around in the kitchen, fuming, pissed at Gods knows what. *I should be the one pissed off.*

She stabbed Asher!

Frustration and anger coiled inside me, but I couldn't blame anyone for what happened. Wendy was acting off instinct. I was quite proud her intuition was still on point for being gone for so long.

Asher was pissed off with me for not telling him that she was back. The hurt in his eyes was something that I don't think I'll ever forget. The image was burned into my retinas for the rest of my life. I was already plotting a way to see him again, and now I had to add groveling, too. A groan escaped me as I rubbed my hands over my face. Regret and grief punched a hole through my chest. This was a fucking mess.

The thunderous bang of a pot hitting the counter echoed through the house, reverberating through my skull and making my head throb. "Fucking hell."

Forcing myself off the couch, I searched for the menace, seemingly trying to destroy my kitchen in her fit of anger. "You know, throwing shit isn't getting anything done besides creating headaches, right?" I asked from the threshold.

If Wendy's glare could have killed a man, I wouldn't be standing. Her face was flushed and her hands were shaking. She wasn't just mad. She was furious.

"Did you know keeping your mouth shut and leaving me the fuck alone is better for your health?" she snapped, her hair auburn locks bounced around her face. She still had on the clothes that were smattered in Asher's blood, making my skin itch with the need to tear them off her. *I* was the only one allowed to draw his blood, and the blatant reminder that she wore it with pride irritated the living fuck out of me.

It was almost comical watching her bluster around the kitchen. But I knew her anger could be violent. We've done this dance before. We both grew up on an island where violence is the answer to everything. I could see her need to let out her fury, but my kitchen was not the place for it.

"I think you should sit down and have a drink. The last few days have been exhausting for everybody and we need to talk," I stated as I took the knife out of her hands that was violently trying to open a coconut.

"No fucking shit. You just left me here with pirates!! The same pirates we used to kill for fun!"

Shaking my head, I grabbed her wrist and pulled her to the cabinet that held the whiskey. "Make us something to drink. Captain should be here soon. We can all talk when he gets here. In the meantime, chill the fuck out," I gritted out.

She wrenched her arm from my grasp, her eyes fixed on mine. "Fine. How about you tell me what the hell is going on between you and Asher? I'm not stupid. Spill it. Because I really don't think your darling Captain would like to know that you are fucking one of the Fae."

"Who is doing what?!" a deep voice rumbled from the living area and my stomach plummeted through the floor.

Fucking hell, my life couldn't be easy for just one day. Having Wendy here was going to create more chaos than this was going to be worth.

"Nothing." I clenched my teeth, shooting a glare at Wendy. "You will pay for this, dear sister," I whispered into her ear. The threatening tone wasn't to be missed. She would learn her place here. She may have been Pan's favorite, but with him being dead, she was nothing but a spoiled brat and now had a target on her head.

"It didn't sound like nothing. Now answer the question. Who is fucking the Godsdamned Fae?" James' face was getting mottled with anger.

"No one," I grunted, "My sister here is jumping to conclusions." There was no way I would admit to Cap that I was in a relationship with Asher. It was one of the unspoken rules of Pirates' Cove. Don't fuck the Fae.

"Pfft. Anyone with eyeballs can see something is going on between you two. And I haven't been here in years." Wendy scoffed as my ire rose. I clenched my jaw shut before I said something I would regret.

Cap just stood back on the threshold and watched the two of us argue like we were his personal entertainment, pushing my annoyance levels higher.

"You don't know what you're talking about," I spat out before walking away from her.

The good news was my kitchen wasn't a complete wreck. I could still work around the mess Wendy had created to be able to make something for us to eat. Gathering supplies, I ignored the tension that was growing in the room. I didn't want to deal with it and cooking was an excellent way to keep my mind off things while I figured out how to get Wendy home, beg for Asher's forgiveness, and tell Cap about the goings on at the palace. Wendy was going to be a pain in the ass about going home, though. When I stumbled upon her and Asher in the woods, the look in her eye told me she was staying. I don't know what he told her, but she wasn't happy.

She wasn't supposed ever to come back here. None of us were. Pan had only brought me back because I had begged him to. I was only supposed to be here for a few days. Days that turned into years of nightmares.

The island wasn't a horrible place to play when we were kids. Yes, there was violence, but what we did was nothing compared to the atrocities that have happened since. This place has become its own hellscape of the paradise it used to be, even with the man-eaters.

A glass clinking against the counter brought me out of my musings. Wendy's eyes, the same color as the whiskey she had poured, were lined with small wrinkles that showed her age and worry.

Cap had made himself comfortable at the table in the middle of the room, his boot-clad feet resting on the nearby chair, his head tipped back, and his eyes closed. I knew better than to know he was resting. The man knew everything that was going on in this room. He was just comfortable with me and wasn't too worried about Wendy.

He should be. The woman was a menace to society and had a *throw now and ask questions later* attitude before. It had gotten worse with age.

"I think we need to talk," Wendy stated flatly, her earlier anger gone. Whiskey does wonders for the Darlings.

Cap scoffed from across the room. "Truer words have never been said." He raised his glass to his lips and looked the two of us over. "You know, I have a feeling you two have a lot to hash out, but I also need to know what happened before I got here. So, why don't we start at the beginning?"

My jaw clenched as I wondered how we could start our story. It was going to confuse the fuck out of anyone we told. Each of us had a different experience here than the other. But we all loved it. Hell, we flourished here. Our true selves could come out to play, while at home, we had to put on a facade and play the part of well-kempt children when we were feral at our core.

Wendy shuffled toward the table, sitting across from Cap, a heavy sigh billowing from her lips. "To start at the beginning would take too long. Let's say we made enemies here in our teens and the only person able to set things right is missing."

"He's dead, not missing. I don't know why you refuse to believe it," I interjected. Her blind faith that Pan was alive was going to get us killed.

"He can't be dead. The island would cease to exist without him and his magic," she retorted matter-of-factly. She wasn't wrong. That was what Pan told us, but the fact that he has been gone for so long and no one has seen nor heard from the man in over twenty-some years, would lead one to believe she was wrong.

Cap's raised his eyebrow in question. "Who are you two talking about?"

"Peter Pan, of course," Wendy stated while sipping her glass.

"Peter Pan? The legend? Wendy, did you hit your head?"

"Actually, yes. On your ship. But that's the least of the offenses that happened to me on that ship," she spat, fury marring her features.

What the hell happened while I was gone?

"Whoa, ho, ho. Back up." Grabbing my glass, I came around the island and sat between the two at the table. "Explain." I pointed between the two of them.

After Wendy ranted to me about her treatment on board the ship, my glare toward James was getting colder as the grip on my glass got tighter. "Grim did what?" I gritted out between my teeth.

"He—"

"I heard you the first time, Wendy! I want to know why he thought he could do so in the first place when I had already told the man to back the fuck off."

Cap's eyebrows rose again as if it were all news to him. "I had no idea of any of that."

Wendy scoffed, her arms crossed her chest as she glared at the captain. "I bet you didn't. What was it you said? Oh yeah. 'Grim would love to get his hands on you.'"

"I didn't mean it in that way, you bitch! He had already tried to kill you. Why would I think he'd want to fuck you?" Cap snarled across the table, the two spitting venom at each other.

"The fuck you didn't—"

"ALRIGHT! ENOUGH!" Slamming my hands on the table, I stood up. "Grim will have his hands on a platter the next time I see him. End of discussion. You two," I pointed at the both of them again, "need to start getting along. Now." Sitting back down, I grabbed my glass of whiskey and shot the rest back. "Do you want to know what happened at the palace while I was there?"

Cap's eyes snapped to mine, anger rippled off of him at being ordered about, but I didn't give a fuck. He couldn't control his crew, so now I would handle the problem. He knows he has no control over me. I just let him think he did. I could kill him before he even thought about it.

He waved his hand through the air. "Please, enlighten me. You apparently don't care if your sister hears," he ground out, his jaw clenched in hidden fury. Good, let him simmer.

"The more she knows, the better for her health. I would prefer for her to return to London, but I have a feeling she would find a way back here until she could find Pan."

"Damn fucking straight. You all don't give two flying fucks about him," she gritted out.

"The only reason you care is because you two used to fuck," I deadpanned.

"It was more than that, and you know it," she seethed, her teeth bared.

She's right. I know it was more than that, but the longer she was here, the more likely Tink would find her and exact her revenge. Whatever that may be. The woman went mad a long time ago.

"Anyway," I got up and went to the bar, grabbing the bottle of whiskey, "the usual orgy was well in hand when I got there—"

Wendy's chair screeched across the floor. "ORGY! What the *hell* has happened since I've been gone?!" she exclaimed as she started pacing the floor, her hands raking through her already disheveled hair.

"A lot. If you would sit down and shut the fuck up for ten minutes so that I can finish my report, I can fill you in on Tink's bullshit," I spat, reclaiming my seat. Gods, the woman was infuriating.

"If you told me this when you stopped by, I wouldn't be so angry!"

"I kept this shit from you to keep you safe!"

Wendy stalked back toward the table, leaning into my face. "See how far that got! I am still here and you're still full of bullshit!" Her face was flushed with anger.

My chair flew back, hitting the hardwood. As I rose to my feet, fury coursed hot through my veins. My fists firmly planted on the table as I leaned back into Wendy's face. Fuck her. "Everything I have ever done here was to survive. Everything I may or may not have told you was to keep you safe! So, you can scream obscenities at me all you want, but the truth is, none of this would have happened if you and Peter had kept your hands to yourselves!"

The little gasp that left Wendy's mouth was all I heard as I left the room, going outside to recollect my thoughts. Gods, why couldn't she just shut the fuck up and listen?

The night air was balmy, clinging to my already fevered skin like a blanket, suffocating me. Rubbing my hand over my face, I walked down to the beach, one of the places on this island that still gave me a sliver of peace.

The sand was still hot and the triple moons shone brightly against the waves. The sound of gulls settling in for the night and the crickets chiming through the nearby woods washed a sense of calm through me as I replayed our conversation.

The need to hurt something surged beneath my skin. The rage I tried like hell to keep contained, fought to break free from the constraints on my mind. Soon... soon I would let him out to play.

"She's settled in the kitchen, taking her anger out on some unlucky vegetables you had in your pantry. Remind me never to get on her bad side. She can handle a knife."

I scoffed at James' statement. "Should see her use a bow. She has a wicked aim, too."

"Duly noted. So, I can see you all seem to have your issues that need to be sorted out, but would you finish your report from the palace? Then, I can tell you what happened when Asher and I met up." His voice strained with leashed anger.

Something was wrong, but he wouldn't tell me until I had finished with what I had to say. I might get lucky enough to know what the fuck has been going on since I left.

Clearing my throat, I went through everything that happened at the palace, including seeing the kids. Kids that shouldn't ever be in a setting like that. Bile rose in my throat at the thought of what other things those kids are going through.

"Teenagers? Where the fuck did they come from?"

"I don't know, but I feel the Fae are playing a bigger game than we know."

Cap stared off into the distance, deep in thought. "That makes me wonder what happened to our prisoner. Asher and I arrived at his cell. Striker and Savage were dead, and the man was missing. When I was interrogating him, he called himself a lost boy. Whatever that means."

My head snapped up. "Lost Boy?"

Cap's head nodded. "Yeah, you heard of them?"

"The Lost Boys were a gang of kids that Pan brought to Neverland to play until they became too old. It's impossible that there are any here."

"Are you sure this Pan didn't bring more kids here?"

"He's dead. They're all dead. I know. I watched them die."

Chapter Twenty-Three

JAMES

A low, burning rage flowed through me as I pondered all the happenings that have come to light in the past week here in Neverland. As I sat in my cabin, the whiskey burned my throat as I took a big swig to calm my slowly fraying nerves.

Watching Smee with his sister had a burning hole of sorrow burrowing into my chest. One that I would love to wrench out and get rid of forever. I, too, had a brother who could press my buttons. I never would have thought that I would miss the fucker, but after seeing the two together, it had an ache forming between my brows. Maybe if the asshole were still alive, I wouldn't be in the predicament I was in.

I poured myself another glass as I grumbled under my breath. Alis was brought to me by a woman claiming that she was my brother's lover and had a child. The child had become sick and she needed help. Why she hadn't thought to come to me sooner was a mystery that I would never understand.

"Please... Help her..." the woman in my office pleaded with me as I took in her appearance. She had long, dark hair and curves for days. Her dark eyes were wide. Afraid for her or her child? I couldn't tell.

"And how do I know she is my brother's? He made no mention of a child before he disappeared," I said, both angered at the audacity of this woman and perplexed that she would keep the child a secret for so long.

The woman's face flamed beet red. "You could take a DNA test. It would prove she is your niece." Her answer was rushed as she tried to maintain her composure. What did my brother see in this woman to have had a child with her?

Nodding, I mulled over the idea. I could do that. But what do I get out of this? Another burden? Shaking my head at myself, I beat myself mentally for the thought. If she was my brother's, then she is the only thing left of h im.

"Is she with you?" I asked, resigned to my fate.

Nodding quickly, she left my office and returned shortly with a blonde, curly-haired waif of a girl wearing a blue sundress and black dress shoes. The shock rattled me to my core.

The girl could have been my brother's twin.

As the girl drew closer, her shoulders hunched and eyes filled with tears, I could see the dark circles under her large, dark-blue eyes, lined with equally long dark lashes in stark contrast to how pale her skin was.

Sick. The woman wasn't wrong. The girl needed help.

Standing up, I came around my desk, kneeling before the girl, taking in her features. She had freckles sprinkled across her nose that have faded with time. Her lips were pursed as if in thought as she gazed at me, both wonder and curiosity playing behind her eyes. I could see her adventurous spirit wanting to play in that gaze, like my brother's, but her body kept her from living her life.

With my mind made up, I stood, making eye contact with my brother's lover. "No. No testing is needed." I made my way back around the desk, praying I wasn't making a mistake by taking in this child.

The fading memory gave me pause. Alis was brought to me before Tink recruited me, her treatment not working as well as we all had hoped, her body slowly fading into the wraith she was the last time I saw her.

Was bringing her really going to be best for her? Her body was so fragile the last I saw of her, over three weeks ago. My time at the hospital with her was getting sporadic, but it wasn't my fault. Not really.

Drake and Tink's demands were becoming more of a pain in the ass than anything, taking up a lot of my free time. The crew was becoming more and more inebriated in their addictions, most not having half a brain cell to fly the ship anymore, and recruiting new members was out of the question. The Fae brought me my team. The one time I tried to make my own crew... Well, I have scars reminding me who I work for.

Tiger Lily was my primary mode of moving between the realms to visit Alis. But the woman had become scarce in the past few months, and finding her had become near impossible.

Sighing, I downed the rest of my whiskey and got to my feet, anxious about the deal I made with Neverland to heal her. Waiting on a message from Asher that she was safe at The Sanctuary and that I could visit her felt like ten thousand paper cuts were flayed across my skin and rubbed in salt.

I hated it. I hated depending on other people. I hated that the only way that I could save Alis was to bring her to the one place that was just as likely to kill her.

Leaving the ship, I brought the dinghy to shore as we had only started to rebuild the dock. Fucking Wendy. Fucking Neverland. Something was stirring on the island, leaving a hard rock in my stomach.

"There were kids there, James. Barely teenagers, watching the Fae fuck each other in blood." Smee's words rang clearly through my head as I made land. The rock in my stomach sank further and bile rose in my throat as I clenched my jaw to not vomit at the thought, the need to hurt something rising in me. The beast rattled in its cage.

I would have never thought kids would be here. I knew Asher had Fae children in his house, but now I wondered whether they were indeed Fae, human, or both.

The only way to get the answer was to ask, but I don't think I was going to like the answer I received. Which would I rather do? Remain ignorant of what Asher was up to or have the knowledge of all of what Tinkerbelle's misdeeds were. I had a feeling she was hiding a lot more than she let on. Only everyone has a snippet of information and everyone else is tortured into silence.

A shiver coasted down my spine as my body remembered the last time I was left at her mercy. Never again would I incur the wrath of Tink. It wasn't worth it. It took me months to recover, and only with the help of Asher and Smee did I even survive it.

I slowly made my way down to the dock that held the dinghy for Crocodile Creek. Going back to see the room where my men were slaughtered wasn't really on my to-do list, but I needed to clean it and try and figure out what happened and why. Hell, I would love to know how the Fae found out about my torture chamber. I hadn't had to bring any there before, and the only people who knew were my trusted few and the dead. My trusted few quickly dwindled into none.

The revelation that Smee was related to the Wendy woman that we were all told to kill on sight was a betrayal I never saw coming. But the more I got to know Wendy, in the few encounters I had with her, the more I realized she might be the way to save Neverland. The island itself sighed with relief when she made land, like it was almost happy that she was here. It made me wonder what the hell Tink had against her. The fact that she didn't want to talk about it gave me pause. What could have been so bad that you didn't want to talk about your own stories of Neverland?

Skull Rock shone in the moonlight, the eyes even darker now than in the sun. The shadows moving across the limestone added to the eeriness that was my playground. Tying the boat to the dock, I quickly made my way to the entrance, my knee twinging in pain at the quick movement, lighting the lanterns as I went.

I couldn't stand the fact that I had to bury two of my friends and not tell the rest of the crew about their demise. If I had a mole in my crew, I needed to find out who—and fast. But that was going to be a tedious process of trying to figure out which lowly addict was desperate enough to be bought by the Fae.

The room was still saturated in their blood. The smell of death and rot permeated the air, forcing a gag from my throat. I grabbed the bucket that was still sitting there from my session with Chip and made my way to the bottom of the cavern to fill it.

The sound of the water lapping at the edge of the rock was soothing, something I hadn't let myself feel for a long time. Only Jane was able to soothe my soul of hurts. Her thinking she was going to be able to leave left an empty hole in my chest. The need to keep her close was becoming an itch under my skin that couldn't be scratched unless I brought her here so she couldn't escape me. The need to bend her to my will and see the error of her ways. To see her become what she truly was. Mine.

Gods, this woman was beautiful. I could only be grateful that I found her when I did a little over a year ago. I could only imagine what those dim-witted fuckers would have done to her if they had gotten the two girls alone that night.

Anger still riddled me at the thought. Until I could exact my revenge on them, it would always be there. A deep-seated hatred that would continue to burn until I was able to extinguish it with blood. A slow, malicious smile formed over my face. I couldn't wait until the day that they learned their lesson.

As I trailed my hand over Jane's throat, pride filled me at the collar of bruises marring her skin, marking her as mine. I don't know what had gotten into that pretty little head of hers to think that she could leave me, but that would be eradicated quickly. Our earlier conversation still rang hot in my mind, creating a flood of fury and desperation to keep her. And I hated to feel desperate.

Silently, I strode over to the small desk in the corner of the room. The sound of the drawer opening shot through the room. A small shiver of fear that she would be woken by it and ruin my plans had me turning to study Jane's form.

Her breathing was still slow and soft. She'd probably be out for another hour.

Pulling out the long, velvet-wrapped box, I switched on the small lamp and opened the case to look at the necklace that was inside. A small pulse of magic flitted through my fingers as I lifted it out of its home. The thin, leather band was going to look perfect wrapped around her pretty little neck. The green of the emerald faery pendant matched her eyes, adding the perfect touch. The matching ring was hidden underneath the necklace. It was the key. The only way to get the collar off was going to be to take my finger, because the fucker wasn't leaving my hand.

A small smile crept over my lips at the look of contentment on Jane's face. The thought of collaring her had my cock thickening. The need to take her again had my heart pounding against my ribcage.

Slipping the thin strap around her neck with her disgruntled groans as I moved her head slightly, a small chuckle left my lips. Those groans were going to be more apparent when she woke up. Too bad I wasn't going to be here to hear them.

Taking the ring, I locked the small mechanism in the back in place, letting the pendant settle at the hollow of her throat. My raging hard staff begged for relief as I stared down at my girl. Mine.

The bed dipped underneath my weight as I settled myself behind her, my one hand wrapping lightly around her throat as the other gripped my cock, lining it up with her entrance that was still soaked from our earlier tryst.

A low moan vibrated from my chest as I watched her pussy swallow my length. Fuucckkk... I could look at this sight every day and not get tired of it.

Seated deep inside her, I pulled out slowly, searching her face for any reaction to what I was doing. Her eyes fluttered lightly and I stopped, watching her chest as her breathing returned to normal. I was going to have to be careful about this.

Ever so slowly, I pressed back inside her. Her walls clenched around me and I gritted my teeth to keep from waking her. I needed to say the enchantment for the collar to work, but Gods, I just wanted to fuck her. To see her eyes roll back as I took her again and again, reminding her of who she belonged to.

As I got into a torturously slow rhythm, I wrapped my hand around her hip, snaking my fingers through her slick folds to circle her clit. I didn't need her to come with me for this to work, but godsdammit, I was going to do it anyway. Hell, I didn't need to fuck her at all, but just the thought of claiming her as mine in all ways set my blood on fire that I wasn't going to ignore the need to do so.

Working her body as she lay asleep had my cock twitching inside her so that I could turn her on so easily. Even in sleep, she couldn't resist me. Her eyes started fluttering as her breathing picked up. "James…" she sighed, still half-asleep as her pussy started fluttering against my cock, pulling me in deeper. A groan escaped me as I pressed my face into her neck. She was almost there.

Whispering against the lock, I started the enchantment that was ingrained in me by Drake when he told me about the collar.

"In realms where shadows dance and dreams unfold,

through ancient magic and secrets old,

this pendant stakes Neverland's claim,

it's magic shielding through night and day."

A small flash of light emanated from the pendant as I worked Jane's body to orgasm, her walls clenching down on my cock. White heat traveled down my spine as I came inside her once more.

She wasn't escaping me now.

A slow smile crept on my face as the memory replayed in my head, my cock growing hard as a plan slowly formed. Bending down, I started scrubbing the blood off the floors.

Jane will be my queen. She doesn't have a choice.

Chapter Twenty-Four

WENDY

The string on the bow was pulled taut, the tension singing down my arm and shoulder as I held the arrow steady, my target in sight.

The brightly colored bird would have once been camouflaged by the towering flowers and trees that made its home. Now, it stood out like a sore thumb among the dulled and wilting blooms. Neverland was slowly losing its magic. The island dying became more and more apparent the longer I was here.

We needed to find Peter and bring the magic back.

Letting the arrow loose, a rustling in the brush had the bird taking off, a bustle of feathers falling behind as my arrow just missed the fucker.

"Should have let it go two seconds ago and I wouldn't have scared it off."

"Or you could have waited two seconds and I wouldn't have missed," I sniped as Michael entered my view.

It had been a few days since everything blew up in his kitchen with Captain Barrington as an audience. The tension that had settled between us had been thick and wrought with glares and loathing. I couldn't fault him for thinking I was the reason Peter wanted to leave, but it wasn't my fault that Neverland was falling apart. I didn't know why it was dying, but we needed to find out before we all ended up as its victims.

Michael rubbed his hand over his scarred face, a sigh falling from his lips. "Do you always have to be a brat about everything? It gets tiring."

"Do you always have to be a pain in the ass? I am not a stranger to this island. I know the dangers, probably better than most of those men you have in town who think they're badasses, but really, they're just wannabe pirates with addictions."

Since arriving, I had been to the bar in town a few times to hang out with Talia. The place was littered with men and women who seemed to have zero aspirations in life except to be high and drunk all the time. It was disheartening.

What had happened in the time I had been gone? The place went to hell in a handbasket with no sure way out.

Michael had moved into the clearing. Picking one of his daggers off his person, he nonchalantly flipped it through the air. The amount of practice it had to have taken for him to master that left me in awe. I wish.

"You're not wrong. Most of the pirates in the cove are addicts. But what you don't know is that they didn't start out that way. Most came here after making deals with Fae, their payment being to work on the island. What they didn't know was that there was no way out. So, they live every day high as fuck to forget that they chose to be here and that they will die for their choice as well."

Surprise flitted through me. So, the Fae are making bargains now. The thought was unsettling, leaving a knot of apprehension in my stomach. It wasn't right.

"We used to run the island, prank the pirates, and kill the man-eaters. What the fuck happened?"

Michael stared off into the brush and his eyes glazed over as if he were a million miles away from here. He saw what had happened here over the years and knew what was happening. I needed to know what he knew.

"Michael. Please tell me what happened."

Violently shaking his head, he turned to me as anger darkened his features, chasing away the melancholy in his eyes. "There's nothing to tell. Everyone we knew died and the Fae took over, turning Neverland into this prison." The dagger flew from his fingers hitting a tree, the bark splitting as purple sap oozed from the wound.

"There's more to it than that. Why won't you tell me? I need to know. I need to know everything if there's any hope of finding Peter!" I practically shouted. He was purposely hiding everything. I didn't know whether it was for his sanity or mine, but he wasn't helping by keeping quiet about it.

The muscle in his jaw ticked, his teeth bared and his breathing uneven, his eyes dark, and his pupils shot wide. His features morphed into a man that was no longer my brother. I now understood why people in the Cove feared him. His once playful air was sucked away by this beast of a man that they called Smee. This was the man he had turned into to survive this hellhole. This was the man who reveled in violence and he had set his sights on me.

"Smee, you must kill the wolf, or he will eat you whole..." Pan yelled into my little brother's face, holding down the offending animal. It was already half dead from a fight with a man-eater and most likely wouldn't harm us, but Peter gave no chances to be proven wrong.

"If you want to be initiated into the Lost Boys, you must kill it," Peter stated more calmly this time. My little brother's tears trailed down his face. He didn't want to kill it. I could see it in his face. But if he didn't, Peter wouldn't bring him back, banishing him from Neverland forever.

The slash of the knife came down swiftly, blood spurting from the wound as the wolf howled in pain. Again and again, the knife came down, and slowly, a smile formed on my brother's face. No longer Michael, but Smee, the boy that killed for Pan.

The memory flashed through my mind as an inkling of fear flitted through my body and settled at the nape of my neck. My body tensed for a fight as Smee approached me, crowding my space. We were chest to chest, my will against his, and I refused to back down. I refused to accept that my brother, in any capacity, would harm me.

"They all died, Wendy," he snarled in my face, his voice low. "I watched them burn! No one, and I mean no one, survived the fire, including Pan. Stop asking to search for him. He's dead."

Taking a step back in shock, I stared into my brother's eyes, wondering what the hell happened to him. When did he turn into this monster of a man? "What fire? What the hell are you talking about?"

Turning on his heels, he left the clearing, leaving me to catch up. Throwing my bow over my shoulder, I raced through the woods, refusing to let this argument go. He wasn't just going to ignore me. I would search for Peter myself, with or without his help.

Was I more likely to die that way? Yes.

Did I want to do it that way? No.

Would I? Most definitely.

It would take an idiot not to see Neverland slowly fading. Its light was slowly dying. But from what I remembered, Peter and Neverland could not survive without the other. They were two halves of a whole.

"He's dead. I watched them burn." My brother's words echoed in my head as I finally caught up to him on the trail, leaving a sense of hollowness in my chest.

No. I refused to believe it. Until I saw Peter's body, there was still a chance he was alive.

The trail Michael led me on was overgrown and barely there anymore. The dull-colored ferns and vines created a tangled mass of death and slow rebirth as we made our way through them. The ground was covered in new life, trying to grow and make its way upward, but the shading from the overhead foliage kept it from gaining momentum.

It gave me hope that Neverland wasn't dead yet. It was trying to fight, to live. We just had no idea what we were up against.

The silence between us was deafening. I hated it. As kids, we all relied on each other and talked all the time. I had hoped it would be the same if we ever met again. Apparently not. It left a stinging hole in my chest that my brother didn't trust me anymore.

"Where are we going?" I asked, deciding that talking was better than the tension growing between us.

"You'll see when we get there," he grunted, clearly still pissed off.

"I used to say that when I was taking Jane somewhere as a surprise. I feel like this isn't a surprise I want to see, though." I half-laughed, finding the irony fitting. My heart cracked at the reminder that I may never see her again and tears stung my eyes.

Michael sighed as he slowed his pace. "Jane. Is that the name of one of my nieces?"

"Jane is my daughter by birth. She was the blonde in the photos you were looking at. Julie has been her best friend since they were little. Her parents kicked her out as a teen and she came to live with us. I consider her my second daughter and Jon considers her a niece. I don't see the harm in you thinking that as well."

Nodding, he pushed through the brush, the tension not nearly as taut as it was. Deciding that the girls were a safe ground to talk, I told him memories of when the girls were small and would play faeries in the backyard. Or when Jane tried to jump off the roof, claiming she could fly. She broke her right femur after that accident, leaving a nasty scar that she covered up with a tattoo when she turned eighteen.

We carried on that way for what seemed like miles. He would ask questions about the girls and how they grew up. I would tell him stories of what trouble the two would get into. Laughing, we remembered the trouble we would get into here in Neverland.

"We had some good times here," I said wistfully. "I wish the island hadn't changed. I think Jane would have loved it."

"It's a good thing she'll never have to experience it, Wendy. No one should have to." Michael sighed as he stopped moving forward. "Wendy. I know you don't want to believe that Pan is dead, but..."

My heart was racing out of my chest as he trailed off. Where were we? What did he want to show me? I know we didn't just trek halfway across the island in this Godsforsaken heat for nothing. He had his reasons, but I don't think my heart was going to be able to handle what he wanted to say.

Steeling my nerves, I pushed through the last of the brush and stilled as shock took over my body. The tree we all played in as kids was gone. Only a burned-out stump remained with the surrounding grounds burned to ash.

"What happened, Michael?" I asked as I took a step toward what once was Deadman's Tree.

"The day that Pan brought me back," he choked, as tears clogged his voice. "We found the tree already in flames. The smell of burnt wood and human flesh was everywhere. The man-eaters were crawling out of the woods toward the tree when Pan picked me up and flew me to Skull Rock to keep me safe. He went back to save what Lost Boys he could. He never returned."

My heart sank with each word he said. Tears ran down my face as I took in what was our home. Tears for the friends we lost. Tears for the years that Michael had to endure this alone. Tears for the man I loved.

"Why did you bring me here?"

"I needed to show you proof that Neverland isn't what it used to be. That it's deadlier now than it was back then. That there is no way Pan is still alive."

"You came back to London to say goodbye," I stated, staring off into the woods. The chill in the air surrounding this area was eerie and unnerving.

Michael walked slowly into the clearing, stopping beside me. "There is something happening here, Wendy. Nothing good. Neverland is dying and we can do nothing to stop it."

"Did you ever find their bodies?" I asked, turning to him and changing the subject.

He shook his head. "There were no bodies. It was assumed the man-eaters ate them, leaving nothing behind."

Shaking my head, I took in what he said.

There was no body. The man-eaters usually left bones and scraps of meat behind. Pan very well could be alive.

Hope took root in my chest as I took one last look at the stump that held so many memories. "So, no one has seen Peter's body in over twenty years. There's no real proof he's dead." I looked up at Michael, gauging whether I should voice the rest of my thoughts. When he remained silent, I continued. "Neverland is dying. It's losing its magic, but what if it's because Peter is still alive and slowly dying himself? What if he needs help?" I let my questions hang in the air.

"Wendy, it's a fool's errand to go searching for him. I have a team that has been scouring this island for decades with the same thought. He isn't here." His voice was flat as he turned to go back into the Never Wood.

My feet moved swiftly beneath me, catching up to my brother. "I am not saying you're wrong, Michael. But until I see his body, I won't give up looking for him. I can't."

Michael shook his head, moving through the brush. "You're in love with a ghost, Wendy. A shadow that haunts your dreams. Just give up!"

Anger coursed through me that he would give up on Peter so easily. There had to be something he was missing. Catching his arm, I pulled him to a stop, my heart beating wildly in my chest. "Just let me stay until we figure out why Neverland is suddenly dying if it hadn't been before. Just let me help you," I pleaded, praying he wouldn't send me back to London. Not yet.

"Wendy, you can't stay here. It isn't safe... You have no idea what you're up against anymore."

"Then tell me," I pleaded once more. A dull, red petal as big as my head came floating down between us and one of the suns peeked through the hole left behind.

Glancing up, Michael sighed, resignation in his voice. "Fine, but don't say I didn't warn you."

Chapter Twenty-Five

SMEE

"I am not going to London this time, Cap'. I have some business to attend to here," I stated as we loaded the last of the Dust onto the Krok.

"What happened to taking your sister home?" he asked as we heaved the last trunk into the hold.

"She has talked me into keeping her here to see if she can help us fix Neverland's magic. At least for a week or two," I said, my stomach in knots that I had agreed to such a thing. We were both dead if word got to the Fae she was here.

Cap grunted as if he was only half-listening to what I was saying. He hasn't talked to me in the past few days, except for the necessary things to keep the Cove running smoothly. He hadn't even announced the deaths of our crewmen to the rest of the crew, which had my teeth on edge. I didn't know what game he was playing, but it was starting to leave a knot of tension between us, which didn't bode well for the Cove.

"Do I want to know what your business is?" he asked, skepticism laced in his voice.

Usually, I would put my business aside to ensure everything ran smoothly as they sailed through the cosmos, but today, I had a meeting I couldn't miss. "You know," I said, waiting for him to protest. It wouldn't have done anything. I would still follow through with what was planned, with or without his blessing.

We kept eye contact until he acquiesced to the notion. "It needs to be done." Resignation rang deep in his voice as he climbed the stairs to the main deck. "I just wish it didn't have to come to this."

I nodded my agreeance, but there was no use in setting laws if you didn't follow through on the threats. That was asking for trouble.

The main deck was in a flurry of activity as the men and women of the crew were setting up to get on their way. The ship's black sails were unfurled and lightly waving on the Never Sea's breeze. The salty breeze was calming, but my anticipation for what my night had in store was singing through my veins. No amount of trying would calm the beast inside, except for blood.

I had been waiting all week for this and was itching for the ship to leave the harbor. Then I had free reign of the Cove until Barrington came back.

After grabbing a few items from my cabin, I half-ass saluted James and strode off the ship. I needed to get Wendy from the house first. I needed her to be a part of this. She needed a wake-up call to see what life was like here anymore. That if she wanted to survive, she had to let out her demons. To let Moira come out to play once more. I knew she was in there. I just needed to prod her out and let her know that the blood and violence were as necessary now as it was back then.

My blood rushed in my ears as I strode through town, and time grew nearer to Grim's demise. The bastard thought that he could touch

Wendy and get away with it after being told to leave her alone. She was family, and no one touched what was mine.

"Wendy!" I called through the house as I opened the door. We didn't have much time. I knew where the man was now and didn't want to miss him. Having to search for him wasn't on the to-do list tonight. "Wendy!" I called again, but the house was seemingly quiet. Where the fuck was she?

The sound of a door slamming upstairs hit my ears as I paced the living room. "What the hell, Michael? I was taking a nap," she sniped as she was putting her long, auburn hair up in a ponytail.

Rolling my eyes, I grabbed her hand and dragged her out of the house. I didn't really care what she had been doing. We were going to be late.

"What the hell! Where are we going?" she yelled as we quickly returned to the town square.

"Wait here, I have a surprise," I said, leaving her in the middle of the square as people milled about, watching us curiously. It was rare to see me alone with a woman, let alone dragging one along behind me. The last one was a mole who thought she could get extra Dust from the Fae in exchange for sex. We don't deal with that around here. Well, except me. Only I was allowed to fuck a Fae.

I strode through town quickly. The crew who was left here scrambled out of my way the closer I got to my destination. I could feel my face morphing into the man that this Cove feared. Michael wasn't well known, just an unfettered Smee. But Smee on a mission... he was cold, calculating, and dead inside.

My blood was rushing with anticipation as I entered the bar. The man in question was leaning over a table, inhaling the drug that was always at hand. Disgust must have marred my face as I approached. The people in the bar quickly moved out of my way as I stopped in front of Grim. His body relaxed as he reclined in his seat. Dust would do that.

"Ah, Smee... What can I do for you? I am quite sure the Krok is supposed to be underway to go to London, shouldn't it?" he asked, oblivious to the fact that everyone else felt the chill in the air from my icy exterior. Or he was really good at ignoring it to make himself feel more alpha than he really was.

A true alpha wouldn't touch a woman while she slept. Hell, a real man wouldn't touch a woman without permission at all. The fact he felt comfortable enough to do so said a million things that I didn't want to contemplate. If I did, he would die, and not just be maimed.

He was to be punished, as per law, but telling that to my violence was hard going. That's why Wendy was there. To see that her aggressor was punished for his wrongdoings, but also to pull me back before I killed the fucker.

Grabbing the man by his collar, I lifted him to his feet. His breath plumed into my face, smelling of rum, sex, and fear. Good, he knew what was coming. "Let's go. You have a date in the town square. There is someone I would like for you to meet."

Grim had the audacity to stand to his full height as he shook free of my hold. He wasn't as tall as I was, but definitely broader. If he thought he could intimidate me, he was dead wrong. It wasn't doing shit but pissing me off. My fury was already stoked to a high degree. The urge to harness this man and put him on his knees until he learned his place burned through me, my fingers twitching to hurt the fucker. His surrender was going to taste so sweet.

"I am not going anywhere, Smee. I haven't done anything wrong." The lie rolled off his tongue with ease, leaving a small apprehension in my gut.

Fury mottled my face as I stood up to the man who had the gall to lie to me and think he could get away with it. I could feel the evil smile creeping over my face. The delight in watching this man get turned into a blubbering mess was going to be my favorite flavor to date.

Unwrapping the rope from my belt, I felt the man in front of me tense as I unfurled the last bit. He was coming with me one way or the other. He didn't have a choice. The smart choice, to keep a little bit of dignity, would be to face your consequences head-on. Grim wasn't that smart and was high as a kite right now. Lucky for him, he might not even feel his punishment until he came down from it.

"To the square." My voice deepened, as ice filled my veins. Cold. That's all I was.

"No," Grim stated indignantly, drawing his sword. "I told you! I have done nothing wrong!"

Only someone who was guilty was going to fight this hard about it.

I shook my head as I took in the man's stance. His red-rimmed eyes were blown wide as they shifted constantly about the room. His footing was one of the laziest stances I had seen in a long time. He had become too complacent. Too comfortable of his place here in the Cove. He needed to be brought down a few pegs.

I stood still, letting the man make the first move. His sword slashed toward me as I stepped out of his way. As he stumbled forward and fell into a nearby table, everything clattered to the floor as he sprawled in the wet mess.

Internally rolling my eyes, I picked the man up and brought him to his knees, wrapping the rope around his hands and neck. If he didn't want to walk, then dragging would do.

The gurgling and gasping for breath coming from behind me as I pulled the offender into the middle of town was music to my ears. I could only hope it would also bring Wendy as much pleasure to hear.

The murmurs ringing through the crowd grew louder the closer we got to the square. It wasn't every day we had entertainment. Especially without the captain to witness. It leaves most of the town unsettled, which is what I want. They need to know that just because we aren't present, doesn't mean we aren't watching.

Wendy was standing in the same spot I left her. Her eyes widened in fear. Whether it was me or the sight of Grim being dragged behind by his neck was to be determined.

We halted as we came before my sister. I slowly inched the rope toward my body, pulling Grim with it, and threw him at her feet when he was close enough. "Is this the man? The one who touched you?" I asked, brusquely. I knew it was. I just needed her to admit it to the crowd.

The gasp that came from the crowd as she nodded her ascent had my face alighting with a dark smile.

"What does that slut have to do with me?" Grim spat blood at Wendy's feet, his lip curled in disgust toward her.

Pulling the man's head back by the scruff on his neck, I made him stand before her. "What would you like to happen to him?" I gave the question to Wendy. His fate lied in her hands.

The man's eyes bugged out of his head as I pulled the rope tighter around his throat, the realization that I wasn't in charge. It was the woman whom he had assaulted who held his life in her hands.

"Let her out, Wendy. Let her come out to play."

Fear took over her gaze as she registered what I had asked of her. To let out the woman that Neverland feared. The woman who was just as deranged as Pan.

Shaking her head back and forth, she searched the crowd, looking for what I couldn't possibly know. No one here would help her. They wanted to see the show.

"Weennnddyy..." I sang her name. "Let go... If you want to survive, you know you have to let her out to play. Let her get her revenge."

"No. I can't. I put her away for a reason, Michael."

"Michael isn't here. And Smee would like to play with his old playmate."

She slowly realized that the only way out of this was to play along. I wanted to see Moira.

Ever so slowly, her body loosened. She closed her eyes as if she was concentrating on the demons inside her. Good. She needed to let them loose. Let them come out to play. Let them wreak havoc on the island she loved so dearly. It might keep her alive.

Her eyes popped open and her usual whiskey-colored irises were now dark forest green. Her swagger quickly followed suit, becoming more predatory and less prey. The sight of a malevolent smile crossing her face had mine matching hers. "Anything?" she asked, her voice deeper, more sultry and deadly.

The look of terror filled Grim's face as she matched my energy. "Anything besides death. Barrington wants him kept alive."

"Are you doling out the punishment, or can I?" Moira asked. Glee lit her eyes as I nodded.

"You are more than welcome to do whatever you feel fits."

I had forgotten how violent my sister could be. Watching her move up to the man who was now shaking in my hands, she leaned down into his face and smiled. Her teeth bared in impending violence.

"You will learn today what it means to mess with a Darling."

Chapter Twenty-Six

JANE

Tick... Tock...

My nerves were strung as tight as an acrobat's rope. One single fray and I was ready to snap.

When Jules and I arrived, the club was in full swing. The music was thumping and bodies were grinding against each other as we fought to forget our woes.

Coming home from the hospital after Alis' abduction, the hospital had put me on leave until I was cleared of all wrongdoing. No one believed my story. I wouldn't have believed it if I hadn't seen it with my own eyes. Now, I need to apologize to Uncle Jon for calling him crazy the other day about Neverland.

He had asked me about Dust, which was odd. He said he had patients who mentioned the stuff, but couldn't find any studies. So, he wanted to see what it does to a person's psyche. I didn't have much to tell him. It's just that it made Jules super high and we both had weird hallucinations.

Then he asked if I could get a sample of it to take back to the labs. That favor was what had my gut clenched in nerves and fear.

But where did the ticking come from? It was like something unlocked in my brain that night that I couldn't shut back up. It was on the verge of driving me insane.

I never got a chance to ask him about Neverland, as he was called in for emergency surgery. I have been left to stew in my thoughts and memories that had me spiraling for days.

Tick... Tock...

I shook my head and returned to the present and away from the memories that plagued me. No matter what I did, they always found a way to creep back into my thoughts. All my memories and thoughts had twisted into nightmares of glowing eyes and malicious smiles. No, I must keep reminding myself that I can't do anything about Alis and people's eyes don't glow.

Jules went off to the bar in search of drinks while I stayed on the wall by the door, searching for the faces of the men I knew should be there. And one I was desperate to see.

James had been nowhere to be found and never came to the hospital after Alis' disappearance, which was a red flag on its own. The fact that I hadn't been able to find him in the crowd tonight had my already frayed nerves skyrocketing and the butterflies in my stomach lurching. Trying to escape through my throat, bile rose at the thought that tonight was a mistake.

I searched the crowd to find the men who gave me the Dust last year. It shouldn't be too hard to find them. It would be convincing them to let me have some. Without them present, however, was the problem. They wouldn't let anyone take the drug outside of the clubs. It was all hush-hush insider secrets.

My gaze flickered over the sea of faces, most of them familiar to me at this point. My heart was slowly sank to my feet in despair. I was afraid I might not get to see James tonight to tell him what happened to Alis.

Jules bounced back into my view, drinks in hand, as she returned to my side. Her smile dimmed as she neared. "What's wrong, cupcake?" she asked, handing me my rum and Coke.

"You know what's wrong. Everything is wrong and I don't want to do this." Tears clogged my throat as the week's past events pressed down on me, my shoulders sagging under the pressure. I wanted to drown in my sorrows until there was nothing left. I wanted to bleed out all my mistakes and grieve the fact that I was never going to be enough to save anyone.

I went into nursing to help and save people. And all that has come from it was pain and suffering. I have lost more patients than I have saved. Hell, my own mother has gone missing and I can do nothing to help her. The cops have done nothing to help find her. They literally threw her case to the side, leaving me hopeless and bereft.

I only wanted James to hold me and tell me everything would be okay. But that wasn't going to happen. He probably was avoiding this place, blaming me for Alis' abduction. I would, too. I should have done more to get to her, but it was like I was stuck in quicksand and nothing I did could move me from the spot I was rooted in.

Tick... Tock...

Jules took my open hand, shaking me back to the present. "Come on." Her dark hair swayed across her back as she pulled us to the dance floor. "Let's just let go for a little bit, then we can go looking for the guys," she yelled into my ear over the music.

We let the crowd guide us to the dance floor, swaying with the beat and let ourselves get lost in the rhythm of the melody floating around us. The beat was slow and ground me back to myself.

I loved dancing. It always helped me clear my head and relax. Raising my hands above my head, I let the music lull me into a trance. The drinks kept coming and my worries from the last few days flowed away with them. Sweat beaded on my brow as Jules and I got pushed further into the center of the dance floor, letting the crowd ebb and sway with us in its grip.

TICK... Tock...

The resounding bangs of the ticking had my hand gripping the side of my head. I hadn't heard it so loud since Alis was taken. I still haven't figured out why I only heard it loud sometimes and not others.

The drinks in my system had my face flushed and my body hot. All my worries were at a low. Except for my want for James. But I was quite sure I was just horny and needed a good fuck.

I glanced up at the spot on the balcony where he was always watching and paused. James wasn't there, but a beautiful redhead was standing next to a man with skin as dark as night. I had never seen them here before.

The woman's hair was in a fancy updo, her cheekbones sharp enough to cut glass. Her bright, green eyes were glued to the necklace that was still around my neck. Tearing her gaze from me, she leaned into the man, her lips against his ear as his gaze found mine. There was no expression on his face when he answered her. The woman stepped up to the railing, a long-fingered hand wrapping around the banister as she glared down at me.

A thrill of fear crept up my spine as I made eye contact with the woman. I couldn't tell you what her problem was. I had never met her, but her instant hatred had me on edge. We needed to leave—

TICK... TOCK...

Now.

The banging gongs in my head were giving me a migraine and the redheaded woman sending me death glares was not my cup of tea tonight. Most nights, I could deal with jealous women, but tonight was not it.

Wrenching my gaze from the people on the balcony, I went to grab Jules and panic slowly rose in my gut as I found she was gone. What the fucking hell? Not again.

My gaze shot to the balcony once more before I started making my way through the crush of bodies and found it empty. It was as if the two weren't ever there.

No. I was buzzed, not insane. They were definitely there. The fear and panic in my gut told me I was in danger and needed to leave, but I wasn't leaving Jules behind.

Frantically, I searched the faces of everyone as I pushed my way through the crush of bodies, my anxiety rising that Jules was missing, too. Everyone I loved was disappearing to Neverland, and from the stories I remembered, I would never want Jules or Alis to experience it. I don't want to experience it.

TICK... TOCK...

My breath was stuck in my throat. My lungs ached as I tried to get a lungful of air. The ticking in my head, loud as fuck, made my eyes hurt. The faces around me blurred as I spun in circles, trying to find Jules. She had to be here.

We came together, we left together. That was the rule.

Glancing back up to the balcony, I prayed that James was there. Instead, the woman with the red hair was back. Her haughty stance and upturned nose had my gut rolling as she watched me.

The press of sweaty bodies against mine had my stomach turning, bile burning my esophagus at the urge to retch all over the dance floor as I pushed my way to the entrance. I needed air.

Seeing the edge of the crowd, a rush of adrenaline had me pushing myself against the tide as I fell through the throng of people. Pain stabbed through my leg as I righted myself, my ankle halfway twisted in my heel. I knew I shouldn't have worn these damned things. Stupid dress code.

Hissing through the pain, I stood up straight and limped to the bar toward the seat always reserved for James. The empty chair was both a relief and a reminder that he wasn't there. Shaking my head to clear it of the depressing thought, I sat down and studied my hurt foot, the constant throbbing telling me I probably sprained it.

Groaning, I waved to the bartender until he nodded and brought me two glasses—my usual rum and Coke and a whiskey on the rocks for James. Shaking my head, I yelled, "Can I get a bag of ice? I twisted my ankle." Again, he nodded as he turned away and went off to grab me what I needed.

No. What I needed was to find Jules and get out of there. Where the fuck was she?

TICK... tock...

The fucking ticking was pissing me off. Why couldn't it be fucking useful and tell me where my friend was instead of just bonging inside my head for no reason, like hot and cold? That would be nice.

I grabbed the bag of ice that was set on the bar and placed it on my swelling ankle, hissing at the cold against my fevered skin. I was going to kill Jules when I found her.

As I sat there, I scanned the area for my friend's face while I let my ankle rest. I would have to hobble to the entrance at some point to leave, but it wouldn't be anytime soon.

The adrenaline I felt just moments ago was slowly draining out of my body, the pain in my ankle growing and shooting up my leg. All I wanted to do was sleep.

I would leave Jules here if I wasn't such a good person.

Placing the ice on the bar, I stood up, ignoring the lancing pain as I put weight on it and started to make my way towards the bathrooms. The one place she could be.

Slowly limping my way across the club, I was careful of the spilled drinks and cups as I skirted around the dancing people. My heart was stuck in my throat. This was the only place she could be. The private rooms were for the owners and elite members, things we were not, and she wasn't gone long enough to be in one of those.

The hallway was empty and the hairs at the nape of my neck stood on end. That wasn't right. There was always a line.

TICK! TOCK!

The gongs were back, louder than ever, ringing through my mind.

"Hello, pretty girl. Long time, no see."

Whipping around, fear seized my chest as the bile I had been fighting all night came back up, scorching my throat. The blonde man from my nightmares, the one I was supposed to be seeking out, came out of the shadows.

The Dust was no longer on my mind. Uncle Jon was going to have to figure out how to get some himself because this wasn't worth it. I couldn't do it. Fuck this. I just wanted to go home.

"What do you want?" I asked, my voice steadier than I thought it could be. Two points for me.

"I hear that you and your friend... Juliette? Was that her name? Well, it's no matter. We heard you were looking for some Dust."

TICK! TOCK!

Shaking my head, I denied it. I didn't want it anymore. I didn't want to be near this man at all. Backing up, I slowly came to the realization that there was nowhere for me to go. Trepidation sank low into my back as I felt the wall behind me. Blondie hadn't moved from his spot in the corner, but the look of lust and anger on his face said I wasn't going to get anywhere without a battle.

"Now, don't be coy. We both know that Barrington was only going to be able to keep you safe for so long."

Tremors worked their way through me at the way he eyed my body, his tongue slowly dipping out of his mouth, wetting his lips as if he couldn't wait to get his hands on me.

Disgust and terror held me fast as I quickly scanned the area. A water fountain was in the corner and the door to the bathroom was across from me. No one had come out of it in the whole time we were here. Maybe there was no one in there? But that made no sense with how busy the place was...

TICK! TOCK!

My mind was racing a mile minute as I thought about everything that had happened since we got here. My instant want to leave, the woman glaring at me, twisting my ankle, Jules missing...

"I see you are finally figuring it out there, darlin'." The man's deep voice rumbled across my skin, my stomach tightening at the sound.

"Where's Jules?"

"Tsk. Tsk." He straightened himself from the wall and started making his way toward me. "I think the better question should be, 'Where's your boyfriend?'" He stopped a breath away from me, I had nowhere to go.

I was trapped against the wall and my ankle was screaming as pain shot through my leg from standing on it for so long.

"I don't have a boyfriend," I snarled out—not that I knew of. James and I had never made anything official, and his not showing up for tonight or for Alis' disappearance made me believe he was done with me.

TICK!!! TOCK!!!

"Oh! Well, then, that will make this so much easier."

Raising his arm, I had no time to react before I felt the sharp sting in my neck and everything went black.

Chapter Twenty-Seven

LILY

One would think that after years of doing this, I would finally get over it.

I haven't.

The guilt that settles in my stomach every time I leave these kids in the old treehouse makes me sick. There was something wrong with all of it. What the hell could the Fae need these kids for?

Pan was no longer here to play with them and give them adventures to live on, and I have not seen any of these kids in the woods or out and about while traversing the island. The Fae were up to something, but I couldn't investigate it without getting caught in the crossfires of Tinkerbelle's rage. The bitch was more conniving than a fox and I had the scars mapping my body as a constant reminder. I have no idea how she garnered so much power, but someone needed to take her down.

It wouldn't be me, though. I couldn't fight Tink if I wanted to. All I could do was pop into the next space I opened. That only worked for so long before I got tired and had to rest.

Turning away from the sleeping children, I slowly walked toward the stairs leading up to ground level, the scuffing of dirt beneath my shoes the only sound. I grasped the small handle of the door above me and gave a slight shove to prop the door against the stump as I climbed out.

The area around Deadman's Tree used to teem with life and laughter. Now, it was encased in shadows and haunted by the ghosts of good times past. The lives of the Lost Boys lost in the fire still haunted me. We never found out what started the fire, but the tree remnants, a blackened and hollowed-out stump, reminded everyone that no one in Neverland is safe. Even Peter Pan wasn't safe from the wrath of the island if it so chose.

The air was stagnant as I crossed the scorched grounds, approaching the tree line. This part of the island was eerily quiet, as if Neverland itself was scarred by the violence that took place here. The island had always had an air of malevolence, but what happened here was malicious and evil. The balance of the island had been upset and never returned to normal after that night.

I broke through the brush onto the hidden trails, the dew from the jungle sticking to my arms as I strolled past. A burst of energy caressed my skin, the leaves next to me rustling as the magic blew past. The scent of burnt ozone filled my senses, reminding me of the smell of my portals.

Pulling a thread of magic from my center, I sent tendrils out in search of the magic that was being played within the area. It had to be close, but trying to figure out where it was would be the problem. The trees and foliage provided good cover for anyone trying to hide themselves.

The swirling sparks of blue and orange wound their way through the jungle with ease, taking me back the way I came. Who was at the treehouse? The Fae come closer to daybreak to collect their children, so who the hell was there?

The sounds of men's voices carried across the open field, causing a shiver to coast down my spine with uneasiness.

"Fucking hell, she would lead us here…"

I made a quiet snap of my fingers and pulled my magic back into me, my head swimming with the excess, blurring my vision. My stomach rolled at the voice that shouldn't be here.

Quietly, I lowered myself to the ground, making a small hole in the ferns to peek through and immediately I saw what I felt.

It was a portal, like the one I just closed earlier. Three men were walking into the clearing. Two had women in their arms, and I would recognize the other one anywhere.

Drake.

Fucking bastard was using my magic. No wonder I was tired all the fucking time.

The wet dirt beneath me soaked my front. The cold was almost a welcome reprieve from the heat of the anger brewing inside me as I watched the three men.

Drake was clearly irritated by whatever was happening, his finger twirling his ring. His only tell. It was the only way I knew if I was getting under his skin. After being together for so long, you learn all the quirks of the other until you loathe them.

Me? I despised this man.

No, not despised.

Hated. I hated him with a fire that would burn me from the inside out if I couldn't be rid of him soon. Whatever he was doing now only added more fuel to my rage.

"Well, you two will have to trek to the palace from here. Make sure they arrive in one piece. Tink has plans for them." My husband's voice raked down my spine. Gods, he was vile. Not only was he forcing me to transport children here for Gods knows what, but now it's women?

And what the hell would Tinkerbelle need with these two women anyway? They couldn't have been here before. That was impossible. No one leaves Neverland alive since Peter went missing.

So, what the fuck was going on? What did I walk into?

I craned my neck ever so slightly to get a better view of the men who came with Drake, but they were already walking through the tree line. A blonde head with curls was draped over the blonde man's arm, her hair bouncing slightly as he trudged through the wood.

A zap of energy crossed my skin as the portal closed, my eyes snapping back to where the hole was. Drake was gone.

I let out my breath as I slowly stood, my body aching and cold from lying in the mud.

Quickly, I crossed the ashy field in the direction the two men went. The breeze that blew around Neverland picked up, blowing my hair into my face.

SHADDOOOWWW...

A chill swept through me as the wind blew past. I didn't hear that, right?

Glancing ahead of me to where the men disappeared in the brush, I watched the wind blow through the trees, making its way to wherever they could have gone. Terror and trepidation filled me as I ran to catch up, praying the island wasn't really talking.

SHADDOOOWWW...

No. It was. Another chill ran through me. Neverland hasn't talked in over twenty years. Who the hell did Drake bring here?

Running as quietly as I could through the wood, the men were easy to track. It wasn't going to be easy getting to the palace from here with two unconscious girls in tow. Why didn't they leave them in the stump?

I caught up to them in no time. Skirting around them, I ensured they weren't alerted to my presence. I wanted to get around them and meet them halfway. I wanted to get a good look at the girls' faces.

I ran ahead, my hair in my face as my mud-caked clothes clung to my body. Gods, I wanted a soak after this. As I slowed, I came to a small clearing with a shimmery, white boulder in the middle. The grass was soft and a mellow green. The copse of trees shimmered in speckles of gold and silver from the dew. The breeze flowing through the opening was cool and calming. It was the perfect spot to rest, and I was counting on them to use it.

This spot used to be a little sanctuary for the Lost Boys to play with the pixies without fear of the pirates or man-eaters getting to them. It was one of the places protected by the Krok. But she has been long dead, her body decaying beneath the rock placed in her honor. She would lie upon the boulder for hours, sunbathing, as the boys frolicked and played under the sister suns while Pan would play on his flute.

The Krok herself was not Fae, mermaid, or human, but a tiny part of each. She had this sense of protectiveness over the humans on the island. No one knew why she felt this way. It was just accepted that you didn't touch them when she was around. Or you faced her wrath, usually losing a hand, tongue, or leg—whatever she felt like eating that day.

Sitting on the same rock that she used to lie upon brought back some good memories that made you feel warm and fuzzy, pulling you into their embrace for a short spout of happiness before melancholy and reality hit you. I don't know how Krok died. No one did. Nibs, one of the Lost Boys, found her here while he was out hunting pirates. A little bit of the island died that day. That was the day that I believed that Neverland started to fall. But it was hard to tell. The Fae had so many tricks up their sleeves that Neverland could have been falling for a long time before it came to light for all the rest of us residents to see it.

The sound of muffled voices and brush moving had my attention at the edge of the clearing. A small smile formed on my lips. I knew they wouldn't be able to resist this little haven.

"You know, I am getting really sick and tired of this bullshit. Why couldn't he just take us to the palace? *Nooo...* gotta walk half the island with two unconscious who—"

My eyebrow quirked at the Fae that walked through the tree line. Arron and Madok. They were a couple of Drake's grunts—pissy ones, at that. This was going to make my life so much easier. I couldn't take the women from them. That would garner too much attention and time. Besides, I would have to explain myself to both Drake and Tink, and I would prefer to avoid both.

"Hey, boys." I sat up on the rock as if I had been there all night contemplating life and not following them around like a dog. "Whatcha got there?"

The two men were broad-shouldered and looked human. If it weren't for the glow of their eyes, I would have assumed that as well. Madok had dark, wavy hair that curled perfectly to cover his pointed ears. He carried a girl with long, dark hair and a slinky black dress. She was missing a shoe and her makeup was smeared down her face, creating a map of what she probably went through before he brought her here.

The other man, Arron, held a girl with curly, blonde hair, a pert nose, and lush, red lips. I recognized her almost immediately. Jon's niece and Wendy's daughter. That meant the other girl was the friend that lived with them. Protectiveness came rushing through me like a tidal wave. I had watched them grow up from the shadows, and to see them here, I felt fear crashing through my senses. The intense need to get them home was palpable. Jane was missing both her shoes, her one ankle turning blue, so I would assume she wouldn't be able to walk even if she were conscious. Her dress looked torn at the hem. The collar around her neck was a statement, though. She belonged to someone on the island. Even more peculiar.

Fury roiled through me at the treatment of these women before they even arrived here. What the fuck did my husband do to them?

"Tiger Lily... What are you doing around these parts? Isn't your place on the other side of the island?" the blonde asked.

Damn it, I didn't think they would know where my whereabouts on the island usually are. "I decided to visit this little shrine for old times' sake," I said coyly, twirling a strand of hair around my finger, trying to make myself look like a smaller threat. I may be able to take care of myself against a Fae, but two? That was a death wish.

"Well, could you be so kind as to transport us to the palace since your husband could not? It would make all our lives easier. And I'll put in a good word for you with Tinkerbelle," Arron tried to barter. Apparently, he was the brains of the operation and not very good at it.

"I could. But what do I get out of it? A good word with Tink means nothing to me. I am already in her services, so nothing in that regard could entice me."

Madok readjusted the girl in his arms. I could tell they were getting tired and needed my help to get to the palace before the girls woke up. I don't know what business Tink has with these women, but it wasn't good, especially if one was already claimed. But if they woke up and tried escaping these men, their fate would be just as bad. If I wanted to help them, I needed to know where they were. If they were at the palace, I could find them. If they were let loose on the island, I may never find them to take them home.

Watching the gears turn in the men's heads, I jumped down off the rock and sauntered across the grass to them. "How about you tell me who these women are and what Tink's intentions are with them, and I will take you to the palace?" I glanced up at them, their minds running through all the possible outcomes of giving me this information.

On the one hand, nothing came of it and we'd all go our merry way. On the other, they died. Meh. Didn't matter to me which way it went for them. They were scum, but I wanted to know what the fuck Drake was up to.

"Why do you care?" Madok asked, his voice rumbled from his chest.

"Because I want to know what my husband is up to. And the fact that I am just nosy." I tapped my finger on his nose, just to irritate the shit out of him.

"Don't touch him," Arron ground out between clenched teeth, the muscle in his jaw ticking as he also readjusted the girl in his arms.

Oh. They were lovers. This was going to make this so much more fun.

Moving behind Madok, I came only up to his shoulder, but it was the perfect height to tease the man's neck. Running my hand through his hair, I traced a small kiss on the back of his neck as I held Arron's gaze. Madok tensed beneath my hands. "Oh, come now, we could have so much fun."

Arron gnashed his teeth as his eyes lit with anger and lust. Too bad I was off limits, and they knew it. "Fine," he snapped. "The girls are Jane and Juliette. They are playthings of Barrington's. He pissed off Tink, so this is her repayment to him." He moved the girl in his arm to go over his shoulder, her ass hanging out in the air. "Stop touching what's mine," he gritted out, his eyes lit on my hands.

Lifting my hands, I drifted back away from them as I pulled the little magic left in me and opened a small portal. The flickers of orange and blue on the edges were fading fast.

"Hurry, my cocksucker of a husband used all my magic to get you here. That's all I have left."

The two men wasted no time in moving through the hole before it closed behind them, leaving me out of breath and my hair stuck to my forehead with sweat from the effort.

Falling to my knees, I lay in the grass and closed my eyes.

Fuck.

Chapter Twenty-Eight

JAMES

I was late getting to the club tonight.

The plan was to talk to Drake quickly about the events in Neverland, grab my girl, and head back to the island.

Was I going to ask Jane to come with me? No.

Did I care? Also, no.

The club was starting to close. The crowds slowly made their way off the dance floor and the music echoed around the mostly empty club as it wound down for the night.

My stomach sank as I realized the time. Jane better still be here. If I had missed seeing Jane, there would be hell to pay.

The bass was making everything vibrate, and due to the lack of bodies in the room, my teeth were on their way to falling out of my skull.

Drake waited at the top of the staircase, his black suit blending with the backdrop. The effect made it look like his head was floating at the top of the stairs. I would have been disconcerted if he hadn't done that trick on me before. Now, I am used to his little antics that he tries every now and then. The good news is that when he does it, he's in a good mood, making prying for information much easier.

"Tink was told about the dosage dilemma." His voice was deep, almost vibrating, as I hit the landing.

Nodding, I looked up to him and concern flickered through me at the statement. It wasn't a question. He knew I told her. It was to be expected, but how he worded it said more.

I was tall at six feet two inches, but Drake made me look small. He was five inches taller than me and built like a linebacker. His suits had to be tailored to him because no one made suits in his size. "Can we talk in your office? I have had some things come up and would rather talk to you about them than anyone else."

Waving his hand behind him towards his open door, I made my way to the room that I hated being in. It always felt two sizes too small, especially after Drake entered the room. He took up so much space, and the power that oozed off his body made the room feel like it was pressing against you with no room to breathe.

I sat in the chair across from him as he sat behind his desk. "This has got to be interesting," the Fae stated as the chair creaked under his weight. "I don't think you have ever had a problem before that you needed my help with."

"Make no mistake, I don't need your help, per se. But I need some clarification on some information that has come to my attention."

"I will try to answer as much as I can."

Leaning forward, my elbows rested on my knees and I dove right into the deep end of the shit, hoping that he would help. "I had a stowaway on my ship the last time I was here. The man claimed to be a 'lost boy.' Do you know what he was talking about?"

Drake's eyes flashed with surprise as he quickly masked his features into one of indifference. "No. The Lost Boys died years ago." His tone fell flat as he maneuvered his chair closer to the desk.

Nodding my head, I continued. "Well, he said he came from Tink's castle and was looking for a woman as payment."

The man's brow rose in curiosity.

"I think he said Wendy... Wendy, something..."

"Darling," he finished with a sneer, his hands clenched into fists as he finished her name.

"Yes! That's it!" I clapped my hands together as if I had forgotten her name. "He said that Tink would be over the moon with glee if she ever got her hands on her."

"Wendy," he snarled, "started the downfall of Neverland. If she had never come there and taken Pan, we wouldn't be in the mess we are in now. But there is nothing to be done about it now." Annoyance was evident in his voice. "What exactly is your question?"

"Is there a bounty on her head? A reward perhaps for finding the Wendy woman?" I asked.

Drake raised his fist to eye level, playing with his wedding band, and I looked down at mine, reminding myself that I needed to speed this up. "Not that I am aware of. Tink was gracious enough to let the woman live if she never returned to the island. I don't know why this man thought he would garner a reward for bringing her back."

I sat back in the chair and took in what he said, studying the man before me. He was irritated, if not by my questioning, then something else. He rarely, if ever, played with his ring, a sure sign that something was amiss. A knot had formed in my stomach long before I arrived and sat like a stone in my middle. Drake was hiding something.

"Men in the castle seem to think they can be rewarded for her head. I want to know why I wasn't informed if a new game was afoot. I could at least ensure they weren't stowing away like rats on my ship to find her."

"I have no idea what you are talking about, so I am of little help." He shook his head, standing abruptly as if to finish the conversation. "Anything else I can help you with?"

Nodding, I stood as well. I couldn't stand staring up at the man. I still had one more question. "Who is he? Peter Pan?"

Drake's eyes snap to mine, anger glistening in them. Not necessarily directed at me, the anger more of a past hurt that the man didn't want to revisit. "Peter was an old friend. Legend said he and the Island were one. That one cannot exist without the other, which is odd, seeing how the boy-turned-man died. How can Neverland exist if he does not anymore? It begged a lot of questions that have no answers, or answers no one wants to hear."

"So, he couldn't leave Neverland? Even if he wanted to?"

"Only for short periods of time. Nothing longer than a week. But that also became his downfall. He would disappear for a week and then return for a few days, just to return to London and the Wendy girl. The more time Pan spent here, the more he grew up. After he became a man, he disappeared, and we all presumed him dead after so many years of no contact."

"So, you have no proof that the man is dead? Just that he disappeared? So, he could be alive?"

"No. He couldn't be alive. He can't stay away from Neverland. It's in his blood. The magic calls him back, but he hasn't been seen in a long time."

"But you already stated the island and him are one, and if one is dead, the other should die too. So if Neverland is still there, that begs the question, how?"

"That is the question. One I have no answer for and I don't want to go digging for it. The cargo was settled, though?" he asked, abruptly changing the subject.

Nodding, I noted the sudden shift in Drake's demeanor. Agitated. Irritable.

"Yes. Everything should be set for you this week. Tink said she upped the dosage for you and everything was in order when I left the ship."

"Good. I will dig into your stowaway to see what may have prompted this sudden search for a banished woman," he stated flatly as he motioned toward the door.

Irritated that I was being dismissed, I didn't get much in the way of answers, but I did learn more about Neverland and the man Pan.

Opening the office door, the music was still blaring, the bass thumping its beat in time to the vein beating in my forehead as I saw the club was now empty. My temper flared at the fact that I had missed seeing Jane.

"If you're looking for your little nurse, you will find she is not here." Drake came up from behind, surprising me. Usually, once our meetings were done, they were done.

I took a quick glance at the Fae, but kept my eyes on the dance floor. A knot of apprehension settled at the nape of my neck. "What's that supposed to mean?"

"Ask your queen what she has done with your precious darling..." he trailed off, a malevolent smile plastered on his face.

Hot fury took hold as I grabbed the man by the throat, shoving him against the wall. The spilling of his magic flashed across my skin, but

I paid it no mind. The burn only added to my rage. "What does that mean?" I growled out between clenched teeth.

Drake chuckled darkly. "Careful, one might think you're in love with the little sprite."

Red filled my vision as I drew back my fist. The Fae's power flashed like lightning across my body, a scream of pain torn from my lungs. The burn from his magic flayed my skin. Blood trickled down my body in rivulets as he threw me across the landing. My head slammed against the concrete and stars filled my vision as more blood ran down the back of my skull.

I just fucked up.

Groaning, my body was held immobile. I felt Drake's magic as it pricked and tore at my skin, new wounds were ripped open as my heart raced in my chest and fear overcame me. I was a dead man.

Drake strode over, straightening his suit and playing with his cuff links.

"If any harm comes to her—"

"She was delivered earlier tonight." He bent down, his body shadowed mine, a reminder that I was nothing compared to him. "You only have yourself to blame."

Terror crawled through my middle and burned my throat. "Did she say why she wanted her? Of all the girls here, it had to be her?" Defeat was in my tone. There was no way she was in Neverland. If she was and Tink had her, she was as good as dead. And that was not something I could accept. Ever.

The Fae's hand shot out and gripped my throat, squeezing the little bit of air that I had. "When you said that the man was looking for Wendy, I was quite surprised by the truth that came from you, as that was not the story I had been told."

Spitting blood at the bastard's feet, I moved my head to show him the fury that was raging under my skin. "Why would I lie to you? You can smell lies," I spat.

Tightening his grip, I gasped. The burn in my lungs for air raged against the need to kill the fucker before me. Drake lowered his face towards mine, his breath hot against my skin, the smell of mint covered blood had my stomach roiling in disgust. "What was most intriguing, though, was that you never mentioned that the man succeeded and Wendy was, in fact, in Neverland."

My heart was thundering in my ears as its staccato beat railed against my ribcage. How the hell did he know that?

"Yes, we know she's there. The only question is, why did you keep her there? Why didn't you bring her home?"

Staying silent, I kept glaring at the man. I had no answer other than she talked us into staying. And that was not something the Fae would like to hear, especially from me. But regret was churning hot in my stomach that I hadn't. Maybe Jane wouldn't be suffering if I had followed my gut to bring her home.

"Ah, yes, well, it is no matter now. Tink has what she wanted. Something that would cause you the most harm."

No.

"I will let this... indiscretion, we will call it... go. But I need a favor from you in return."

Anger burned brightly behind my eyes, tears slid unbidden down my face from the pain ratcheting my body, the lack of oxygen and the burning sense of failure deep within.

"But I will collect that at a later time."

The instant relief and burn in my throat from Drake's hold had shivers wracking my body as I choked on air, trying to get a full breath.

"Better hurry. You may just be able to see your love one last time before Tink destroys her." Drake laughed as he walked back into his office, leaving me in a puddle of my own blood and tears.

Fuck!

Chapter Twenty-Nine

JON

The hospital was in crisis mode all day. Between emergency brain bleeds and my regular patients, I felt like I had been run over by a truck. My upper body ached and a low twinge in my lower back needed to be massaged away. Too bad I had fucked up with Isabella. She had hands that would do wonders for my body. I just knew it.

Groaning, I made my way into the house. Dixie yawned from the couch as I made my way to my room. Such a great guard dog. I shook my head at her.

Jane should be out at the club tonight as she did every Friday, but tonight, she was supposed to bring me back a little bit of that drug she had mentioned. Guilt had been eating at me for asking her to do so, but she was my only option that I knew could get the stuff without alerting the police to it and trusted not to screw with before I could test it.

I shucked off my clothes as I made my way to the en-suite bathroom, turning on the water as hot as I could manage. Maybe some heat would help soothe my tense muscles. I rolled my neck along my shoulders as I stepped into the shower, the steam caressing my chilled skin.

I needed time to think and figure out what the hell was happening. Every time I turned around, another wrench was added to my already stress-filled life. All I wanted was a drink and a good fuck. But I can't seem to manage to do that, either.

The warmth sank into me as the water sluiced down my body, washing my day down the drain. Finishing up, I grabbed the faucet handles when I heard Dixie barking downstairs. What the hell was she barking at?

Quickly drying off, I wrapped the towel around my waist, threw my glasses on my face, and grabbed my pistol from the nightstand. I went through a lot of screening for this damned thing and my gut was right. It would come in handy at some point.

Dixie's barking became quiet as I quietly descended the stairs. The smell of something burning tickled my sinuses. What the fuck? Was something on fire? Alarm rang through me. There was no way something was on fire. I just got home.

Fuck. Fuck. Fuck.

I rounded the corner where I could hear Dixie playing. Anger coursed through me as I thumbed the switch off my safety. Who the hell dared to enter my home?

Cautiously, I stopped outside the door to my office, a woman's voice emanating from inside. What the hell?

I let out a calming breath and quickly stepped around the doorway, my gun pointed into the room. My breath caught in my throat at the sight in front of me.

Dixie was prancing around a dark-haired woman that was bent over in the middle of the room, her perfectly rounded ass in the air. The woman who had been haunting my every dream and every nightmare for the past twenty years was in my office, playing with my dog, her voice low and husky. Her laughter echoed around me and sank into my skin, turning me on in ways I didn't think were possible.

I missed her fiercely.

Lowering my weapon, I cleared my throat. "Lily," I stated, my voice strained. Here was the woman I had been pining after for years and I couldn't talk. My throat clogged with emotion that I didn't want to come to the surface.

As she turned toward my voice, her eyes widened as she caught sight of me. Her sudden intake of breath as she apprised herself of my body reminded me that I was only in a towel. A blush grew up my neck as I felt blood rush to my cock at her slow perusal of me, tenting the towel around my waist.

"Jon..." She licked her full lips, her gaze grew heavy the longer she stared. "It's been a long time."

The longer she stared, the harder my cock got and Gods, if I didn't want to bury myself in her. Or have her on her knees, those luscious, pouty lips of hers wrapped around my cock as she gagged on my length. The thought had my throat dry out, and if there was a way for more blood to rush south, it did, my member heavy with need.

Coughing, I pointed to the couch with my gun. "Make yourself comfortable. I'll be back." I turned to leave, already halfway out the door.

"No need to cover yourself up now. I have no problem with your nakedness," she stated, her voice thick with lust.

With my hand on the doorframe, I angled myself back to her. "No, but if I don't, I am likely to fuck you on the nearest surface and I would rather keep my head attached to my body. But thanks, anyway."

"Such a shame." I heard her mutter as I walked back up the stairs, my mind racing with questions.

Why the hell was she here?

Hell, how did she get here?

How did she even know where I lived?

Grabbing a t-shirt and a pair of jeans, I quickly got dressed as I rushed into the bathroom to brush my teeth, threw in a fresh pair of contacts, and combed out my hair. It might not be super long, but it was still long enough to snarl, and Gods, I hated it when that happened. I don't know how women dealt with it.

Butterflies danced through me, making me sick with nerves as I neared my office again. I may not know why she was here, but I wouldn't make a fool of myself thinking she came to see me. Not after she ran from me just last week. With Wendy missing, most likely in Neverland, and Michael and Lily both suddenly popping back up, something was wrong and I needed answers.

As I rounded the corner, my already racing heart pounded harder against my ribcage at the sight before me. Lily was curled up on my couch, her breathing low as Dixie was lying by her feet.

If this was punishment for something I did in a past life, just kill me now. I couldn't handle watching the woman I was still in love with sleep in my office with my dog. It was a tease of the life I could have had, and my heart was ready to burst from seeing a glimpse of what could have been.

Grabbing a blanket off the back of the chair Jane usually slept in, I laid it on top of Lily and went behind my desk to do some paperwork.

Did she seriously come here to sleep? Doubtful. Lily had a reason for everything she did, so if she was asleep, she wasn't sleeping in Neverland, which meant something was wrong.

Letting myself get lost in my patients' records, I didn't realize how much time had passed until Lily stirred from her position on the couch.

Watching her lithe body stretch along the sofa, I got a nice view of her body and what it would look like underneath me.

Fucking hell.

I took my time closing my computer and got up from my chair. Rounding my desk, I leaned against its edge while waiting for her to get her bearings. Her hair was slightly mussed from lying down and she had a nice flush on her cheeks. Thoughts of recreating that flush on my own sent another rush of blood straight to my cock.

Rolling my eyes to the ceiling, I counted down from ten. At this rate, I would have the worst set of blue balls known to man.

"What are you thinking about there, pretty boy?" Her voice, low and husky from sleep, had my cock twitching within the restraints of my jeans.

"Nothing you want to know."

She shrugged her shoulders and got up from the couch, sauntering towards me, her hips swaying in a rhythm that made me want to grip them and never let go. "We need to talk."

"You think? Why are you in my house? Hell, how do you even know where I live?"

"Magic," she said as she waved her fingers in front of my face, because that was an excellent explanation for everything.

"Right." My ire rose like an itch under my skin that needed to be scratched as she was half-assing her answers. It made me want to claw my eyes out. "Well, as much as I would love to have a little reunion with you, my niece should be arriving home soon and I would much rather not have to explain who you are and where you came from. So please, tell me what you want." I wish she would tell me she came because she finally got rid of that damned husband of hers, but I knew better.

She tensed up and backed away from me, her eyes skittering all over the room but never landing on me. "That's why I am here, Jon. Oh, Gods, you're going to hate me. I never should have fallen asleep."

My eyebrow quirked up in question as trepidation sank through my middle.

"Jane isn't coming home. Tinkerbelle has her. That's why I am here. I can't rescue her by myself and no one from the tribe will help me," she spit out as fast as she could. Her breathing picked up as her nails started raking marks up and down her arms.

Horror filled me as what Lily just said registered.

"What do you mean Tinkerbelle has Jane? She was supposed to be at the club."

"She goes to Tinkerbelle's club. Magique. I only know Captain Barrington is a player in all this, which was why Tink took her. Jane is his plaything." Again, she was rambling and making no sense.

"Barrington? Who the fuck is that?"

"Captain Barrington is Hook's son. The old pirate is dead. But still, I have no clue about how Jane ended up with him."

"So why did you come to me? Why didn't you go to Wendy or Michael? They're both there in Neverland?"

She screwed her face, perplexed. "They're in Neverland? Since when?"

"Michael has been there since Pan was last here for twenty-some years and Wendy was taken last week. We don't know how she got there. The only clue was Toodles' marble bag. Jane was convinced there were drugs all over it, but when I got to the house, it was all washed away in the storm," I explained.

"What do you mean Michael has been there for twenty years?"

"The last time Pan was in London, he took Michael to Neverland. They never returned."

"Michael can't be alive then. Pan and the Lost Boys died," she stated as if it was fact.

I shook my head. "You're wrong." Pan might be dead, which led to many problems, but I just saw my brother.

"No. I can prove it to you."

I scoffed. "How?"

The smell of burning fabric filled the air as blue and orange sparkles swirled in circles around Lily's hands, forming a hole in my office and burning the edges of my rug. Dixie was barking at the chaos as my ears popped from the shift in pressure.

What the hell? Lily has magic? Could she have always done this? The questions spun in my mind as she gripped my hand and pulled me into the hole she created. Faraway, I heard her call for Dixie, but I wasn't paying attention.

In front of me stood a field with a burned-out stump in the middle.

I would recognize the area anywhere.

It was where most of my nightmares started.

My heart sank to my feet as I realized two things.

I was back in Neverland, and Jane was in greater danger than I could have ever imagined.

Chapter Thirty

JANE

Tick… Tock… Tick… Tock…

Why the hell wouldn't this nightmare go away?

Tick… Tock… Tick—

Shadow…

Fear spliced through me as I jolted awake. My heart raced in my chest and I opened my eyes to darkness. There was nothing to see but the inky blackness all around me. The air was damp and cool, and the drip of water somewhere off in the distance was the only thing telling me I was awake.

I ran my hands down my body and found I was still in my dress from last night, albeit torn, but still wearable. My feet were numb from the cool dampness surrounding me, making me shiver as I wrapped my arms around myself to create a little warmth.

Where the fuck was I? Wracking my brain, I tried to remember what happened before I woke up, but nothing came. Just the constant drip of water. There was no light, no other sounds besides my breathing.

Listening to the drip of water, I relaxed as little as I could. Slowly, the aches and pains that riddled my body took over my mind. My ankle throbbed and my neck was sore, which were two of the most annoying hurts. I felt like I had been run over by a truck repeatedly.

I tried to trudge up my memories from last night, but all I could remember was going to the club and then everything went blank. The lapse in memory left me bereft and disconcerted. My memory was almost always spot on. I needed to know and remember everything that was happening with my patients. So, not being able to remember what happened to me and how I ended up here filled me with a dread so profound it felt like a vast chasm had opened inside me. And I was on the edge, ready to fall.

I had been sex trafficked. There was no other explanation.

Tick...

Fear made itself a home deep in my chest as my eyes slowly adjusted to the pitch-black surrounding me. Searching the darkness from where I sat on the cold floor, I tried to find anything that would give me a clue to where I was.

Slowly, I turned my aching body and the sight of a slight glow on the wayside of the wall lit a small ball of hope inside my chest. That wasn't just there. I could have sworn I wouldn't have missed it. I cried out in pain as lightning shot through my leg as I got my feet under me.

Fuck! Oh, Gods, that hurt!

Putting my hands in front of me, I slowly limped toward the glow. My body screamed at me to lie back down, but the adrenaline in my system told me to move and figure out a plan of action.

As I approached the light, I realized it was a flame held in a sconce that reflected shallowly off the white, marble-like wall behind it. Forcing myself to keep moving forward, I felt a cold metal brush my arm before

I ran face first into metal bars, the clanging echoed around me as pain ricocheted through my face.

Tock...

Gods, I was in trouble.

I gripped the iron bars and laid my head against them, the pain slowly fading. Was I in a cage? No, more like a cell. Panic fluttered in my chest, but I swallowed it down quickly. Panicking was the last thing I should have been doing. I needed to figure out where I was and why I was here. My hands roved up and down the bars. The rough edges against the overly smooth wall were an interesting contrast, especially with nothing but touch guiding my way.

The glow was still far away, but the more I focused on it, the more detail I could see around and behind it.

The walls were white with gold streaking through them like marble, but the coloring was off, and the sheer amount needed to make a wall of it was impossible. There was no way that was it. Looking further to the left, a wooden door with more iron filigree appeared. What was up with all the iron? After further inspection, more light came from under the door.

Tick...

"Hello?" I called out, praying that someone would answer. "Hello?" I yelled out again. There was no way I was in a dungeon without a guard. That wasn't how it worked in the movies, anyway. But then again, maybe they were overly confident in themselves and didn't think I'd be able to escape.

"Are you trying to get yourself killed, girl?" a voice rasped. A shock of adrenaline and fear washed through me as I jumped in surprise.

"Who are you?" I asked, my voice trembled slightly as fear took over my body.

"Why do you care? We are all here to die anyway. I would prefer not to anytime soon." The voice sounded like they had smoked way too many cigarettes in their life and had permanently developed a hoarse throat. Which also made it hard to discern if it was a man or woman I was talking to. Their attitude sucked ass, though, so I guess it didn't really matter.

"Well, I like to know who I am talking to."

"Doesn't matter. Besides, the less anyone knows anything about you here, the better the outcome for you."

Tock...

James had said the phrase to me once a few months ago, and his deep voice rang through my mind.

"Where I come from, names are powerful. The less anyone knows about you, the better. Even your name could mean great harm will come to you if you give it out to the wrong person," he stated as he wrapped his arms around me tightly.

It sounds like something my mom would tell me about faeries when I was a kid. But I wasn't going to bring that up. That would make me look insane, and I don't want to lose the one man that brought me a little bit of sanity.

"So, my name could put me in danger, where yours brings me power? How does that make sense?" I asked, genuinely confused.

"Yes." A dark grin came over his face as he looked down at me. "Tell anyone my name here or anywhere you may end up, and it should grant you some protection. But hopefully, you won't ever have to use it."

I shook myself of the memory and brought myself back to the present. The movement had my brain sloshing from one side of my skull to the other like I was still drunk. An impending headache had started to form between my eyes as I continued to stare at the flame on the other side of the wall.

Tick...

Stroking up and down the whole cell door until I felt the spot where the lock would be, I felt around, gauging what I already knew. I was going to need a key. But to get the key, I would need a guard to come in, and apparently, there were no guards around to hear me.

I groaned, turning away from the flame and headed back to where I had started or hoped I was going toward it. I couldn't tell in the darkness before me, my eyes trying to adjust to the lack of light again.

I should have used the wall and moved around the cell, well, what I am assuming is a cell, to get back to where I started. Sometimes, my brain worked slower than it should, but at the moment, I wasn't going to give myself shit over it. This wasn't a situation I ever thought I would have been in.

Escape. That's what I needed to do. Not only did I not know where I was, I was injured and not in any condition to run away, which made the situation even more dire.

Tock...

The room spun as I turned around to see what was in the cell. The little light that came off the torch did not help me see. The tiny bit of light that did make it into my cell made out the outline of the bed of straw I was lying on when I awoke, which now made sense as to why my body ached so much. Well, I had been kidnapped. I shouldn't expect great accommodations.

Sighing, I went back to my "bed" and laid down. Thinking was going to be my only friend because, apparently, the other prisoners were unhelpful. But then again, they may have already tried to escape and found out that there was no point. But no, I wasn't going to think like that. I need to believe I could get out of here.

TICK...

"Where is she? Where is this girl you say woke the Island?" A female voice rang out down the hall.

"Your Majesty, the Island talked to her. I swear I heard it right before I came to you," a male answered.

Island talking? To whom? That makes no sense. Islands can't talk. Gods, nothing makes sense anymore and my brain was about to implode. From the throbbing or the ridiculous conversations, I have yet to decide.

"Neverland hasn't spoken in over twenty years. I doubt it started talking to this girl," the singsong voice came again.

Neverland?

No!

TOCK...

I couldn't be...

"I'm telling you, there's something different about her."

"Are you questioning me, Goran?"

"Never, Your Majesty! I just want you to keep an open mind. Please."

That man, whoever he was, must be gutsy. I don't know if I could ever talk to the Queen of England the way he was talking to his. Hell, I don't even know who *she* was, but she sounded important. But also, this woman is the one keeping me hostage.

TICK! TOCK!

The footsteps stopped and light filled my cell, blinding me. I cried out at the sudden glare, my eyes welled with burning tears. "She doesn't look like much," the woman said. I don't know why, but it pissed me off.

I blinked rapidly to adjust to the bright light and a wave of awe overtook me. I didn't want to stare at it, but it was hard not to. It was just a ball of light, floating in the middle of the cell, illuminating everything. It chased away the shadows and brought to light all the stuff I couldn't see and I wish I never had.

The floor was stained red with blood. And a lot of it. There were chains with shackles attached to the wall to the left of the cell door. To the right, there was water trickling down the wall. I don't know if it was purposeful or not, but I wouldn't trust anything that ran down the walls of this place. The amount of bacteria would probably kill a person. It was interesting, though, that the walls themselves were smooth and white marble. White that was stained pink and speckled with darker notes of red. The floors, though, were made of brick. They weren't just stained with blood. They were saturated with it. Who knew how many people had died in this room alone?

TICK! TOCK!

My eyes finally landed on the woman at the door and my jaw dropped.

No. It wasn't possible. The first thing that caught my attention were the huge, gossamer wings springing from her back.

Faery wings.

Fae.

Neverland.

Shaking my head, I continued my perusal of her. My eyes caught on her strawberry blonde hair piled high upon her head and a small crown pinned around the small bun. Her green eyes were huge and lined with dark lashes. Her complexion was flawless, and, if circumstances were different, I'd ask for her secrets, but it was probably just being Fae.

Terror seized me as recognition hit me like a freight train.

It was the woman from the club.

Her black dress ended on the floor, hiding her feet, but when she moved, you could see they were bare.

The man behind her had horns coming from his forehead and curved upward. His dark hair was long and fell past his shoulders. He wore what looked to be leather, but that couldn't be it. The Fae were supposed to be harmonious with nature, and killing animals was against their nature. But this is all stuff my mother had told me when I was a child, so I could be remembering wrong. His eyes were black as coal, with what looked like black veins moving out and around his face to his neck and body. His aura was menacing and fear clenched around my body.

Fight or flight was taking over as I looked at the pair. If that was the woman's guard and enforcer, she had to be worse. Her light appearance was a mask to hide the demon inside.

"Who are you, child?" the woman spoke, her singsong voice lilting gently across the cell.

TICK... TOCK...

Wincing at the ticking in my head, I looked at the pair staring at me. There were questions in their eyes, but there was no way I was answering their questions. Taking the ticking as warning bells that were always ringing in my head, they were now full-blown sirens.

This happened right before Alis was taken, I thought to myself. Maybe the ticking was trying to help me?

"Keeping quiet isn't going to help you, dear. You should probably tell me who you are so I can best help you." The woman's high-pitched voice grated on my nerves.

"Is your voice always that annoying?" I asked. Stupid of me to antagonize my captor, but damn her voice.

Laughter comes from her throat, which might have sounded like the tinkling of bells if its sinisterness didn't seep through.

TICK! TOCK!

Wincing again, I knew I was in trouble. "Silly girl." Her voice was much lower, almost a normal tone. Still a little high pitched, but being Fae, I guess that can't be helped. "You really need to learn about who are dealing with. Maybe I'll let my guards have their fun with you for a bit. Teach you a lesson in manners. When I come back, I want answers."

The smile on the face of the man behind her turned dark as trepidation and fear wound through my middle.

TICK!! TOCK!!

TICK!! TOCK!!

The light in the middle of the room went out and the sound of the door creaked loudly as it opened, my heart pounding a mile a minute. She wasn't serious? Fear slid down my spine as I backed up as far as possible before hitting the wall. The silhouette of the man was illuminated as he entered the cell, slamming the door behind him.

"Oh, come now, little mouse, don't be scurrying away now. We are going to be having a lot of fun." His deep voice reverberated around me.

No...No...No...

I searched the darkness that I was now blind in and tears formed in my eyes, blurring my already nonexistent vision. No. I wasn't going to cry. I couldn't. I was stronger than that.

"All you had to do was answer Her Majesty's questions. But here we are. I am almost glad you didn't. I'm not going to lie, little mouse, I have been watching you sleep and have been fantasizing about your taste."

TICK!! TOCK!!

The ticking rang like gongs in my head and I slid down the wall to the floor. How was I going to fight and save myself with this debilitating noise in my head?

Hands wrapped around my upper arms and pulled me against his chest. He smelled of dirt with the coppery undertone of blood. It made me want to gag. Leaning down, he buried his face in my neck and took a deep breath.

"Ah..." he whispered in my ear. "You smell of coconuts and the salty winds of the sea. You smell of the Island. I think my queen may be mistaken. You might just be the key. But as you won't tell us who you are, I'll just take my time getting the answers out of you."

TICK!! TOCK!!

TICK!! TOCK!!

Terror took over. No! Clenching my teeth, I grabbed onto the Fae's shirt, which was not made of leather, it just looked like it, and brought my knee up as hard and fast as I could.

The man let me go in a shout of pain, bending over to clutch himself. I ignored the lightning shooting up my leg as I ran to the cell door. Grabbing the iron bars, I pushed and pulled against the door, but it wasn't moving. It couldn't be locked! He was on the inside.

Dark chuckling came from behind me as I was pressed against the cell bars, my body pinned. The Fae's hard cock on my ass had bile rising in my throat. Oh Gods, this just turned him on. "Oh, my dear mouse. Now we get to have real fun. There is no escape. Magic may be gone from Neverland, but some of us can still make use of what's left. And you just pissed me off." Pulling away from me, he grabbed my hair and pulled me back across the cell. My screams echoed off the walls, my scalp on fire as I reached up and dug my nails into the man's grip. Trying to reach the man's arm and get him to let go was almost useless. I used up my one chance of surprise. He wasn't going to let me get that chance again.

TICK!! TOCK!!

TICK!! TOCK!!

The ringing in my head was beginning to annoy me as much as it was helping. I know I'm in danger. The man threw me against the far wall, the chains rattling as I landed on them and pain ricocheting through my body. Terror seized me once again as I realized what his intention was.

Trying to get up, adrenaline made me move. I was able to make it to my knees before the man kicked me in the ribs, white-hot pain exploding inside. I rolled over toward the wall, clutching my stomach. Once again, the man grabbed my hair and pulled me up. My body was nothing but scorching pain and I had a feeling it was going to get worse.

TICK!! TOCK!!

"Now, you will start talking, little girl. I have all night and many ways to take information from you. We can do this the easy way or the hard way," he said as he locked the cuffs around my wrists.

I glared at the man who was taking pleasure in torturing me. What kind of sick bastard does that?

"Tell anyone my name here, or anywhere you may end up, and it should grant you some sort of protection..."

This was going to be a long shot. Surely, they don't know who he is here. This was Neverland. He couldn't possibly know of this place.

"James. James Barrington... Do you know him?" My voice shook with fear as I asked the question.

A dark rumble of laughter came from the man's chest as he lowered himself to my face. His breath, smelling of sex and blood, made me gag. "Why yes, yes, I do. Why do you care?" He flicked the charm that was on my necklace.

"He stated that I would have protection if I gave his name. That no one would touch me."

"Did he now? That's entertaining, seeing as he's the reason you are here."

My stomach dropped into my feet as everything from the past year between him and me flew through my mind.

He brought me here.

My heart shattered as I watched the man smile, his teeth stained yellow, and I came to the realization that I was going to die because the man I loved betrayed me.

Chapter Thirty-One

JON

A rock sat in my gut at the carnage that was before me.

Lily had let me wander the area of Deadman's Tree. The vast tree house I had called my second home was nothing more than a blackened stump standing sentinel over the haunted grounds. The area surrounding the tree was eerily quiet, as if Neverland itself was carrying the ghosts of the lives lost in the fire.

"How long ago did this happen?" The question came out unbidden as a slow anger built in me. I didn't know how this happened, but it was quite evident that it was intentional. The loss of my childhood friends in such a violent and vicious way had the need for revenge, building a low fire in my veins, the need for violence burning slowly.

I had done a good job in London, keeping my violent tendencies buried deep within. It was also one of the reasons I became a surgeon. Cutting into people helped to keep those urges at bay. Now they were back, pressing against my psyche. The need to punch something or someone had my hands clenching into fists and the muscles in my jaw ticking in rhythm to my raging pulse.

Lily quietly walked up next to me, her hand gently brushing mine. Her soothing presence sent a wave of calm through my senses. Ire rose in its wake that she still had this effect on me.

Turning my head, I quirked an eyebrow in her direction, waiting for her answer.

"Around twenty-four years ago, if I remember correctly." Her voice was low, as if she didn't want to disturb the spirits still residing here.

Twenty-four years ago.

That was around the same time Pan brought Michael back for one last rendezvous. One that never ended for him. Guilt ate at me that I hadn't come back to find him, but without Pan or pixie dust, there was no way here.

Or I thought there wasn't.

I glanced over to the dark-haired beauty that brought me over with magic. Magic that she didn't have when we were kids. I had more questions than answers.

"Well, this doesn't prove to me that my brother is dead, " I said, irritated that she was keeping secrets.

Lily shook her head as if what I was saying was just me being in denial. "He was here when it happened. No one survived." She waved her arm toward the stump.

"And I am telling you, you're wrong."

Her look of bewilderment slightly amused me, lifting my spirits a little higher than the depression they had sunk into.

"What more proof do you need? They all died! Including Pan!" She waved her arms, clearly exasperated, as she stomped back into the trees, my dog sitting patiently for us.

Why the hell did she bring Dixie here? How does she even know her name?

So many questions swirled through me as I ran to catch her. "I know Michael's alive," I stated as I stopped before her.

"How?!"

"Because I just saw him a few days ago!"

Taken aback, Lily peered up at me, her eyes searching mine for the lie she was looking for. "That can't be. That means that..." Her sentence trailed off as she gazed back at the stump.

I let her contemplate whatever it was that had her mind turning. It would be a lot to find out that someone you thought was dead was not.

Her eyes were wild as she glanced back at me. "We need to get back to camp. I have to talk to the Elders. This changes everything."

Trepidation crawled down my spine, settling into my lower back at what she wanted me to do. "Whatever you say, princess." As she marched past, I bowed and waved my hand before me, Dixie happily trotting alongside her. I gritted my teeth and forced myself to follow.

I forgot how humid it was in Neverland. A sheen of sweat immediately coated my skin and I looked down at what I was wearing. The jeans were going to make my life hell. If I would have known she was bringing me back, I would have worn something different.

The recent rain had softened the ground beneath my shoes, and I was reminded of when we used to frolic through these woods with no worries except when we ran into the man-eaters or pirates.

Moving through the brush and branches, Lily was ten steps ahead of me. Dixie pranced beside her, sniffing everything, never glancing back to see if I kept up with them. Grunting, more to myself than anything, I quickly made up the distance between us and pulled her to stop, my grip firm on her arm. "Whoa, whoa, whoa. We are going to talk. I am not going to just follow you everywhere on this fucking island just because you say so."

"What the hell are you talking about?" Lily spat at me.

No, I wasn't doing this again. I wasn't letting her take charge like when we were kids. That almost got me killed and I have a death threat on my head this go around.

"We need a plan. We need to be a team. And I refuse to follow you and trust that I will not be led into a trap."

"You seriously think I would do that to you?" she exclaimed, exasperation written across her face.

"You lied to me the first time around. Why would this time be any different?" I growled out. It's not only my life on the line this time, but Jane's and Jules' as well. Wendy and Michael can fend for themselves. They know the island and its tricks. The girls did not, and they were my main priority.

She stood at her full height, a few inches shy of mine, her chest brushing against mine. "I didn't have to find you and tell you where the girls were. I could have just left it as is and let you wonder for the rest of your days. I didn't have to do anything about it. I am doing *you* a favor. You should well remember that before spouting off that I am trying to get you killed. I offered you a way to save them, and here you are, treating me like I'm the threat. I am not the enemy."

My dick twitched at the sight of her anger staining her cheeks pink. Her breasts heaved against my chest as she fumed and my breath caught in my throat. Goddammit. No. She wasn't mine to have anymore.

I gently pushed her away to get my bearings and took in what she said. She was right. I was treating her as the enemy. To my heart and sanity, she was, but she didn't need to know that. The girls deserved better than me being an arrogant asshole to the one person I know trying to help them.

Letting out a silent breath, I looked Lily up and down. "You're right. But I am not keen on barreling through the Never Wood without knowing where we are going and why."

Lily stepped forward, back into my chest, as if she couldn't physically pry herself from me. Her big, brown eyes gazed into mine as she leaned forward, her lips almost touching mine. "I guess you'll have to learn to trust me," she said, barely grazing my lips with hers as she stepped back and started walking back up a path only she knew.

Blood rushed to my now straining cock, wanting the one thing it had desired for so many years, and all I could do was stare after her perfectly round, swaying ass.

"Are you coming, or are you just going to stand there?" I heard her yell in the distance. Fuck, I needed to get my ass in gear and my head on straight. I have no idea where I am on this island anymore, let alone where she was going.

We were going to need to work on our communication skills. At the rate we were at, I was going to end up dead in no time. I may have grown up here, but times have changed. And as much I want to boast about staying in shape, Neverland was its own challenge.

Running through the brush, trying to make sure nothing hit my face, I caught up to her in no time, sweat rolling down my face and neck. "I don't remember it being so hot."

"Yeah, since Pan 'disappeared,'" she moved her fingers to make air quotes, and I wondered how long she had been bouncing between the realms, "and the Fae took over. The island has changed a lot. It being hotter is the least of your worries."

"What do you mean?" I asked, curious to know what had changed since I had last been here. I also wanted to know what I would face in the coming days as I tried to find my niece.

"The man-eaters, or cannibals, whatever, aren't as prevalent now as they were before. The pirates are now in league with the Fae and are full of tricks, willing to do anything to gain the advantage. They care little about anyone but themselves."

My gut twisted at what she said. This wasn't the Neverland of our childhoods. It was a totally different world and I was dreading to know it.

As the brush started to thin out, I could see the opening where Lily led us. Apprehension sank into my bones at what we were up against. Not paying attention to what Lily was doing, I ran right into the back of her, the both of us falling into the clearing. Catching myself before I landed fully on top of her, I looked down and smirked. My member, still hard from our earlier encounter, was now pressed into her ass, and I heard her gasp from underneath me. Gods, have I wanted to hear that noise again. Too bad it was going to end too soon.

Lily looked back at me, her dark hair falling over her shoulder, anger simmering in her eyes. "If you would kindly remove your cock from my ass and get off me so we can get the camp, that would be great," she whispered, her teeth bared.

A smirk crossed my lips as I bent my head low to her ear. "Just a fair warning. If we get anywhere private where I get to have your ass, I will be taking it. I have dreamed of it for far too long for you to tease me about it." I thrust lightly into her ass before I lifted myself off her. I couldn't tell you if the small gasp that left her lips was because of my promise or my actions, but either way, my cock twitched at the sound. I couldn't wait until I got her to myself.

Scrambling away from me, the sudden change from her earlier behavior set my teeth on edge. What? She could be the one to provoke, but couldn't handle it returned? Maybe she just wanted to see if she could still get a response out of me after all these years. Maybe she was regretting her decisions from so long ago.

Gritting my teeth at the thought, I admired the gorgeous, pink flush to her cheeks. Her chest was rising and falling rapidly as if out of breath. I felt a smirk form on my face as I watched her get as flustered as I was, and it was returned with a scowl and the rolling of her eyes. If they could have rolled back any further, she would have seen her brain. "If you want to roll your eyes, I could help with that," I told her as she started to walk away. Probably for the best. The way I felt right now, I would just take her up against the nearest surface and say fuck it.

"My Gods, is the only thing you think of is sex?" she berated me.

Only when it comes to you.

I scowled at that thought. Probably something I should keep to myself, but I wasn't very good at keeping secrets away from Lily. Never had been. "You're right. We have bigger things to worry about." I caught up to her and whispered in her ear as we walked side by side to the camp up ahead. "But I will make good on my promise. Don't you worry your head about that, princess."

I moved away from her as she whipped her head towards me, shock written across her face. "We won't be doing much once we get to the encampment. And I'm still married. You'd best remember that."

"Says the woman who almost kissed me a few minutes ago. Maybe you should remember that for yourself because, at the moment, I don't give a fuck," I stated as I marched ahead of her.

I could feel Lily rushing behind me to catch up. Ire struck through me at her words. No, I didn't forget she was married. In fact, the last time I was here, I was banished and told never to talk to her again.

The moon shone brightly as if mocking the way my heart was shattering.

The Chieftain glared down at me like I was worth less than the dirt beneath his feet. "You are henceforth forbidden to see or talk to my daughter, Jon Darling." His deep voice boomed across the camp. "She has been spoken for and will be wed in two weeks' time. She does not need you filling her head with promises and lies."

"But I love h—"

"You are too young to know what love is. Now leave us before I decide to make an example of you."

Apparently, saving their precious princess wasn't enough for them to let me love her. No, the Fae was allowed to, though. A sneer crossed my face as I thought back upon the day I found out who her betrothed was.

"Are they still sore about me wanting to take you away from Drake? Not that it worked, obviously."

"You're lucky you're even alive. I overheard what they were going to do to you if you stayed. Trust me, I am risking a lot by bringing you back here. Not only are the girls' lives in danger, but so is yours."

The silence stretched taut between us. Clenching my jaw from saying anything else that might land me in even more trouble, I started moving my feet to get a move on. No use in standing here staring at each other when the girls were Gods knew where with Gods knew who. If anyone on the island knew who Jane was, she was as good as dead if we didn't find her and fast.

Chapter Thirty-Two

JAMES

I had ordered everyone off the ship as soon as we made land. The need to be alone in my torment had every bit of sanity leaving my body.

My arms were braced against the side of the bar, staring into the glass of whiskey I had poured as if I could scry Jane's location on the island.

No.

I knew where she was. I had been there before. My own blood stained the floors of that dungeon, along with countless other victims that Tink had wrought her anger upon.

No!

My arms swept and swiped everything across the room as anguish and fury fought for dominance in my chest. My vision blurred as I sank to the ground, leaning against the wall of the ship. Pain shot through my body as my blood stained the floor.

She needed to be okay. Tink wouldn't do anything to her if she knew what was best for her. If that cunt even thought about touching a hair on Jane, I would wring her head from her body with my bare hands as her blood cooled where she stood.

My only consolation was that I had put that enchantment on her when I last saw her.

Sitting in the broken glass, my thoughts returned to my conversation with Drake. Tink was pissed off that Wendy was here, blaming me for her presence, which it wasn't. It was the damned missing lost boy's.

What made him so desperate that he was willing to face death for bringing Wendy here in the first place? What was Tinkerbelle doing to the people in her palace besides fucking them?

Then, there was the problem of figuring out who killed two of my best men. How did anyone even know they were there? Was it Chip? Or was it someone else?

Questions spun through my mind. The alcohol burning through my veins wasn't helping the dizziness that had started to settle in. I needed to see to my wounds that were still seeping blood into my floor, but I couldn't be bothered.

The hollow ache in my chest grew deeper at the realization that I couldn't help Jane without a confrontation with Tink. One that would lead to both of our deaths. This was why I avoided relationships. I never should have started anything with the girl when I found her last year. But she probably wouldn't have ended up faring any better with Arron and Madok than she is right now.

Gods, this was fucking mess.

Slowly, I got to my feet, the sharp pain of glass cutting into my palms added to my mental tally of hurts, as I headed toward the cabin door. I needed to know the reasons for Tink's hatred of Wendy and if there was anything to do besides handing her over in exchange for Jane. Because it had crossed my mind, but I knew Smee would kill me before that happened.

As much as I would like to think I could take him, the man had a dark side that I try to avoid. It made me look like child's play. I don't know what he experienced growing up here, but he thrived in violence, the ragged scars running down his face a testimony to his violent past.

I grumbled as I yanked the door open to the deck and stumbled down the docks. Running my hands through my hair, I made my way through the little shanty town, my ire rising at the happy sound of a flute playing in the tavern as I passed. My world was falling in shambles and my crew was having a party. Fuck them.

Salt sprayed off the waves of the cove, sticking to my skin and burning my open sores. The scent of the night air filled with jasmine once again reminded me of Jane, keeping me slightly sane. Picking up my stride, I found myself in front of Smee's place. The one man I trusted, and this time, I was getting answers.

Raising my fist, I pounded on the door to his house. The holes he had for windows made it easy for me to hear him and Wendy talking inside, clearly ignoring my presence.

"Smee! Open your damned door before I bust it down! We need to talk!" Birds scattered at the booming sound of my voice ricocheting off the trees.

Seconds later, the door opened and Smee's face appeared, crossed in concern. "What happened?" he asked, worry dripping from his voice as he looked behind me toward the cove.

I pushed my way around him as I sank into one of his sofas that he brought over from London. "Tink has my girl and I want answers. Now."

Closing the door behind him, Wendy entered the living area as I glared at the both of them. My anger simmered under my skin, waiting for the perfect moment to burst. This was their fault. If she weren't here, this wouldn't be happening.

"Oh, my Gods! You're bleeding!" she exclaimed as she caught sight of my wounds.

"It's fine," I growled out. I didn't want either of them touching me. This was my burden to bear. My penance for failing Jane.

Wendy sat on the opposite sofa, her legs tucked under her, as Smee stood behind her. The two looked like they had worked out their problems. Good. Now, they could help with mine.

"One of you better start talking. I want to know what the hell happened." I didn't know if I wanted the long or the short version, but the fact that I was being blamed for Wendy's presence and it had Tink pissed off enough to steal what was mine has my already tightly leashed anger lashing out to be released on the two keeping secrets.

"Why don't you start with what the hell happened to you in London? Then we can tell you what you're asking for," Smee stated cautiously. "You said Tink took someone?"

"My girl. She has my girl," I gritted, barely containing my fury at my redirected questions.

"Okay. Do you know why Tink took her?" Smee asked, flopping down on the opposite side of the sofa from Wendy.

My rage was boiling just beneath the surface as I lifted my hand, pointing. "This bitch. Tink took her because of Wendy," I growled, my voice almost unrecognizable.

Wendy and Smee's faces fell, her eyes widening into saucers, reminding me of how Jane sometimes reacts in our conversations. Smee rose, cursing as he grabbed an empty glass off the table and threw it across the room, shattering it.

Why the hell is he pissed? *My* girl is the one in danger. They were both here perfectly fine. His outburst ticked my fury up a notch, my fists clenched and my jaw strewn shut as I watched my first mate lose his shit.

"Who was she?" Wendy asked, her voice still soft.

"It doesn't matter who she is! She is mine! And I want her back!" I snapped, my anger getting the better of me.

Smee turned quickly toward me, his finger pointing at my face. "Don't talk to her that way! She was asking a question and your anger is misplaced. Tink is the problem, not us. If you want answers, then leash yourself," he stated between clenched teeth, spittle flying from his mouth as he reined in his own anger.

My chest heaved as I forced myself to breathe through my nose to better calm myself. He was right. Arguing wasn't getting us anywhere. Closing my eyes, I focused my mind on Jane and her bright, green eyes shining with delight as we danced, or her body flushed as she came on my tongue. I would have her back soon. I would not fail her.

Smee sat back down in the place he vacated as he glanced at Wendy. "Tell him, Michael. People are getting hurt because of us." Wendy nudged him.

"I'll start at the beginning," Smee, Michael, whatever his name is, started. "Wendy, our brother Jon, and I were brought here by Peter Pan. Our parents were always working and we were left to fend for ourselves most days, so they never noticed when we went missing. Anyway, having been brought here, we quickly learned the way of the island. What faeries we could trust and which ones to watch out for. Tinkerbelle used to be our friend when we were kids. We would all play and have a great time. She would look out for us and warn us of incoming danger from man-eaters or the pirates coming to play tricks on us. Well, over the years, we grew up, and because Peter spent a lot of time in London with us, about as much time as we spent here, he also started growing up. Pan brought me back one day without Wendy or Jon, and the night we arrived, the tree house was on fire. I can still smell the Lost Boys burning—their screams for help as they died. Pan flew me to Skull Rock, saying he would save them. He never came back. None of the boys made it out alive."

I carefully kept my face blank as the picture Smee painted made my stomach roll. What the fuck happened here before I arrived?

"That doesn't explain Tinkerbelle's hatred of Wendy. She's the reason for all of this," I stated flatly.

Wendy uncurled herself from her perch, leaning her elbows on her knees with her hands clasped before her and her head bowed as she took a deep breath. "Tinkerbelle believes I stole Peter from her. She has hated me since we started coming here. I never did anything to her. She has just been a jealous bitch over the fact that Peter loved me and not her."

The air in the room became stagnant as Wendy's words hung between us. Tinkerbelle started all of this over a boy?

"So, what happened?" I asked, the second half of their story missing.

"Peter never came back with Michael like he was supposed to. But as we could not get to Neverland without Peter, we had to tell our parents that he had gone to a friend's house. They sent out missing person fliers and all the works, searching for him when they realized he had never reached his supposed destination. Only Jon and I knew where he was and knew there was no finding him." Wendy stopped, sucking in a breath. "After so long, he was pronounced legally dead. I found out I was pregnant shortly after and worked my ass off to be able to keep the baby. Tinkerbelle showed up one night, looking for Peter's shadow, and ransacked my apartment. She was adamant that I had stolen it and came up empty-handed. Afterward, she threatened that it would be our lives if we ever showed our faces back in Neverland." She blew out a breath as she leaned back against the cushions. "I had no real intentions of returning as much as I wanted to find Peter. I knew my and my child's lives weren't worth the effort. Michael had repeatedly stated it here, and now I know it to be true. Peter is most likely dead." A small tear fell down her face as her eyes turned distant.

Tinkerbelle was looking for a shadow? How the hell do you lose your shadow? Wendy had a child? More questions burned through me, but I could tell that Wendy was done talking. I got enough out of the two to know that Tinkerbelle started all of this because she was a jealous cunt.

And I was no closer to finding Jane.

Chapter Thirty-Three

MICHAEL

Hefting the bag of goods over my shoulder, the trek through the wood had become a hot, sticky, and plain old pain in the dick to traverse. If it weren't for seeing the man I had been craving for weeks, I wouldn't be making this trip.

I needed to talk to Asher. Not only about what had happened with Wendy, but also about everything happening in this hellhole since the last time I saw him. He was the only one I truly trusted with my life—no one else.

I loved Wendy, but we had been separated for so long and I couldn't get over the fact that she nor Jon ever came to find me. Even though, logically, I knew they couldn't, the little boy inside me still felt betrayed by it, which I knew I needed to work on and put behind me.

As I drew near The Sanctuary, the sounds of children playing were like music to my ears. I loved to see the kids playing and enjoying the island for what it was supposed to be. An escape from your everyday life. If only they knew what we adults protected them from, would they ever know the true danger they lived in.

One of the few pixies left in The Hollow chased the kids, their tinkling bells floating and mingling in the children's laughter as they fought over what looked like a ball. But seeing as they all had games, they made up as they played, who knew what was going on?

Shaking my head as joy filled my being, I went up to Asher's offices. He was always doing something, making lists of needed items from London or the castle to keep things running smoothly, cooking for the kids, or plain old working on the treehouse.

"Michael?" Asher asked before I made it through the door, his voice sending pinpricks along my skin.

"Yes..." I chuckled as I came into his office, tossing the bag of goods he had requested. The cost to Barrington, losing his girl for getting these goods, sent a pang of guilt through me. I didn't know the woman who had Barrington under her finger was, but she didn't deserve to be in Tink's bad graces. No one did.

The sound of the bag hitting the floor reverberated around the room, making Asher cock his eyebrow at the weight of it. "You carried that all the way here by yourself?" he asked, concern laced in his voice.

I shrugged my shoulders as I made myself comfortable on the sofa he had. "It wasn't anything to bring it. Besides, I didn't want anyone else here when I came to see you," I admitted. I needed to see Asher alone and I couldn't do that if I had a crewman up my ass. I would much prefer it to be the man across from me.

Sighing, Asher got up from his seat to stand before me. His body surrounded me as he leaned down, his hand lightly squeezing my throat. Blood rushed to my aching cock as he brushed his lips against mine. "Thank you." One more little squeeze had my breath catching, my lips begging for more than a taste, as he stood back up, grabbing the bag off the floor.

The bastard knew how to push my buttons and Godsdammit if he didn't have me panting in the first ten minutes of being here. Sometimes I loathed him.

I shifted my position to relieve some of the achiness in my loins. I spread my arms across the back of the sofa, my legs spread to give me some breathing room. Asher turned back to me, his gaze lingering over my form, a small smile touching his lips. Cocky motherfucker.

Clearing his throat, he went back to setting everything on the desk, meticulously checking everything off his list.

"We need to talk," I said. Guilt had been eating at me since the last time I had seen him, bleeding out from Wendy. He had refused to let me help him and I needed to clear the air. As much as I wanted to fuck this man, I needed to know we were on the same page.

Grunting, Asher turned back to me. "Yes. Why don't we start with your sister being here, shall we?" Anger crossed his features as he crossed his arms, closing himself off from me. He was still pissed.

Gritting my teeth, I stood up. I wasn't going to be able to have this conversation sitting still. "She was found in the hold of the Krok the last time we made port. A man who claimed he was a 'lost boy,'" I shook my head at the notion. Fucking bastard thought he could call himself one of Pan's friends when he had never met him had ire twisting in my gut. "He had thought he could buy his freedom from Tink with Wendy. When you happened upon her in the woods, I was coming to find her. She was supposed to return to London, but has somehow talked herself into staying here a bit longer."

"Of course she did. Why didn't you tell me this before I went to see Barrington? It would have shed a lot of light on what we came upon in Skull Rock," he said, irritation ringing in his tone.

"I was hoping to avoid the whole thing and pretend she never returned in the first place. But Tink somehow got wind of the fact that she was here and now Barrington's girl from London is paying the price." Wringing my hands, I paced a hole into Asher's office floor.

Surprise lifted his features as he came to stop my pacing. "What are you talking about?"

"Barrington had a girl he would see in London when we made port. Tink thinks he purposely went in search of Wendy and is punishing him by taking the one thing he cared about."

"That may be because I have the one other thing he cares about," Asher sighed.

"What?"

Heaving a sigh, Asher motioned toward the door. As we moved through the halls, the light of the suns illuminated all the little crevices. I had a feeling of home wrap around me, even through the worry that had wormed its way through my body.

As I stood on the threshold of the main playroom, Asher moved around me toward a small, wraith-like child. Her head was bald and her blue eyes sunk in as she sat in the middle of the floor, playing with a couple of dolls. "Alis. I would like for you to meet a friend of your uncle."

Uncle? Barrington had a niece? The thought punched a hole in my gut that he had kept her a secret from me. But I couldn't blame him. I had kept my own, and now look where we were.

The little girl wobbled on her feet as she stopped before me. I bent a knee to reach her height and took in her sickly state. Extending a hand, she strongly grasped mine, surprise flitting through me. For being so small and thin, she was strong.

"I'm Alis," she stated matter-of-factly as she shook my hand.

"Michael," I answered in kind.

"Hmm… my nurse at home had an Uncle Michael. She said he died before she was born, though." Her voice was light and airy, almost Fae-like. It was eerie. It didn't fit with the Fae here in Neverland, but something about her wasn't entirely natural, either.

Curiosity coursed through me. "What was your nurse's name?" I asked to keep the conversation going.

"Miss Jane. She told me stories of this place. She said her mom told her about adventures that could be had in Neverland. I am so happy she wasn't wrong."

Shock sank into me. Jane. Wendy's daughter. Barrington's nurse. Surely, he wasn't fucking my niece. That would create much more hell for us than we could have ever anticipated.

Glancing up to Asher, I cleared my throat and brought my attention back to the little girl. "I am glad you are enjoying your time here, Miss Alis." Standing, I motioned to him that I was leaving the room, my mind racing in ten different directions.

Making my way back to the office, I took time to breathe. It could just be a coincidence, and Barrington just knew Jane, and he wasn't fucking her. Gods, I could only pray that that was the case. But with the shit storm that had been raining here the past week, I doubted it.

Asher came up behind me, the warmth of his body easing into mine. "What was that about?" he asked, rubbing the backs of my arms.

"Jane. I am quite sure that Alis' nurse is, in fact, my niece."

The man's hands tensed as he took in what I said. "Niece? Which one of your siblings reproduced?"

Sighing, I rubbed my hands over my face, turning around. I needed to see Asher's face when I told him what I suspected. "Wendy."

Shock radiated from his face as he connected the same dots that I did. "Fuck."

Nodding, I moved across the room and settled back onto the couch. "If Jane is, indeed, the girl that Barrington is a mess over, this whole island is screwed."

"Tink can't find out who she is."

Shaking my head, I placed my face in my palms. This was a fucking mess.

Coming over, Asher sat down beside me, his arm wrapped around my shoulders as we both thought about the fucking hell that was about to be wrought on the island.

Slowly, coming out of my depressed stupor, my body was tingling as Asher traced patterns up and down my body. The sensation was both calming and exhilarating. My breath started to catch as his hand made its way south, unbuttoning my pants to rub my semi-hard staff. His hands wrapped around the sensitive flesh, pulling a moan out of me.

Gods, I have wanted this for so long.

Settling more comfortably against him, his chest to my back with his cock pressed hard against my lower back, he kept up the pace on my now raging hard cock. "Gods, you don't understand how good that feels," I moaned as Asher's other hand came up to my chin, tilting it to look up at him.

"I think I do." His voice deepened by desire as he took my mouth. His tongue clashed with mine as he sucked the air from my lungs, grasping, teasing, and pulling on my length with vigor.

Moaning, I started to thrust into his palm, the need to chase my orgasm at the forefront of my mind as he kept up with his pace, precum leaking down into his hand.

"Fuuuckk... Yes," I groaned as he moved his hand to my throat, squeezing, my pulse jumping in his hand to the time of my thrusting.

He ran his hand down my cock, cupping my balls as he made his way further south to play with my ass, anticipation singing through me.

His finger, sticky with my precum, pressed against my hole, slowly working its way in, pumping in time to me thrusting the empty air. "Are you going to be my good boy and come for me?" he whispered as I moaned in response.

Yes... yes...

The tinkling of bells flurrying into the room had both of us groaning in pain. Godsdammit. Just one time, I would love for Meera not to interrupt us.

"Wait... Meera... slow down..." Asher said as he slowly pumped a second finger in my ass, making me feel full, apparently not caring that she was interrupting us this time.

A low moan escaped me as he kept up the teasing pressure, turning me on more than I had before. If I wasn't sure before if I was into people-watching, this little display proved I was.

"Shhh... you're being distracting." Asher clenched his fingers against my throat as he pushed harder inside me.

Fuuuckkk.

Keeping myself as quiet as possible, I let the sensations of Asher's finger fucking my ass wash over me as he tightened his hold on my throat, my hips moving of their own accord now as he kept up his conversation with Meera.

"Don't come yet," he growled and continued his punishing pace, still conversing with the pixie.

A high-pitched moan escaped me and Meera flew out of the room.

Asher's eyes lit back to mine, both anger and desire mixed on his face. Leaning down, he whispered a kiss against my lips. "Now, you may come, pretty boy." He sighed into my ear as he let go of my throat, and I let myself go.

The room spun the higher my orgasm took me. Spurts of cum stained the front of my pants as Asher pulled his fingers from my ass. Gods, that was the hottest thing I had done with him in a long time.

Coming down from my high, I slowly moved off the man that had seen to my needs. Asher got up and started to pace the room.

"So, what was that about with Meera?" I asked, clearing my throat.

A sigh left his lips as he stopped pacing to look at me. "Tink didn't take one girl. She took two," he said, licking his lips.

"Okay..." I said tentatively. He was hiding something from me.

"The island is awake. It's calling to one of them."

Shock sank into me. Neverland only talked to those who belonged to it.

Pan...

Then Wendy...

Jane.

Chapter Thirty-Four

LILY

As we entered the camp's protective circle, a low voice came behind us. "Tiger Lily."

There was no going around this. I knew we would be confronted as soon as we crossed that circle. My presence was more than welcome. I am one of the ones that laid the circle. But Jon, as much as I loved him, I couldn't hide his aura from the circle and those that guarded our borders.

Squaring my shoulders, I turned and faced the man who had addressed me. "Yes, Hunter?"

"You know the rules. We cannot let outsiders in the encampment, especially ones who were banished," he snarled, his eyes sending daggers toward the man behind me.

Jon moved to come between me and the guard, which made my heart pick up at his protectiveness, but right now was not the time. I put my hand up to stop him as he looked at me expectantly, not saying a word. He knew the gravity of the situation. How he left and how the Elders treated him before would make this situation sticky.

"Yes, well, you aren't my father and I have my reasons for bringing him here. He isn't going to harm any of us, so piss off."

"Your father has already been alerted to the newcomer. It would be best if you didn't keep him waiting."

Fuck. I forgot the guards and their connection to the Elders. They would make my life harder than it needed to be. I should have left Jon at Deadman's Tree and foregone all this mess, but I didn't know if the Fae had picked up the children yet and I didn't want Jon to know what I was a part of.

Gods, this day was going to hell in a handbasket.

"Well then, we shouldn't keep them waiting, shall we?" I turned and motioned for Jon to follow.

The walk to the Elders' tent was silent and taut with tension. I knew Jon was burning with questions, but I had no answers.

The Elders' tent was on the other side of the encampment, which meant we would have to make our way through the village. I had hoped to avoid all that by just running to my tent and grabbing the few things I needed before leaving quickly and quietly, but Hunter had to ruin that plan.

"Not much has changed," Jon stated quietly, almost in a whisper.

"No, it hasn't," I sighed, letting go of the anger that had slowly built inside me since our fall in the woods. I couldn't be mad at him. I was more upset with myself for not considering the consequences of bringing him here.

As we passed, the villagers' stares and snippets of whispers grated against my skin. The feeling of someone brushing my hand startled me. Glancing down at my fingers, I saw Jon had caught up and was looking at me from the corner of his eye. Was he trying to comfort me? A blush crawled up my neck as the memory of him pressed against me and his threat had my thighs clenching.

And here I was, trying to get him someplace alone to talk. Great idea. We were alone in the woods, but I could never trust a sprite not to be listening in to our conversation. Clearing my throat, I glanced back up ahead and caught sight of the Elders' tent.

Get your head on straight. We can't be going in there thinking about the man's dick, even if it was a great one.

"Are you going to tell me what to expect before we get there, or are you letting me go in blind?" he asked, again, quietly from my side.

I just shook my head and kept silent. I didn't even know what we were in for, so how could I tell him what to expect?

As we approached the tent flap, I could see his eyebrows raise from the corner of my eye. The guard outside nodded and opened the doorway, letting us through. The inside was dark, but the immediate relief from the humidity was welcoming. There were lanterns set up around the outside edge of the tent. A little way in front of the lanterns were logs made for sitting. Everything was in a circle. An unlit fire pit was at the center of the tepee and would remain that way unless a ceremony was performed.

Three people were standing at the far side of the structure, away from the entrance. The one I recognized immediately was my father. As the Chieftain, he would be here for the meeting and to reprimand me for bringing Jon here in the first place. Most likely saying that I am breaking my vows to the wretched Fae husband of mine, which I am not. I have not done a damned thing that Drake himself hasn't done.

Waiting for the Elders to turn so I knew who I was talking to today, I brushed my hand against Jon's, needing the grounding he gave me. He was the only one who could comfort me. My greatest regret was giving that up and didn't wait for him. His hand turned over, entwining his fingers with mine, reassuring me. Quickly dropping his hand after the quick squeeze, I cleared my throat, hoping the Elders would hurry up with whatever they were whispering about across the way that was more important than my punishment for bringing Jon here.

My father snapped his head towards me, disappointment written across his face. "Have we forgotten our manners, Tiger Lily?" His gravelly voice carried across the tent.

"No, I just had something caught in my throat. Please take your time. We're just going to sit over here." I pointed toward a log and started to make my way over when a force of wind encircled me and lifted me up and towards the people in the back of the tent.

Jon shouted out in surprise, panic, or fear, I couldn't tell, over the wind whipping around me and blasting my eardrums. I was placed down gently before the woman, our Shaman, who used her magic to relocate me. It was a power show to remind Jon and me who we were talking to.

An older man, Misu, located to the right of the Shaman, looked me up and down, looking for something I could only guess. "You are weak. Why?" he asked, his voice soft, almost soothing.

Holding back the grumble that wanted to pass my lips, I sighed. "I have been tasked with a lot lately and haven't been taking care of myself properly," I answered. It was the truth, but only some of it.

"No. Your powers are weakening. Why?" the Shaman asked. She was always so much more perceptive than I would like her to be. But, then again, when you commune with spirit, you would know things and hiding anything is nearly impossible.

"I found out some things and need to figure them out," I answered. I don't know if they knew about the joining of my and Drake's souls when we got married. But right now wasn't the time or place to ask. I don't need Jon going off and ruining our chances of rescuing Jane. We needed to get out as quietly as possible.

The Shaman's eyes rolled into the back of her head, the whites the only thing I could see, sending a shiver down my spine. The feeling of power rushed over me, embracing me tightly. My skin felt taut and goosebumps appeared across my bare flesh as her power pricked and prodded at me, as if she was trying to get under my skin and into my very being. My hair whipped around my face as the wind from the Shaman's powers picked up and I tried harder to get inside me, to feel out my problems and needs. I had learned a long time ago to block out what the Shaman did, but my mental capacity was at a breaking point. The fissures were slowly cracking along the walls I had created in my mind to keep everyone out and to keep myself safe. If she kept this up, my dam would break and there would be no going back. Everyone would know what I have been up to these years. My stalking of Jon, the use of the men in our tribe to do Tink's bidding, the bond that was between me and Drake, and his abusive ways.

No. I couldn't let her in. I couldn't let them know about what was going on. The tribe would stand against Tink and her minions. She would kill them with a flick of her wrist and then me for disobeying her.

No. I couldn't do that. I needed to live, keep this barrier strong, keep everyone safe, and keep Jon safe.

Jon.

I pried my eyes and glanced toward the man that had once held my heart. No, he still did. He never stopped. There was no going around it. I am in this mess because of my love for the man and I couldn't let the tribe or anyone else on the island get to him. He was my only reason for being.

His eyes were wide with fear and I could see his lips moving. Straining my ears, I could barely hear him over the tornado of power whipping around me. "LILY!" His voice held the terror his eyes conveyed. Fear for me.

"STOP!" I screamed at the top of my lungs. "Just stop! I'll tell you." Defeat entered my being. At least this way, I wouldn't have her in my head and would get to keep some of my secrets.

The wind came to a slow standstill. Raising my arms, I untangled my hair from around my face to look at the Elders and a sigh escaped from my lips.

"Lily!" Relief flooded Jon's voice as he ran up and wrapped his arms around me, keeping me whole. I brought my arms around him and sank into his embrace, letting him mend a couple of breaks in my being that only he could.

The tension in the room ratcheted higher as the Elders stared on at our embrace. I didn't care. I needed this. I needed to know he was there, that everything would be okay. That we were going to find a way out of this mess. A mess I created, but still.

Letting out a breath, I stepped back and looked up at Jon, his brown eyes lined with concern as his hands came up to hold my face. "Are you good?" he asked softly, almost a whisper.

Nodding my head, I turned and faced the group that was glaring at us at this point. And truthfully, I didn't blame them. I had been keeping a great many secrets, and this was just the tip of the iceberg.

"Tiger Lily. It seems you have been lying to us as to your whereabouts. Explain." My father glowered at me, flicking a quick glance at Jon before returning his dower expression to me.

"I haven't. Per Tinkerbelle's request, I have been going to London to pick up the goods she wants ferried between our worlds. I just happened to find out my husband was also using my well of magic." I let the statement stand. I wanted to see the Elders' reactions to the news that Drake had access to my magic.

Anger passed over my father's face and through the whole group of Elders. The only one left unsurprised was the Shaman. And she was the first to speak. "Yes, that happens when you marry a Fae. They become part of you, and you of them. You should be able to access his powers as well. Drake cannot hide his magic from you as you were bonded at the soul level. It is a surprise that he had kept it a secret for so long."

Fury swept through the crowd before me as embarrassment flushed my cheeks. According to the spirit woman, I should have known what I was getting into when I wed the Fae at sixteen.

"I believe you have forgotten that I didn't have a choice. It was do it or Jon died," I growled out between clenched teeth. I wasn't going to be belittled for something they decided for me.

"Wait," I heard Jon say beside me. "You were forced to marry that bastard?" His anger was apparent as red blotched his cheeks. His eyes hardened, daring me to recant what I had just said.

"Yes..." I glanced at him under my lashes, waiting for my father to say otherwise to save his reputation. Looking at my father, though, his features showed nothing but remorse and anger. He was usually better at hiding his emotions, but having it out in the open that the Shaman held back vital information from the tribe peeled his mask away, leaving him raw and unfiltered.

"Why is the Darling here?" one of the Elderly women in the room asked, changing the subject.

"Drake used my magic to transport a woman here, not realizing I was close by when he did it. That was when I learned of his ability to use me. I tracked down the woman's residence and found she was living with Jon.

He was frantic about finding her and I offered a way to retrieve her. Why she is here and what Drake was doing with her in the first place, has yet to be found out," I answered as matter-of-factly as possible. No, I wasn't going to disclose that the woman was another Darling. That would put the whole council into an uproar.

"Who is this woman to you?" a man asked, directing the question to Jon. "She cannot be your lover, as we have seen how you and Tiger Lily are still quite close."

"A coworker," was all he said.

Good boy, was all I could think. A slight smirk lifted at the corner of my mouth at that thought. Maybe I should try praising him later for that.

"Is there something amusing to you?" asked my father. Of course, he wouldn't miss the twitch of my lips.

"No. I want this done so we can be on our merry way and get Jon and his friend back to London, where they belong."

My father just stared at me. I kept eye contact with him, not wanting to be the first to break it. I wasn't going to bow under the pressure anymore. They now know that the Fae have been using me and our beloved Shaman knew about it the whole time. They had bigger fish to fry than worry about what I was doing with a Darling.

"The Darlings are not supposed to be here. You had better be careful where you step and with whom you trust. Apparently, even our own cannot be trusted, " my father said as I watched the Shaman woman shirk slightly at the remark.

She wasn't going to have a good time coming to her. I knew what my father's wrath could bring. I was his daughter and had been on the receiving end more times than I could count. I could only imagine what hell he was going to bring to the woman who stated I had no choice in my future. Maybe if we all had known what would happen if I was married to a Fae, we wouldn't be in the predicament that we were in now. That made me wonder if the Shaman was in Tinkerbelle's pocket or just out for her own agenda.

"Also, I have come across some information that you would probably like to know," I stated before I could be dismissed.

My father's eyebrows rose. I didn't often come across information that he didn't already know. "And what might that be?"

"Michael Darling survived the fire of Deadman's Tree. He has been on this island for the last twenty years."

Surprise filtered across the Elders' faces as murmurs filled the tent.

"There were survivors? How do you know this?" the Shaman asked, bewilderment written across her face. Not much can be hidden from a spirit woman, but this showed that she didn't know everything and wasn't as powerful as she believed herself to be.

Jon stepped forward. "Because he visits London every so often. I don't know how he gets back and forth, but I can guarantee he is alive."

"So, the Pan may still be alive as well?" one of the Elders asked.

I shrugged. It was speculation, but it was one that brought hope.

"Very well, go find your Darling's friend. Then we can discuss this new information." My father dismissed us, and I quickly grabbed Jon's hand and bolted for my tent.

Chapter Thirty-Five

LILY

I will never know how Tinkerbelle had tamed the elemental sprites to do her bidding. They used to be malevolent tricksters, but now they are nothing more than messengers for *Her Majesty*.

The little fire sprite flew out of our nightly bonfire to tell me Tinkerbelle wanted to meet. My stomach dropped when it popped up before me, praying Jon didn't see the interaction. I didn't want to explain my ties to Tinkerbelle if I didn't have to.

Leaving Jon at camp was probably going to piss him off if he found me gone, but I couldn't risk bringing him to the castle with me. I knew he would be angry with me for leaving him behind while I went into the lion's den where his niece was, but he was safer with my tribe than barging into unknown territory looking for the girl.

Tinkerbelle's castle was on the side of one of the few mountains on the island. There weren't many, but enough that if you didn't know which one you were looking for, you'd end up hiking the wrong one.

One of the benefits of portal magic was I could pop on over when needed, saving me the hassle of the climb. The Fae were lovely enough to put in stairs, but I am in a hurry. And if Tink does have the Darling girl, then being invited in was a much better idea than sneaking.

Looking up at the wood doors inlaid with veins of gold magic, I hesitated, instantly chilled by the snow flurries falling around me. I don't know where this snow had come from, as it hasn't snowed in years, but it can fuck right the fuck off. I was not made for cold. I don't think this island was at all and would die quickly if the weather had kept up the way it was.

Shaking my body to get rid of the chill, I sighed. I needed to get my head on straight. No thoughts about the man I had brought here. No thoughts about the Jane girl. Nothing but business. After this meeting, I can go wandering for a minute.

Inhaling deeply, I grabbed the cold knocker, the frigid metal stinging my hand as I let it fall, banging against the door and echoing all around. The sound scared some crows out of their nests a little way away. Why they stayed around the castle, I would never know.

The doors slid open, almost of their own accord, as no one on the other side would greet me, not that I wanted someone to be. The Fae were once tricksters that were fun to mess around with. Now, I avoided them at all costs. The monsters they have become were worse than any nightmare I could imagine. This is also why I am concerned about the Darling girl and going to find Jon in the first place.

As much as I was still in love with him until I could be rid of Drake, there was no way to be with him without repercussions. Another reason I left him behind. I couldn't risk both of our lives when his being here could easily be misconstrued. He was here to retrieve his niece, nothing more. Even though both of us desired the other with a fierceness that had never dimmed, it was to be my perpetual punishment to watch the man I loved be with other women until the day I died. Sadly, I was still married to one of the Fae and could not break out of that oath without one of us dying. But being bound to each other meant the other was likely to die as well. It was a difficult situation, and I wasn't sure how I would get out alive. That was a problem to solve on a different day.

Today, I needed to find out what Tinkerbelle wanted from me.

Walking into the foyer, I felt like the walls were closing on me. The walls were white quartz with gold veins of magic running through them. They looked like marble, but quartz was made for magic and held it much better than the other rock.

The magic in the gold veins in the wall called out to those who had magic, pulling you towards the Heart of Neverland. Being as depleted as I was, it was hard to ignore the pull. The little magic I had left screamed at me to be released.

Ignoring the pull in my body to go right at the main corridor, I took a left, straight to the throne room where I knew Tink would be awaiting me. I haven't the faintest idea why she always put on this big show of being in there. We all knew her powers and didn't want to test them no matter where she was. The throne room was more to feed her ego and give the impression of insignificance to those who entered. After being brought here so many times, the grandeur wore off and was just another stale room that held nothing but lies and blood.

The walls in the throne room were more smoky quartz than white, but the gold veins of magic were just as strong. The magic pulsed and the golden veins moved of their own accord within them. It was as mesmerizing as it was eerie.

The floors were made of black marble, as it was throughout the palace, but the magic that coursed through the walls avoided the floors as if it didn't like being walked on. It was always a thing of curiosity to me. One would think the floors would be the first place the magic would flow, as it could touch most of the magical beings through their feet, but alas, the magic must have a problem with being below other people.

Tinkerbelle's throne was empty at the far end of the room. Curious. She was always here waiting for me, especially when she had called for me. Trepidation sank into me as I perused the room.

Slowly making my way up to the empty seat, I looked about the room, taking in different things I had never noticed before. Things I would have noticed if not for fear of looking up from the floor when in Her Majesty's presence.

The ceilings were made of glass or maybe transparent crystal. The snow outside melted as it hit the still-warm panes, making rivulets. My eyes observed the water trailing down to the ends and falling off the ledges.

My thoughts wandered back to Jon. Was he doing alright with everyone at the camp? When we were kids, we played for days and had little problems. But that was before we grew up. That was before he professed his love for me and begged my parents to give him a chance. Since then, everything has changed. Not only did we grow up, but my feelings never subsided. And apparently, neither did his. He still loved me, whether he wanted to admit it or not. Even though I was married to Drake, my parents still did not approve of his being here, especially with me.

They knew of my late-night comings and goings to London. They knew why I was gone when I was supposed to be in bed. But there was little they could do about it. I was now a grown woman, and what I did in my spare time was of no concern to them. At least, that's what I kept reminding them. I have also told them multiple times that nothing will happen between me and Jon while he was here, but I am not sure I can keep that promise.

Just his presence made my body heat and my core clench. I know I haven't been fucked in a long time, but that was my own doing. Drake was more than willing to do the job. I just refused to let him put his hands on me. Just the thought was like dousing myself in cold water.

I shook my head, ridding myself of my thoughts, and brought myself back to the present. I took my eyes off the ceiling and studied the empty throne. I had never seen it without Tinkerbelle sitting in it, so I was never able to just study the chair in its entirety.

The chair's body was made of glass, and its legs were shaped like the claws of a crocodile—an ode to the Guardian who once watched over Neverland. This was interesting, seeing as Tink and Krok rarely got along.

The rest of the throne almost looked like a winged back chair, but the arms did not attach to the back. That must be for Tink's wings to slip through and to sit more comfortably. I had always wondered how that worked and seeing it now made much sense. The back of the throne had etchings that shone through the front, looking to be a map of Neverland. But I wasn't close enough to see for sure. I didn't want to get too close to the chair, as my luck would have it. She'd see me and then behead me for looking.

Stepping away from the chair of power, I scoffed to myself. I went behind it and looked out the window that overlooked the gardens. Most of the faeries had moved indoors to avoid the cold. I couldn't blame them. Neverland wasn't made for the cold.

Listening to the ice pellets lightly hit the windowpanes, I let my forehead rest against the cold, trying to figure out where Tink might be. She was never late, and now I was getting worried. I should be rejoicing that she wasn't here, but the longer I waited, the more my stomach twisted into knots.

The pull of magic toward The Heart was getting stronger and the need to visit the sacred space was getting harder to ignore. My magic pulsing beneath my skin felt like its own entity trying to escape my body. I wish it would. Too bad it was just as trapped as I was.

I concentrated on the cold on my face and let out my breath to calm myself, fogging the window. The difference in temperatures was something I could focus on that was outside myself, and the pull lessened slightly at the distraction.

A knock resounded through the room, jolting me from my half-assed meditation. Quickly moving away from the window and back to the center of the room, where I was supposed to be, fear clawed at my throat that I had been caught. Not that I had done anything wrong, but standing behind the throne was not a thing to be done. Tinkerbelle never lets anyone stand behind her, let alone me, whether she was here or not.

Kneeling in front of the throne, I waited. The knocking continued. What the hell? Where was that sound coming from? Turning my head, I glanced behind me to see if anyone wanted to enter the throne room, but no one was there.

The knocking was getting louder, echoing all around the crystal walls, ringing through my ears. I clamped my hands over them, hoping it would help to dampen the noise. It didn't. After another set of deafening knocks, I noticed the veins in the walls glowed brighter when the knocking sounded.

Terror was slowly making itself a home inside my chest as I waited for the next round of knocks. The doors blew open behind me and Tinkerbelle blew into the room. Her magic bowled me over until I was pressed hard up against the wall, the gold veins of magic dimming as they reached out to me.

What for? I could not say. I was not someone of power.

Tinkerbelle stomped her way to the throne, anger pulsing off her frame in waves as she settled onto the seat I had just studied, her wings splayed out behind her. She clasped her hands around the ones at the ends of the chair arms as if she needed to hold someone's hand.

The look of maliciousness on her face sent the terror that had already wormed through me into a full-blown panic. The glint of evil and malice in her gaze made me kneel right where I was, praying she would forgive me for whatever wrongs I may have done.

Tinkerbelle glared down her nose at me, disdain dripping from her eyes as if I were the reason for her problems. Maybe I was. She relied on me to get her 'lost boys' from London.

"Stand." Her voice was deeper than usual and vibrated with energy I hadn't heard from her before.

I forced myself to stand away from the wall as her magic lessened. My knees shook with the effort, my heart racing through my chest, fear closing off my throat. I did not dare speak in her presence without her permission. The last time she was this mad, I ended up in the dungeons for a month at the mercy of her guards because I let a child go.

I could only imagine what she would do if she knew I brought a Darling back.

"Tiger Lily, you know you are one of my most trusted friends."
Friends?

"And that I would do quite a lot for you."
Doubtful.

"So it was quite a surprise when I heard that a Darling was back in Neverland. You wouldn't know anything about that, now, would you?" Tinkerbelle's gaze bore into mine, her eyes flashing from blue to silver and back to blue. She was pissed.

I don't know who tipped her off, but they would die when I found out. Right now, I needed to figure out how to get out of this situation without dying myself.

Slowly shaking my head from side to side. Clearing my throat, more to steady it and waste time than anything, I said, "What are you talking about, Your Majesty?" I feigned ignorance, praying to the Gods that she couldn't smell the lie on my breath.

Her eyes flashed back to silver. I was answering incorrectly, but I wasn't sure how to navigate this situation. She was always like a box of dynamite, and you never knew when one of the sticks was burning or how fast before they all went off. "The Darling girl! I felt the Wendy girl's presence as soon as she arrived. How long have you known she was here?"

Wendy? That's who she was talking about? Slight relief slid through me, the tension in my shoulders loosening. She didn't know about Jon and I just found my way out of this mess.

"Wendy? I have been at the camp and going back and forth to London to see Drake. I had no idea that she had come back. How did she arrive here? No pixie dust was left to fly and I certainly did not bring her here..." I trailed off, hoping Tinkerbelle would apprise me of the situation, as Jon hadn't said much about how his sister got here.

"Barrington brought her here," she sneered, her face twisted into one of disgust. "He kidnapped one of my lost boys, killing his guardian, before torturing the boy for information on how to get to me. That's why I brought you here. I want you to find out what they are up to and report it back to me. They are more likely to trust you than one of us faery folk."

Ah, there it was. She needed a spy. Glancing up, her eyes were back to their normal shade of deep blue, her voice higher to its normal range, but the energy around her still vibrated with the fury she was barely restraining.

I had to tread lightly here. I knew there was no way to deny her this request without becoming a suspect of treason, and I hoped to hold out a little longer on that suspicion. But that meant I would also have to betray Jon in the worst of ways.

My heart started breaking at the thought that I wasn't even going to have a chance at mending our relationship, or if I did, I was going to break all the trust to keep myself alive.

"What do I get out of this?" It was bold, but the Fae were always about making deals. I was doing her a favor, so if she did not pay me, she would be in my debt, which was unacceptable.

Tinkerbelle looked down her nose at me. She already knew that bartering for my life was out of the question. She already had that. That's why I was working for her in the first place. No. She would have to give me something that was just as important to me as this exchange of information was to her.

"I will release you of your marriage and bond to the Fae. Drake will no longer be your husband and you will be free to do as you please," she stated with an evil glint in her eye. She knew she had me. That was the one thing I would do anything for.

"My understanding was that bond couldn't be broken without one of us dying. And in turn, the snapping of the bond would most likely kill the other in the process. Hence, the mate bonds among the Fae have been dwindling. No one wants to die because of the other," I stated. I wanted to be sure I wouldn't die at the end of this to get what I wanted.

"There are ways around it. You can be assured that you will live through the snapping of the bond if you do this favor for me. I want all the information you can get about why the Wendy girl is here. Or if she leaves, even better," Tinkerbelle reassured me. All I had to do was get close to Wendy.

A shiver coasted down my spine at the thought that I had to purposely seek out the vagabonds that lived on the southernmost part of the island. I had been avoiding the captain as I couldn't help him transverse the realms anymore. My magic too depleted to do so. And now I knew why.

"So you just want to know why she is here? Is that all?" I asked. I could easily guess why she was here, but I wanted to know precisely what Tinkerbelle was looking for so I could get that information as quickly as possible and get out of my bond.

"Yes. I want to know why the Wendy girl is here and how she got here. I want to know all about her life in London for the past twenty years without her darling Peter Pan. I want to know everything there is to know about this girl so I know how she ticks. I want to know what it is like to be her." Tink's eyes were wide as a crazed gleam had come over her face. It was the most I had ever seen her express in such a long time. Wendy had cracked Tink's usual cool and collected facade, which was fascinating.

Nodding my understanding, I looked back to the floor as if it had become the most interesting thing in the room. I didn't want to ever see her look at me with that look in her eye. I knew it was directed at Wendy, but seeing how unstable she had become was unnerving. "I will do my best," I agreed, my heart sinking at the deal I had just made. I may have the opportunity to get away from Drake, but it will be at the expense of losing my heart and the one I truly love.

I could only pray that I could get away with both.

Chapter Thirty-Six

JON

Lily disappeared at some point in the night. I left the tent to search for her, but was pushed back and told she would be back. She had business to attend to elsewhere. Doubt sank into me, but I let it go. I didn't know what her life was like here anymore, so I couldn't be too judgmental when I had been gone for so long.

I settled myself back into her furs as her scent engulfed me. The sound of wolves howling outside granted a level of comfort I had long since forgotten as I thought over everything that had happened since I had been back. From what I had gathered, Lily had been forced into marriage with the fucking Fae bastard. And not only that, but he had also been bound to her soul and magic, leaving her exhausted and tied to him for the rest of her life.

The thought that she would die before we would ever be allowed to be together had my barely stitched-together heart ready to tear at the seams.

No. Denial rang through me. There had to be a way out of it. I wouldn't let Drake win. She had just burst back into my life and I wouldn't let her go easily this time. We were barely kids when this all played out. Now, we were grown and able to fight for what we desired, and I would die before I let her go again.

But would I? I had so many questions that needed to be answered and Lily was the only one who could answer them. For example, how did she know Jane was my niece? How would she have known where I lived if she hadn't seen me in over twenty years? Why does my dog treat her like a friend? Why did she run from me last week?

More questions than answers swirled through my mind, making me dizzy with the drama that has become Neverland. There was also the matter of no one knowing that my brother had been alive on this island for the past twenty years. Where the hell did he hide? Did he know what happened to Pan? To Wendy? The only way to answer *those* questions was to find him and I didn't even know where to start.

A twinge in my lower back had me turning from side to side, trying to get comfortable on the hard-packed earth. The furs were not doing much to help alleviate the pain. I pulled some furs to the wooden chair Lily had set up in the corner. If I wanted any sleep, I was going to have to get used to the barbaric ways we used to sleep. My childhood body didn't care. My mid-thirties body was screaming at me like it was in a nightmare.

The furs made the chair ten times better than it was as my body slowly relaxed. A shift in the air as the tent flap opened had a waft of warm air enter the tent. I peeked my left eye open to see Lily's silhouette.

"Where did you go?" Her body tensed at the sound of my gruff voice.

Her sigh carried across the room as she shuffled around the small living space. The rustling of clothing being removed was the only sound she made before she straddled my lap, her face pressed against my neck.

My hands snaked around her tight body. A groan rumbled from my chest as blood rushed south and my breath caught in my throat. Good

Gods, she was naked. I don't know what I did in a past life to deserve this, but I was thanking whatever the powers may be that I could experience this.

"We should go to Pirate's Cove to see what Captain Barrington says about all this."

My eyebrow quirked at her redirection of my question. I know I had to trust her to get Jane back, but her dodgy behavior had a rock sitting in my gut.

"Sounds like a good place to start. From what you said, he was the reason she was taken and I want to know why."

Lily snuggled deeper into my lap. "Perfect, we can leave first thing in the morning." Her lips pressed against my pulse, slowly moving up behind my ear and sending shots of fire through my body straight to my aching cock. A groan tumbled from my throat.

A low moan escaped her as she ground down on my member, creating a friction that I was hard-pressed to ignore. Her lips pressed against my Adam's apple, sucking it into her mouth. Her tongue laved at my skin as her hand snaked south, unsnapping my jeans so that she could grip my now raging cock.

I knew we shouldn't be doing this, that this would only end in heartbreak, but I was tired of waiting. Lily was mine in every way but in marriage. As much as I want to break that bond, I don't know if there was a way to, and right now was all we had before we were sucked into the troubles of Neverland.

Grunting, I grabbed her ass, molding the perfect globe in my palm. Gods, I had only dreamed about this for the past twenty years and to be able to hold her had my cock aching.

Picking her up, her legs wrapped around my waist and her pussy ground against my bulge as I moved us toward the bed of furs. A moan

left her lips as she rubbed herself against me, filling me with the need
to hear more.

The furs were soft as we made ourselves comfortable, my lips
tracing patterns along her throat. Lily's breath was shallow as I kissed
my way down her body, her back arching into me, putting her breasts
on perfect display. Pulling one of her nipples into my mouth, I sucked
hard, feeling it pebble under my ministrations. My cock twitched
as her moans of pleasure hit my ears. Playing with her other breast,
plucking at her tightened bud, I slowly moved my way over to suck
on this one as well, nibbling, and sucking, and pulling until she was
writhing in need.

"Jon, please..." Her moans filled the air as she tried to move my
head south.

A dark chuckle rumbled from my chest, vibrating against her
nipple as I pulled long and hard, staring at her flushed cheeks and
heavy-lidded eyes. "This is my time, Lily. I have waited twenty years
for this. You're going to have to wait."

A groan of disappointment escaped her as she slowly relaxed under
my touch. Good. I was going to taste everything before I let her come.

Slowly moving up her body, I tasted every inch of skin, trailing
kisses and sucking on spots that she reacted to, careful not to leave a
mark. I didn't need Drake knowing what we had done, as much as I
would love to mark her body up as mine.

Capturing her lips with mine once more, she sighed into me,
wrapping her arms around my shoulders, pulling my hair, and
scratching at the nape of my neck. "Will you please fuck me already?"
she breathed into me, her tongue tracing my lips.

"Are you so eager to have my cock that you can't wait?" I asked,
pulling her full, lower lip between my teeth.

A hiss fell from her lips as she moved her hand over my abs and into my jeans, squeezing her hand around my engorged shaft. She pulled and rubbed, forcing a groan from my chest. "Yes, I am," she moaned, her hips grinding into mine. "I have watched you fuck so many women that I hate myself. I have needed you since you left, Jon. Please... Just please, fuck me," she admitted. Shock made me lift up to look into her eyes.

"You've been stalking me?" I asked. I felt invaded, but was turned on by the fact that she had watched me, which left me confused.

"How did you think I knew who Jane was and who to look to for help?" Her question begged my critical thinking skills to come to the fore and put away the want to fuck her senseless.

"No." All those times I had smelled her scent on my pillow, all those times I woke up to the bedside messed up. She knew who Jane was. She knew my dog's name. Everything was coming down, crashing around me. The realization that she never had left me alone left me feeling violated.

Standing, I moved to the other side of the tent. I needed space. I needed to think.

"Jon... it is not a big deal..." she started, rising from the floor.

"The fuck it isn't, Lily! You invaded my home! You literally slept next to me! I thought I was going insane!" I pulled at my hair, the fire of strands being torn out of my scalp a welcome sensation to the bottoming out of my heart. "You realize that if you were caught, I would have been the one getting the shit end of the stick, right? Not you?" I paced the floor, my thoughts spiraling out of control.

She was there the whole time. Watching me from the shadows. All those times, I thought someone was there. It was her.

"Jon." Lily's hands softly pulled at mine, forcing me to stop tugging at my scalp, halting my erratic pacing. "I was overly cautious when I visited.

I didn't do it all the time. I couldn't, even if I wanted to. My magic doesn't work like that," she started explaining. "Once a week, I would sit in the bar you frequented. I just needed to see that you were alive. That Drake hadn't done anything to you since I last saw you." Her voice rose with every word she said, her eyes wide with panic and fear.

"Why the fuck would he?! I had no way of seeing you!" I exclaimed, my anger rising, a heated flush creeping up my throat.

"He knew I still loved you," she said quietly. "It was the only way to keep me in line. I would have left him a long time ago if I could have. But since your life was always dangled above my head, I... He's a monster I wish I could be rid of..." she trailed off as she turned to the back of the tent.

I needed air. I needed to breathe.

Shaking, I watched as she hugged herself, trying to pull herself together. I couldn't do this. She stalked me for twenty damned years. She violated my trust. Disgust filled my being as I stalked out of the tent.

Chapter Thirty-Seven

ASHER

The castle's magic felt like the brush of an old lover against my skin, welcoming me home. At one time, that's what I would have called this place. Now, it was a shell of what it used to be—a hollowed-out husk filled with malice and lust.

A little earth sprite interrupted my morning walk of The Sanctuary grounds to tell me that *Her Majesty* requested my presence as soon as possible. Rolling my eyes at the use of her title, I had to contain my excitement as I realized this was the perfect opportunity to find the two girls that Meera stated were here.

Having had to leave Michael without notice left a pang of guilt running through my middle. It couldn't be helped. If I had told him my plan, he would have insisted on going and I couldn't risk Tinkerbelle finding out I had more than one weakness.

No. Whether I was there or not, he was safer there than anywhere else on this island. Did he need my protection? No, most definitely not. Did I like that he was in danger a lot of the time? Also, no. He was mine, and the Fae protected what was theirs.

A shiver ran down my spine as I entered the throne room, apprehension settling at the base as I wondered what Tink could want of me. She never called for my presence unless she needed something of me, and I don't have much left to give.

The sister suns lit the room through the vast, ornate stained-glass windows behind her, giving Tink an ethereal glow. Her strawberry blonde hair fell down her body in waves and a crown of ornate flowers and gold adorned her head. Her pale green dress fell to her bare feet, inviting anyone to look at her body.

Fighting the urge to roll my eyes at her antics, I gave a quick bow and placed my gaze squarely on hers, refusing to look at her mostly nude display. Should I ignore what she was purposely putting out there? Probably not. It was an excellent way to get on her wrong side. Did I want to see her naked body? No. I had seen it so many times, and most of the time, it was not of my own accord that I had to experience it. It left a bad taste in my mouth.

"Asher. I am so glad you could get here within the day. I had hoped you would." Tink's high-pitched voice rang through the atrium. It was the only thing that didn't change when she changed sizes.

When Pan was still alive, Tinkerbelle was a little pixie-like Fae, if pixie is what you would call her. She was the only Fae that could change her size at will. We all put it down to the fact that she was Pan's faerie, so she was her own breed. When Pan died, she was in her human-like form and has remained that way ever since. The only thing she could hide, at will now, are her wings. Sometimes, she had them on display, but most of the time, she had them hidden as if she were ashamed of them. Today, they were hidden.

"I would hate to keep you waiting. What is it that you require of me?" I asked, purposely not using the title she expects of everyone. I refused to accept that she was a queen. More powerful? Yes. Queen? Never.

Irritation flitted across her face, her right eye twitching slightly. The only tell she has. One she has never been able to control. I found it amusing that I could get under her skin so quickly. "I require nothing. Just your opinion on a matter."

My eyebrow cocked at her statement. My opinion mattered little to her, always throwing it to the wayside. My desire to keep with tradition was an old way of thinking and she often reminded me of it.

"I want to celebrate the Autumn Solstice. We haven't done it in so long and I do miss the old traditions we held." She continued. "Do you think the rest of Neverland would like to do the same?"

Surprise flit through me as my thoughts raced back to years ago. Back when we all lived in a semi-peaceful harmony. The Solstice was one of the four times every year that the island got together and celebrated without threatening violence toward the other persons. It was when we all put on our best finery and partied in The Hollow from dawn to dusk for days. We haven't celebrated the life of Neverland since Pan died. What was she up to?

"We haven't celebrated The Solstice in years. Why now?" I asked, both curious and apprehensive at the notion. She never did anything without a reason. Most were lessons. This would be no different.

"I believe you have heard that the Darling woman is back. Wendy..." she spat, disgust rolling off her in waves. Nodding to her, she continued her tirade. "Captain Barrington thought he could bring her here with no repercussions. I have a gift and figured it would be the best way to present it. A way to punish them both and bring faith back to Neverland."

Trepidation slid down my spine as fear for what she had in store formed a knot in my chest. This wasn't good. My thoughts turned to the girls that she had in her dungeon and horror filled my being. She was going to use the girls as punishment.

My only solace was that I had sent Meera ahead to find them. The doors to the dungeons were magicked to change locations, so one never knew where they were. Meera was always able to find them. It was how I got a lot of information about the goings on in Neverland and Tink's plans. But the stakes were just raised and Meera's mission became more urgent. She needed to get those girls out fast.

"So why did you need my opinion?" I asked tentatively, poking at the actual reason she asked me here, bringing my attention to the woman at hand.

"I just wanted to know if you thought it would be a good idea. You are the one here who loves to stick to traditions," she sang-songed.

Her voice grated on my nerves, pricking at places I would rather keep buried.

"Well, that would be a good way to get the island together. The morale ha—"

The doors behind me flew open, the power coming through the other side blowing past me and knocking me to the ground. My body slid across the floor, caught in the torrent of magic, before pain exploded behind my eyes as I was slammed against the wall before I could even harness my magic to combat it.

"Goran..." Tink's voice sing songed along the walls. "What have you in such a tizzy?"

The man's hands were clenched into fists, his jaw tight as he fought for calm. He failed. "The girl... she still won't talk. Short of taking limbs, I am at a loss. She has been abused and tormented in all ways possible, yet all she calls out for is fucking Barrington."

Curiosity flickered across Tink's face as I watched from my spot on the floor, apparently forgotten. "I gave you a toy to play with and you are telling me you can't break her?" Irritation tinted Tink's voice, ratcheting it to a higher pitch than it already was, piercing my ears. Her power lashed out in lightning strikes, flaying my skin like knives. Sharp pain radiated from the cuts left behind, blood staining my clothes.

My gaze wandered around the room, landing on the guard who had implied he couldn't get information out of his prisoner. His fate wasn't any better than mine, being the main line of fire, and his moans of pain echoed around the chamber.

Heaving out a low moan, Tink's sharp gaze landed on me as surprise lit her face. She had forgotten I was in the room. "Asher, please forgive my outburst," she said, her tone even as she waved her hand in my direction. "You know where the infirmary is. Get yourself seen before you leave."

Hot anger coursed through me at her dismissal. She called me here for what appeared to be nothing, inflicted damage to my person, and then waved me off as if I was a bothersome pest. My hatred for the woman sank deeper into my middle, a rock that was becoming more of a burden to handle the longer I had to watch her slowly strangle the island and become an overindulged, petulant cunt.

Pain flared across my body as I stumbled toward the doors. I wouldn't trust her staff to treat a paper cut on me, let alone the damage she inflicted. What stung me the most was that she thought I needed her healers to help me.

I was a healer. I just needed rest.

"Get up, you dim-witted fuck," Tink called to Goran as I got closer to the threshold. "Move the girl t—"

The smell of burning ozone tickled my nose and the sound of electricity zapping the air next to me drowned out whatever she was ordering Goran to do. Irritation skittered along my skin and I couldn't hear what she had planned for the girl.

Only one person on the island could open the portals, so why was Lily coming here?

The opening widened, the sounds of people arguing in the background as a huge man appeared. My surprise was overridden by the sudden need to hit something—specifically a man's face.

My hands were already clenched into fists from the pain ratcheting my body, but now my fingernails were creating bloody moons into my palms to contain my hatred of the man in front of me.

Drake was once my best friend until he decided that working for Tinkerbelle was a better cause than trying to save Neverland.

"Asher," he stated coolly.

Nodding, I cleared my throat. "Drake."

His arched brow showed he was either amused by my state of duress or curious about what happened. At one time, I would have been able to read his expressions. Now? I try to ignore the bastard.

"Do I want to know what is in store for me in there?" he asked under his breath as if I would forewarn him of Tink's temper.

Glaring at the man in front of me, I turned to leave the room as Tink's high-pitched voice rang out. "What the fuck? What is this? A party?"

Drake chuckled and moved into the throne room, brushing past me. A hiss escaped me as pain flared at the contact, reopening the wounds that were trying to heal as fresh blood coursed down my arm.

"Your Majesty, I come to you with some bad news..." I heard Drake proclaim as I left the throne room.

"Can't be any worse than I have already heard."

"I have reason to believe the other Darling is here..."

"WHAT?!" Tink's shrill scream pierced the air and a magic rush brushed against my body as I fled the room.

I needed to find Meera.

My steps were slow and careful as I ignored the agonizing pricks of my slowly healing wounds and took in the scenery of the passing windows. The petals from the Everblooming Starberries were wilted and drying up. It wasn't a good sign when the one plant that had always held fruit was dying. Neverland needed its magic back.

The need to rush back to The Sanctuary and Michael before he left pounded a fierce rhythm through my veins, but Tink made that trip nearly impossible. He'd be long gone before I returned. I would be lucky to find Meera before leaving this prison.

Grumbling to myself, the hall was quiet as I lumbered down the corridor. The smell of old blood permeated my senses, my stomach rolling at the thought of all the violence that had happened in these walls. There was a reason I left.

Turning right at the main hall, my eye caught on a small child's foot peeking out from behind a statue. Curiosity had my brow quirking. No Fae children were supposed to be in the palace. That was my job. I raised them in The Sanctuary to help them grow as their magic grows with them. It was the deal that I had made with Tink to maintain my sanity and peace.

Stopping in front of the statue, I pretended to study it. Then I heard the child's pulse quicken and the sweet smell of fear permeated the air. What the hell? It smelled human.

Kneeling, I ignored the pain shooting down my body as I came down to the same level as the child. The boy was startled, eyes widened in fear, his breathing shallow and fast. A small gasp was the only sound that came from him as I took in his appearance.

He was small and no older than six years of age. Bruises marred his skin. Different shades of yellow to black covered his face and neck. His hair was blonde and matted with dried blood and dirt. He was thin, but I couldn't see his bones. Not yet, anyway. A few more weeks of going through whatever hell he was experiencing here and he'd be dead.

Cold fury for the human child ran through my body, a tremor of violence shaking my frame. Who dared to harm the child? Fuck! Why was he here in the first place? Thoughts swirled through my mind as I took a deep breath, forcing myself to relax my shoulders and calm myself.

I knew what I looked like. I wasn't small and probably looked just like the monsters that abused him in the first place.

"Are you hiding?" I asked, weaving some of my magic into my voice, letting it settle into the boy's psyche to calm him down.

Watching my magic slowly work into the boy, I studied him as he slowly nodded, his body loosening under my spell.

"Did you want help?" I asked, pushing a little more magic into it. I needed him to be relaxed around me if I wanted to help him, and I couldn't do that if he were ready to flee at a moment's notice.

The boy's shoulders relaxed as he took a tentative step closer to me.

"Henry!!" A sharp, shrill voice sounded down the hall. The boy shirked from me and squeezed himself smaller and further back behind the statue. Quickly standing, I made myself appear to the Fae, who was striding down the hall, as if I was studying the statue. I pulled onto my magic, letting the scent of oak and pine, the smell of home, cover the boy's fear. I wasn't leaving him. That wasn't happening.

"Henry! Where the hell is that boy?" The woman hadn't seen me yet, too focused on finding the missing boy.

"Lost something, have you?" I asked the woman coming closer to the statue. If she happened to look behind it, the boy was fucked.

The woman was startled, her long, white hair flowing around her thin body, her wings tinkling as she moved. "Asher! I'm sorry I didn't see you there." Her voice held an air of breathlessness as if she had been running. She stank of sex and violence as fear leeched off her body in waves. What the hell did she have to be afraid of?

"You didn't answer my question," I responded, ignoring that I had no idea how the hell this woman knew me.

"Nothing of importance. He'll be dealt with accordingly when he is found. He has a knack for escaping his room and making a greater punishment for himself. It is of no consequence," she stated, her voice wrought with haughtiness.

My earlier fury for the boy came rushing back. The need to protect him from harm sang through me. The fuck did she think she was going to do to this human? Quirking my eyebrow at her, I pulled my magic from within, engulfing her with it, forcing the spell under her skin to permeate her being. The woman's eyes glazed over as she relaxed, her breathing evened out, and her shoulders slumped.

"Why is a human child here in Neverland?" I asked, digging my magic a little deeper into the woman's psyche. She was already in my clutches, her magic no use against mine.

"They are nothing but toys," her voice light, almost melodic.

Anger flitted through me. "What do you do with these toys?" I gritted out, my fists clenched tight. My knuckles were white and I could feel the blood seeping under my nails from digging into my fleshy palms.

"Play with them. We must train them first. That's why we get them so small."

Rage flashed through me as I gripped the woman's head and twisted. The satisfying crack of her neck felt like heaven in my hands.

She'd live, of course. Her head needed to be taken clean off before she died. When she woke, she probably wouldn't remember this conversation at all. She would be baffled as to what happened. Good. Let her ponder why her neck was snapped.

Turning to the boy, I knelt once more to his level. "Did you want to go someplace safe? Where other kids play?" I asked, holding my bloody hand out so he could see I meant him no harm. It probably wasn't the best idea, but I couldn't let the boy stay here.

The fear in Henry's eyes lessened as he peered around my body at the woman on the ground behind me. I could only pray he didn't watch me 'kill' her. Nodding his head, the boy put his tiny hand in mine. Swiftly lifting him into my arms, I ignored the tiny pricks of my still-healing wounds as I marched to the front of the palace.

Meera would catch up at some point. I could only pray she found the girls in time.

Chapter Thirty-Eight

JANE

Pain blossomed through my body. Nothing didn't hurt. Silent tears fell from my face as memories came to the forefront of my mind.

I knew the Fae were tricksters and monsters, but I never thought it was that bad. It was like he took all his anger and aggression out on me, and I couldn't stop it.

My voice was hoarse from the amount of screaming that came from my throat as the man pounded into me over and over. My body was nothing but holes for the man to use and torture me with as he tried to get information out of me.

Tick...

I never told the bastard my name. The last thing I remembered was the man saying he was coming back with others and I had better be ready to answer their questions.

I don't have any answers for them. I refuse to tell them who I am. Being stubborn is my only friend. Like yes, I could end my torture, but really, would it be any better for me if they knew I was Wendy's daughter? Probably not. If what my mom and uncle had said was true, my head would be rolling before I took my next breath. It was best to keep my identity to myself. A little more pain was better than death, right?

Groaning, my arms shook with the effort to sit up. After a while, the man unchained me, realizing I had no strength left to try to run from him. It was a good ploy on my part, but it wasn't faked. I was indeed exhausted. But I needed him to release me so I could try to find a way out of here.

Using the wall, I slowly stood up, crying out as the cuts on the bottom of my feet screamed in agony.

"You are a stubborn one, aren't you?" A small voice came to me out of the pitch-black of the cell.

I jumped, fear skittering down my spine, my heart racing as I searched the inkiness surrounding me. "Who are you? Where are you?" I said aloud, my head whipped around to try and find the source.

A little light flew in front of my face. "Right here."

Tock...

Screaming as I jerked back from the faery, I hit my head against the wall behind me, pain exploding in my head as stars filled my vision. Moaning, I rubbed the spot, trying to keep my eyes on the ball of light in front of me.

"Who are you? What do you want?"

"I am Meera, and who are you?"

Distrust filled me. "Why do you want to know? Are you another ploy to get my name and get me killed?"

"No. I am genuinely curious. Most don't survive the night with Goren. Most give in or die. You have done neither. It is most curious."

"Well, I am not most people," I groaned as I slid to the floor. I just wanted to sit or lie on something more comfortable than the cold, brick floor.

"That is noticeable. That is why I am here."

I looked over at the little faery floating in the air above me. Curiosity made me want to know more, but every fiber of my being told me to keep quiet. Besides, I had little energy to deal with the little sprite.

"Ugh. Since you aren't being forthcoming, I'll explain why I am here and why you should trust me."

"Good idea," I groaned, my body screaming in agony.

Tick...

"The other prisoners said you were calling out for someone. Not your name, but for a person. A James. Do you have a last name for this James person?"

"Depends. What do I get out of it?" I answered. I wouldn't give away his name freely, even if he did hand me over to these monsters. What I remembered from Mom's stories was that the Fae loved bargains. I just never thought I would end up in a place of faerytales bargaining with a faery.

"Your freedom."

My eyes bugged out of my head. That was too easy. There was no way this little Fae was going against their queen to get a name. And it wasn't even my name. It was my lover's, no, *ex*-lover's name. What could they do with it? Bring him here? He was the reason I was here. He didn't care.

"That doesn't seem like much. What's the catch?" I ask.

"You know, for someone that has never been here, you seem to know a lot about us, Fae. You know not to give out names and not to trust us. But us little Pixie folk cannot lie. So, if I say I will give you your freedom, then I shall. If I say you can trust me, you can. I mean you no harm." Meera's voice was light and airy, but her pleading with me to trust her made it higher pitched and almost hurt my ears.

Tock...

"Still, what's the catch? I want to hear what the catch is for his name."

"There is no catch. You give me the name and I unlock the cell door. What happens afterward is up to you."

"Why do you want to help me? Out of all of us here in this dungeon, why me?" I asked.

The little pixie flew up to my ear as if she didn't trust anyone not to overhear, but then again, all the prisoners probably overheard this whole conversation. "The island has been silent for over twenty years. Since you have arrived, it has awakened. And to see you here when you should be out there is heartbreaking. I believe you may be the person who will heal the island and bring us back to our former glory. But don't tell anyone. That is my own thoughts," she whispered.

Doubt wormed through me. An island talking? What the hell is going on?

When I arrived, one of the first things I remembered was the guard saying the same thing with suspicion in his voice. There was no way an island could talk, let alone be talking to me. And her crazy ass thoughts that I was going save it was going nowhere.

I was going home. Fuck this shit. Mom was right. This place held nothing but nightmares and broken dreams.

At this point, the need to escape this place was essential. Whether I was a savior or not, I wouldn't survive tonight if the guard brought his friends. And all she was asking for was the name of my lover. We didn't harbor any real feelings towards each other, right? We left on very uncertain terms the last time we saw each other in London. The next I knew, he had handed me over to these creatures. He didn't care about me.

"James Barrington. His name is James Barrington." The sudden intake of breath from the little sprite made my head whip in her direction. "Do you know him?"

Tick...

"Yes, I know him. Everyone knows him. Goran is going to be in so much trouble." She laughed, the laughter sounding like little bells tinkling. It must be a faery trait, irritating as it was.

"What do you mean by that?" I whispered, confusion misconstruing my face. The pain shooting through it reminded me it was all bruised to hell.

"You will learn soon enough," Meera answered.

I huffed. Whatever. He didn't mean anything to me anymore. Right? Yeah, that was why my heart was still shattering and I still had a little spark of hope that he didn't do it. "The door?" I asked.

"Ah, yes." She flitted to the door, her light dimming to almost nothing as I watched her climb inside the locking mechanism. Was she seriously that small? Time seemed to slow as she took her time to unlock the door. After what seemed like forever, but was probably only a few minutes, the lock turned with a click and she reappeared, covered in grime and no longer glowing. "Tell no one what happened here. I will be your best friend here, but no one can know. This castle holds a great many secrets and I am trusting you with mine."

Before I could thank her, she was gone.

Tock...

Not wasting any time, I went to the cell door, ignoring the agonizing tremors wracking my frame as I pressed against it, praying the hinges didn't creak. Surprisingly, they didn't. I wasn't going to ponder why they did it with Goran and not me. There was too much to think about and it wasn't that important.

Staggering through the corridor, other prisoners approached the doors, begging to be freed. Most were gaunt, their bones protruding from their skin and their stench unbearable. Some had age-old wounds that were festering with maggots and rot. The training in me was tearing at me to stop and help them, but if I did, I wouldn't be able to help myself.

If the Fae treated their own this way, I could only imagine what they had in store for me. Last night, it looked like peaches compared to this squalor.

As I came to the end of the corridor, a small voice—a woman's—caught my ear, but it wasn't torn and hoarse like the other prisoners.

Creeping toward the back past the stairs, I peered inside the cell. Shock rang through me as I saw Julie sitting on the floor, her head bowed and soft cries hitting my ears.

"Jules..." I whispered, praying she heard me through the thick door.

Her dark hair whipped toward me, her eyes bugging out of her face. Her dress was dirty, but mostly intact. Her makeup ran down her face, her bruising matching mine, but she looked to be in a better state than I was.

"Jane! How—What—Where are we?" she whispered frantically as she approached the door, wincing as she stepped across the blood-soaked brick.

Adrenaline shot through me as I knew I wasn't leaving her behind. But the keys to this fortress were going to be hard as hell to find.

A tinkling of bells shot around me as I watched Meera disappear into the lock. The little sprite shot out, sitting on my shoulder, her one wing bent painfully backward. The door to the cell flew open as Jules crashed into me, sending shock waves of pain flittering through me.

"You will owe me a favor, but I can see that you two came as one," Meera whispered as she tugged on a piece of my hair.

"Jane... are you... what happened?" Jules took me in, her eyes not missing a mark on my body as I did the same to her.

"I'll tell you later. We need to get out of here," I stated as we turned and slowly crept up the stairs, stopping at the wrought iron door. Taking a deep breath, I let it out and opened the door slowly, the hinges squeaking as I did. Wincing, I prayed no one was on the other side.

Tick... Tock...

Letting out a breath I had held in fear, we hurried to the far wall with the windows and looked out. Neverland was more beautiful than I could have ever imagined. Except the creatures that inhabited the place made it a hell in paradise.

Looking out, it looked like the entrance was down and to the right from where we were. Interesting setup. I guess I wouldn't have considered looking for the dungeons' entrance on the second or third floor. I would have assumed they were lower.

Sighing to myself, I made myself move, holding Jules' hand as we crept down the hall. If we wanted out of here, we needed to move fast. The walls were dotted with a fire torch here and there, but it was still hard to make out where we were going. I didn't want to get lost, but the appearance of no other Fae made my stomach uneasy.

Finally, the corridor opened into a stairwell. There had to be another way down. I didn't trust going down the main walkways. That was a sure way to get caught, but seeing as I had no other option, I started trekking our way down, stomach churning with adrenaline and fear.

The stairs ended on another floor, this one with what looked to be a red carpet. But upon closer inspection, it was red moss. It was soft against my feet as I walked down the hall. I heard voices and took a sharp breath as I flattened myself against the wall. A mirror was across from the door and my reflection stared back at me. FUCK!

Tick! Tock!

The door we were passing flew open. The only thing stopping it was our bodies. I moaned lightly against the discomfort as we hid behind the door. My ears perked up as I heard the woman's voice in black from within the room.

"Rabbit, make sure to send the queen my regards. I do miss her terribly."

Rabbit? Queen? What the hell?

Jules and I stared at each other, our breaths mingling in the humid air. Her eyes widened in fear as determination to get her out of this hell hole sank into me. "My mom... she's somewhere on this island. We need to find her," I whispered, fear sinking into me that we may not escape this prison.

"How? Where are we?" she whispered back so faintly I could barely hear her.

"Neverland. We are in Neverland—"

"Will do, Your Majesty. Thank you for your hospitality. I shall take my Alice and leave at once."

Alice? My Alis?

Peering through the crack between the door and the wall, the man came out of the room, a child in his arms. He was dark-skinned with a shock of white hair. He was wearing what looked to be an old vest with a clock attached by a chain. The last thing I would think a man named Rabbit would look like.

More footsteps came from inside the room and stopped by the door. Terror trapped my breath and my hands clasped tightly with Jules as we silently prayed to Gods who might not even exist. The doors moved slowly, closing silently, and I let out my breath, shaking with fear.

The man with the child was gone. Only our reflections in the mirror across the way remained. Where the fuck did he go?

TICK... Tock...

Shit. We needed to get out of here.

With the door closed, the two of us bolted, following Meera to the next flight of stairs. Jules was running faster than I was, my lungs burning with the effort to keep up. My legs felt like jelly and my feet screamed in agony the harder I ran.

Turning to move down the hall, I ran right into a wall of straight muscle. Looking up, I found it was the guard from last night, anger gleaming in his eyes. "How did you get out of that cell?"

"The door was open." It's not a lie, but it's not the whole truth either.

"JANE!" Jules yelled back.

"RUN! DON'T STOP RUNNING!" I screamed to her as Goran picked me up like I weighed nothing and threw me over his shoulder. My fists beat into the back of him, but I knew it was going to do no good.

"Find the other girl," Goran yelled to another man passing in the hall.

"NO!" I yelled, beating against his back. I could only pray that Jules got out of here and found Mom.

TICK! TOCK!

Chapter Thirty-Nine

JULES

Neverland. I was in Neverland—a place of faerytales and where kids don't grow up.

Never in my life would I have thought I would have ended up here. When Jane's mom would tell us about this place, I always pictured little faeries from books and a beautiful jungle to go on wild adventures. Not a dungeon with creatures that have horns from their heads and my best friend's screams echoing in my ears.

The bruises and blood marring her body and her dress barely hanging onto her frame had fear and rage boiling beneath my skin. I don't know what those creatures did to her or why, but I wasn't going to leave this Godsforsaken place without her.

Shaking my head, I focused on the little fluttering ball that would hopefully lead me to safety. I had to trust Jane and she trusted this faery thing, even though my gut told me to run from all of it.

As the two of us rushed out of the castle, Jane's screams still rang in my ears to run and the only thing on my mind was finding Mom. But as we emerged into a dark, dilapidated garden with a glass dome overhead, all thoughts flew from my head at the dark beauty surrounding me. It was a deserted greenhouse.

I had never seen such an immense amount of beauty wilted and rotting. The flowers looked like they should have been neon-colored and bright, but something was missing. Some of the enormous flowering plants towered over me, with their petals drooping so low they brushed my head as I ran past. The once-leafy stems dried up and cried out for help. Did no one take care of this area? Would anyone come looking for me in here?

The crashing of bodies through the brush behind me sent a jolt of icy fear through my veins. I guess that answered that question.

My arms pumped harder and my legs moved faster as I heard the tinkling of bells up ahead, the faery's small glow coming from between two rocks. How the fuck was I fitting in there?

Shaking my head, I pushed myself to reach the small alcove as the sounds of the creatures following me came closer.

"We can smell you, little one. Your fear has the sweetest scent... most tantalizing... I wonder how she tastes—" A low voice reverberated around me.

"We aren't allowed to taste her. Only the blonde." Another voice echoed through the atrium.

Jane. They were going to eat Jane.

Terror seized me at the picture painted in my head of Jane being taken apart and devoured by these creatures. No. I had to help her. She stayed and helped me through some of the hardest parts of my life. I couldn't leave her to die at the hands of these monsters.

Crashing into the small alcove where the faery was, her light went out as she pushed against my back to keep moving. I braced my arms against the rocks on either side to keep myself in place. I needed to save Jane.

The little faery was quite strong, pressing herself against my back, the tinkling of her bells getting louder, almost as if she was getting mad. If she was talking, I couldn't understand a word she was saying. She must have her own language of bells she communicated with, which did nothing to help me.

"Stop!" I hissed. A flurry of red glowing wings came into my face, her high-pitched bells almost grating on my ears. "I need to help Jane! I can't leave her here!" I whispered frantically. I just needed a place to hide out until the beasts passed.

"She's over there— I heard her talking," one of the creatures bellowed.

The flurry of red pulled on my dress to get me moving into the dark wall. "Where are you taking me? This is just a wall! I can't go through it!" I whispered harshly as I raised my arms in front of me. Stepping forward, a tingle lightly shot through my fingers as I touched the crumbling wall. As I pushed against it, my hands went right through what should have been solid bricks, sending little shocks of electricity down my arms. Pulling back, I glanced down at the now pink ball of light still pulling on my dress, my brow furrowed. It wasn't a wall. I could walk through it and get away. I could leave this castle of horrors— but I couldn't leave Jane.

Find Mom!

"There! She's in the alcove!" The crashing of plants and stones jolted me out of my reverie.

No, no, no, no, no...

I needed to find a way out of here and back into the castle. I needed to get Jane.

"The fucking pixie is with her... Stop her!" the other man shouted as the sound of a rock whizzed past my head and fear spiked through me.

Pixie?

A sharp cry escaped me as unexpected pain exploded in my shoulder and my body jolted forward from the impact. Turning to see what had happened, I saw a rock lying behind me with the two offending beasts were not far behind.

Horror seized me as I took in their monstrous appearance. Tusks protruded from their mouths and spikes trailed down their arms. They were taller than anything imaginable. Their heads were topped with greasy hair, hung in dirty strands that fell into their faces. But their eyes glowed with a hunger that said they would do more than hurt me when they caught me.

The pulling on my dress shook me back to myself and I ran headfirst into the wall of electrical magic. The sparks that floated against my skin were almost welcome until I fell flat against a hard stone scraping against my cheek, my face stinging and wet from both blood and dirt.

Gasping, I forced myself to my knees, the gravel embedding itself into my skin as I took a moment to take in my new surroundings and saw nothing. It was so dark I couldn't see my hand in front of my face. The only light emitted was from that little faery—sorry, pixie—and there wasn't much to be seen but dark rock.

Peeking behind me, it was just as dark as it was in front of me—more inky blackness as if the creatures following me hadn't existed.

Relief that the creatures didn't follow me sang through my body as I fell forward, my hands scraping against the rough rock, tiny cuts blossoming on my palms.

Sorrow punched a hole in my chest and tears streamed down my face at the realization that Jane was stuck there. A sob was wrenched from my throat that monsters like that had been torturing her the whole time we had been here. My best friend, my sister, was stuck in that hell hole and her main concern was getting me out. What the hell did I do to deserve a person like that? What person did it make me that I didn't go back to save her?

Find Mom... Jane's panicked voice rang through my head.

Jane's mom took me in as a second daughter. Since we met when we were little girls, we were inseparable. As I grew older, my parents started to care less and less, leaving me to my own devices as they were too busy getting their next hit to worry about me. So, I clung onto the one family that gave a shit about me, and here I was... in a place that shouldn't exist, running for my life from creatures only my nightmares could create.

Where the hell could Wendy be on this island?

Where was this faery—I mean pixie— taking me?

Slowing my breathing, I took deep breaths to calm myself, focusing on the pixie fluttering before me.

Her color was no longer red, but pale yellow with a pale blue tinge outside her glow. Staring at the little creature, her face was downtrodden, almost sad, like she also felt my pain. Maybe she did. She was trying to get Jane out before she stopped and found me. But why Jane? What was so special about her that everyone was after her?

Too bad I couldn't understand the little sprite in front of me. It would have helped a lot if I had asked her some questions. Shaking my head, I rubbed my cut hands over my face, the sting burning through my face and arms.

If this is only the beginning of Neverland, I don't think I want to know the end.

Getting to my feet, I groaned as the pain in my shoulder made itself known once again. I don't think it was severely hurt—just overly bruised and hurt to move. I ignored the shock of pain that lit down my arm and made a show of putting on a brave face. If Jane could do it, so could I.

"Where are we going, little pixie thing? I can't understand you, but you have made it clear that you don't wish me harm, so I will put my trust in you to get me somewhere safe."

The pixie nodded vigorously, her light changing to that of a light pink before she flew down the passageway.

Following slowly, the pixie came back to flutter a few feet in front of me to light my way. We must have been in a cave system under the castle. The rocks were cold and wet. The walkway must not have been well used as my feet were cut on sharp edges that I couldn't see. My blood made the walk more difficult along with the shooting pain through the soles of my feet.

The tunnel felt like it took forever to trek through, and it probably did with how slow I was walking. Pain emanated from my every step until tears, once again, fell from my face. Half sobbing, I pushed myself to keep going. I couldn't help Jane if I didn't get out of here.

The pixie stopped in front of me, halting my progress. Her tinkling bells were soothing to my ears at this point. Her hands motioned for me to sit down, but I wouldn't get back up if I did. Hell, I couldn't get back up.

Shaking my head, I took another couple of steps forward before my legs gave out from under me, the ground scraping along my face and hands, flaying the skin that was already ragged and raw. My whole body was a bloody mess and I couldn't do it anymore.

Despair sank into me as the realization hit that I was stuck here. Jane would die an excruciating death and I would bleed out before anyone found us. Curling into a ball, I laid my head back against the wall and let out all the crushing sorrow and misery that had taken root in my chest. A gaping hole that felt like my being was ripped into two.

My parents were right. I was a failure. I would never amount to anything and was as hopeless now as I was when I was a baby.

I don't know how much time has passed since I reopened my eyes. I had cried and screamed. My body was still shaking and my throat was hoarse. My eyes were swollen and gritty from my dried-up tears. Blinking, I tried to regain my vision. The realization that I wouldn't be able to see anything anyway, as the little pixie left me a long time ago after trying to console the emptiness that couldn't be contained, left a gaping hole of hopelessness in my chest.

Groaning, I tried to get up. A feeble attempt, really. I couldn't bring myself to put much effort into it. We were all dead anyway. There was no point in trying.

My body felt like it was on fire. The cuts in the bottom of my feet sent shocks of lightning up my legs. The slices in my ass added to the ache of my hips from sitting on a hard surface for hours, to the pain still radiating from my shoulder, and to the small abrasions on my face and hands. I was a bloody mess.

I stared off into the darkness, trying to find ways I could get out of here. Crawling was my best bet at the moment. My hands were already fucked up, but it was better than trying to use my feet. Glancing to my right, the way we were headed before the pixie deserted me, I saw a tiny light.

Was that always there? Was I always this close to the end?

No. I couldn't have been.

Was that daylight? Or was it something else?

Questions were spinning through my mind faster than I could keep up.

The little light was getting bigger with the shape of humanoid figures behind it.

Fuck!

Adrenaline shot through me. I needed to move. I needed to get out of here, now.

Standing, I swallowed my moans of pain as I turned to my left to go deeper into the cave system to escape whatever fresh hell was coming my way. Not that I would get far, but it was better than facing whatever was coming.

"Stop! We're here to help you!" A woman's voice rang out, echoing around cavern walls.

The light approaching me halted in front of me and I recognized the little pixie from before. She came back.

A sob I didn't think was left in me came unbidden. Gods, when did I become such a crier?

Turning, I looked to see who my saviors were.

"Jules?"

I knew that voice.

"Uncle Jon?"

Chapter Forty

JANE

Tick...Tock...

My teeth were chattering with either fear or cold. I couldn't tell anymore.

This wasn't the same cell I was just in. The stone floor was covered in water, the icy cold sinking into my bones. The silence that rang through the place was deafening.

The ticking of my mind was my only solace. At least that hadn't left me.

Staring up toward what I assumed was the ceiling in the darkness, my hair floated in the water around me as I lay on the floor. I couldn't sit anymore, my hips too sore to put pressure on.

I prayed that Jules got out, that the little faery, Meera, had helped her. I could only imagine the punishment she would endure if she had been caught.

I still didn't know why we were given over to these monsters in the first place.

A payment? Faeries loved bargains. Did James bargain our lives for something that could benefit him?

Water splashed into my eyes as I shook my head. The burn added to the list of hurts I had on my list. He wouldn't have done that. He was too possessive of me to give me up willingly.

From what I could remember, the Fae couldn't lie, so what the guard said had to be the truth. I was here because of him. My chest ached at the notion that he was the reason I was here and my eyes burned with tears that wouldn't come.

"Gods, why am I such a fuck up?" I asked the empty room, my voice echoing back to me.

"Who says you are?" a male's voice rasped from within the dark, shocking me. Instantly sitting up, I scanned the darkness for whoever answered me.

"Who's there?" I asked, my limbs trembling in fear. If someone else was down here and couldn't escape, my likelihood of survival was looking pretty grim.

"No one of importance," the man said, his voice barely carrying to my ears.

"Me neither." I laid back down in the water. The smell of death permeated my nose, but at this point, what didn't smell of rot in this place?

"Who said you're a fuck up?" the man asked, apparently not giving up on my earlier statement.

"I did."

Tick... Tock...

"Well, since you are here with me, I would have to attest to the fact that, yes, you fucked up."

"No shit. Thanks for that," I snarked. Whoever the man was had a sense of humor. "How long have you been down here?" I asked, curiosity getting the better of me.

"Too long," the man sighed as his voice tapered off.

"Great... So, the deranged woman keeps us down here for her own entertainment?" It was more of a statement than a question. She wasn't keeping us down here for much else.

"Sadly. Most don't live very long."

"Why are you still alive?" I asked, genuinely curious and fearing the answer.

"I can't die."

Surprise flitted through me at his answer. Who the hell couldn't die? *TICK... TOCK...*

The banging in my head matched the sound that reverberated around the room, my heart racing in my chest as I jumped into a sitting position once again. Someone was coming.

"Ooooh, Jannneee..." The sing-song voice tinkled through the room, grating against my skull as fear spiked through me. Gods, I would love to treat her to a new voice box. The thought brought a small smile to my face.

Slowly, realization sank into me as I replayed what she was singing. My name. She found out my name. Thinking back, I wracked my brain to how that could have happened. I never said it, not once. Not in all the sessions that the monster Goran had with me. Not with the little faery that had helped me. How?

"JANE!" Jules' voice resounded in my head as I remembered being carried away. Jules said it. Fuck me.

A bright light shone in my face and a scream wrought from my throat as the burn of light scalded my eyes. "What's so funny, Jane girl? I don't see a reason for you to be smiling..." the woman trailed off as I whimpered in pain.

Fucking hell, this bitch. I don't know what I did in a past life to deserve this, but I was tired of it. "Maybe I was just imagining your head on a stick? Seems like it would do a great job of scaring people off," I snarked, holding my temples, praying the radiating pain would disappear soon.

TICK! TOCK!

"Well, I could put yours up instead. But that will have to wait. I am not done playing with you yet."

I slowly opened my eyes, adjusting to the brightness that shone from the floating ball that the woman seemed to be able to turn on at will—more magic.

Taking in my surroundings, I suddenly wished I hadn't opened my eyes. My stomach sank as I vomited into the pool of bloody water and entrails that I had been lying in. My skin, stained in the bodily fluids of others, had another wave of bile forcing itself out and adding to the mixture. I wanted to die.

TICK! TOCK!

I was horrified with myself for not knowing what I was lying in and with the woman in front of me. She had this room specifically for her own pleasures and I was her next target.

"Humans... So fragile..." the woman's shrill voice added to the pain radiating from my head, the ticking getting louder the closer she got.

"Maybe... But at least I know I'm not a deranged psychopath. Therapy would do you great," I spat as I heaved the last remnants of my stomach.

The woman towered over me as I knelt in the filth of her past victims, her power rolling over me in waves, my breath catching at the pricks of power pulling at my skin. "You are an interesting creature. You refused to tell Goran your name after days of torment. You were able to escape my cells, your one friend getting away, and now you have the audacity to tell me that I am insane? Do you have a death wish?" she asked, confusion filling her voice. It was almost as if she hadn't had someone stand up to her before.

TICK! TOCK!

"No, but at this point, what does it matter? No one will know if I live or die here anyway. If I get one last laugh in before I die, then so be it. At least I know I irritated you to my last breath." I had no idea where this bravado came from, but it was doing wonders for my self-confidence.

Magic blew me up against the wall, stars filling my vision as pain exploded in the back of my skull, matching the migraine the ticking had already given me. My skin was on fire as she blasted me with her power. Another scream wrenched from my chest as I tried to catch my breath.

"All I want to know is why Neverland is talking to you," the woman said as I splashed into the entrails.

TICK! TOCK! TICK! TOCK!

The ticking grew louder and more insistent, as if I could do anything about it. "I don't know...what you are... talking about," I answered, trying to get a breath.

Lightening skittered around the room, flaying my skin from the muscle underneath. My screams echoed around us, piercing my ears.

A growl erupted from the maniacal faery as her eyes turned silver and her hair a deep red. A glow around her body formed, the color a red so deep it was almost black. Wings erupted from her back as she flew toward me, her long fingers gripping my throat, squeezing the little bit of air I had left in me.

"I am tired of your games. Who— Are— You?" she growled into my face, her breath smelling oddly of mint. At least she didn't smell of the death that everyone else around here did. If I had to go, at least I got one last good smell before I died, even if it was my tormentor's breath.

TICK! TOCK! TICK! TOCK!

"No one important." I struggled to get out between my clenched teeth. Her grip on my throat tightened as I fought her arm to get some air. My eyes bulged and everything in the room faded to grey, almost like a black-and-white film, as her nails dug deeper into my skin. All she had to do was tear out my throat and I'd be done. This whole thing would end and I would be at peace. I almost wished she would.

The sudden drop into the cold water had me gasping for breath. The burn in my lungs had hot tears streaming down my face. My throat was on fire, the need to quench the burn the only thing on my mind. The icy water waved around me, reminding me that the answer was right there. But the thought of drinking other people's blood had bile rising in my throat once more, adding to the inferno inside.

TICK! TOCK!

A zap of lightning tore a gash in my face and another scream of pain ripped from my chest. Her long, chilled fingers gripped my jaw, forcing me to look at her. Wonder had taken over her face in place of the earlier anger. "What are you?" the woman asked, curiosity filling her tone.

Confusion riddled my brain. What the hell was she talking about? "Human. Unlike you," I spat. The grip on my cheeks tightened, her nails creating divots in my skin. The burn of fresh cuts had a hiss escaping from between my teeth.

"No. You're not." She threw my body into the fetid water. The taste of blood and entrail coated my tongue and insides, my stomach instantly regurgitating the substance as I tried to sit back up.

What the fuck did that mean? I know what I am. The woman was insane. That's all there was to that.

Is this what happened to the others before me? Were they tortured slowly as well? Were they made to go insane like the monster that stood before me? No, the man said no one lasted long. How long was she going to keep me alive? Was I going to be able to withstand her torture for that long?

I had to hope that Jules found Mom and she came looking for me before too long, or I was going to end up like the dismembered bodies floating around me.

The woman moved away from me, clearly over the fact that I wasn't answering her. I could only pray she was done with her questioning for the day. The light went out, coating me in darkness, as terror seized my limbs. Only the red glow of her body lit the room.

TICK! TOCK!

The sounds of chains rattling on the other side of the chamber had my ears perked. A low moan echoed around me as the faery turned attention to the man.

"Come now, boy. You know what is required of you," she said, her body blocking my view of him.

"No," he protested, his voice hoarse.

A slap resounded around the walls, ricocheting in my head. What was she doing to him?

"You will service me. I don't care that you don't want to. You never do. One day, you will learn to enjoy it."

My stomach twisted at what I was hearing. She was raping him. That's why he was alive. She used him as her own sex doll. Horror filled my being as my stomach rolled and I gagged. The sounds of her moaning filled the chamber and my stomach lurched as I dry heaved into the water.

TICK! TOCK! TI—

Suddenly, I was lifted out of the water, the air of the room brushing past my body as I was slammed against the wall. The man's head was buried beneath her dress as she rode his tongue, her eyes hooded with desire. The violence that had been painted on her face was eased with pleasure.

"Maybe you need to be coerced a different way," The woman stated, her eyes lingering on my body as a malicious smile twisted her mouth.

Terror filled me once more. No. Nononononononono...

I struggled to move, to speak. But her magic held me in place, my mouth sealed shut. The feeling of icy cold sparks pricked at my body. My nipples hardened at the cold and the woman's gaze heated at the sight. Her hands moved between my thighs, my dress a tattered mess, no longer covering much of anything.

TICK! TOCK! TICK! TOCK!

"Maybe violence won't get you to talk, but the promise of pleasure will..." She slid her fingers through my folds, my stomach lurching at her touch. The feel of her pressing inside me had a groan of discomfort escaping me. "You'll enjoy it, I promise."

The need to get her off me was screaming in my mind as I tried to fight against her magic. It was no use. It was like being held down by straps and weights. I was at her mercy. Hatred filled my eyes as she played with my body and I forced myself to think of anything other than what she was doing. Tears streaked down my face as I thought of James and what he would do to her if he found out that she was touching what he considered his, bringing a little bit of peace to my mind even though I knew it didn't matter. He gave me to her.

Her moans heightened as the man worked her to orgasm. I could only hope he would hurry up and get us both out of this torture. The woman's shout of pleasure filled the room as she came, her head falling to my chest as she took one of my nipples into her mouth, sucking until she was satiated.

"Well, that was highly satisfying. Maybe I'll keep you," she whispered, licking a trail of my tears from my cheek, repulsion filling me with the need to vomit.

Slowly, I was floated back to my side of the chamber and laid into the bloody water. Her echoing giggles rang in my ears long after she had left.

Tick... Tock...

Chapter Forty-One

WENDY

"Where is it?!" Tinkerbelle hissed as she tore through my flat.

"I don't know what you are talking about. I don't have anything of Peter's here. He left and never came back." I crossed my arms, exasperated. Why she thought I had Peter's shadow, of all things, was ridiculous.

How the hell do you lose a shadow?

"I know you have it! You're the only one he'd trust with it besides me and he didn't give it to me." She tore through my closet and dresser as if I would wear the damned thing.

What the fuck was going on?

"Tink, I promise you I don't have it. I haven't seen nor heard from the man in months. It has to be in Neverland somewhere."

The faery turned her head toward me, the glare in her eyes dark and malevolent. The realization that she would hurt me felt like I was dunked in ice. She stood to her full height, her power lashing out at my body, but I stayed firm. I wouldn't cower before her.

"It better be. If you or your brothers ever show your face in Neverland again, your heads will be the price paid."

"WENDY! Get up! We need to head to town now!"

Michael's voice jolted me out of my memory, my heart railing against my ribcage as a cold sweat beaded my brow. The memories here were only getting worse and I was losing the little sleep I was getting to be woken at obnoxious hours. My brother rushed into my room, throwing clothes at me as my brain slowly tried to understand what was happening.

"Jon's here. We need to go."

I grabbed the clothes that were thrown at me, falling out of the bed at the same time as pain ricocheted through my body at the impact. "What?! How?! Is Jane here?" I prayed to the Gods that she wasn't. This was the last place I would ever want her to be.

"He's with Tiger Lily and another girl. The girl is pretty beaten up. They're on the ship. LET'S GO!" He turned and slammed the door behind him, giving me privacy to change.

He had only been back from his trip to what he called The Sanctuary for a few days. His relaxed and carefree demeanor was suddenly gone, replaced by the man I had grown used to seeing around here.

Quickly changing into the navy blue blouse and black jeans, I pulled on the knee-high boots that Talia had gifted me and I rushed out the door, running my fingers through my tangled hair as I met Michael at the door.

"How did he get here? Why is he here?" I asked as we locked the house up behind us.

"I don't know. But it doesn't bode well that we are all here."

My heart sank at Michael's words. He was right. The only reason Jon would come back here, with Tiger Lily, no less, would be if something awful had happened. I could only pray that he came looking for me, but my gut was twisted into knots that something else was wrong.

More horribly wrong than what you did to the Grim? My conscience hasn't left me alone about what we had done to the man who assaulted me. What *I* had done.

My gut churned with regret that I had let my inner demons out to play that night. I let the island get to me and let loose on a man who may or may not have earned that rage.

Yes, he had touched me. Yes, he had promised more violence. But I had endured more in London than what he had done to me here, and I never acted on my murderous tendencies there. Confusion muddled my brain at what was happening to me the longer I was here and I didn't like it. I was out of breath by the time we got to the ship. I hadn't been back to the ship since we docked. The Crimson Krok had a black hull with matching black sails, the wood creaked as the waves pressed against it. The sails were rolled up, but the wind on the sea was still strong, pushing the waves angrily against the ship, sending sprays of salt water into my face.

The crew for the ship was crowding around as I ran up the gangplank. Pushing the bodies of men out of my way to see what the hell they were staring at. I gaped when I caught sight of my brother holding the body of a girl I loved as much as mine. Juliette.

Barrington was standing close by, his face of shock and despair. This must be the girl he was looking for. I didn't know Jules was seeing anyone, but she wasn't one to tell me about her private life. We were close, but she was closer to Jane than me. But the two were inseparable. Where one was, the other wasn't far behind.

"What happened to her? Where's Jane?" I exclaimed, worry and panic flooding me as I rushed up to Jon. My hand ran over her head, sticky with blood, taking in how bloody and mangled her body was.

"I don't know," Jon ground out, tension wracking his frame. "Where can I put her? She needs medical attention and I can't give it to her if I am holding her."

"What do you mean—"

I was interrupted by the jangle of keys that Michael brought out as he crossed in front of us. "Follow me," he said.

Grunting, Jon and I quickly followed our brother, readjusting Jules in his arms to the back of the ship and up a flight of stairs. The room was almost an exact replica of the captain's quarters, which I had stayed in. It was just smaller.

Michael pulled back his bed cover and Jon laid the girl down as she groaned in her sleep.

Jon rolled up his sleeves and got to work assessing her injuries as my mind spiraled with questions and fears. "What are you doing here, Jon? Where's Jane? Hell, why the fuck is Julie here?" I asked again, desperation leaking into my voice as the need for answers clawed at me.

"I need you to leave me alone. I can only help one person at a time and I need to get Jules to stop bleeding. Go ask Lily. She'll have more answers than I do," Jon growled out as Michael brought over a first aid kit.

"Right... go ask the woman that betrayed you for answers. She is as likely to help as a Godsdamned codfish!" I yelled, fear and worry combining into a torrent of anger.

"Don't talk about her like that!" Jon turned, snapping at me. "She's the reason I am here at all! So just go talk to her, Wendy!"

Taken aback, I stomped out of the room, knowing he would make sure Jules was okay. However, I needed to know where my daughter was, and apparently, my brother's ex had the answers.

"TIGER LILY!" I yelled as I stormed down the stairs, anger and fear for my children swirling into a mix of desperation and violence.

The woman was standing close to Barrington. Their hushed voices carried across the ship as she stepped toward me.

"Hello, Wendy-Bird. It is nice to see you aga—"

I didn't let her finish her sentence as I pulled my fist back and sent it flying at her face. The bitch had broken my brother's heart multiple times just to bring him back here, and now my daughter was missing, the other beaten bloody, and her being the only one with answers had my gut churning with the need for violence. To let Moira back out to play.

"That was for what you have put Jon through for the past twenty years, you cheating fucking whore!" I spat as I followed her fall to the deck, straddling her hips, gripping her shirt, and pulling her face to mine. "Where the fuck is my daughter?!" I gritted out, my teeth bared as she started giggling, blood spewing down her lips and chin, splattering on my shirt.

"Ask Barrington. He is the reason she is here after all..." Lily's eyes danced with a mixture of mirth and malice as she glanced between us.

I let go of the woman's shirt, her head cracking against the bloodstained deck as more giggles escaped her. She was fucking insane. Why the hell did Jon trust this cunt? Standing, I turned to the man in question. "What the hell is she talking about, Barrington?"

"I have no idea." The man's eyes were white, widened in shock, his voice grating on my last nerve.

My ire rose, an itch under my skin that made my muscles twitch with the need to hurt something. Anything. Spinning back to the now standing Lily, she was leaning against the railing, wiping the blood from her face, blood stained her teeth as she bared them to the captain.

"Of course you do, Cap'. Neither of the girls would be here if you hadn't brought the Wendy girl back. Tinkerbelle is in quite a tizzy about that," she said as she hoisted herself on the ship's edge, nonchalance rolling off her in waves.

What the fuck was she talking about? Confusion rolled through me as I glared between the two, waiting impatiently for answers.

"Jane is mine! Tinkerbelle has no right to touch her!"

"Jane is nobody's!" I screamed at the man claiming to own my daughter. "If anything, she is mine! My daughter! Mine to protect!" My voice failed me as I fell to the deck. Realization hit me like a freight train to my heart, pulling me down to the depths of hell.

Barrington was a mess about a girl the other day. The girl he had been obsessively searching for was my daughter, Jane. Tinkerbelle had her.

My heart was beating so fast it hurt. My breathing shallowed, tears streaked down my cheeks, and blood rushed through my ears, drowning out all sound as panic took hold. My heart was falling apart into tiny shards, my fingers clutching at my chest as if I could hold my heart together in my hands. Desperation to find Jane took root in my chest, fighting against the panic closing in.

I could only pray that Jane remembered all the rules I had told her as a child to be able to survive that wretched bitch.

The sound of a door slamming shut shook me. "What the actual fuck is going on here?" a man's voice roared as he stormed down the steps. Smee was here.

Could anyone here tell the difference between the two men? I wondered as I watched him saunter to the party, his gait predatory.

"Did you know?" I whispered, barely able to find my voice, my throat sore with unshed tears.

"Know what?" Smee asked, bewilderment crossing his face, a flicker of my brother coming to the surface.

"That Jane was here the whole time? That Barrington's girl is my daughter?!"

Smee's eyes slowly morphed from a calm, calculating menace to a man of fury and violence. His features flickering between panic and rage. His jaw screwed shut, the muscle in his jaw jumped as his hands clenched and unclenched, his gaze never wavering off the man he called a friend.

"Is that true?" His low voice rumbled across the ship, a knot of fear settling in my gut at the sound. "I had a feeling when I met your niece that you knew Jane. I had hoped it wasn't what I thought it was." Smee's voice held the promise of violence that only had my body vibrating with fear. As much as I would love to believe he would never harm me, I don't know this man. The man who took over my brother's body at will. The man who would cause chaos and destruction to protect himself and his own. I don't know what happened to my brother, but this man terrified me.

But what hurt worse was that he had suspected it and had not said a word. I thought I could trust him, but I was wrong.

Barrington stood up to the man before him, not at all fazed by what he saw. He was expecting the anger, the restrained violence. "I didn't know Jane was related to you. When I found out she was missing, I just wanted to find her," he stated, his voice even, calm, as if he was talking down a killer on the edge. He probably was.

"You never told us her name. Why?" Smee asked, relatively calm.

The wind from the Never Sea picked up, carrying his question away on the breeze. Water rose above the sides of the ship, the spray wetting my fevered skin as a gasp escaped me from the sudden cold. The seas swirled higher and the cyclone of water and wind carried itself on board the ship.

My heart beat a staccato rhythm against my ribcage, shock entering my system as I watched the torrent of seawater slowly morph into the shape of a man—a ten-foot-tall man made of water. The man was made of the sea, with pieces of seaweed and coral floating within his body and fish swimming along the currents as if they lived there.

It was the first time I had ever seen something like this in Neverland. Terror once again seized me as I realized my brother was right. Neverland had changed.

The seaman opened his mouth, a booming voice echoing around the cove.

"HER MAJESTY, THE QUEEN, WOULD LOVE FOR THE MANY PEOPLE OF NEVERLAND TO COME AND WITNESS THE MAGIC THAT THIS WORLD HAS TO OFFER. TO ALL WHO ARE PRESENT, YOU ARE ALL INVITED TO THE SOLSTICE BALL IN ONE WEEK'S TIME AT THE PALACE. THERE WILL BE FOOD, DRINKS, AND GAMES TO BE HELD FOR EVERYONE TO ENJOY. WE HOPE TO SEE YOU ALL THERE!"

My hands shook as the man fell into a puddle on the deck, slowly spilling off the sides. The fish and coral inside the man were left to flounder on the wooden boards, littering our feet.

"That's why I didn't say her name. She has spies everywhere. That's probably how she knew Wendy was here," Barrington answered, all of us silenced by the knowledge that Tink was everywhere.

And we were just invited to her home.

Chapter Forty-Two

MICHAEL

"No! The answer is no."

"You can't tell me where I can and cannot go, Michael! We needed a way into her inner sanctum and she practically invited us in to play. To let this chance go would be stupid!" Wendy yelled across the room, her arms flailing in every direction. She was right, but there was something off. I couldn't quite put my finger on it, but Tinkerbelle, inviting everyone on the island to a ball that hadn't been held since well before we came here, had trepidation sitting like a hard knot in my gut. Something wasn't right.

"She's luring us in. She has a plan. I don't like that we are just pawns to whatever she is planning," I sniped back. She wasn't going to listen to reason. She wanted Jane back and it was driving her closer to the brink of desperation that I couldn't pull her back from.

All of us were in James' quarters. I couldn't stand to look at the man I called my friend. If I did, I was going to kill him. My blood was boiling with fury and disgust. Every time we were waiting on his ass to get back to the ship, he was too busy fucking my niece. I knew little about her, but the thought made my blood boil.

"Well, I'm going. I need to find Jane. We'd know where she was if Jules were in any condition to talk. I'd say our best bet is to play Tink's games." Wendy got up from the sofa and went to the bar.

The very empty bar. All the glasses were gone and the decanters were empty.

Glancing over to Barrington, his body was tense with frustration and his eyes lined with worry. Searching his face, I noticed that there were dark circles under his eyes, his eyes themselves bloodshot. He hadn't been sleeping. Maybe he cared for Jane more than I gave him credit for.

"Truthfully, I don't think it's a good idea for any of you Darlings to go," James said, rubbing his hand over his face. "The woman has a death threat on your heads. To show up in her palace would be instant death to all of us. And I prefer to keep my heart in my chest, thank you."

"Exactly," I grumbled as I flopped down on the man's bed, flipping my dagger in the air and catching it.

"But Wendy is right. It's the only way we will find out what the hell she wants with all of us. We could all go in separately. I would have to be in the main room as Tink would expect me to be, but the Darlings, she wouldn't expect them to come. It would be stupid on their part. They could search the castle while everyone was distracted at the party," James explained, pacing the cabin.

His idea wasn't bad. But it wasn't the greatest. If we were caught, we were all dead.

I had never seen James like this. He was always calm and collected. But it was clear his world was unraveling and he had no anchor. It made me wonder how far he would go to keep Jane safe. It was apparent it was tearing him apart as his hands ran through his hair, pulling at the ends.

"And who is going with Wendy?" I asked.

"I'll go," Jon piped up, his arm wrapped around Tiger Lily, her face swollen and bruised from Wendy's hit. Curiosity was biting at the bit to know why the two were so cozy. She left him heartbroken for another man, a Fae at that. And here they were as if the past twenty-some years had never happened.

"And how are the two of you going to get into the ball without being noticed? The Fae will recognize you immediately," I said. I wanted to know the specifics of this plan. I wasn't going. I wasn't going to play into the game. I refused.

"They can dress up as part of your crew," Tiger Lily interjected. "It wouldn't be hard to make them into the addicts that roam the island. And no one will look at two drunken pirates as much of a threat."

"And if we get caught wandering, we can claim we got lost in our drunken stupor," Wendy finished the idea.

It wasn't a bad plan, really. I just didn't like it.

"What are we doing with the girl in my room?" I asked, praying they would agree with me on my plan for her.

"The girl? Do you even know who she is?" Tiger Lily asked as she leaned forward, her elbows on her knees and her hands clasped in front of her.

"No, I have never met her before. But seeing as she is important to Jon, Wendy, and Jane, I want to ensure she is safe. And the safest place on this island is The Sanctuary," I stated, flipping my dagger in the air again. The movement bringing me little peace.

"It's the safest place, yet you kept me here? Why is that?" Wendy asked, perplexed as she moved to stand in front of the windows that panned the back of the room.

"Because I needed to keep an eye on you. For some odd reason, you have an unhealthy obsession with a dead man and would run off half-cocked, killing friends of mine if left unattended." I flipped the dagger in my hand, the soothing rhythm doing little to calm my nerves. "Quite frankly, Wendy, you're a menace."

"No, Moira's a menace. I am quite sane, thank you, " she said as she continued staring out the windows at the slowly setting suns.

Cap was going to create a trench on the floor with the amount of pacing he was doing. "Who the hell is Moira?" he asked, confusion written on his face as Jon and Tiger Lily gasped at the name.

"A friend," Wendy said, tension ratcheting in the room, taut and thick.

"When did she arrive?" Jon asked carefully.

"A few days ago. Smee brought her out to play."

Lily had stiffened in her spot next to Jon as he leaned into her, trying to comfort her as James stopped his movements and glanced between us.

"Will someone please explain what the fuck we are talking about?" His voice was tinged with anger and annoyance.

"We all had to have alter egos to survive Pan. We called them our inner demons, as they only wanted to play when violence was needed. Jon was Starkey, Wendy was Moira, and I was Smee. If you ever paid careful attention, you would know the difference between us," I stated flatly.

"I noticed yours. You just never gave me your real name," James stated, his eyes flicking between my siblings. I'd watch out for them, too. If he thought I was bad, they were worse.

"How were you planning on getting Juliette to Asher's?" Lily asked, breaking the tension and returning us to the topic at hand.

"I was going to wait for her to heal then take her there. Why?"

"Her wounds are going to take weeks to heal," Jon stated. "If you're that concerned with her safety, maybe you should take Lily's way," he suggested, tracing his fingers up and down her arm.

"Lily's way?"

"What way is that?"

"What the hell are you talking about?"

"Why would you suggest that?"

Everyone clamored at once, all of us vying to be heard over the other.

"STOP! Fine, I'll take them. But there is to be no talk about it afterward. Agreed?" Lily exclaimed as she stood, putting her hands on her hips and glaring at each of us in turn.

Shrugging my shoulders, I agreed, but to what, I am not quite sure.

"Go grab the girl, Michael. Once you come back, I'll tell you what to do."

Nodding, I slid my knife back into my thigh sheath as I slid out the door and quickly made my way to my cabin. The girl, Juliette, was softly snoring in the bed, her body curled into a ball and her bandages looking like they needed to be changed already. Something I could do when I got her to Asher's.

No, something I needed to do. I needed to see that she was healing correctly. Lifting her into my arms, I cradled her to my chest as I returned to Cap's room. The smell of blood and antiseptic filled my senses, but under that was the faint scent of vanilla. I wondered if she would smell as sweet after she was healed. Confusion warred through me at the sudden need to keep the girl safe. I had never had such a visceral reaction to anyone except Asher and now I was questioning myself.

The door was still open as I carefully entered the room, everyone's eyes on Tiger Lily. Sighing, she moved to the center of the cabin, her hands in front of her. A breeze blew around us, raking a shiver down my spine. Magic. She had magic.

Fear slid through my gut, not just for me, but for the girl in my arms as well. What the hell did I sign us up for?

Watching as blue and orange sparks flew from the woman's fingertips, a small circle formed in the air in front of her, growing bigger and bigger until a person could walk right through it. The scent of burnt ozone hung in the air as I stepped closer to the spark-encircled hole. Peering into it, the other side showed the gates to The Sanctuary. Awe took over as I wondered how the hell she was doing this.

"I can't keep it open for long. Just step through and you'll be there," Lily said, heaving out a breath as sweat beaded on her brow.

Nodding, I readjusted Juliette in my arms and walked through the hole she had created. As soon as I was through, it closed with a snap, the rancid smell lingering in the air.

I don't know how she acquired that kind of magic, but I was grateful for it. It just saved me a two-day trek across the island.

A low moan escaped the lips of the beauty in my arms and my cock twitched at the small sound. Oh, if only it were me creating those noises for another reason than her pain.

Grunting, I shook my head to make my way through the gate and started my small trek through the front gardens to the door when a fluttering of pink flew into my face. Meera's arms flailed about her as her high-pitched tinkling told me she was flustered. The worry lining the little pixie's face told me another story. She knew this girl.

Anger flashed through me at the reminder that she was injured and that was why she was here. I knew it wasn't Meera's fault, as the pixie was only big enough to trick a person into doing something for her, but it still irked me that the girl was hurt in the first place.

Dashing ahead, Meera opened the door to the treehouse and flashed up the stairs, leaving little specks of dust in her wake. Once upon a time, we used to use the pixie dust to fly, now if any of us were found flying, it was an instant death sentence. Tink's ruling that flying away from Neverland without a proper purpose, you know, those of her own wishes, would cause significant harm to the island.

It was a bunch of bull shit, but I would rather keep my head attached than not.

Slowly walking up the stairs, careful to make sure Juliette's head didn't hit the walls as I made my up to the infirmary, I made note of all the cuts marring her face and body. I had watched Jon meticulously sew her deeper cuts and then bandage her up, so I knew where every little mark was on her body. But to calculate the exact amount of blood that would be drawn was my own little desire. Whoever caused this would have a long, slow death.

Asher's voice could be heard in the distance talking to the pixie. Envy cut through me, souring my already dim mood that the man could speak to her and I couldn't understand a damned thing she said. It would make life so much easier if I could hear her.

The door to the infirmary was open. Asher was on one of the beds, making it ready for me to set the girl down upon. The window at the far end of the room let in a gentle breeze and the scent of jasmine and Asher floated in the room, calming my nerves slightly.

"Meera said she handed her off to Tiger Lily. How did you get her?" Asher's gruff voice came from behind me as I laid her down, propping her head against the pillows, causing my heart to race. This man was going to kill me one day with my heart palpitations.

"They took her to the ship."

"Who's they?" Asher interrupted.

"Apparently," I continued, irritation flitted through me, "Lily brought Jon here to help find the girls, and they were on their way to the Cove when Meera found them." Running my hand over Juliette's dark hair, I felt comforted that she was found before any lasting harm came to her. "We don't know what happened to her. They found her like this."

Asher grunted as he moved quickly to the first aid cabinet by the door. The sounds of him rummaging, looking for Gods knew what, was the only noise in the room besides the girl's light moans. Her face was pinched in pain and her hands were starting to twitch. Maybe a nightmare? I wouldn't doubt it. I no longer slept because of my night terrors.

"Meera said she was in the castle's dungeons with another girl. I assume Jane, as the girl refused to give her name. She said it was like she knew the rules of Neverland and Fae. Meera found it quite peculiar."

"Peculiar?" If Wendy and Jon did anything right, teaching the girls never to give their names was it. But that begs the question: If she freed Juliette, where was Jane?

"Her words, not mine. Anyway, she freed the blonde, and when the blonde found this girl, she knew they came together by how they dressed and addressed each other." The tinkling of bells from across the room interrupted Asher's narrative. "Like sisters, she said." He continued. "But as they were making their way to escape, the blonde was caught and told the girl here to find Mom."

"Wendy. She was told to find Wendy."

"I thought Wendy only had one child?" Asher asked, confusion pinching his features.

"She does, the blonde in Meera's story. This is Jane's best friend, but Wendy raised her like a daughter. She lived with them."

"You're saying Tinkerbelle has a Darling in her dungeon?"

Nodding, I let Asher take in what that meant.

"Fuck all!"

My chest was hollow. Like a hole had been punched through me and my heart taken out. Jane was in the palace's dungeons, so at least we knew where to start looking for her. But we don't know how long she has been there or if she was even alive at this point.

Stomping back to the bed, Asher dumped bandages, antiseptic, and a clean overshirt for her to wear. Jealousy punched through me, quickly followed by confusion that he would see her naked body. I didn't mind Jon looking. He was a doctor and only ever had eyes for Tiger Lily, but Asher was mine. But glancing over at the girl in the bed, a wave of need heated my blood, not for Asher, but for her, leaving me torn.

I grabbed the scissors from the kit and slid the edges against her torn dress. This is something that girls would wear to the nightclub. I had seen plenty of dresses like it at Magique when I went inside, which wasn't often. Unease slid in my gut at the thought—thick and slimy.

Was she there? Was that how she ended up here? Was she with Jane when this happened? Something was amiss and I wanted to know what the hell it was.

As I finished cutting the dress off her body, Asher's sudden intake of breath had me glancing back at him. Fury burned into his features as he took account of all the marks on her body. He felt the same way I did when I saw the damage done to her. Absolute rage.

If this is what she looked like, I had no doubt Jane was in a worse state, if she was even alive. The need for violence boiled under my skin—the need to lash out at whoever caused all this spreading, like a cancer through my veins.

Asher pulled me aside, taking me out of the room as Meera flitted about organizing the bandages that would be needed. "I can smell your need for vengeance, but the scent is distracting me. Go find something to do while I take care of her. We can plan out how to kill the person later."

Relief that he understood me, both sides of me, I nodded and left The Sanctuary, looking for something to hunt and sate my needs.

Chapter Forty-Three

JON

Lily stopped, grabbing my arm and forcing me to look at her. "Seriously, you can't go. Drake will be there, and if he finds out you're here with me, we're both dead."

Ah, yes, the threat of her husband again. Yet here she was, being the biggest cock tease. We had already discussed that we couldn't let anything happen between us, and here she was, bringing up her bastard husband again as if I had any choice in coming here. She practically kidnapped me.

Rolling my eyes, I strolled across the yard to Lily's tent, Dixie running up to me, her tail wagging. At least one of us was having a good time. The people in the encampment were more than happy to watch my puppy and she made quick friends with the few children here.

"JON!" Lily's voice rang out behind me. I groaned as I ignored her. We weren't having this discussion where others could hear. Hell, they probably still could in her tent, but it was a matter of privacy, even if it was fake.

The sounds of her footsteps running to keep up with me made a sly smile form on my face. I knew she didn't like being ignored, but sometimes, she needed a reminder of who she was talking to. And it wasn't the boy she fell in love with when we were kids.

After taking the time to think about her actions, her stalking me, and all the other enumerable things she had admitted to doing, I came to accept it. Even when we were kids, she wouldn't let me play with the other girls in the tribe, proclaiming me to be hers. Now, it seems like her love for me may be closer to obsession, but I can't judge. That would be calling the kettle black. I would have done the same if I was in her shoes.

Entering her tent, the coolness of the air inside was a reprieve from the dual suns that had been blazing down on us. I don't remember it being so hot when we were kids, but the island had changed a lot since then, so it wouldn't surprise me if even the environment changed because of Pan's disappearance.

I turned, waiting for Lily to enter her home, my arms crossed. I didn't want to fight about this, but there was no way I wasn't going to the ball. The plan she had laid out was perfect and only now was she having second thoughts about it because of her maniacal husband.

As she burst through the threshold, I rocked back my heels, waiting for her to tear into me with all her excuses. At this point, I didn't care if Drake was there. It'd give me the opportunity to maim the fucker, but my main reason would be to locate my niece. She was the reason I was here in the first place and the one I needed to keep my head on straight for. If finding Jules was any consolation, it was that Jane was still alive.

Lily stopped a few feet in front of me, her hands on her hips, her head cocked to the side as if waiting for me to start the argument. There wasn't one to be had. She had no say.

"Well... Are you going to say anything?" she asked, her hands flying in the air, exasperated.

"There is nothing to say. I am going. I need to find Jane. The more eyes we have there, the better. Michael will stay with Jules for now, and Wendy and James will also be going. I don't see what the deal is at this point."

"Drake will kill you the moment he sees you."

"Who the hell said we were going together? Did you forget the part where I am supposed to be part of the crew? It was your fucking idea, Lily!"

"I don't want you there at all. Drake is a possessive asshole, and if he gets wind that you are on the island, I'll pay for it in spades," Lily argued, desperation filling her tone.

Cupping her chin in my hand, I made her meet my gaze. "No, you won't because he won't find out." Leaning down, I grazed a small kiss across her lips, a small smile forming on hers as I pulled away. "I promise."

Her arms wrapped around my neck, her fingers playing in the strands of my hair as she pressed her lips against mine, her tongue darting out, licking, sucking, and nipping at my bottom lip. Sucking in a breath, my tongue met hers in a dance of heat and desire. The need to feel her body melded with mine was the only thing on my mind.

"Are you going to make do with your promise?" she whispered huskily, the sound wrapping around me and pulling me into her orbit. She climbed up my body, wrapping her long legs around my waist and grinding herself against my cock.

A groan rumbled from my chest at the fact that she had been thinking about my threat for the past week. It explained why she had been playing hot and cold since she brought me back to this Godsforsaken place. But doing so was a danger neither of us could afford. Drake would have our heads if we got caught, but Godsdammit, the temptation was almost too much to ignore.

If she wanted me to fuck her, she'd have to beg.

Grabbing her perfect ass, I lifted her off me and placed her in the chair as she spread her legs so I could kneel between them. Bringing my lips down to hers, I could feel her breath mixing with mine, my tongue sneaking out to lick along her plush, bottom lip, her breath catching at the contact. Pressing my lips against hers, a growl rumbled through my chest as the taste of berries and wine fell upon my tongue.

Her hands groped my hair, pulling my body against hers. Our lips crashing together in a rush of restrained desire as we licked, nipped, and sucked. Thrusting my tongue through her parted lips, I plundered her mouth, taking what I had wanted for so long.

Lily rose, pressing her full breasts against my chest. Her hands roamed my body, burning a line from anywhere she touched straight to my cock. I was being driven mad by my need to bury myself in her perfect little cunt.

A moan escaped her as she continued to ravage her luscious lips. Pulling back, I gazed into the face of the woman that had haunted me, her lips swollen and eyes blown wide with lust.

A smile bloomed on my face.

She can pretend that I do not affect her outside of this tent. In here, she's mine.

Tearing her shirt off her body, the shimmer of magic swirling under the tattoos marking her skin had blood rushing south to my already raging cock. Snaking my hand slowly down her body, I cupped her heavy breasts in my palms, her hardened nipples tempting me to play with them. Alternating between pinching and pulling, Lily arched her back silently, begging for more. She had no idea the amount of begging she was in for.

Slowly tracing my way down her body, I explored her. It has been over twenty years since I have seen her like this, and I was going to take my time and relearn everything there was about this new Lily.

Lifting herself up, I pulled her pants down her body, revealing the one thing I was desperate for. Spreading her thighs, I leaned back on my heels to look my fill. Lightly stroking her clit, a hiss came from her lips as she bucked toward my hand, her pussy already soaked.

"All this for me?" I glanced up at her face. Her cheeks flushed as her breasts heaved with a heavy breath.

"Yes..." she sighed, reaching for me. A glint of light glanced off her wedding ring, sending a cold shock through my system, dousing me in reality.

As much as I wanted to do this, to fuck her until we were both panting and spent, the threat to our lives wasn't worth it. The reminder that she wasn't mine yet had me taking a step back. Cool rage simmered in my veins. When I finally fucked her, she was going to be mine in every sense of the word.

Shaking my head, I changed my course. If I couldn't fuck her, then I would make sure neither of us got what we wanted.

Grabbing her hands, I pressed them down toward her precious little cunt. "Show me... show me how you play..." I wanted to play with her. I wanted to touch her, but the reminder that she wasn't mine had me taking a step back. I may have promised to fuck her, and I will, but I want her on my terms. And the reminder that she's not mine yet had an icy rage filling my veins.

Lily sat up, a dark look in her eye and a sly smirk on her face as she spread her legs wider, one knee on the arm of the chair with the other foot flat on the floor.

Shaking my head of my dark thoughts, I leaned back until I sat on the rugs before her. Pulling my cock out of my jeans, relieving myself of its tight constraints, I pumped myself as I watched Lily snake her fingers through her curls down to her tight entrance. Pressing two fingers inside as she pumped in time to my hand, I groaned.

My gaze stayed on her hand as she slowly removed them from her hot cunt, dripping with her slick as she pinched her clit, pulling then flicking it. I stared, mesmerized, as she repeated the pattern before circling herself and dipping back down to pump herself again.

My cock jumped in my hand as precum sluiced down, coating my length, pumping myself in time to her ministrations.

Her free hand moved up her body, cupping her breast and pulling and teasing her nipple. Her breathing became uneven as her eyes closed.

"Eyes open. I want you to keep your eyes on me as you fuck yourself. I want you to see what you're doing to me," I growled out. I wanted all of it. I wanted to watch her come. I wanted to see her eyes blown wide and her full lips gasping my name as she came all over the chair. But she wasn't mine yet.

Her eyes snapped back to mine as she moaned, her fingers moving faster, and her breathing became erratic.

"Stop!"

Groaning her disappointment, she removed her fingers, lightly brushing her clit, her body convulsing. She was on the precipice. Just one little push and she would fall into rapture. "Please..." Her high-pitched keel had my cock twitching, the need to finish this torment for both of us within reach. "Please..." she pleaded with me, her lust-filled eyes frantic with need.

Getting onto my knees, I came towards her, placing myself in between her legs once more, the smell of her sex filling my senses. "No. You don't get to come." I leaned into her ear, my hand wrapped lightly around her slender throat. "I have had twenty years of blue balls because of you. You will do well to know how it feels."

Squeezing her throat, I tweaked her nipple as I rose from my spot, my cock now on proud display before her. Her eyes widened as she realized she wouldn't get what she wanted.

"I will finish this—" she stated breathlessly, her hand moving to do just that.

Grabbing her wrist, I pulled her up my body, my hard cock pressed against her soft belly. The need to bury myself so deep I wouldn't know the way out was close to taking over. "No, you won't. You don't get to come until I tell you to. And you haven't earned it. Until you get rid of your husband, you will be edged until you are nothing more than a blubbering mess begging for release."

Letting her go, her eyes now widened with shock as she sat back down. Slowly, her breathing went back to normal, but her body was still flushed and her nipples still hardened, begging to be sucked. My mouth watered at the sight of her.

"You know, normally, I am in charge, demanding these things. Why am I so turned on when you do it to me?" Her voice was small and quiet.

I tucked my aching member back into my pants. I was going to need a cold douse of water. Soon. Leaning down, I tucked a piece of hair behind her ear and searched her face. She was genuinely confused. "Because you have always submitted to me. I am the only one with access to your mind, body, and soul."

Standing, I buttoned my jeans and exited the tent into the balmy night air.

The sounds of little paws running in the dirt were a reprieve to my senses as Dixie ran up to me. Kneeling, I gave her much-needed attention that I hadn't been able to give her the past few days. Guilt for ignoring her gnawed at me.

"Come on, girl, we're going to see Wendy." Dixie started prancing and galloping ahead as she heard my sister's name. She always was her favorite.

Making my way through the encampment, I ignored the whispers of Lily's people. They always had something to say and it was never anything good.

I kept up my pace, walking through the magical barrier they had erected. It was an unpleasant feeling, like having your breath sucked from your body and then immediately refilled. But what was more off-putting was that they needed it in the first place. It wasn't there when we were kids. It left me with a sense of foreboding as we slowly traversed the woods back to Pirate's Cove.

I couldn't handle seeing Lily right now. It was probably for the best. As much as I wanted to fuck her, she was still married and she even said I had a death threat on my head. The reminder made walking away from her that much easier.

The Never Wood was cooling off for the night. The sister suns had set and the triple moons were coming out to light up the night. Fireflies danced as the wilting blooms of the trees and vines tried to glow. When we were small, the glow of the plants would light our way, letting us play at any time of the day. Now, the faintness of their light was disheartening, leaving the shadows of the island to take over.

A flutter of leaves behind me gave me pause and a shiver of trepidation snaked down my spine. Searching the dark, the fireflies continued winking as Dixie stopped playing and went on point.

Something was out there. Fucking hell. I didn't have anything to defend myself with, and I knew better than to have been walking out here without one, but I was too wrapped up in my head about Lily. I didn't think anything of it. Now I wish I had.

"Jon Darling?"

Fear skittered through me as my name was called through the dark.

"Who's there?" I asked, ignoring the question. I wasn't stupid enough to say yes to that. I may not have been here in a long time, but the rules remained the same.

A dark chuckle erupted from the jungle, the sound surrounding me as the press of magic against my skin caught my breath. I couldn't move. I was being held in place. The feeling of being dragged down and anchored had blood rushing to my head and I lost feeling in my extremities.

Dixie had started growling, circling me, as she tried to place the threat. She wasn't going to find it. The magic made sure of it. The poor girl was going to die if she didn't leave.

"Jon Darling. I never thought I would see you again. Yet here you are." A smile shown in the dark, a clash of white teeth against a black background. There was only one man on this island that was that dark.

Drake.

Terror seized me as I realized I was fucked. My heart raced in my chest, beating against my ribcage, trying to escape its fate. He was going to kill me for being here, for being with his wife.

The man stepped out of the darkness, his suit finely pressed and just as dark as the rest of him. His golden eyes glowed and he smiled maliciously.

"I have hoped to see you again. I will make sure your stay here is quite enjoyable."

Holding the glare I had at the man, with a flick of his wrist, I felt his magic press harder against me, choking me. The sounds of Dixie growling, barking, and whining sent fear for her rushing through me as everything went black.

Chapter Forty-Four

LILY

It has been days since I last saw Jon. Anticipation sang through me at the chance to see him. I needed to know he was okay.

My body flushed hot as I remembered the last time I saw him. Gods, I had never been so turned on and pissed off in my life. But the man wasn't wrong. We shouldn't have been tempting that line and he probably saved our lives by leaving that night.

The castle was teeming with life, more than I had ever seen. The Fae were all decked out in their finest, and depending on the court they were in, you could see what they thought was most appropriate. But everyone was wearing a mask of some sort, which was disconcerting, in the least. You would not know who you were talking to until it was too late.

The Earth Fae wore green and gold leaves, with gold filigree woven through their auburn hair and horns. The women wore sheer gossamer gowns that fell to the floor, leaving trails of fabric and leaves behind them. The men wore shorts made of leaves and vines that wove around their bodies.

The Water Fae wore different shades of blue, if you could say they were wearing anything. The women had various shades of shells covering their breasts and sheer organza fabric in shades of blue, green, and purple that were bound at the waist with more shells as the fabric fell to the floor, giving the illusion of waves of the Never Sea. Their legs were also covered in tiny shells that shimmered as they walked. Silver filigree was woven through their long silver locks, their hair color giving them away. The men also wore barely anything; their pants matched the women's skirts, only they tied off at the ankle. The men had shells covering bits and pieces of their upper bodies, catching the light as they moved through the halls.

The Fire Fae wore shades of red, from a deep wine red to a vibrant, almost garishly bright red, with shades of oranges and yellows thrown into the mix to soften them. The women wore dresses covering everything, from their necks to their toes. Nothing was left uncovered. The dresses were slim and hugged their figures beautifully. They all looked like little bits of flames wandering the castle, as if just their state of dress could illuminate the darkest secrets that the walls held. The women's hair was piled upon their heads, the red of their locks falling in waves and curls to their waists, even with them being pulled up, with copper strung up, holding a lot of their hair in place. The men wore red suits and looked out of place in the castle. Unlike the women, their red hair was cut short, with copper filigree weaving around their horns. Their eyes were pure black and gave the air of danger as they passed. They reminded me more of the tale of demons the humans in London spun to their children. And maybe they were what the humans were talking about. Who knew?

The Air Fae wore white gossamer gowns that flowed about their bodies, silver and glitter abounding everywhere they went. The glitter was more likely to be pixie dust that was no longer useful to us here, so they used it as magic glamour to make them look even more beautiful than they already were. Their wings glittered as they walked by, making little tinkling noises as they moved.

The pirates were wearing their best. The men were wearing tuxedos and the women were wearing evening gowns. They all looked to put their best foot forward. The pirates looked out of place amongst the faeries surrounding them. Noticeably, all of them were weaponless or seemed to be. To be without a weapon here on the island was a great act of trust, praying that the Fae would play by the rules tonight.

My tribe all came wearing our best: animal hides and leather, feathers in our hair, and headbands. Keeping our war bonnets at home, we decided it was best to come and see what Tinkerbelle was up to before we wore our war gear. It's best not to start a fight when one isn't needed.

Lost in the glamour surrounding me, I lost track of where I was until I felt someone entwine their fingers in my hand. A jolt of adrenaline went through my body as I tugged my arm to free myself before I heard *his* voice in my ear. "Now, *darling*, we don't want anyone here to think we aren't getting along now, do we?" Fear chilled me where the adrenaline had heated my skin. What was *he* doing here?

Looking up, I was met with the golden eyes of my husband, his smile disarmingly bright against his dark skin. My heart raced out of my chest as he bent low and grazed his lips against mine. "Good girl. Now, if you behave all night, maybe I'll let your little boy toy go."

My eyes widened as his words slowly registered in my head. "What are you talking about?" I hissed in his face as he pulled me towards the dance floor where a few of the Fae and pirates had started dancing to the music floating around us. Sweat beaded along my hairline at what he was implicating. Pulling me flush against his body, his hand pinched my waist as the other gripped my hand so hard I almost yelped.

"Oh, darling, you didn't think you could get away with bringing your ex-lover here and me not finding out, did you?" Drake asked, his voice low so no one could hear our conversation.

My breath hitched at the realization that he had found Jon. My stomach sank to my feet as bile rose in my throat, the acid burning my insides as my terror chilled me. My eyes widened at what he was implicating. I had lost many good men because of his jealousy. "I don't know why you concern yourself with my doings. I was helping him, nothing else."

"And why, my pet, do you reek of him?" he practically growled into my ear.

"Because we have been close together for almost a week. Also, I am under Her Majesty's command to get close to the Darlings, so I am." I didn't think he'd be able to smell him on me. We hadn't seen each other in days, so it made no sense. Using Tinkerbelle as a scapegoat was risky, but I couldn't let Drake know that he was here because of me, for my own selfish reasons. As far as I knew, Tink had no idea that all the Darlings were here—just Wendy.

He spun me out from his body, then pulled me back in violently. "Don't forget, dear, that you are mine," he spat loud enough for anyone close to us to hear. "Mine to hold, mine to fuck, and mine to bleed. Don't push your luck because you will find your Darling in pieces by the time I am through with him."

"You bast— " His grip was on my throat faster than I could finish my sentence, cutting off my air as my lungs burned.

"You want me to be a monster?" He leaned into my ear as I choked on the need to breathe. "Then I'll be one."

The words I had said to Jon rang through my ear. My heart sank into the ground, realizing he had been watching me as I had done to Jon for so long. He didn't smell him on me. He had been watching everything we had done together and now we would pay for it.

He released my neck as the doors to the front banged open. The party stalled and the music went quiet as two men strode through.

Arron and Madok.

The sniveling little snitches. Gods, their noses must be so far up Drake's ass that they couldn't pull their heads out if they wanted to.

I gasped at the sight of the man being dragged between them. His head was hung low, but I would recognize that hair and body shape anywhere.

Jon.

My heart beat against my ribcage as I took him in. His body was limp, blood stained his clothes, and it looked like a gag was wrapped around his mouth.

"What did you do to him?!" I exclaimed, stepping toward him as Drake grabbed my arm, pulling me back against his body. His cock hard against my ass made my stomach roll.

"Nothing that wasn't warranted. I mean... he did try to fuck my wife. He's lucky I haven't cut off his hands for touching you, my sweet." Drake's fingers glided through my hair as he moved it to the side, slowly kissing my neck.

Disgust filled me as bile rose in my throat. I could only pray that he would just let us go with a beating, but I know this is only the beginning of our punishment. "We never fucked," I growled under my breath.

"I don't believe you," he hissed into my ear.

Staring out into the crowd, I watched as the Fae moved closer to watch the show that was about to be put on. They always did love a good, violent punishment, and most of them hated me, so it was going to be something to relish in their eyes.

I caught sight of my father standing at the back of the room, his eyes distant as he stared at the wall in front of him, not paying any attention to what Drake did to me. I didn't want to hope he would step in to help, but his blatant display of ignoring me sent a pang of betrayal through my being.

"I don't know who you're searching for out there. No one is going to help you," Drake whispered into my ear, sending chills down my spine as his grip tightened on my body, rubbing himself against my ass, reminding me that I was his.

I was expendable.

My gaze roved the faces of the crowd, everyone blurring together as tears filled my vision with sorrow for both myself and what I had wrought upon the man in front of me.

A movement from the back caught my attention. A tall man with dark hair was moving through the crush of bodies to get to the front. Captain Barrington. Fury lit his gaze as he took in our circumstances. Shaking my head, I silently told him to stand back as a small woman came up behind him.

Wendy.

What the hell was she doing here? She was supposed to be searching for Jane.

Her gasp was almost audible in the silence ringing around the room. With her hair dyed blue, her outfit screamed pirate princess. A dark blue corset around her middle as the train on the skirt billowed out to a black. Her menacing glare completed the look, making her blend in with the rest of the pirate crowd. I wouldn't have guessed it was her if I hadn't seen her a few days ago.

A loud tinkling of bells rang through the hall and dread filled my being as Tinkerbelle herself rounded the corner into the room, her gaze on the situation in front of her. Her laugh echoed off the walls as she came closer and stopped in front of Jon, her hand held out, cupping his chin to bring his face up to hers.

Jealous rage filled me as she touched him, but Drake's rough hands held me back from confronting her.

"Jon Darling. How marvelous that you decided to join us," Tinkerbelle exclaimed. "I am so glad I arrived in time for whatever Drake has planned for you two." She turned toward me, fire in her eyes. "Tiger Lily. I had thought you would know better than to bring another Darling here. But it was only a matter of time before you betrayed your husband, wasn't it?" she questioned as she raised her hand.

Watching the hand move toward my face, I could do nothing as my husband let her slap me. The fiery sting of flesh on flesh had a shout of pain escaping me as Jon got up from his crouch on the floor, fighting to get away from the two Fae holding him. He had no chance.

Drake held me up as Arron and Madok wrestled Jon back to his knees. Another Fae came forward to stand just to the side of the men as if waiting for something. Drake's tongue licked my neck, leaving a wet trail behind. His hand inched around my front, cupping my breast and pulling at my nipple as revulsion rolling through my stomach.

The man's cock was still raging against my ass as if watching the two of us being punished was turning him on. I would have gagged at the thought if I could have, but my throat was dry, and terror seized me as I watched a pair of Fae move a bench in front of us.

Suddenly, a wave of cold realization hit me.

This was planned.

He had planned this with everyone here and their payment was to watch.

Drake forcefully bent me down over the bench as another pair of hands wrapped a rope around my wrists, tying them against the front. My breasts smashed against the hardwood, my ass in the air. Drake slowly unlaced my skirt, baring my ass and pussy to the crowd, shame burning through me.

I could hear rustling, the sound of fists hitting flesh and grunts of pain from behind me. The only image running through my mind was Jon being beat back into submission to watch my punishment with everyone else.

Guilt ate at me as I listened to what I could only imagine was Jon being beaten to a bloody pulp when the snick of a whip caught my ear, terror seizing my body taut.

Drake's rough hand rubbed up and down my ass, pressing a finger into my pussy. "Maybe you'll think twice before letting another touch what's mine next time," he growled as a resounding slap hit my rear, a gasp leaving my mouth from the sting.

The hiss of the whip ringing through the air was my only warning before it hit. A scream wrenched from my lungs as the next hit came down. Under the sound of my screams were the yells and grunts of Jon trying to get in the way, only to be subdued by more violence.

I couldn't tell you how many times Drake hit me, my back, ass and legs were screaming in pain, my flesh hanging in strips baring the muscle and bone beneath. My blood dripped on the floor in time to my ragged breathing as I faded in and out of consciousness. My vision blurred from the amount of tears that rained down my face.

I couldn't do it anymore.

Groaning, I felt a hand cup my ass, the sting of pain was almost welcome at this point. I deserved it. I was the reason for all of this.

A second hand joined the first, spreading my ass cheeks wide. Pain radiating through, a shot white hot pain clouded my eyes. The feel of a man's tongue licking the blood running down my asshole had me trying to clench my thighs shut.

No. He wouldn't.

Grunting behind me, Drake slapped my ass cheek, rendering another cry from me, my voice so hoarse from screaming it came out almost nonexistent. Pulling back from me, I felt a light reprieve. Hope ignited in my chest that he was done.

The sound of Drake's belt unfastening killed that butterfly of hope as horror rendered me stiff. I couldn't move, I couldn't scream. I was at his mercy.

"I would fuck your lovely cunt, sweet wife of mine." A grunt was heard from behind me again as another hit was rendered on Jon. "But I refuse to let my cock be wettened by another man's cum."

"We never had sex," I whispered, my voice torn and my throat sore.

"Then let this be a warning to you both," he continued, ignoring my plea of innocence. "Maybe you'll remember that you are mine!" Spreading my ass again, he used the blood that was still trailing down my body as a lubricant around his length before shoving into my tight hole. A scream rent from me that I didn't know was left.

Pounding into me, the sound of his flesh hitting mine, pain radiated everywhere. I couldn't think anymore. I couldn't do anything anymore. Letting the pain take over my body, I fell into the black abyss that had been calling for my release.

Chapter Forty-Five

JAMES

This was a horrible idea.

Wendy shouldn't be here. We were all in for a world of hurt if she was found. But there was no talking her out of it. She was determined to find Jane. Jon was supposed to be here, but no one had seen him since he left with Tiger Lily almost a week ago. I had to hope he was with her or we had even bigger problems.

The castle was overflowing with Fae, leaving a rock of unease in my stomach. The acrid taste of bile sat at the base of my throat as I realized that Jane was here somewhere with these monsters. I could only hope and pray that she was still alive.

I didn't care what condition she was in when I got her back. I just needed her breathing. I would rain hell on anyone who had touched her, but I needed her safe first.

Watching the Fae mingle, drinks overflowed their glasses and the smell of food tickled my senses, making my mouth water. No. You don't eat or drink anything the Fae offered you. That was a sure way to owe them a favor. No matter how thirsty or hungry you get, you ignore the pain until you get home.

Wendy knew the rules, so I didn't have to worry about her. I was worried about my crew, but the looks of wariness they gave Wendy had me on edge.

"We need to split up. There's no use looking for her here. She won't be here. Tink would have her someplace safe until she was ready for her. Search the corridors and all the rooms," I bent and whispered into Wendy's ear.

She nodded, her gaze filled with the promise of violence if provoked.

The woman beside me gave off the waves of a predator stalking her prey. Her eyes glanced up to mine, her usual brown eyes now a dark shade of green, and it hit me. Wendy wasn't here. This was Moira, the one Smee had warned me about.

I hadn't seen hide or hair of Grim since coming back to the Cove, but the whispers around town told me he was still alive. My crew now gave Wendy a wide berth when we found her a suitable evening outfit. Curiosity was burning at the back of my mind about what she did. What she was capable of.

A commotion in the middle of the dance floor caught my attention. This was supposed to be a night of fun and games. What the hell was going on?

The front doors banged open and the sound of a man being dragged resounded through the now-silent hall. What the fuck?

Pushing through the throng of people, shock rang through me at the sight before me. Arron and Madok had a man between them. His head was bowed and his body slumped in defeat, a gag wrapped around his head.

My gaze moved to the people they were facing, fury boiling in my veins at the sight before me. Drake held Lily back by the throat and my eyes moved back to the beaten man. Recognition hit me in the gut. No one had seen Jon because Drake had him.

Lily's eyes found mine as I went to grab my revolver hidden in the back of my pants, her head moving quickly from side to side, saying to stand back. I didn't trust the Fae not to pull something of the like, but Lily telling me to stand down had trepidation settling like a rock in my throat. Something was wrong.

The sound of a gasp rang out in the nearly silent room came from beside me. Glancing over, I found Moira standing there with rage and violence dancing in her eyes. Grabbing her arm, I pulled her to the front of the hall as the first sounds of torment started, the sounds of flesh tearing and screams of pain filling the hall.

We needed a distraction. This wasn't what we had in mind, but I would take it. We could heal the two later— if they survived.

Asher stood in the hall, watching from the corner, as if he didn't want to be a part of that torture as well. None of us did.

"What the fuck? We need to help them!" Moira hissed at me. Her voice was deeper than Wendy's. More sultry, dangerous.

Asher's eyes flicked to the woman beside me, his eyes widening in shock. "Moira. It's been a long time since you came to play. We have missed you."

"No, you haven't. You all are a bunch of bigoted, bullheaded monsters that need to be put down."

Asher nodded. "Some, yes. The animals in there, most definitely. But you won't harm me. You enjoy my company too much," he snarked at her, poking the beast.

"I really wish we could keep up with your little reunion, but while everyone is watching Jon and Lily get taught a lesson, we have time to search for Jane." My voice was low and I pulled them down the hall.

"A lesson? Is that what that is supposed to be?" Moira's voice reverberated down the hall.

"Yes." That was all I was going to say right now. I wasn't in the mood to explain what she couldn't figure out.

"Meera's been searching. She said she was in the walls. I am not quite sure what she means by that," Asher reported, ignoring Moira's question as well, bringing us back to the real reason we were here.

The tinkling of bells floated from behind us as if the devil himself wished her here. She came. I hated pixies. "What the hell is she saying?" I asked, my patience running thin. We needed to find Jane, and fast.

"She's moving. Someone has her. She's hurt. That's all she knows. She lost the trail at a wall. There is something behind the walls that we can't get into," Asher explained, defeat in his voice.

"You used to live here. How do you get into the walls?" I asked, impatience spilling under my skin. She was here. Alive. We needed to find her.

"Tink magicked the castle after I left. The doors change periodically, so you never know where anything is. The only rooms she keeps the same are the throne room and the infirmary," Asher explained. Dread filled me with every word he said.

"So, this is a fool's errand? We will never find her?" Moira asked, her voice husky with restrained fury. I can see why Smee told me to be wary of her. But I wanted to see what she was holding back. To see the violence she was restraining.

Searching the woman's gaze, I saw the wheels turning in her mind. She was plotting. Moira was more dangerous than Smee because she thought everything through, taking the best possible route and executing her plan. She was dangerous because she would see to it that nothing would stop her.

The sound of people filing into the hall had us pressing against the walls.

"Where is everyone going?" she asked as I was about to say the same thing.

"Her Majesty has a gift for all of us in The Heart," Asher replied.

The Heart? What the fuck?

Asher's intake of breath was almost lost in the commotion of the crowd surrounding us, pulling us along with them.

"What's The Heart?" I asked low, praying he heard me. The pressing of sweating bodies against me had my ire rising and the need to push everyone off. But I needed to play the game if I wanted to see Jane again.

"The Heart of Neverland. The place was closed off soon after Pan went missing. It used to be a place we worshiped. The place where the Magic of Neverland was stored. I don't like that she is taking us there." Asher's voice was low and held concern.

We were all fucked.

The palace halls were filled to the brim with Fae and humans alike. Searching the area for hidden threats, I started picking out smaller humans. Ones that shouldn't be here.

There were children... Smee's voice echoed in my head.

The more I searched, the more I found. My stomach twisted into tighter knots than it already was, the need to hurt something becoming something that might happen sooner rather than later.

"Do you see them, too?" Moira's voice came from beside me, her gaze flicking to the kids I had also spotted.

Nodding, I put my hand on her lower back, pressing her forward. We couldn't help them. Not now. Soon though.

First, we needed to find our own.

The crowd slowly started to thin out. The palace halls becoming darker, the veins of magic in the walls pulsing brighter. It sent a sense of dread through me. What were we walking into?

The sounds of gasps and horrified whispers hit my ears as we entered the doors. Moira halted beside me, alongside Asher, horror painted on their faces.

"Pe—" One of Asher's hands slammed over her mouth as she started to speak.

My eyes moved to where theirs were locked, shock and disgust rolling through me. A man was hanging in chains, blood dripping from the many wounds that were inflicted upon him. What was worse was the constant flow of magic in the air, the current blowing against us, left a cold chill along my exposed skin.

In the middle of the room was a floating ball of what looked to be water. The insides of it churned with black shadows and the outside was wrapped in black veins of magic.

"What is that?" I asked Asher.

"The Heart of Neverland."

"Is it supposed to look like that?"

"No," was his only answer as he slowly removed his hand from Moira's face, her eyes glaring daggers at the man. "We need to keep to the shadows. Don't get too close. The magic is unstable."

"Who is the man chained to the ceiling?" I asked, afraid I already knew the answer.

Moira looked up at the man, unshed tears shining in her eyes.

"Peter Pan."

Chapter Forty-Six

JANE

*T*ick... *Tock...*

I was done. I didn't want to feel anymore.

Trying to keep my eyes open anymore felt like a chore. The dragging feeling of unconsciousness felt like glorious bliss. I couldn't feel anything when I wasn't there for it.

What did I ever do in my life to deserve this? Why was this woman torturing me this way? Just letting her minions do what they wished with me. Sometimes, she would join in, and the look in her eyes told me she got off watching me in pain.

The queen, they called her. I just called her a raging, maniacal bitch that needed to be put down like the dog she was. But being chained up and starved for who knows how long now, I have little chance of getting the opportunity to do so.

Gods, would I love to carve her up the way she has me. To watch her blood run down her face and body to the point that there was none left.

I never thought myself to be a violent person. I was only ever patient and loved to heal people. I went into nursing because I wanted to help people, particularly children. I loved kids. They were so innocent and loved with no expectations. But this bitch, this fucking cunt, could die. And I wanted to be there when it happened. It would be even better if I were the one holding the weapon to make her life a living hell as mine has been.

TICK! Tock...

Letting my thoughts run on the path they were on, I didn't hear the door above open. The sudden light shining in my eyes blinded me as I scrambled out of the light and back into the dark like a scared animal.

Is that what I have become? Someone so small and scared that I didn't want to be found?

"Tsk, tsk. Come now. You know better than to hide from me, little morsel... I will always find you and take what I want anyway."

The voice made my stomach curl in on itself. The man wouldn't leave me alone. Curling my knees closer to my chest, I stayed in my corner. He was going to come and grab me anyway.

The sound of his shoes scraping the floor was like nails on a chalkboard in my ears as fear clawed up my throat. Not again. Please, not again.

TICK! TOCK!

The man stopped right in front of my feet and glowered down at me. My wrists were yanked by the chain, pulling my body up with it. My body rubbed against the man, acid burning my throat. The urge to gag was barely suppressed as I was backed against the wall and his body was pressed against me, his member hard, pressing into my middle. I turned my head to the side, not wanting to look into his face. Grabbing my jaw, he brought my face back to look at him. I refused to make eye contact and stared down as far as possible.

"One of these days, you will appreciate all the time I spend with you, little...morsel..." He licked my face as a shudder rang through my body. "See, even your body is starting to react to me," he said, mistaking my shiver for pleasure.

"Hurry up, Goran, Her Majesty wants her now. Don't play around." Another male's voice carried in from the doorway, just out of view. My body tensed. *She* wanted me.

A sigh came from the man's lips and fell over my face, the smell of mint assailing my nose. At least the man brushed his teeth before coming down to see me, I guess. The man pulled back from me and fished a key out of his pocket. Hoping he was going to take the blasted cuffs on my wrists, I held them out to him. A chuckle came out of the big man. "Nah, you aren't getting the chance to escape again. The cuffs stay on." He bent down and unlocked the chain from the wall.

Pulling me against him once more, he grabbed my face and kissed my mouth, forcing his tongue through my lips. Letting him enter, I bit down on the intruding piece of meat, blood filling my mouth. He pulled back so fast I didn't see his hand coming at my face. Stars sparked against my eyelids as my neck snapped to the side. I knew that was coming, but it felt good all the same.

TICK! TOCK!

"Do it again. I dare you, then you'll see the true meaning of pain," he growled into my ear, blood gushing out of his mouth and now smearing my cheek. Pulling the chains, he hauled me harshly into the hallway where the other man I heard was still waiting.

The man looked me up and down, disgust marring his face. I knew I was a mess. I hadn't showered in forever, I had blood dried all over my body, both mine and others, bruises marred my skin, I hadn't eaten since I was brought here, my body nothing but skin and bones, and I was naked. I was a sight for sore eyes and didn't even care anymore.

"She's going to be pissed seeing that new mark on her face. You just couldn't hold your temper, could you?" the new man said.

"She bit me. Fucking animal deserved it."

Rolling my eyes, I looked at the door at the top of the stairs. I barely remember the last time I saw daylight. The thought of the sun made me smile. Who would have thought something so small would mean so much?

TICK! TOCK!

The unknown man lifted his arms and the bag in his hand fell open as he placed it over my head, tightening it around my neck. Panic settled into my body, my breath coming in short, hot bursts. "Sorry, but Tink requested that you come up with your face covered." The man sounded almost apologetic, as if that was a thing these monsters even knew of. It didn't help to relieve anything as I hyperventilated in the mask. I couldn't breathe, the mask being sucked into my mouth, and I couldn't stop.

"Fuck! She's going to pass out before we get her up the stairs," the man said.

Goran put his arms around my knees and hefted me over his shoulder. "Whatever, that's her problem if she doesn't want to know what's in store for her."

His words sank into me and terror seized my body. Tremors racked my frame as he carried me up the stairwell. Where were they taking me? What the hell does he mean? The realization that she might try to kill me this time sank in. A new panic sank in as I started punching the man's back as best as I could with my hands locked up. I started kicking and squirming as much as possible to escape the Fae, but the only noise out of him was grunts. Like I wasn't doing more than annoying him.

TICK! TOCK! TICK! TOCK!

We turned left and then up some more stairs, my body slowly giving out, betraying me. I had little energy left and whatever was ahead of me would be bad. Letting my body relax as much as possible, I listened around me for other people. Doubtful they'd help, as I was being carted around naked, she probably cared little about what may happen. Her people were loyal to her and willing to do heinous things to keep her happy.

Wherever we were, though, it was eerily silent. The rattling of my chains echoed through the halls, muffled slightly around my ears, was the only thing I heard.

The man holding me stopped suddenly and the new man knocked on a door. It sounded like heavy wood, but who knew? I couldn't see anything and everything was half muffled anyway.

Being jostled back up his shoulder, the man grunted and went through the door, I assumed. As we started moving again, the sound of whispers came at me—a lot of whispers. That's why the halls were quiet. Everyone was in this room.

TICK!! TOCK!!

"Ah, the main course of this evening's events." That voice. I cringed and ducked my head against the man's back, grabbing his shirt, not wanting to be let down. I'd rather deal with him than her.

The man grabbed my hips and lifted me as if I weighed nothing, which probably was closer to the truth, and threw me on the ground. Stars filled my head as it hit the floor. My teeth clacked together and I bit my tongue. *Karma for biting his,* I thought to myself.

"Get up, you cunt!" The woman's voice rang through the hall as she landed a kick to my stomach, sharp pain radiating through my center. My lungs burned with the need to breathe, making me roll into myself.

The rancid bitch was going to pay one of these days. I just needed to bide my time. Forcing myself into a sitting position, pain ricocheting through my body, I slowly got to my knees and stood, my legs shaking with the effort. The bag on my head was still in place and I turned toward where I heard her voice last. I wanted to face her. I didn't want to see who else was in the room to watch me or get whatever punishment she had decided I was being dealt next.

"Now, I know you all saw that Peter here is still alive and well. Well, mostly, anyway..." Her high-pitched laugh rang around the atrium. "I have another surprise for you all."

Peter? As in Peter Pan? The man my mother was obsessed with?

"Captain Barrington betrayed us all by bringing back the Darling woman," the woman practically growled, my heart beating loudly in my chest. Barrington. James. Did he take my mother? What the fuck? "And I thought that it only be fair that since he thought he could destroy what we created here with her help, he should sacrifice something of his own as penance to Neverland." Wrenching my neck back, my tormentor ripped the bag off my head, light glaring into my eyes as pain exploded in my head.

I had wanted the sun. I had prayed for it, but this was too much. Screaming in pain, I closed my eyes and bent over, bile rising in my throat at the sudden pain and heartache.

The cunt grabbed my hair and pulled me back into a standing position. "Nuh uh huh... open your eyes, girl, and look at everyone lusting to see your demise. Maybe, just maybe, this will appease the

Island and give us a little semblance of the order we once had," she whispered into my ear, disgust rolling through me.

Looking around, tears streamed down my face as I locked eyes on the one man I had prayed would find me. Next to him was a woman with blue hair and dark green eyes. The longer I stared at her, the easier it was to place the known features.

Mom. She was here. Where was Jules?

The sounds of water hitting the floor resounded in my ears, bringing my attention to the giant, floating water ball in the middle of the room. Wait... when did I miss *that*?

Shadow...

The name that had haunted me since before I had arrived here echoed around the room, wind slapping against my bruised and bloody face, stinging my eyes, hot tears adding to the sting.

My frame trembled as I tried to back away from whatever was coming. A giant, shadowy figure emerged from the water on the floor, forming a humanesque void.

Two reptilian green eyes glowed from the depths of where its face should have been. Its sights set on me.

Chapter Forty-Seven

JANE

The water monster's eyes were glowing gold as it crossed the floor. Its hands and feet were in the shape of crocodile claws, similar to the one on my side. The sounds of snapping and clicking came from its watery body as it staggered toward me.

TICK! TOCK!

Scanning the crowd, my heart beat against my ribcage, trying to flee out of my chest as if it could outrun the monster in front of me. There were people everywhere, most with glee in their eyes, and my stomach turned. They were going to enjoy my death.

My eyes caught James', who was standing stock still in the middle of the crowd, his eyes never leaving mine. Fury burned within his gaze as he took in my damaged body, finally resting on my neck, where his collar was missing. Goran had torn it off my neck ages ago. I couldn't have been bothered to care until I saw the look of death in James' eyes.

"Where's the necklace, Jane?" His voice rang out from the crowd.

A small giggle came from the bitch that was floating in the air, watching everything with glee below her. "Oh, that little strap. I got rid of it. The protection enchantment only works if the other party recites the verse back to you." Another round of giggles rang around the room as dread sank into me.

I tried to circle slowly around the floating ball, away from the creature, without startling it, my legs shaking with the effort toward James and Mom. The words the bitch was saying sank into my psyche. He had tried to protect me. He didn't send me here.

"Oh, yes, that's right. Drake only told you what you needed to know. You marked her as yours, making her an easy target for my wrath. But we had a fail-safe and only told you half of what you needed to know. The spell wasn't any use against us, to begin with."

If my heart could sink any lower, it would. He tried to protect me from these monsters, but they just played him a fool and marked me as a target instead.

I backed away from the creature in front of me, slowly making my way toward James and Mom. They were my only hope of surviving this. My mind was still swirled with thoughts of how Mom ended up here with James in the first place. Were they together? Bile rose in my throat at the thought. No. James was adamant that we were exclusive. Then how? Why?

The feel of sparks licking my skin as the water ball turned with me had my stomach drop to my feet. It was acting almost sentient. Alive. The black veins encompassing it stretched toward me, flicking against my already bruised and broken skin. It sent excruciating shocks of electricity through my body, setting my insides aflame with heat, contradicting the frigidness of my extremities.

My vision blurred, everything turning into the shades of grey I had become accustomed to over the past few days. The lack of color was different this time. The bodies in the room were white while the creature in front of me was pitch black, its eyes shining a green gold as it stared at me. Usually, everything looked like a black-and-white movie.

Shaking my head, I tried to ignore the agonizing sensations wracking me as I took another step back, ignoring the change in my vision. I just needed to survive this, and then I could figure out the rest.

The creature stopped suddenly, cocking its head to the side as if listening to something no one else could hear. Fear skirted through me. It was thinking.

TICK! TOCK!

The creature shook its head and the clicking grew louder the closer it took another step toward me. Terror slowly seized my body. My shaking legs were only going to hold me up for so long. I was exhausted and there was no way I could fight this thing. Glancing behind me, relief flooded me when I saw the circle's edge. I'm only a few feet away from Mom and James. Only a few feet away from freedom.

"Don't bother trying to get him, dear. He can't help you." A maniacal laugh rang around the room. Gods, that woman needed to be shut up. What did she mean he couldn't help me? "The people around you are held back by a magic circle, little Jane-girl. So the Krok can't hurt anyone, but you. The most Barrington can do is scream your name, as you have done his for the past two weeks. He'll get to watch your demise. The guilt that he's the reason you died, eating away at him for the rest of his days."

TICK! TOCK!

No, no, no, no, no...

My gut churned with fury that I was being used as a pawn and nothing else. *Shadow...*

The word reverberated around the room, soaking into my psyche. I couldn't do this anymore.

"I do have to say, though. I do find it very fitting that the girl with the symbol of the crocodile painted on her body will die by the very creature she admired."

Ignoring the psycho woman, the sounds of chains rattling brought my attention up to the ceiling, a gasp leaving my throat at the sight. The man from the dungeon. He hadn't been in the room with me for days and now I knew why. In the light, I could see his features and they were haunting.

His eyes were closed, but you could tell they were sunk in. His skin was a ghastly hue of white, like he hadn't seen sunlight in so long that he had lost all his color. His wrists and ankles were chained to the ceiling in a position that I would imagine would look like if one were flying, the skin around the shackles torn and missing. His body was gaunt and bony. He was so emaciated that I could count his ribs under all the blood, dirt, and grime that covered his frame. Falling from his sides were small tubes that hung from his frame, connecting to nothing, which had my nurse brain wondering what the fuck he was attached to on this primitive island. His hair was a long, matted mess of dried blood and whatever else that was in that dungeon. On top of his head was a crown of iron thorns, fresh blood trailing down his face as tears fell from his eyes.

Was that Peter Pan?

Shadow...

"Jane! Come on, you're so close!" Mom's voice encouraged me to keep moving, and a tiny flicker of hope ignited in my chest. I couldn't trust the Fae. I had to believe that I could escape this hell.

"Jane. Don't let the thing out of your sight." James' voice was a soothing balm to my panicked state. He was right behind me. "You should be able to cross the circle. She can keep people out, but someone from the inside can break the circle and get out." Nodding my ascent, I took another step back, another foot closer to the edge.

"Don't be filling her head with silly notions, Barrington," the Fae woman called out. "I have learned since the last time you and I went round. The Jane-girl is my plaything to do as I please."

TICK! TOCK!

"I don't believe everything that is told to me either. Everyone lies. As you should know," he called out, baiting her, fury simmering underneath it all.

Her annoying laugh rang out again, making me wince as the creature cocked its head at me. Its glowing eyes were calculating, watching, waiting for me to fuck up. As long as I was standing, I was fine.

"Should I tell you about how sweet she tastes? Goran and I quite enjoyed her cunt. He even pleaded with me for her to remain alive to keep as his personal toy. Too bad she's destined for an early death. It would almost be worth it to watch you be in pain knowing she was being fucked by a better man than a traitor."

Fear and shame intermingled in my gut as she told everyone here what she had done to me and planned for me if I didn't die. Between the two choices, I'd choose death. I had chosen death a long time ago. But I wanted to watch the woman suffer first. It was my only reason for living anymore.

"Peter! Do something!" I heard Mom's voice over the loud clicking of the beast.

I glanced back toward her, horror overcoming me as I fell backward, stumbling on the uneven ground. The creature snapped into action, a flurry of wind and magic pressing against me.

TICK! TOCK!

"PETER! SAVE HER!!" Mom's panicked voice rang out in the atrium.

Scrambling back on my hands and knees, I tried to right myself, but it was too late. The creature was stronger and faster than I was. Its icy claws dug into my ankle, pulling me back from the edge of the circle, screams being torn from my lungs. My bloodied fingers scrabbled for purchase against the cold floor, my already broken nails digging into the dirt and brick, sending a sharp pain through my wrists and up my arms.

More high-pitched laughter filled the room as I screamed in terror. "Peter can't do anything, Wendy Darling. See, he has no power here. I have made sure of that."

"MOM! JAMES!" A blast of magic blew over me, scraping my skin raw as a roar from the ceiling shook the room.

Pan...

TICK! TOCK!

The creature let go of my ankle, allowing me to scramble for the circle's edge. The magic swept around the room like a tornado, pressing everyone against the walls and floors. The screams of terror and pain pierced my eardrums and I covered them to block out the sound.

The ball of water in the center of the room lit up gold, fighting with the black veins engulfing it. The creature shook its head in confusion as it stared at me, its gold eyes shifting to turquoise and then back to gold.

The magic rushing over my skin flayed me as I tried to push against it. I needed to move. The longer I stayed here, the easier prey I became.

As if moving through thick mud, I slowly inched forward, the magic in the room keeping everyone in place. Time was standing still as the two magics fought for dominance. Tink against Pan. Captive versus tormentor. It was a battle of wills and magic that wouldn't end well for anyone.

TICK! TOCK!

As suddenly as it started, the magic ceased. My lungs burned with the effort to breathe and my mind was too slow to realize I should have been moving.

A scream was rent from my battered body as I was hoisted in the air, landing on the creature's shoulder. Its claws dug into my thighs as it returned to the now black ball and fear sunk into my being.

The creature took one last step toward the water ball of magic. My screams filled the room as the iciness of the water enveloped me, burning my lungs from the inside. Everything started fading as I took a breath, my lungs filling with the vile black shadowed liquid surrounding me.

Shadow...

The ticking finally stopped.

Chapter Forty-Eight

PETER

*S*hadow...

The voice of Neverland woke me from my stupor.

I was in the air. Was I flying? No. I lost that ability a long time ago.

The sounds of chains rattling in my ears as I tried to move my dangling limbs told me I was still bound. Why? What was going on?

Shadow...

Searching the area below me, the name being called out by Neverland itself circled the girl in my cell—the only person who could withstand Tink's wrath.

She had my Shadow. Why hadn't I been able to see it before? How did she end up with it?

I glanced around the room and caught sight of a woman with bright blue hair and dark green eyes. I knew those eyes. Moira.

Wendy.

She cried out to the girl—to me.

"Peter! Do something!"

I could hear Wendy screaming at me to help the girl, but I couldn't. My magic was drained. Tink took it days before she brought me here.

"Peter! Save her!!"

Moving my gaze to the screaming girl, the spirit of Krok stalking her made my own heart beat erratically.

Krok was dead... How was she here?

My Shadow had been missing for the past twenty-four years...

"MOM!! JAMES!!" Jane's voice echoed in terror as she tried to crawl away from the creature, but her body was failing her. She couldn't keep up anymore, not after the past week of torture from Tink and Goran.

Mom...

The last time I saw Wendy...

Tink's maniacal laughter rang hot in my ears as she watched the display of Krok coming for the girl.

Fury, an emotion I hadn't felt in so long, surged through me and the center of my chest burst with the need for violence. The chains holding me against the wall burned my skin brighter than it had in years, wrenching a shout of pain from my chest.

Shadow. Jane. Mine.

Magic was buzzing beneath my skin, burning in my veins so hot it hurt. I had forgotten what it felt like to feel Neverland. To feel the need to fly. To Crow.

The sound of pain burst through my damaged windpipes, burning my throat as my magic expelled itself. My magic rushed through the room, crushing everybody against The Heart's walls, but Krok continued her path toward Jane. My magic inadvertently pushed her closer to the monster approaching her.

If Krok got a hold of her, Neverland was done for.

The thought that the girl I had watched get tortured for the past week, grateful it wasn't me, had bile crawling up my throat, burning my insides at the shame and guilt of not protecting her. She was a part of me.

A man in the crowd shouted, trying to move, but my magic pressed everyone into submission. It demanded penance.

Pulling on my magic, trying to bring it back into myself, I struggled against myself. Against Neverland.

The Heart was glowing brighter, my magic swirling in torrents around the room, mingling with the magic of Neverland. It took everything I was giving it and Neverland suffered because of me.

No, because of Tink. None of this would have happened if she hadn't taken my magic.

A growl of impatience reverberated around the chamber as a scream of terror echoed alongside it. My heart plummeted as I watched Krok grab the girl's ankle, pulling her slowly across the floor, blood trailing behind them. Watching in disbelief that no one could help her, I roared my rage into the atrium, letting Neverland feel my fury.

To put my will of letting the girl go against the will of Tink's.

The only problem was that Tink had stolen my magic for so long that Neverland almost didn't recognize me anymore, sending waves of guilt through me. I should have tried harder to escape. But Tink had grown too strong at the time I went to London.

Jane's terror-filled screams echoed alongside my magic as she fought against Krok's Shadow, kicking as hard as she could and scrabbling at the stone floor with no chance of purchase. Krok wasn't affected by her efforts, slowly making her way across the floor, pulling the girl over her shoulder. The snap of magic silenced Jane's screams as I lost connection with The Heart.

I had failed. Tears sprang into my eyes as defeat took over, my body sagging in its chains.

Maniacal laughter rang out around us as we watched on in stunned silence.

"If I knew I was getting revenge on the Darling woman and Barrington simultaneously, I would have better prepared for this." Tink's laughter rang around the room as everyone slowly got to their feet.

The smell of my burning flesh filled the room from where the iron touched my skin.

Wendy's eyes met mine, anger and betrayal flickering in her eyes. But under all of it, confusion and a spark of something else.

"The twist of Wendy indeed having the Shadow of Neverland in the guise of a baby was truly something I never saw coming, though." Tink's eyes moved up to me, appraising her handiwork. "Peter, you naughty boy. You never told me you had a child. All of this could have been avoided if I had been told."

The thought of what she would have done to Jane as a child had disgust rolling through me and hatred filling my being. Fuck her.

I will find a way to get my Shadow back. I will save my daughter.

I had to.

Epilogue

Welcome home, Little Shadow...

Welcome home...

Acknowledgements

I want to start by saying thank you to you, the reader. This wouldn't be possible without your support and love for crazy stories.

For my family, for always being there and listening to me for the past year, telling them about my weird Peter Pan story. Then helping me flesh out the ideas I couldn't pull out of my head. You guys are amazing and are loved and appreciated more than you know.

To my customers who have been watching me write and edit for the past few months, always asking where I am at and keeping me on track. To Joe and Sandy for asking me daily and holding me accountable for all of my actions, even my lazy ones.

To my ARC readers, thank you for understanding that I was running behind, forgiving me for giving out a half-edited product, and not using it against me.

A huge thank you to Hannah for squeezing in my final edits at the last minute. You are the real hero! You will never know how much you are appreciated.

Lastly, thank you to Vicki Pettersson for creating House of Ink and believing that all of us in the group are more than capable of writing amazing stories. The people I have met in this group are amazing, and their stories are as fascinating as mine. To Tara, Jess, and Bianca for being my beta readers and the rest of the group for being an amazing support system and dealing with my daily posts and rants. You don't realize how much this group has formed me into the writer I am and will become. This is only the beginning.

About the author

Emberly Jade is better known for her drink-making skills than her story-telling and is looking to change that.

Living in the wilds of Northern Michigan, she spends her free time building her garden and kayaking in the summers and her winters cozied up with her dog, reading and writing dark, fantastical stories.